TELESHOP USA

TELESHOP USA

ISBN: 979-8-9863956-6-1 (Hardcover)
ISBN: 979-8-9863956-7-8 (Paperback)
ISBN: 979-8-9863956-8-5 (Ebook)

Published by Richards & Jones

www.stashcairo.com

TELESHOP USA

BY

STASH CAIRO

RICHARDS & JONES

For my mother and for Gicky

CHAPTER ONE

Oklahoma City, Oklahoma. Summer 1987.

The Dealmaker

The Dealmaker awoke with a severe hangover late Monday morning. His head, thumping like the beat of a mariachi band, sent pain throughout his forty-three-year-old skull. Drawing himself up, he leaned back and glanced across the room to the bureau's broken mirror.

The taste of stale beer, cigarettes, and the bitter/numb feeling of old cocaine moldering in his mouth held him slumped against his bed's backboard, unmoving.

Bitch.

The Dealmaker sat there for a few more minutes. He had to urinate, but the aggravation of getting out of bed versus the bearing of another ache left him wavering. Eventually, his bladder won. He hauled his corpulent carcass from the bed in his motel unit to the matchbox toilet, farting proudly along the way.

If the Dealmaker had observed his surroundings (which he hadn't) or deigned it important to ponder the way in which he lived, he might have noticed the general stench of decay hanging about his room. He would have seen the pizza boxes, milk cartons, laundry, beer cans, bills and sundry scattered about as if an earthquake had recently struck.

The Dealmaker would have replaced the broken mirror on the dresser and fixed the cracked glass of his only window to the outside. Not that the view was much — overgrown weeds leading off to a fetid creek. Still, the principle remained. And besides, it wouldn't always be summer. Oklahoma City could get mighty chilly in the wintertime.

Standing over the toilet, scratching his hand over his beard, the Dealmaker glanced at the clock on the bathroom vanity. 10:15 a.m.

Fuck.

He finished relieving himself and, without shaking, climbed into the shower. The hot water poured over his body, dissolving the sleep from his eyes and removing some of the smell of stale booze.

Ah.

While lathering soap over his chest, the Dealmaker felt the urge to urinate again. He let go of the stream and continued washing, glancing down as his urine mixed with shower water, collecting and swirling down the drain. It made him recall a joke he once heard Rodney Dangerfield tell an audience in Las Vegas. Rodney said he knew a guy who had so much class, he got out of the shower to take a piss. The Dealmaker chuckled, until he remembered his wife was sitting at the table with him that night. She had that sanctimonious look on her face, the one she might as well have had tattooed there. He stopped thinking about Rodney Dangerfield.

Finishing his shower, the Dealmaker jumped (or at least tried to jump) from the bath. He struck a match, lit a Camel and inhaled the nicotine-laden smoke deep into his lungs immediately feeling its invigorating relief.

Who needs sex!

He threw on a pair of less-than-clean boxers, his watch, a cheap pair of pants, and a shirt and tie that matched the trousers in style. The last thing the Dealmaker did before he left his mangy motel room was to kick the ancient baseboard air conditioner and turn it off. The old machine stopped with a sputter, the sound of the now shutting door echoing to an empty room.

The heat hugged the ground, moving up the Dealmaker's body until it enveloped his head. Never in the best shape even on a cool day, sweat seeped out his pores, staining his Walmart dress shirt and starching its collar with his perspiration.

The motel sat off I40, at the county line outside Oklahoma City. Tractor-trailers kicked dirt into the broken-up parking lot, causing miniature whirlwinds. Soaking wet and choking with dust, he shook his head and glanced up at the motel's sign. It read, "Best Value Inn, Jack and Ruth Miller, Proprietors." He didn't have a clue who Jack and Ruth Miller were. A guy named Ahmed owned the motel. The Dealmaker didn't give a damn one way or the other. Ahmed minded his business, and besides, he sold full-strength beer under the table at the front desk. Best Value Inn was in a dry county.

The Dealmaker walked to the office and opened the rickety, old door. Ahmed stood behind the counter reading a copy of *USA Today*. He glanced up when the Dealmaker entered and opened the Coca-Cola cooler by the cash. After moving several boxes around, Ahmed pulled out a six-pack of Olde English Malt Liquor and handed it to the Dealmaker.

"Rent's due yesterday," said the owner.

The Dealmaker grunted and ripped one of the cans out of the plastic. He opened it and drank it all the way down. The cold beer made him pause for a moment, just a moment, before considering what in the name of J.C. he was doing living in this cesspit. Then he crumpled the first can and tossed it into the trash. Opening his second, he lit up another Camel.

The Dealmaker walked out of the office toward his car, swinging the six-pack by its plastic. He stopped and looked back up at the sign.

Three fucking months.

§

Mary-Anne Warner

"Jesus H. Christ!" Mary-Anne Warner ran down the long, office corridor toward reception.

Where is he? Where is the prick?

She was a thin, small-busted, middle-aged woman of medium height with dark brown, almost black hair. Her angry eyes sat in a taut face that brooked no argument. While dressed in an expensive, tailored suit, her feral features couldn't hide a pulsing tick. The involuntary twitch announced Mary-Anne's desperate need of a cigarette.

Several visitors glanced up from their newspapers and looked at Mary-Anne, surprised. Rosa, the receptionist, kept her head down and said nothing. She knew how excitable Mary-Anne became even on a good day. Today was obviously not a good day.

"Rosa, has he called? I've got the Triboro Media people in from New York and my number one salesman isn't here. He's going to miss his shift!"

"No, ma'am; he hasn't called," replied Rosa, keeping her voice calm and modulated. No sense in making the woman even more frantic.

"I swear that bastard's sole purpose in life is to piss me off. He should have been here two hours ago. Have you tried his car phone?"

"Ms. Warner, he hasn't had a car phone since his wife threw him out three months ago."

"Shit! Call me the instant he walks into the building."

Rosa nodded in reply and answered the buzzing telephone. Mary-Anne turned around and flung herself back down the corridor, sprinting toward the guests waiting in her office.

I'll get the sonofabitch if it's the last thing I do. Please God, before I die, let me put the boots to the fucking Dealmaker!

She stopped in front of her office door in the executive area of the building. Its sign read, "Mary-Anne Warner, Vice President." A picture frame, hanging nearby, reflected her image. Mary-Anne swept back her hair and composed herself, her eyes taking in the picture—a collage from last year's Christmas party. There in the center stood the Dealmaker, a drunken leer on his face, his cohorts laughing like idiots while he hoisted a large beer to the camera.

Prick.

§

The Dealmaker

A car swerved in front of the Dealmaker, its horn blasting. The driver spewed out some vague curse, the tone changing like a Doppler shift; he didn't pay a lot of attention. The Dealmaker was on his third can of Olde English Malt Liquor, the second can now occupying the floor with the rest of the six-pack.

"You're in Big Country Land, KGOK Oklahoma City, Oklahoma. Classic Country twenty-four hours a day, Charlie Pride from 1969 with ... "

The Dealmaker twisted the tuning knob of his radio in vain, finally thumping it. The radio only got one station.

Fucking music.

He used to have a BMW 750i. Now, he drove a beat-up 1974 Dodge Duster, purchased without much deliberation from Honest Phil's Used Car Emporium—"Check out the competition, then y'all come back to

Phil's. He'll make it right!"

The Dealmaker appreciated Phil. Like Ahmed, he also minded his own business.

Even with the windows rolled down, the sun beat onto the car's black, imitation leather interior. Sweat drenched his shirt, making it resemble a dishrag. Bargain Malls and Warehouse Outlets ringed the Interstate.

The Dealmaker looked at his watch. 10:40 a.m.

He wondered if he'd make it.

§

Mary-Anne Warner

"Ladies, Gentlemen, if I may have your attention for a minute." The crowd of twelve stopped speaking and looked at Mary-Anne. "If you'll follow me, we'll head over to production."

Twelve corporately dressed men and women filed out of the office and took up position behind Mary-Anne. The men in their Armani suits, the women dressed in Anne Klein. Did any of the corporate climbers ask if it was a coincidence they all wore gray?

§

The Dealmaker

Minutes before start time, the Dealmaker's battered wreck pulled into his company's driveway. He turned off the ignition and climbed out of the car, the engine knocking like a machine gun for several seconds.

The Dealmaker walked, carrying his beer-belly and himself, from the asphalt-covered parking lot into the building's reception room.

Rosa stared up from her desk, looking anxious. If Mary-Anne had a meltdown, the entire staff would know about it within minutes.

"Ms. Warner is very upset. You're supposed to be in a meeting with the—"

The Dealmaker cut her off with a wave of his hand. "Good to see you too, Rosa. Weekend? Not bad, but I had to work. Feel like somebody is stomping on my head. Yourself? Great. We should have lunch sometime. See ya!"

The Dealmaker opened the lobby door and passed through it. From behind him came Rosa's worried voice. "But, Dealmaker, it's five to eleven!"

He ambled down the office corridor toward the production area, knowing he would make it with seconds to spare. Several people smiled at him as he walked through the building.

"Hey, Dealmaker, how's the boy?"

"Jesus, Dealmaker, were you messed up last night!"

"Dealmaker, Mary-Anne wants your balls on the whipping post. She's p-i-s-s-e-d!"

He smiled and continued walking, past the accounting department to Scheduling, through the buyers offices next to the executive suite and skirting across the creative department while wondering who came up with their name.

Christ, if creativity was snot, those assholes couldn't blow their nose.

In the distance, at the end of the hall and through an archway stood production. The Dealmaker saw a group of people clustered around what looked like Mary-Anne.

The woman in question turned and saw him, her face freezing in a grimace. "Ladies, Gentlemen, if you'll excuse me, I have to speak to someone."

Mary-Anne smiled and approached the Dealmaker who was

slowing to a stop. "Where the fuck have you been? No don't tell me, I can smell the answer."

"Mary-Anne, I'm not in the fucking mood. Give me my show and let me get to work."

"Work? You haven't even met with the director, let alone reviewed the products! I was going to have George go on in your place."

Mary-Anne motioned to a man off to her left, leaning against a wall. He smiled sheepishly and waved at the Dealmaker. The Dealmaker nodded in return.

"You know, I am your boss; I could suspend you."

"Mary-Anne, it's the end of the quarter and we're behind. I don't think so," replied the Dealmaker with a biting grin.

Before she could respond, a woman from production came running in a panic. She was in her twenties, gamine, and wore a headset. "Dealmaker, you're on in ninety seconds. Hook up."

He strode away from Mary-Anne and took a wireless microphone from the other woman's hand. "Susie, I left my headset in the lounge."

"It's okay, I've got one," replied the tiny woman.

The Dealmaker wrapped the speaker around his ear and down his shirt, walking toward the podium. Mary-Anne rejoined the group of corporate climbers.

"This should be exciting," said Mary-Anne, trying to minimize her anger. Her face, frozen with an affected smile, gave it away. "That's the famous Dealmaker and he's on in thirty seconds."

The assembled crowd stood chattering. On the studio's far wall the "Live Set" sign lit up and they stopped.

The Dealmaker sat in the anchor chair and pushed his intercom switch. "Who's in there and what are we doing, I feel like shit."

"It's Mark. We're starting off with the Capodimonte tulips and featuring the Spray-On-Scalp at the bottom of the hour. And no wonder you feel like shit—do you remember what you did last night? We're on … "

In his headset, the count of his audio operator sounded while the floor director signaled.

"Roll music, cue announce tape, coming down live in five, four, three, two … "

Across America, in the highways and byways of the blue rinse crowd, from coast to coast and parts in between, TV screens faded up from black.

"*Live from Oklahoma City, Oklahoma, TeleShop USA brings you the Markdown Man himself, the King of Bargains, the Emperor of Value … Dealmaker Dave Leonard!*"

The tally light over the camera turned red as the Dealmaker raised his head with a smile beaming from ear to ear.

"Well, *arby-dar*, it's the old Dealmaker coming at ya from TeleShop. Friends, I've got to say, we've gone a whole lot of miles together over the last few years, but today really takes the cake. I spent a lot of time working on the show, hunkered down with our president Billy-Ray Newton and tried to squeeze in the odd extra special or two. You know Billy-Ray, he can be tight with a dollar, but I think we got the better of him. I can't remember seeing this much great merchandise in a long, long time. Let's kick it off with a favorite of the Dealmaker—hand-painted, hand-fired from the south of Italy, the Capodimonte Tulips; they are gorgeous and only fourteen dollars and forty-four cents!"

In the control room, the crew activated the onscreen graphics. Frank, the audio tech, brought up the background noise cart, letting it play at a low level. When the price appeared on his monitor, he hit the applause cart. A cheering crowd clapped for the amazing deal on the Capodimonte tulips.

Frank looked on in startled fascination. "How does he keep this bullshit up, day after day?"

"It's Dave. The Dealmaker's a legend," the director replied, answering what should have been a rhetorical question.

"Mark, he didn't even look at the show."

"So what? If the Dealmaker tells people it's a winner, they believe him."

"There's a sucker born every minute."

"You got it."

"So remember friends: When you want quality, look for Capodimonte. If you know someone in the hospital, or even, God forbid, not long for this world, brighten up their day with a tulip. Real flowers die. Capodimonte is forever. We'll be right back."

CHAPTER TWO

Robert MacKenzie

Robert MacKenzie sat in TeleShop's reception area absorbing its tension. At twenty-five years old, he stood about six feet tall with short, sandy brown hair and nervous hazel eyes. Robert had positioned himself in the brown, fabric chair, his back erect, holding his lean frame stiff while hoping he expressed sincere determination. He stared about the room, praying nobody would notice the beads of perspiration that had begun to break on his forehead.

I need this fucking job.

Assorted salesmen filled the other seats. They rested in a variety of positions, all hoping they projected confidence to spare. The successful ones, resplendent in their crisp-pressed suits, exuded sangfroid. By contrast, their less successful brethren had faces clouded with worry and apprehension.

Robert waited, absorbing the room's atmosphere and wondering about his own place in the hierarchy.

Across from him lounged a handsome, trim man, his face a mask of nonchalant poise. The creases on his trousers glinted like razor blades in the fluorescent light of the reception room. His sample case waxed jet-black and polished, balancing its mirrored finish against his alligator shoes. You could almost hear him say, "Stirred, not shaken."

Next to James Bond slumped a tense and anxious man, his demeanor showing off his ill-fitting jacket. He personified a bush-league Willy Loman (if that was possible); they loved him in Amarillo.

What am I getting myself into?

While Robert pondered his fate, the reception's street door flew open and in walked a large, burly man. He appeared about fifty hard-years old. He smelled of beer and fatigue; sweat drenched his shirt and his tie gave the impression it may have been fashionable in 1975. By comparison, he made Willy look like 007.

The receptionist spoke to the newcomer. The man grumbled a sharp reply then pulled open the office door and lurched inside.

"That's our top host, Dealmaker Dave Leonard!"

Nobody so much as glanced up from their newspapers or took their eyes from the ceiling. Instead, the supplicants remained sitting—awaiting their destiny with practiced calm. It wasn't the first time Bond and his crew had watched this drama. Occasional pandemonium was part and parcel of TeleShop's groove. The receptionist, detecting the room's ambivalence, lowered her head and went back to her responsibilities.

Robert remained in his chair, drumming his fingers against the armrest, wondering why he ever bothered to apply for the position in the first place. He had spent the last nine months in Phoenix, working as a security guard in a downtown condominium. That is if you could call the center of Phoenix "downtown." It wasn't Greater Boston—his home—with its parks and restaurants and nightlife. Phoenix was more like a city that had sprung into being in the last thirty years. Everything was new and bland. The skyline reflected a combination of homogenized

Mexican and humdrum modern architecture. It was all ridiculous since the total isolation of the desert stared back constantly from the outskirts of the city giving the expression "out of town" a new relevance.

Before Phoenix, he'd lived in Los Angeles, working in an adult video store on Sunset Boulevard. He enjoyed the excitement of working in the semi-licit environment, even living in a rent-by-the-hour motel only blocks from his work.

But the job's seediness heightened the sense of profound isolation and alienation he often felt for others. The only people he got to know were the prostitutes who worked his block. They were sad people in many ways, although often no worse than the "regular" people he met on his travels. But it was a shabby existence and he felt the concern in his mother's voice every time they spoke, so now they rarely did.

What am I doing here? This is insane; they're going to know I'm full of shit. My résumé has more hot air than a balloon and I've got more balls than brains.

If the network had gone to the trouble of investigating his references, they would have found they didn't exist. Robert had always had a talent for re-creating himself as needed.

Sitting in TeleShop's lobby, he steeled himself for the inevitable, allowing his panic to have its moment before it mattered.

He was tall and decent-looking. With a gift for self-invention, he could spin his experience selling magazine subscriptions door-to-door into an adventure—he had to.

I'm not going to spend the rest of my life as a goddamn security guard.

In his head, the voice of Delroy Jackson, the man he worked with in Phoenix, repeated what he'd told Robert the night he had first heard of TeleShop USA.

"Hey, MacKenzie, I've got a job for you. TeleShop needs new on-air people."

The clock above the surveillance monitors read 3:20 a.m. as Robert glanced up from his book.

"The what needs what?"

"TeleShop. You know, the shopping channel? The one from Oklahoma City. They had an ad in *The Sun* yesterday." Delroy put down his newspaper and turned to Robert.

The oppressive quiet of the security office maintained its stony silence. Outside, the empty driveway, leading to the condo's entrance lay still; the access gate hadn't moved in over two hours.

"Never heard of it."

"Ah, I forgot; you don't have cable. It's hardcore; my fiancé is always ordering stuff from them. She even bought our engagement ring there, and what's more, she didn't bother telling me until it was too late. When I came home from work one day last year, she was wearing the damn thing on her hand. Told me it only cost three hundred dollars and she loves me and all. Next thing I know, I'm saying I'll pay for it because we're supposed to be getting married."

"What's that got to do with me?"

"C'mon, I've heard you bullshit with the tenants — you know how to talk. And you're good-looking for a white guy. Besides, you're always saying you ain't gonna be no night watchman for the rest of your life."

"So."

"So call them!" exhorted Delroy, mustering atypical enthusiasm. In the early hours of the morning, maintaining a clear head required effort. Passion was impossible. "The pay can't be too bad. Has to beat the shit out of this place."

"If you're so hot and bothered about it, why don't you call them?"

"Man, they don't want no homeboy like me. And even if they did, I don't know how to bullshit like you. When you're on a roll, it's like poetry."

"Poetry, Delroy?" Robert liked his colleague's description, even as he affected indifference.

"You heard me. Why don't you give it a chance? Didn't you say last week another six months working here was going to drive you right out of your goddamn mind?"

If he had to be a security guard, then working in a condo guardhouse at night was as good as it got. That is, if someone considered doing almost nothing and reading lots of books "good."

"Yeah. You've got a point. But if it's such a big TV network, what the hell are they doing advertising for talent in the newspaper?"

"How the Christ should I know? Yo' big shot, you got better things to do? What you waitin' for?"

In fact, the question was brilliant in its simplicity. He had nothing on the go and limitless time to get there.

Robert's perspiration developed a life of its own, beading furiously and etching down his cheek, heading toward his chin and making a concerted attempt to reach the floor.

"Mr. MacKenzie?"

Robert glanced up from his inner drama with a start and stared in the direction of the voice. "Ma'am."

"I'm Yasmine Dubai, Director of Talent. I work with Ms. Warner."

Robert stood and had his hand shaken with business-like efficiency by a striking young woman. Twenty-six years old, she radiated warmth and charm from her five-foot eleven inch tall and trim frame. A beret held long, brunette hair in a neat braid at the back of her neck. Her teeth glistened like burnished steel, yet her eyes held back the potential malevolence with a seeming vulnerability. She had exotic, Persian features and wore a severe business suit to complete the image.

"Hi," Robert replied.

"Ms. Warner is running late—she's with the Triboro Media people. They're minority investors considering upgrading their position.

They're here on a tour of our facilities."

Robert looked as if only a fool wasn't aware TeleShop had new investors. He shook his head conspiratorially and knowingly as if to suggest he timed his arrival at the office to coincide with the new investor's inspection.

"Ms. Warner asked me to show you around the building until she can see you."

"That would be great." Robert got to his feet and followed Yasmine to the receptionist's desk.

"Rosa, would you please issue a visitor's badge to Mr. MacKenzie."

Robert looked to the receptionist. She was a bored Latina in her mid-thirties, obviously overworked and probably underpaid. She moved about doing eight things at once, answering the phone, directing couriers, ripping copy from the fax machine, all while issuing a yellow security tab.

He took the badge while signing his name on the security log.

"Please, follow me," said his new escort. Yasmine turned and walked through the same door the man in a hurry had entered several minutes before.

The building's entire character changed the moment they accessed its inner sanctum. There was a buzz in the air. They stepped into a long corridor with offices on either side. At the far end stood an archway that opened into a vast space containing hundreds of people sitting in booths, answering telephones. An almost electrical charge crackled down the hallway. Robert glanced back from where they'd come. The lobby door managed to keep the reception room safe from the panic and intensity surrounding him, like a water-tight compartment on a ship. People ran past with intense looks while unseen voices shouted. Robert stared in apprehension, now isolated from the relative tranquility of the lobby.

Yasmine noticed his discomfit and told him this wasn't unusual. "Our business operates on a ten-second basis."

"Ten seconds, what do you mean?" asked Robert.

"It takes ten seconds for our mainframe to update our sales information. We break down each day into a series of individual sales minutes. For revenue calculation, we then examine each minute as a series of six, ten-second episodes."

"Doesn't that ever get the place feeling like an emergency room?"

"Exactly."

Robert's intuition told him it was time to smile and get with the program or forget about the job. "I love chaos," he said with enthusiasm.

"What else is there?" she replied. Yasmine's words, though simple, peeled with unvarnished truth. They bared far more than most would have ever admitted. She couldn't have formulated a more perfect response if he had paid her.

There are moments in everyone's life when awareness strikes with a hammer blow. Destiny is hence; the time is nigh; the cliché is now. Call it serendipity or epiphany; call it happenstance or fortuity. The specific term is of no consequence whatsoever. Robert saw himself at TeleShop—the interview now a formality. He would remain nervous if for no other reason than appearance. But the job was his.

Robert existed for the unstructured, fighting against organization and rules since puberty. It cost him his diploma in high school. That helped to destroy his relationship with his father, a glazier, dead at fifty-two of a heart attack. His dad left behind his own broken dreams and the hope his only son would go to college. His mother still lived in the family home in Shrewsbury, Massachusetts. His older sister (two children and married to a teamster) resided four blocks away. Her carbon copy house mirrored her carbon copy life. She never understood her younger brother and they'd never been close.

Yasmine and I live in the same world; this place is like Beirut. I've been here ten minutes and it's already like being in an asylum.

"Mr. MacKenzie?"

Robert snapped the glazed look off his face and smiled. "Sorry, this place is a tad overwhelming."

"Yes, it's like that the first time you see it. And this is just the office; wait until we get to production. That's when it gets crazy."

In every office and hanging from all parts of the ceiling were television sets displaying, like *Big Brother*, the face of the man who'd barged into the reception room earlier. His image dissolved into a buxom woman smiling while demonstrating some kind of exercise machine. She looked as if she belonged on *The Price is Right*. Robert glanced at Yasmine, noticing a slight curling of her upper lip as her eyes caught the scene from one of the ubiquitous TV sets.

They walked down the corridor, past the offices and toward the archway. A sign hung from it reading, "Television Production." Robert got his first good look into the heart of TeleShop. It was huge; hundreds of people wearing headsets answered calls and took orders. In the far corner was another sign, this one illuminated. It read, "Live Set" and marked the actual shooting boundary. Technicians scurried about moving lights and cables and cameras.

The focal point of the entire process was the man Robert had seen earlier. He sat at an anchor desk, smiling and talking to the camera. His infectious laughter filled the large room all the way to the very back. Robert had trouble reconciling the image he saw in the studio with the disheveled misery he'd seen earlier.

As they approached the arch, a thin, mustached man walked through it and toward them, his shoulders slumped, his head hanging somewhat downwards.

"How was your show, Kirk?" Yasmine asked as he approached.

Kirk's middle-aged features sagged further. He stopped walking and turned to face Yasmine and Robert. "Slow. I swear those assholes don't know a good deal when one hits them in the face."

"They don't appear to have recognized a lot of good deals lately, have they?" Yasmine replied, a measure of concern mixed with a slight menace in her voice.

"Hey, you know what Joe Giannini says. You can't make chicken soup out of chicken shit."

"Kirk, you'd better find the recipe."

In response, Kirk's face went sullen.

"By the way," said Yasmine. "This is Robert MacKenzie. He's trying out for show host."

Robert held out his hand for Kirk to shake. The other man took it perfunctorily.

"A pleasure to meet you," he said without pleasure, turning his back on the two and heading down the corridor. Robert couldn't help but notice how he walked like a beaten man. For the second time that day he thought about Willy Loman.

"Yasmine, the Dealmaker says his show is shit and he needs a drop-in." The same production woman as before approached them and began talking animatedly with Yasmine.

"Didn't Mary-Anne tell Dave we're trying to get away from changing the shows after they're already on the air?"

"I don't know. He's told Mark if he doesn't get a hot product he's going to go to break and talk to Mr. Newton."

Yasmine gritted her teeth. "Tell that asshole he can throw all the temper tantrums he likes; he's not getting a drop-in."

"You want me to include the asshole part or not?"

"Do whatever you feel is best."

The young woman turned on her heels, ran through the archway toward the "Live Set" sign in the distance and then disappeared behind it.

"You'll have to pardon me," said Yasmine. Walking over to an unused desk in the production area, she picked up a telephone. Within a few seconds Yasmine was yelling, a garbled series of invective all Robert could hear.

While waiting for her, Robert walked back a distance into the corridor, his hands in his pockets. Stopping outside an office, Robert glanced inside and saw another middle-aged man, this time black, sitting on a chair and moving his head back and forth between a television to a data monitor, to the television again, and then back to the monitor. A cigarette hung from his lips and a whole tray of butts sat in the ashtray in front of him. For five solid minutes the man never wavered from his routine of TV and monitor. It was like watching the spectators at a tennis match. When a timer appeared on the television set, the man let out a painful sounding gasp and said one word: "Shit."

Robert, not wanting to share the man's obvious pain, turned away, almost bumping into Yasmine Dubai.

"Sorry for the delay, Mr. MacKenzie. If you'll come this way."

"Who's that guy?" asked Robert as they walked into production, his finger pointing back toward the office and the man with his face now buried in his arms. "He's not crying, is he?"

"Jack's our housewares buyer," replied Yasmine. "He's brought in several unprofitable items lately. I'm afraid he's feeling a lot of stress right now."

"Why?"

"The same reason as Kirk. If he doesn't get his totals up, he's gone."

"Been with you long?"

"About a year. I'm not going to lie, Mr. MacKenzie; this place is a steam cooker. If you don't thrive on pressure, you'll never last."

Robert followed Yasmine into the production area. They headed toward the set, walking through the middle of the operators.

"Why are the operators divided into two sections?" Robert asked.

"On our right, they take orders. The operators on our left handle customer service."

"Is the split even?"

"No, it's a dynamic structuring based on call volume. We redesignate customer service operators as order takers during busy periods. It gets crazy at times. Try getting a hold of a customer service rep during a jewelry marathon." Yasmine looked at Robert with a small smirk and a glint in her eyes. Robert returned the smile and nodded, hoping he projected the right amount of confidence and not cockiness.

They walked past two employees setting up a display of the next product to go to air. It was a guitar-shaped clock bearing a picture of Elvis Presley.

Yasmine held open a door and led Robert into the control room. Its quiet contrasted with the set's madness.

The production crew kept the room darkened like a cocktail lounge. Four people worked inside, conversing with a subdued shorthand. In the center sat the director, talking into his headset with a note of exasperation. The audio tech worked on his left, with the character generator operator on his right. Behind everyone stood the tape engineer.

"Dave, I had Susie talk to Yasmine Dubai. ... No, Mary-Anne isn't available. ... For Christ's sake, Dave, they were the people you said were hanging around like a bad smell twenty minutes ago! ... Of course Mary-Anne is still with them; they're major investors aren't they? ... No, I don't think calling Billy-Ray is a good idea. ... Cause he's getting ready to cash out and he's not about to rock the goddamn boat. ... Yeah, she came in here with somebody. ... I don't know who he is; stop being so paranoid. ... She's standing right behind me. ... Oh for the love of God, hold on!"

The director turned around, looking at Yasmine.

"He's in one of his moods, isn't he?" she asked.

"Hung over like a dead horse and feeling worse. He's threatening to walk off air if Scheduling doesn't drop a product into his show."

"What does he want?"

"The Crystal of the Month."

"Fuck him. Give me your headset."

Every month, TeleShop featured a different and unique "Crystal of the Month." TeleShop's "Collector's Committee" chose each multicolored, lead crystal figurine for their special faceting and singular design. Prices ranged from fourteen dollars ninety-nine cents to twenty-nine dollars ninety-nine cents with sizing between one half inch to an inch and a half. The committee agonized over every choice. Each crystal told a "story" when examined as a collection. They debuted in the first week of every month. The figurine was always one of TeleShop's most popular items.

The crystal's truth was rather more prosaic. TeleShop's collectibles buyer selected whatever their distributor had available. The only rule was enough quantity and a profitable margin. She wouldn't have recognized the crystal's "story" if the supplier had stamped it all over their invoice.

The director handed his headset to Yasmine, who slipped it on. Robert disappeared from the scene once Yasmine began talking over the intercom. He was like an appendix — tolerated, but no longer needed.

"You're on drugs, Dave. First, you're not scheduled for the Crystal; the Dragon Lady debuts it tonight in Show #7. If she finds out you've scooped it, she'll cut your balls off and feed them to you for dinner. Second, you know we've changed our policy about drop-ins. No more. They force us to act tactically, not strategically. I don't give a rat's ass about her always getting the better products. Stop whining like a baby!"

The control room door opened and in walked a short, corpulent man. He looked in his mid-sixties and wore a western-cut suit with a bolo tie and cowboy hat. A tall, busty woman, chewing gum and carrying a notepad, followed him inside.

Robert knew instinctively this must be Billy-Ray Newton. His secretary stood with vacuous eyes, her enormous bosom heaving under her tight dress.

For nine months Robert had lived in Phoenix. He still found the cowboy entrepreneurs of the Southwest self-parodying in their appearance. It was the New Englander in him prodding his bemusement. The area's nouveau riche country bumpkins and their floozies were of a piece.

Grinning, Billy-Ray waved to the control room. He whispered something in his assistant's ear that made her giggle.

"How y'all doin' today?" he asked with a distinct Southern drawl.

"Good, Mr. Newton," rose the room's collective voice, with the exception of Yasmine. She continued speaking with the Dealmaker. Yasmine glanced at Billy-Ray, nodding in recognition before returning to her conversation.

Billy-Ray kept smiling and shook some hands before pausing to listen to Yasmine's now somewhat whispered conversation with the Dealmaker. "Say, Yasmine, what's old Dave got his panties in a twist about today?"

Yasmine Dubai removed the headset and gave it back to Mark. She straightened her hair and faced Billy-Ray. "He's upset because he doesn't like his show and he wants a drop-in."

"So why don't y'all give him one?"

"Because as we've discussed, sir, if we give in to the temptation of fixing shows while they're on the air, we sabotage our long-term planning. You're well aware of the problem. Drop-ins of hot products cause sell-outs, which unsettle the flow of later shows, disrupting our merchandising. That prevents us from creating the kind of product mix which enhances our demographic appeal and allows us to watch our gross margins by limiting the sale of low-profit items."

It was love. The way Yasmine stared the rube down. Her eloquence, her prescience. One glance told him she was right, while another look at Billy-Ray told him she would lose.

"Yasmine, girl, you are absolutely right. No *bout adout* it. Hell, it's why I hired ya. Old Mary-Anne needed help and you were the ticket. But y'all do Billy-Ray a favor, just this once; give the Dealmaker what he wants. I got folks here from New York poking around and big sales right about now would sure look nice. Y'all understand what I'm sayin'?"

Billy-Ray had the charm of a Baptist minister at a Mississippi tent revival. With a snap, the magic grin reappeared on his face. Billy-Ray took his assistant by the hand and led her out the control room's other door with everyone forced to accept his decision, knowing it was final.

The room paused as Billy-Ray left, before the quiet hum of activity began again. In the studio, the floor director cued the Dealmaker the break had ended. Dave, sweat beading on his face in the air-conditioned studio, began yammering away afresh about another unbeatable value on yet another unbelievable product.

"You want me to call Scheduling?" Mark asked Yasmine.

"No, but call them anyway."

"The Crystal?"

"The Crystal."

The director picked up the receiver as Yasmine stood behind him. She stared through the control room's glass window onto the studio floor and the Dealmaker, sitting at the anchor desk, laughing with a lady on the phone from Shreveport, Louisiana.

Robert looked at Yasmine, reacting to the Dealmaker's victory.

Her pained expression gave him momentary insight into her inner thoughts —

Asshole.

CHAPTER THREE

Mary-Anne Warner

"So why exactly do you want to work here, Mr. MacKenzie?" asked Mary-Anne, her eyes hard. "It isn't the easiest job in the world by any means."

Robert faced his prospective employer from across her desk. Yasmine sat in a chair on Mary-Anne's right, a clipboard holding his résumé in her hand.

"Well," he began with a lie, "I've watched the show quite a bit. I suppose, I've always enjoyed selling. There's something about the close, moving in for the kill as it were, you know what I mean. This place is completely unique; it almost reminds me of the coliseum. The gladiators are your show hosts and the slaves are your customers. The only difference here is that when the telephones are screaming off the hook, it's like the victims are lining up for you to kill them. I don't know if I can describe it any better than that. I guess I liked the feeling in the air when Ms. Dubai showed me around earlier. This business is something else."

Mary-Anne smiled, folding her fingers into a gesture of prayer.

Yasmine remained stoic, ever the professional, watching and saying nothing.

"In another company, such a frank admission might end an interview immediately. But, as you correctly point out, this isn't 'another' company. We're judged on our sales minute-by-minute, and that doesn't leave us time for a lot of tortured introspection."

Mary-Anne looked over to Yasmine and nodded. Yasmine stood up and went to a filing cabinet in the corner of the office. She reached inside and pulled out a leather pouch, handing it to her boss. Mary-Anne in turn tossed it onto the desk in front of Robert.

"That's a man's shaving and travel kit. We retail it for twenty-nine dollars ninety-nine cents. You've got exactly one minute to come up with some ideas and start pitching it to me as if you were on our network. If you can convince me it's worth buying, I'll give you a chance. If not, we're wasting each other's time. Your minute starts now."

Mary-Anne looked down at her watch.

§

Robert MacKenzie

Robert glanced at Mary-Anne and then at Yasmine. She returned his stare, Robert noting (hoping) a slight smile cracking through her unemotional features before they became impassive again. He unzipped the leather pouch and took a look inside, a well of panic seizing his chest. It was one thing fantasizing about working on-air. It was quite another trying to sell this woman a man's shaving kit while she sat in front of him, his entire trip and a job he knew he must have on the line. It made him feel inadequate and nervous and excited, all at the same time.

Inside, the kit contained a shaving brush, a razor, a pair of tweezers, a mirror, a nail file and had spaces for deodorant, soap. and other toiletries.

I can't pitch this thing cold; this is ridiculous. Who does she —

"Begin, Mr. MacKenzie."

"Ladies and gentlemen, we're back at TeleShop USA and very pleased to present our Sammy Dreydl Men's Travel Kit for only twenty-nine ninety-nine!" Robert began with a start, the words flowing from his mouth. "Beautiful patchwork leather, with a security clasp and the Sammy Dreydl monogram in the lower corner; it'll be a pleasure to finally fit all your grooming products into one, easy-care case."

He ignored his own objections about why he couldn't come up with something to say and surprised himself by concentrating on pulling it off. Robert's mind raced in overdrive as he tried to remember the travel kit's tiniest details.

"Look at the quality of this. Double-stitching, extra-reinforced for durability. It takes up so little space in your luggage."

This was his time and somehow, he might pull it off. The strain made him feel like a man who always bragged about how he would run the bulls in Pamplona, Spain, one day, only now he was there and the bulls were right behind him.

"You know what trouble a plastic bag filled with your shaving equipment can be. They start off the trip fine, but by the end they're all slimy and gooey and ripped and what have you. I'm not joking. How many of you have pulled open a plastic bag filled with shampoo from a leaky bottle? Muck coats your razor, clippers, everything. A wonderful, leather case like this makes it all so unnecessary ... "

He was on a roll, telling them to call now or miss the great buy. He talked about convenience, he spoke about value and utility, he related humorous, if untrue, anecdotes about his own travel experiences. He didn't even notice the expressions on Mary-Anne and Yasmine, he was so focused on selling the shaving kit. If he had, he would have seen them both smiling, confirming his earlier realization. The job was his.

"… not to mention a graduation gift for your son when he finishes high school. Tell him you're proud of him, acknowledge he's a grown-up, only twenty-nine dollars ninety-nine cents. Call now!"

§

Robert MacKenzie

"Like it's spelled on my résumé: capital M-a-c, capital K-e-n-z-i-e."

"We'll need a voided check to direct deposit your salary."

Robert reached into his wallet and produced a check from inside one of the pockets, offering it to the hefty woman who sat at the typewriter next to him. A half-lit cigarette hung from her lips.

Does everybody in this building smoke? Doesn't that violate the health code?

"This won't do; it's from out of state," the big woman said, handing Robert back his check.

"So how am I supposed to get paid?"

"I'd get a local bank account in a hurry. Let us know when it happens, otherwise you're working here for nothing."

"By the way, in all the excitement, I never thought to ask how much a new show host makes. Do you know?"

"Sure thing, sweetie. Trainee hosts make six dollars and seventy-five cents per hour. Here, sign this and go into the room over there and get your picture taken."

"Did say, six seventy-five, for a television job?"

Is she kidding? That's it? I make six twenty-five as a security guard!

"Sugar, you have any idea how many people come in here all full of piss and vinegar figuring they're going to be the next Dealmaker? You last a few months, I'm sure ol' Billy-Ray will take care of you. Now get over there and get your photograph done and be back here at 9:00 a.m. tomorrow."

Robert went over to the photo area and had his picture taken by another bored woman. After a few minutes, she handed him an employee ID card. It was a typical driver's license photograph, making the subject look like anything but himself. Below his name, it read "Show Host." Robert let the card's impact sit for a bit before he walked out the front door, heading toward his car and the motel.

§

Robert MacKenzie

Another hot June day in Big Country Land, Classic Country, twenty-four hours a day on KGOK, Oklahoma City, Oklahoma. Mercury's way up to one hundred four degrees with a bullet and no sign of relief for the rest of the week; KGOK time 3:45, kicking off a six-pack for the girls at Chuggers, check it out and be a part of the action, Monday night special, Bud Tall Boys only ninety-nine cents, you can't go wrong, it's the best party in town. Five locations to serve you including I40 at Exit 35, here's Merle Haggard ...

The drone of Merle's country twang blared throughout his car. Robert knew the song, but recoiled with sudden shock. While he may not have been from Muskogee, he was now most certainly an Okie.

In Boston, June was a study in contrasts. You could have hot muggy weather one day and misty cool the next. Oklahoma was more like a steam sauna. By the time July came around the humidity was so intense that walking was more akin to vertical swimming.

When Robert lived in New England, an air-conditioned car was a luxury, not a necessity. Here, his Honda Civic's interior temperature would boil water. The sun burned through the windshield without relief. Oblivious to the heat, yet another country singer moaned on about lost love.

I have to report for work tomorrow morning. I've got enough clothes to last for a week or two at the most and enough money for ten or twelve days, if I don't eat much. How am I going to pay my rent at the motel, let alone my room back in Phoenix?

Rush hour started around 4:00 p.m. As the time dragged near, traffic picked up. Robert weaved between the cars, excitement with his new job mixing with concern. The combination kept his foot heavy on the pedal. He wanted to call Delroy and tell him about the interview.

Actually, if Robert wasn't back to work by next week, his company would fire him. That notion didn't give him a speck of trouble. It wasn't the low pay; it was the complete and total lack of respect the position received. He'd heard so many derogatory rent-a-cop jokes they didn't bother him anymore. What irked was the reaction he received from women. Several months ago, he was out with some friends at Seagull Inlet, a trendy singles club in Phoenix. Robert saw an attractive woman at the bar who returned his smile when their eyes met. He approached her to strike up a conversation.

"Hi, what's your name?"

"I'm Candace Fedoruk," she replied, looking coy. "What's yours?"

"Robert MacKenzie." He prayed to the pickup gods for a favor. "What brings you to the club tonight, Candace?"

"Oh, I'm here with friends from school. Girls night out, you know what I mean."

"Sure do," Robert chuckled. "Where do you go to school?"

"I'm at State," she replied, crinkling her eyes and dropping her head a touch.

"What are you taking?" asked Robert, hoping (praying) for a major in something (anything) of substance. The attendant hypocrisy of the fact he dropped out of high school didn't register.

"I'm doing a masters in nineteenth-century French literature."

His heart almost stopped. Candace's major was so unexpected, Robert thought he misheard. She had beautiful eyes. The more she talked, the more they glowed—a completely rare and intoxicating combination.

"That's wild. I'm currently reading the second volume of *Remembrance of Things Past*."

"Go away!" Lindsey replied. "Are you serious?"

"Yes, I love French literature. Hugo, Molière, Zola … I thought *J'Accuse … !* was extraordinary."

"Wow, that's so unusual." Candace beamed, her bright smile showcasing dazzling white teeth. "It's rare to find someone who's even heard of any French writers, let alone be familiar with their work. Tell me, what do you do for a living?"

"I'm a security guard," Robert said.

Candace's face froze, dismayed. Any hope of conversation ended.

"At an exclusive condominium!" added Robert, hoping to escape a brush off, but knowing it was imminent.

"Oh, you'll have to excuse me, my friends are calling. I hope we'll see each other later." She picked up her drink and walked away toward the crowded part of the bar, disappearing into the throng.

"Robert, you should do what I do."

He turned to find his friend D.J. standing behind him, half-drunk and grinning.

"And what exactly is that?"

"I tell them I'm in television. It works every time."

It was only Robert's sense of humor that saved him from jumping off a cliff. He was twenty-five years old, had been out of school almost ten years, and he still had nothing but some clothes and a beat-up Honda

Civic to show for a decade of work.

Robert turned into Best Value Inn, a motel he'd picked when he arrived in town the night before. It was close to his new office and its run-down look told him he could afford it. Turning off his ignition, Robert sat in his car for a few seconds, deciding if he should talk to the manager about a weekly rate or go watch television. He decided on the former.

A bell jingled when he opened the screen door and approached the counter.

"Hi, my name's MacKenzie, I'm in Room 15. Do you have a weekly rate?"

A middle-aged Arab male glanced up from his newspaper. "Seventy-five dollars a week, payable in advance."

"Is that the best you can do?" Robert asked.

"Seventy-five dollars a week, payable in advance," the manager repeated, his voice flat and monotonous.

"Okay, I'll take a week."

Robert pulled his remaining money from his wallet and counted out seventy-five dollars. He handed it to the man who put it in his pocket.

"Do I get a receipt?"

"If you want a receipt, it's a hundred a week," the manager said, his eyebrows raised.

"Never mind." Robert sighed. "By the way, I didn't see any place selling regular beer. Where can I pick some up?"

"You can't. It's a dry county." As the manager spoke he opened the Coca-Cola cooler by the counter and pulled out a six-pack of Olde English Malt Liquor. "That'll be six dollars."

Robert paid him, impressed with the guy's complete lack of expression and seeming total unconcern for the law. The manager took the money, again putting it in his pocket.

"I guess a receipt for the beer is out of the question?"

The man didn't even crack a smile or acknowledge the remark. He sat on his couch, opened the newspaper and began reading.

As Robert stepped back outside into the heat, a battered wreck of a car shot past him, kicking up a cloud of dust. Startled, he froze, eyeing the car as it pulled to a stop in front of one of the motel's rooms. The door opened, and a large man pulled himself from the driver's seat, slammed shut the door and walked over toward Robert and the office.

It was the Dealmaker, who by his demeanor, appeared to be in an even fouler mood now than he was this morning. He walked past Robert, opened the office's screen door and went inside.

Dust devils enveloping the Dealmaker gave him an almost Satanic appearance. A cigarette hung from his lips and sweat glistened on his skin. Robert stood, confused, as the office door shut behind him.

Less than a minute later, the door opened again and the Dealmaker walked back outside, this time swinging a six-pack of Olde English Malt Liquor while chugging down one of the cans. The Dealmaker headed toward his car and kicked its left side with contempt as he approached. Stepping over the curb, he fished a key from his pocket and opened the door to Room 7, walked inside, and slammed the door.

Robert stood in the dusty, parking lot and fixated on the Dealmaker's closed door amazed by the coincidence. His entire trip, from arriving at the ramshackle motel last night to his interview this morning, his obvious (and hopefully mutual) connection with Yasmine Dubai, the ambiance at TeleShop, the loquacious Arab motel manager and now the Dealmaker's sudden appearance, felt like an episode of *The Twilight Zone.*

What the hell is he doing here? He's gotta be making decent money at TeleShop. Jesus, they treat him as if he owns the place. Is he meeting a woman? Then again, the receptionist did say his wife threw him out three months ago;

surely he hasn't moved in here?

While Robert carried on his private conversation he edged himself closer to Room 7 until he stopped in front of it. He heard a toilet flush and a loud groan from inside, escaping through the thin walls. The sounds of the Interstate and his own nerves had kept him awake much of the night before.

He rapped on the door, another muffled curse coming from inside the room and the sound of shuffling feet approaching him. The door opened. Standing in the frame staring at him was the Dealmaker, the same look on his face Robert had seen in the reception room that morning.

"Yeah, can I help you?" he asked.

"Uh, well, I don't know," Robert stammered. "You're Dealmaker Dave Leonard, aren't you?"

"You got it, kid. Congratulations on finding me. Have a nice day." The Dealmaker began shutting the door and Robert wedged his foot in the jam.

"Hey, mac — do I owe you money or something?"

"No, you got it wrong. I was at TeleShop today. I saw you in the lobby when you arrived for work."

"Thanks for sharing that with me. Now if you'd please go away."

"I'm sorry, it's just Mary-Anne Warner hired me as a show host. I had an interview with her and Yasmine Dubai earlier. I start tomorrow."

The Dealmaker paused and furrowed his brow, scratching his cheek while staring. "You were the guy in the control room, right?"

"Yes, sir."

"My best wishes on your new position. Now, I'm tired. We'll talk sometime," the Dealmaker replied gruffly.

Robert's awkward anticipation crashed. He didn't know why he wanted to speak with the Dealmaker, but he did. He was still elated from getting the job and didn't have a friend in town to share it with. He supposed he should phone his mother and sister, but he didn't feel up to it.

The Dealmaker noticed Robert's sadness, and more importantly, the six-pack dangling from his right hand, and had a change of heart.

"Alright. C'mon in; I'll let you stay for a few minutes. Mind the mess."

The Dealmaker stepped back and allowed Robert access. Calling the room a pig sty would have insulted the pig. The unkempt quarters resembled the kind of lodging frequented by derelicts: filthy, disorderly, and rank. Observing Robert's reaction, the Dealmaker mumbled an apology and said he didn't trust the motel's maid to clean the place; they'd stolen some change or something. Robert pretended to accept the explanation and sat down on a chair the Dealmaker pulled out for him. The Dealmaker sat on the edge of the bed and cracked open another can of beer, his third since his arrival less than ten minutes ago.

"So you saw Mary-Anne this morning?" asked the Dealmaker.

"Yes, she was busy with some people so Yasmine Dubai gave me a guided tour. I met with the two of them later in Mary-Anne's office."

"So what'd you think?"

"Of whom, Mary-Anne or Yasmine?" Robert asked.

"Both."

"Very nice, very businesslike."

"Yeah, that's for sure. Let me tell you something, kid, what'd you say your name was?"

"Robert MacKenzie."

"Yeah, Robert, you can call me Dave. Mary-Anne's a bitch, simple as that. She'll nail your bag to the wall as sure as look at you. Billy-Ray's getting ready to cash out and move to Florida. That's why Triboro wants to take a majority stake in the joint. Unfortunately, he's got a performance guarantee written into his buyout. If TeleShop's valuation doesn't hit target, Billy-Ray will leave a lot of money on the table. Trust me, he will be one mean bear with one mighty sore ass for the next couple of months. Mary-Anne is a Triboro plant. She wants to hurry Billy-Ray's departure and take over when he's gone and she won't let anything stand in her way. All of us have got to be on our toes: you, me, everybody."

"Really?" Robert said.

"Really. As for Yasmine, she's okay. But unfortunately, she thinks she's tough. Her family's from Iran; they moved to Canada when she was a kid. Tough, like hell! She has a great façade but that's all it is. At least she knows what she's doing; she's got a goddamn MBA from some university back east. Where she falls short is practicality. Yasmine knows the theory but couldn't sell a glass of water to a thirsty man. In this business, sales — every minute, every second — is everything."

"What about Mary-Anne?"

"Tough with a capital 'T.' Don't fuck with her."

"I was in the control room when you had your disagreement with Yasmine."

"Listen, kid. One thing you gotta get straight right now. In this business, you're only as good as your last show. They talk a lot about demographics and broadening their audience, maintaining margins and what have you. But it's all horseshit. All of it. They've been trying to implement this crap since I got here five years ago. That's why they hired Yasmine. Like I told you, she's got an MBA. Her job is to develop a program to fix the place up. The fact is, the second sales tank, all their plans go right out the window and it's back to business as usual. If you take the big picture and don't bitch and scream for products every day, you're screwed! Pure and simple."

The Dealmaker finished off his beer and reached over to grab another can. "Am I drinking alone?"

"Sorry," Robert replied, opening a can from his six-pack. "Cheers!"

"Yeah, whatever. You got a smoke?"

"I'm afraid not, I don't —"

"Yeah, yeah." The Dealmaker stretched across his bed to the end table, knocking several empty cans of beer to the floor. He grabbed a crumpled package of Camels and pulled out a lone cigarette. "There's nothing worse than running out of smokes."

"How about running out of beer?"

"Nope. That's bad, but not as bad."

"What about running out of both?"

"You're right, that's worse!" Both men laughed, hoisting cans of Olde English to each other.

The Dealmaker picked up the telephone and dialed the desk while lighting the cigarette. Ahmed, I'm out of smokes. No, a carton and a dozen Olde English. Of course put it on my fucking tab. What do you mean when? Hold on ... " The Dealmaker looked at Robert. "Kid, you got twenty you could spot me?"

Twenty? Christ, I'm broke. That's food for a couple of days. But can I say no?

"Ah, I suppose."

"Great, I'll pay you back Friday. Ahmed, I'll pay you cash, send your boy over now." The Dealmaker hung up the phone, shaking his head. "Cheap, fucker, you'd think I owed him his life savings."

Robert wasn't sure how to respond. He took a drink from his beer and decided to say nothing.

"It's my wife, of course, the fucking bitch. She's got my balls crushed so hard I can barely breathe."

"You're having problems with her?"

"Problems, hell! She's killing me. Okay, so she catches me in the sack with Debbie Bruin, so fucking what! Does that mean she has to toss me out on my ass? Now my two daughters won't talk to me, the court's garnished my wages so much I can't afford to take a dump in a pay toilet, and I have to live in this shithole!"

"How long has this been going on?" Robert asked.

"Three months. Three miserable goddamn months!"

"Where's Debbie Bruin?"

"Fuck if I know. She was our tenant. Eve tossed her ass on the sidewalk before mine. Okay, so I shouldn't have done it. Hell, a man's a man — how long was I supposed to watch her traipse around the basement apartment unit in her underwear? For Christ's sake, I'm only human!"

"Of course, how much could they expect you to take?" agreed Robert, astonished the man's ravings sounded reasonable. The Dealmaker swept those around him in a maelstrom of turmoil, his energy and chaos ripping a hole in space, distorting reality wherever he went.

A knock sounded on the door. The Dealmaker crushed his cigarette in an ashtray and walked over to answer. A young man, about fifteen, stood in the doorway with a carton of Camels and two six-packs of Olde English Malt Liquor. "My dad says you have to give me twenty bucks," the boy announced with a halting and hesitant tone.

"Yeah, tell your dad I love him too." He turned to Robert. "Kid, shoot me that double, would you."

Robert hadn't heard a twenty described as a double for a long time. His father used the same slang: fin, saw-buck, double, half-a-yard, etc. But that was an even longer time ago. Robert took the bill from his wallet and gave it to the Dealmaker who gave it to the boy.

"Sorry about the money, Dealmaker. It's my dad; you know how he is."

"Don't worry about it, kid. Drop by sometime."

"Thanks, Dealmaker," the young man answered. He passed over the beer and cigarettes and walked back to the office.

The Dealmaker shut the door and placed the two six-packs in a bar fridge next to Rob's chair. Ripping open the carton of Camels, he pulled out a single package and extracted a cigarette.

"Thank you, Jesus," the Dealmaker said, lighting up the cigarette and blowing a long draft of smoke into the air. He took another hit from his beer and turned to face Robert.

"So what about you, kid. What brings you to Oklahoma-fucking-City? You sure don't sound like you were born here."

"Actually, sir —"

"Cut the 'sir,' shit. Call me Dave or Dealmaker or anything at all except sir. And have another beer. Jesus, I hate feeling like the guy I'm drinking with is playing catchup."

Robert grabbed another beer, surprising himself with the speed he finished his first. He ripped an extra can from the tab and handed it to the Dealmaker without asking.

"That's better," said the Dealmaker. "So, what's your story?"

"Well, I'm from Shrewsbury, Massachusetts. That's about an hour drive from Boston."

"Yeah, I know where it is; it's a suburb of Worcester. I like Worcester, got a bar off Main Street at Pleasant serves a great ham and cheese sandwich on rye. Moynihan's Tavern! Haven't been there since the seventies."

"That's right. It's still around. I'm born and raised in the area."

"Lots of schools in the Worcester area," the Dealmaker went on. "I used to work for a company that specialized in printing yearbooks. Got to the point where the sight of another high school guidance office gave me the shakes." The Dealmaker chugged down more beer. The fact he could drink so much and remain coherent was impressive. "You think selling shit to adults is bad? Try high school kids! Christ, they're a pain! You gotta get everything approved eight ways to Sunday and they're never satisfied. Never! God save me from fucking high school student councils."

As the older man finished the drink in his right hand, he picked up the new one with his left, opened it, and poured some down his throat without missing a beat.

"Why'd you leave the printing business?" Robert asked.

"Personal reasons," the Dealmaker replied without elaboration. "Got into craft fairs about ten years ago. My partner and I sold laser art from a booth we'd set up at shows. First three years we made a fucking fortune! Nobody had ever seen our stuff before. By the fourth year, business slowed down and we began to see some competition. By year five, well, let's say I was lucky to be in Oklahoma City one fall afternoon, reading the paper, you know what I mean?"

"Gotcha!" Robert replied, recognizing fate had provided them a common lucky break.

They talked for the better part of four hours, the Dealmaker drinking and smoking, Robert only drinking and trying to keep up. He told the Dealmaker about growing up in New England, his father, and leaving home when he was sixteen. He spoke about coming to TeleShop because his gut told him he could do the job the moment his friend mentioned it.

The Dealmaker told stories about his early days at the network, moving his family from Los Angeles, and the enjoyment he found selling products on television. Robert knew he left a large part of the tale unsaid. The Dealmaker lived in a shoddy motel with no wife, no family and no money, and although he was only forty-three, he looked a great deal older.

"Any chance of getting out from under the support agreement?" Robert asked the Dealmaker, both of them well lubricated from the

Olde English Malt Liquor.

"Fat fucking hope. I have two daughters; one is seventeen and pregnant and the other is a twenty-year-old college student. I've got a wife who hasn't held a job a day in her life. Then there's me—I'm forty-three, look fifty-three, and my high-profile job convinced the judge a celebrity like me shouldn't worry about providing for his family in style."

"Dealmaker, you're right. You got fucked!"

The two men laughed together in a drunken chortle, raising their beers and toasting each other. As the hours passed, the conversation became less coherent and more boisterous. At some point, Robert heard banging on the wall, but chose to ignore it. Instead, he got up to urinate. When he returned, he reached into the bar fridge and saw only two cans of beer left. Robert hadn't realized how much alcohol they'd consumed or how intoxicated he actually was until then.

"Dealmaker, I've got to get out of here. If I don't get back to my room, I'm going to pass out on your floor ... Dealmaker?"

The Dealmaker lay on his back, snoring into the air, an empty can of beer in his left hand, a still-smoldering cigarette in his right. Robert gazed at the man's prone figure and then turned to let himself out. Shutting the Dealmaker's door, he lurched to his room.

God, am I going to feel like a rat-bag tomorrow.

It was his last memory until morning.

CHAPTER FOUR

Robert MacKenzie

Robert's alarm went off at 8:00 a.m. Turning over, he wedged a pillow over his head to hide from the cacophony. He had always hated alarm clocks. They represented the kind of nine-to-five lifestyle he loathed. It didn't matter how mild or muted their chimes sounded, he couldn't stand to hear them anywhere. Years ago, while working as a front desk clerk in a run-down hotel in Boston, he purchased an LCD pocket clock. Its alarm produced the gentlest warbling tone. He detested the job with a passion and for some reason associated his hatred with the LCD alarm. To this day, if he heard a similar sound, even if only in a movie, it made his skin crawl. When he quit the hotel, he left the alarm behind, its thirty-dollar cost immaterial.

Fuck.

Reaching over, he silenced the clock and pulled his body to the sitting position. His feet touched the floor, his head propped on his hands that in turn rested on his legs.

Jesus Christ.

He stood and walked to the toilet, pausing at the dresser. Reaching for a bottle of Excedrin he opened it and swallowed several tablets, washing them down with a glass of water he poured from the bathroom sink. He climbed into the shower, turning on the warm water and pushing his face into the stream. The spray refreshed him before he began the torturous process of dragging the soap across his body and rinsing it off.

I hate showering with a hang-over. Christ, who am I kidding? I hate scratching my butt with a hang-over.

After a few minutes, Robert climbed out and walked to his bed, water dripping from his body. He fell back and lay staring at the ceiling for several minutes. Feeling the roughness of his beard, he wondered if he could get away without shaving. But, on his first day of work, that was out of the question. With a quiet groan he got back to his feet and walked again into the bathroom, reaching for his razor and shaving brush. He didn't know how bad the traffic became during morning rush hour and didn't want to be late.

By the time Robert left the motel, cars packed the Interstate. Although he felt a general sense of nervousness about his first day, Robert knew he had left early enough to arrive on time. Before getting into his car, he noticed the Dealmaker's Duster still parked outside Room 7. Robert paused by the door to listen for any signs of life, but heard only silence. He stood back and walked to his dust-covered Civic while the morning sun began its daily summertime bake-off.

Robert wasn't prone to perspiration overdrive, but the Oklahoma heat pulled every dollop of sweat from his body. He rolled down both front windows and that helped, somewhat. But it also increased the noise. The air in the car whipped about so loudly it drowned out the radio which, upon reflection, wasn't so bad.

If I make it at TeleShop, I'm going to get a new car with air conditioning. This is ridiculous.

Robert's head continued thumping, making him wish he had something stronger than Excedrin to ease the pain. When he finally saw his exit, he glanced at his watch, thankful he was ten minutes early.

TeleShop lay in an industrial mall off I40, east of Oklahoma City. Its nondescriptness matched the ugly suburban commercial/industrial zone which surrounded it. You could get lost among the endless array of anonymous small businesses, all identically neat and manicured. Each unit the same with their illuminated signs and glistening, paved parking lots. Its bland restaurants existed only during business hours. The area emptied after six p.m., and on weekends you were plain out of luck. As for cocktails, forget it, Like Best Value Inn, TeleShop's environs allowed only low-point beer (and even then only sparingly). The verdict? Grim. Very, very grim.

Before entering the building, Robert looked around the parking lot. In one corner, surrounded by a chain-link fence, stood two large satellite dishes. Off to the right of the employees' door sat a loading dock. UPS parked two large trailers against the bay's open doors. Like TeleShop's lobby, the relative calm of the parking lot could deceive the unwary.

As he opened the employees door, Robert expected another near-electric surge when he walked inside.

"ID."

"Pardon me?" Robert replied.

A fleshy, middle-aged security guard sat in a booth next to the entrance. He wore a dirty, smudged, blue uniform with a crooked hat lying loose on his head. A cigarette hung from his lip and his boots were on his desk. The man's revolver lay out of its holster next to his feet.

"Uh, is this what you mean?" Robert asked, pulling the new employee ID from his pocket.

"Yeah, that's it. Make sure you clip it on your shirt."

Robert attached the tag to his breast pocket and was about to walk into the building proper when he realized he didn't know where to go. "Excuse me, this is my first day and I'm not sure where I belong."

"What'cha do?"

"I'm a new show host."

The man displayed a pained expression, but nodded and got to his feet, telling Robert to wait. He picked up the telephone.

"Yeah, it's Hank. Got a new host here needs lookin' after. Hey buddy, what's your name?"

"Robert MacKenzie."

"Okay, wait here a minute. Yasmine Dubai's comin' down to get ya." The security guard put down the phone, sat in his chair and placed his feet back on his desk. He caught sight of Robert looking at him, his posture and his pistol. "It pinches when I leave it in the holster with my feet up, you know what I mean?"

Robert turned away, nodding his head in acknowledgment while waiting for Yasmine. He paced about before hearing the sound of someone coming down the stairs.

Yasmine Dubai wore a beige business suit with a cream-colored blouse and black pump shoes. He'd always loved the professional look, the librarian or schoolmarm outfit. Something about the severity of icily-cut clothes combined with smoldering intelligence always got his attention.

"Good morning, Mr. MacKenzie," Yasmine said with a smile.

"Good morning, Ms. Dubai. You look well today."

Robert deliberately made the comment on Yasmine's appearance, but immediately wondered if it was a good idea. He worried about sounding inappropriate, not only because Yasmine was his immediate supervisor, but also because he didn't know how she felt about flirting.

"Thank you, Mr. MacKenzie. Please follow me, I'll show you to your training group."

Robert wasn't aware there was a training group as he assumed he was the only new show host starting that week. The news didn't make him feel secure.

"How many new hosts will there be in the group?" he asked.

"Six, including yourself."

"And how about this training? How long does it last?"

"Three days. Those of you who survive can expect to shadow an experienced host on Friday and Saturday, and if you're still around, to have a solo on-air shift during the overnight on Sunday."

"You try out a lot of potential hosts?" Robert asked.

"Mr. MacKenzie, it's an ongoing process," replied Yasmine, radiating competence. Beyond her physical charms, she had poise and aplomb to spare.

They ascended to the top of the stairs and walked into the production area from the rear. TeleShop stood on a sloping hill so the front lobby and production area were on the ground floor while the employee parking lot shared space with the warehouse and shipping dock on the lower level. From their position at the far back, Robert looked out onto the hundreds of frenzied telephone operators typing orders onto their data terminals. It was the same madness by the "Live Set" sign as yesterday. Technicians and camera people hustled about with products. On one of the omnipresent television monitors, a middle-aged woman with a dazzling smile talked about a green brunch coat: "A great buy for nine dollars ninety-nine cents!"

Perched next to the TVs showing TeleShop's feed were data terminals displaying the number of calls coming into the building. The current total read one thousand, nine hundred and eighty-eighty.

"One thousand, nine hundred and eighty-eight! Does that mean there's that many people buying *that dress*?" Robert asked, pointing to a TV.

"That's exactly what it means," Yasmine replied.

"Christ, God help us!"

For the first time since he met Yasmine Dubai, Robert saw her laugh. Yasmine's face beamed as her shoulders shook, her head arching back toward the ceiling. Their eyes locked for a moment before they both broke the contact.

"It is God awful, isn't it, Mr. MacKenzie!" She chuckled.

"No *bout adout* it, Ms. Dubai."

Yasmine stopped laughing and looked at Robert, as near as he could tell, an image of respect on her face. She smiled as she spoke. "You do pay attention, don't you, Mr. MacKenzie."

"I try. But please, do you think you could stop calling me Mr. MacKenzie? My name's Robert. And would you mind if I called you Yasmine?"

She paused for a second, a slight, yet wry smile appearing across her lips. "Call me Yasmine. I'll think about the other and let you know, Mr. MacKenzie."

Robert dipped his head in reply as they stopped in front of their destination, a door marked "Green Room #3." Yasmine opened it and motioned for Robert to enter.

Mary-Anne Warner sat at a conference table in the small lounge. Arrayed around the table were five men who looked to range in age from twenty to forty-five. Mary-Anne was at the table's head, a bulky laptop computer in front of her. A projection television hung from the ceiling, its screen attached to the wall opposite. The men looked nervous while Mary-Anne displayed the same intensity he saw yesterday.

"Mr. MacKenzie, please have a seat. I'd like to begin as soon as possible."

Robert pulled out the only chair remaining, at the far end of the table. Yasmine Dubai left the room, closing the door behind herself.

Mary-Anne began speaking.

"I'd like to welcome you here to TeleShop. On behalf of myself and our president, Billy-Ray Newton, I wish all of you the best of luck. Working as a show host is a great job, the money is terrific, the hours are super, and the recognition factor, especially here around Oklahoma City, is very high. However, saying that, I should also mention the odds of any of you succeeding and lasting beyond this training are very slim. In fact, even if you pass the training and make it to air, the likelihood of your being with us even a year from now is even slimmer."

A series of forced smiles and nervous laughter appeared from the men at the table. Everyone thought they would be the exception, the one to make it. Robert believed this himself, bolstering his fears with swagger, as did others.

"I don't mean to alarm you, but the fact is that as much as we try, it's almost impossible to determine who will make a good show host. We've hired broadcasters and found out they couldn't sell. We've hired salesmen and discovered they weren't good on television. The truth is, most of our best people walked in the door one day knowing they had a natural affinity for the job. I hope you have the same feeling. In the interview process, you pitched a sample product and convinced me you had potential. Now it's up to each of you to show you're worth putting on-air. We have only two positions open and we'll only hire the two best candidates."

Mary-Anne paused. Nobody said anything, but the stolen looks and nervous glances continued. The green room barely fit seven persons with the conference table and its chairs. Its oppressive atmosphere shimmered with raw tension. Robert wondered if his companions noticed as well.

"Since we're going to be here for a couple of days," Mary-Anne continued, "we should get to know each other. Let's start with you."

She pointed to the man on her right. He was a thirty-ish, white male with fair, balding hair and a mustache.

"Uh, my name's Reid McBain. I'm from Gallup, New Mexico. I now live in Oklahoma City and work as an announcer at a local radio station. I watch TeleShop quite a bit and figured it might be interesting to see if I could work here as a host."

The smiles continued. Mary-Anne acknowledged Reid and looked to the man on his right and Rob's left.

"I'm Terry Pavão," said a tall man in his early forties. He was well turned out in a pressed, bespoke suit with a matching silk tie. "I've been in advertising for the last twenty years and I've decided on a career change. Creating pitches others use to sell products becomes boring after a while. So, I figured it might be fun to do a little direct-selling myself."

Mary-Anne looked at Robert, her eyes fixing on his with the rest of the room following suite.

"Robert MacKenzie. I'm from Massachusetts, but lately I've been living in Phoenix. My background is direct sales. I hadn't given any thought to working here until a friend of mine told me TeleShop was advertising for hosts. I don't want to sound boastful, but something clicked inside me. I hope — actually I know — I'm one of those people who walks in off the street with a natural affinity."

Robert stopped talking, happy with his directness, a brief and self-assured smile appearing on his face. He looked at Mary-Anne and saw the positive impression he'd made. In the others, he detected some anger and fear, accepting it and understanding he wasn't there to make friends. If he needed to display brashness then he would.

Robert joined with the room, looking across the table to the man sitting opposite. Mary-Anne raised her eyes and waited for him to begin.

"I'm Alan Bennet and I'm like Robert," said a young man about the same age. He wore a cardigan and a tie and spoke with a pronounced New York accent. "I know I can do this job. I've worked in the carnival business for the last ten years. My family has several booths and we tour across the country. I've been a pitchman since I was twelve. I'm looking forward to working at TeleShop and I'm raring to go."

Mary-Anne smiled. Robert thought him a quick study. Next to Alan sat a nervous man in a rumpled suit, his chaotic hairstyle all frizzy and gray. He looked in desperate need of a cigarette. Considering what he'd seen the day before, Robert wondered why he didn't light one up.

"My name is Saul Lowenstein and I've worked for PBS since the early seventies." Saul's voice boomed out of all proportion to his unimpressive appearance. Startled (along with everyone except Mary-Anne), Robert realized he'd heard Saul narrating *Nova* or some such show. Lowenstein didn't come across as a salesman. "The federal government cut back funding for the network. I got laid off from the Los Angeles affiliate three months ago and I've been looking for a TV gig ever since."

Does TeleShop plan to use his dulcet tones in their promos if he doesn't work out as a host?

"And finally, we come to Mr. Bondero," Mary-Anne said turning her head to the final man, sitting on her left.

"Hi, I'm Sandy Bondero. I already work at TeleShop as an order taker. I've been here for two years and I love my job. Ms. Warner is letting me become a show host."

A quick grimace splayed across Mary-Anne's face, indicating something was up. Of the group, Sandy was the most out of place. He was a pudgy kid, appearing about nineteen years old. His face still had acne scars and his hair could have used a rinse.

"Mr. Newton—our president—believes in promoting from within," said Mary-Anne. "Sandy has been asking us to give him a shot as a host, and we've agreed to try him out. If he's successful, he'll be the first network representative to become an on-air personality." Mary-Anne continued smiling in a subtlety condescending manner. Training Sandy Bondero was clearly not her idea and his hope of passing was less than nil.

"Gentleman, now that we're acquainted, it's time to begin. Let's start with the basics. Phone calls come into this building in the form of a wave ... "

§

Yasmine Dubai

"Mom, everything's fine. Sometimes I get frustrated, like right now, but I'll get over it. I mean after all, this isn't life or death; it's a job. ... No, thanks for calling. You always seem to know when I'm down. ... How's the weather in Toronto? ... Same here, hot. ... Give my love to Farrah. ... You too, bye."

Yasmine Dubai put down the telephone and leaned back in her chair to think. Her mother seldom called her at work, yet when she did, her timing was always impeccable.

Yasmine had worked at TeleShop just shy of one year. They'd recruited her at Wharton, shortly before she completed her MBA. Many recruiters stalked the university's jobs fair and most of them were very interested in Yasmine. She had top grades, a respected undergraduate degree and was also a woman *and* a visible minority. She hadn't even heard of TeleShop USA and had never considered working in direct-response television. But she'd also never met TeleShop's Vice President, Mary-Anne Warner.

From their first interview the possibilities presented by TeleShop compelled Yasmine. They were the third largest home-shopping network in the country, achieving that feat with only a sixty-one percent penetration of the US cable market. As Mary-Anne explained, the right change of look and demographic gave them enormous growth potential. Mary-Anne wanted to expand globally, making Yasmine's knowledge of the Canadian and British markets a real asset.

From her perspective, Yasmine recognized Mary-Anne's seething desire and ambition, seeing its reflection in herself. She wanted to use Mary-Anne as a mentor and climb with her through the corporate maze. Although there were parts of her superior Yasmine found unappealing (the vulgarity, the overt pushiness), Yasmine would work around any problems.

"Triboro Media has increased its holding in TeleShop since their initial purchase two years ago," Mary-Anne told her over dinner during Yasmine's second interview. "While they respect Billy Ray's chutzpah in getting the network on the air and admire the way in which he secured financing, they also feel he doesn't have the ability to set TeleShop's long-term direction."

"What do you mean?" Yasmine asked. She sensed Mary-Anne must have already decided to hire her or she wouldn't have entrusted Yasmine with confidential information.

"Triboro brought me on board after making their initial buy to keep a watch on their investment. TeleShop makes a negligible profit. Our demographic skews to middle-aged, lower-income women. We also tend to churn through our customers. Most make their last purchase from us within a year of their first. If we don't expand our customer base, there will be no one left who hasn't already bought or refuses to buy from us in the next five years. There aren't enough low-income women to go around."

"So, what do you need me to do?"

"I need help," replied Mary-Anne. "I'm busy with the purchasing department and the show hosts and I'm stretched way too thin. I need to bring in somebody with impeccable credentials to help me push TeleShop in the right direction. We need to expand our cable base, especially in California. I have to increase the sophistication of our wholesale buyers so I can attract the proper retail customer. In essence, I need you to run interference for me and help me deal with the show hosts and Billy-Ray."

"I don't get it. Why is everybody so opposed to change?"

Months later, looking back at the interview, Yasmine shuddered at her question's naïveté.

Mary-Anne told her nobody hated change like the show hosts. At their worst, they were a bunch of selfish, egotistical children who wouldn't embrace anything that upset their little world. As for management, Yasmine respected and even liked Billy-Ray, but he was an old school entrepreneur who didn't get the difference between running a string of southern radio stations and a national television network.

Yasmine didn't always like the on-air talent very much. They often acted like spoiled babies and she had no time for self-involved narcissism. Her family had endured far too much pain and suffering for her to tolerate conceit in others.

She was born in Tehran to a Bahá'í family. She had one sibling, Farrah, a sister four years her junior. Yasmine's mother, Safia, had a degree in Persian Literature from the University of Tehran, but was a housewife. Her father, Hossein, was a mechanical engineer who worked for the government.

In 1969, when Yasmine was eight, she joined her mother and sister on a "temporary" move to London. Her father stayed behind in Tehran. Political violence against the Shah and general discrimination against those of the Bahá'í faith made life in Iran difficult.

Three months after their move, the family learned of their father's murder. The details were never clear. Either protestors killed him during a demonstration because he was Bahá'í, or the police picked him up at that same demonstration and he "disappeared."

It was so hard without you, Daddy. And I was so alone. We didn't have money. Our Immigration status was unclear. Mom was a wreck and Farrah was way too young to understand. I will never allow myself to be vulnerable like that again.

Yasmine didn't like London. She was only nine when they left Tehran and the months in Britain were the worst. She used to cry herself to sleep at night, asking her mother why her father couldn't be with them. Safia had her hands full trying to raise Yasmine and her five-year-old sister, Farrah. The uncertainty made everyone's life wretched. After half a year of living in cold, drab, rain-soaked England (Yasmine could never think of it any other way), her mother told them they were moving to Canada. On April 1st, 1970, the family arrived in Toronto.

Canada was a complete change from England. Toronto was a much newer and brighter city than London. Yasmine had taken English lessons from a private tutor in Tehran and further developed her fluency while in the UK. This eased her transition after the family's arrival. At some point, Yasmine stopped thinking about her father on an hourly basis.

Toronto's small, but affluent Bahá'í community helped the family with jobs. After five years, her mother saved enough money working in the clothing import business to open a boutique in Toronto's fashionable Yorkville district.

Yasmine's sister, Farrah, remembered nothing of Tehran or London and thought of herself completely as Canadian. She was doing her Bachelor of Science degree at the University of Toronto and was hoping to become a physician.

Yasmine graduated with a Bachelor of Commerce from McGill University in Montreal and won a scholarship to study for her MBA at the Wharton School in Pennsylvania. Yasmine loved the idea of attending school in the United States, viewing it as a fulfillment of her dream. Although Canada had been very good to herself and her family, Yasmine's ambition burned too bright to find success anywhere but the US.

From high school, she dreamed of working as an executive in New York City. Oklahoma didn't figure into the plan. But she could tell Mary-Anne intended to take over TeleShop, and Triboro's headquarters was in Manhattan. Mary-Anne's ruthlessness became obvious by that second interview with the sharing of the confidential information and her game plan. No other position at the jobs fair offered the same combination of intrigue and immediate seniority. There wasn't even a close second. Yasmine took the job.

On Yasmine's desk lay a stack of reports; her terminal's screen displayed a half-completed memo. The filing cabinet across from her held two televisions, one showing the network feed, the other the second-by-second call volume. The combination of the three monitors, desk, chair, and cabinet made for a very crowded office.

Yasmine looked at the network image and noticed the Dealmaker's show had begun. He sat at the anchor desk, grinning and laughing as always.

You're charming, Dealmaker, I'll give you that. But, we need to move on or we'll die on the vine. The old ways of doing business won't work anymore.

Turning back to her monitor, Yasmine massaged her temples before going back to work on her memo:

To: Billy-Ray Newton

From: Yasmine Dubai

Re: Evaluation of new Show Host candidates

Based upon the first day of training, our most promising candidate is Robert MacKenzie, a twenty-five-year-old male originally from Massachusetts. First indications suggest he is one of the rare natural hosts we discover from time to time. His unforced pitches are creative. While Mr. MacKenzie has no broadcast or non-retail sales experience, we have opted to give him a chance and await his performance on-camera All other trainees sit in the middle ...

CHAPTER FIVE

The Dealmaker

"Now, y'all know I think the world of ya, Dealmaker. But the facts are the facts." Billy-Ray leaned back in his chair, a large Cuban cigar in his right hand. "The Triboro boys now own forty-nine per cent of TeleShop and they don't operate the way we do. These New York types are bean counters. They think operating a television network isn't any different from running a shoe factory. Hell, I've owned radio and television stations in the South since the 1940s; it never changes. Your best talent is always half-insane. Had one guy, Mean Bob Eggleton, used to do the morning-drive show on my Memphis station. Craziest mother you ever did meet! Didn't know from one day to the next if I'd find him dead in a bar or dead in a whorehouse. But the sonofabitch always made his shift and his ratings. Christ, he owned Memphis back then."

The Dealmaker sat in front of his boss's giant wooden desk, feeling like death. He'd arrived for work twenty minutes prior and wanted nothing more than to get out of Billy-Ray's office and over to the set.

"I hear what you're saying," the Dealmaker began, "but this is nuts. I can't go to the men's room without wondering if Mary-Anne is hiding in one of the stalls. And my shows … Shit, are they doing this to me on purpose?"

"I got the Crystal for you, didn't I? Had the Dragon Lady in here yesterday afternoon. If she had a gun, I'd be as dead as dogshit!"

"Yeah, I know. Thanks. But what about the long-term problem? Mary-Anne is gunning for my ass. And she's covering herself with Yasmine, letting her do the dirty work."

"Son, I ain't an idiot; I know that! I *had* to take Mary-Anne because Triboro insisted. She came as part of the financing. The stupid woman thinks I don't know where her real loyalty lies. But, Dealmaker, I'm sixty-eight years old and I'm getting tired. I don't want to run this outfit anymore. Problem is earnings are way down and the only people who are giving me a decent price for my stake is Triboro. I hate the pricks, talking down to you all the time! So I didn't finish the fourth grade? I'm still worth two hundred fifty million dollars. Those faceless New York types make me sick, but they've got my nuts in a grip. If I don't get our earnings up in the next year, they can exercise their option to buy me out for a quarter of our agreement. However, if I get our price to the agreed level, they have to buy me out at market value. Son, that's a lot of goddamn money, and I'm not going to piss it away. Y'all understand what I'm sayin'?"

The Dealmaker acknowledged Billy-Ray, raising his hands in surrender. "What about Yasmine? She's making me crazy!"

"Yasmine's a good kid. She's the least of your problems. She's only doing what Mary-Anne tells her, and besides, she believes in her demographics and all. She's got that business school stuff burned into her head. Give her time, she'll learn there's a middle road between theory and practicality. Besides, Yasmine's right. We've gone as far as we're gonna get selling to the old ladies. We gotta change. Okay?"

Billy-Ray took a long drag on his cigar, inhaling and then blowing the smoke out in a ring. He looked back at the Dealmaker, gesticulating with his cigar. "Dealmaker, how y'all fixed for money?"

"I had to borrow twenty bucks from one of the new show host trainees last night to buy some beer and smokes. That tell you anything?"

"Jesus Christ, you sure got Eve all pissed with you!" Billy-Ray said.

"That's only the half of it."

"Not much I can do about that. She's got a court order on me garnishing your wages."

"I know," replied the Dealmaker. "But it's killing me anyway."

"Look, I'll give you some walking-around money in cash. Go see accounting when you get off-air. I'll slip you two thousand dollars. But keep it quiet and don't even tell your lawyer or *I'm* screwed. Understand?"

"Billy-Ray, I love you!" the Dealmaker said beaming.

"Yeah, I'm an old softie at heart. Hey, which one of the trainees were you borrowing the money off?"

"Robert MacKenzie."

"The tall one? He was in the control room with Yasmine yesterday?"

"Yeah, that's him. Turns out we're staying at the same motel. Got a bit liquored up with him last night."

"For God's sake, Dealmaker. Leave the kid alone! Yasmine tells me he was the best of the lot in the interviews. We need some new talent."

"I hear you. Don't worry."

"What's he like?" asked Billy-Ray.

"The kid's okay. A bit naïve. But you know how it is—we won't know shit until we see him on-air."

"True enough. Speaking 'bout on-air, it's time you met with your people and reviewed the show. You're on in ten minutes."

"I'm already gone," the Dealmaker replied, getting up from the chair and heading toward the door.

"Hey, Dave," Billy-Ray said.

The Dealmaker turned and faced his boss.

"You look like shit. I'm serious. Start taking better care of yourself or your money problems won't matter anymore, you understand what I'm sayin'?"

"Yeah," the Dealmaker replied.

"Sure you do. By the way, you know what happened to Mean Bob Eggleton?"

"No. What?"

"Didn't make his shift one morning. We sent somebody over to his house to check on him. Dead. Lying in bed with a beer in his hand. Dave, he was forty-eight. You're starting to remind me a lot of Mean Bob lately."

The Dealmaker nodded and opened the office's door. He passed by Billy-Ray's secretary, wearing another tight-fitting dress and filing her nails. She held a vacant stare, fixated on the window.

Shit.

§

Robert MacKenzie

"So, let's break for lunch. Take an hour. We'll reassemble in this room at 1:30 p.m." Mary-Anne picked up her papers, got to her feet and left the green room.

The trainee show hosts rose and headed for the door.

"Man, that was intense," said Reid McBain. "My head hurts."

"I hope it lets up a bit. I don't think I can face two more days of all this theory," replied Saul Lowenstein.

"I don't think the theory part lasts forever," Alan Bennet added while stretching his arms. "Wait until we start practice-pitching in front of Mary-Anne and each other. That's when it'll get tough!"

The assembled group muttered in agreement as they filed out of the green room.

"Any ideas for lunch?" asked Robert.

"There's a restaurant down the street. I saw it on my way in. Why don't we go there?" proposed Terry Pavão.

The suggestion won by default. The group walked through the aisles of operators toward the employee entrance. They didn't notice a few of them turning their way and the odd chuckle. Show host trainees were a dime a dozen. Their self-image as new elites contrasted with TeleShop's reality. In fact, they were little better than fodder. Regardless, TeleShop's staff always discussed the new hosts, often wagering on who would and would not make it.

"How far's the restaurant?"

"Over the hill by the lights. We can walk it in five minutes."

It took them ten. The group entered the Excelsior Coffee Shop, a local greasy spoon. Truckers and warehouse workers filled its seats, with the trainees grabbing its last remaining table. A gum-chewing waitress filled their coffee cups without asking saying she'd return in a minute for their orders.

"You think we have time?" asked Reid. "It wouldn't look good being late on our first day."

"Relax," replied Alan. "We're all here. They can't exactly start without us, can they?"

"What'd you think of this morning's session?" Terry Pavão asked while taking a sip of his coffee.

"Like I said, intense," Alan replied.

Robert didn't say much, nodding in reply to the banter. When the waitress returned, he ordered a cheeseburger and a chocolate milkshake.

"What do you make of it all?" continued Saul. "I've been in television twenty-five years and I've never heard of this wave and closing stuff."

"That's because you worked for PBS." Robert found the former announcer's total lack of comprehension throughout training frustrating. "Saul, you're not in Kansas anymore. We can distill most of the morning to two points. First, people tend to call in waves; the idea is to generate a fresh wave when the old one subsides. Second, you use the incoming call monitors to analyze when your pitch is successful. If calls increase, go with what you're saying. If they decrease, change it!"

Robert wasn't trying to show off in front of his fellow trainees, but he had a natural understanding of the process. Mary-Anne's speech about call volumes made perfect sense. He also got the notion behind margins, demographics, and product diversity. Robert listened with rapt focus the entire morning. The others evinced varying levels of comprehension.

Saul Lowenstein was like a ballet dancer in a football huddle, clearly in the wrong place. Terry Pavão appeared to understand the process the most, Sandy Bondero the least. The TeleShop order taker wore his feelings in plain sight. His face hung limp, overwhelmed by information beyond his grasp.

"I'm with Alan; this is nothing," Robert went on. "Wait until we start practice-pitching. There are only two positions available and there's six of us. Do the math."

"It isn't fair. There ought to be a law. You shouldn't give a man a chance and then put him in a competition where he might lose. It's inhumane," interjected Saul.

"Yeah, I agree," Sandy replied. "I've been at TeleShop for two years and I deserve this break. I'm as good as anybody else!"

"Hey, guys. That's life," stated Terry Pavão. "You think this is tough? Try advertising. On big contracts, management will put two or more creative teams on the same account. Whoever turns in the best copy, gets to keep their job. People you've worked with for years become the enemy. It's not pretty."

"Is that why you got out?" Robert asked.

"Naw, I got bored. It cost me two marriages. I'm forty-five and I'm tired of the bullshit. My last assignment was creative director of Rogers, Paxton, Goldberg, and Speers; they're the largest agency in the US. After twenty years I had enough. My wife and I split last year and I hit the sauce a bit. It was time for a change."

After ten minutes of waiting, the waitress brought their orders, a fried confection of red meat, potatoes, coffee, and milkshakes. The Excelsior didn't serve gourmet fare and what it did make, it didn't make well. Robert remained the group's most subdued member during lunch. He didn't want to build friendships with the competition, although it had already become clear he was by far the strongest candidate.

Beyond Robert's earlier moment of self-discovery, the group's dynamics were obvious. He didn't need another walk with Yasmine to see the truth. Sandy and Saul were complete non-starters — hopeless. Reid McBain was out of his element. Alan Bennet had potential. Terry Pavão had strength, although something dark lay beneath his exterior.

Sandy and Saul complained about TeleShop, life, and a million other subjects during lunch. Alan and Terry spent most of the time chattering between themselves. What little Robert said was small talk with Reid McBain. The radio announcer had arrived in Oklahoma City three years before. He'd spent the last decade working for small town country radio stations across the South. Reid viewed his current position as the big time, and it sounded like his wife had pushed Reid into answering TeleShop's advertisement. The high intensity morning made McBain very uncomfortable. Robert judged he might drop out by the end of the day.

The group split the check, with Terry reaching for it the moment it hit the table. A quick calculation showed Pavão underpaid his share. Robert always found cheap people untrustworthy, although he elected to say nothing. If Terry was a former advertising big-wig, this was a hell of a fall. What was the real reason for his career change? Pavão may have been hitting the sauce more than a bit.

It was an uneventful walk back to TeleShop. Robert didn't like his new employer's location in the slightest. It was sterile and reminded him of a trip his family took to Epcot Center when he was fourteen. While his parents and sister fussed over the handicrafts available in the Morocco Pavilion, Robert stood by himself, disappointed by the experience. Whenever he'd seen pictures of Africa, it always looked dangerous, from the Arab north to the Kalahari south. Africa was a poorer, more primitive place than America. There were no street sweepers washing the sidewalks in the Casbah. Authentic Africans didn't spend their meager resources on shiny, new clothes or shave their scrubbed-clean faces daily like the Moroccans at Epcot. Humphrey Bogart didn't walk into a Casablanca merchant's stall to buy Americanized trinkets, arranged in neat rows and overpriced.

On reflection, Oklahoma resembled Phoenix, new and unspoiled. This industrial area was a model of enlightened civic planning, with streets laid out in grids and man-made rolling hills to break up the landscape. It could have been anywhere.

The hot sun continued beating down on the trainees as they walked back into TeleShop's parking lot. As they entered the building, the air conditioning swamped over them. It took away his languor and helped him face the next few hours of competition.

"ID."

Hank the security guard still lounged in his chair, his feet and pistol again on the desk. Robert and company showed their new employee badges and walked back upstairs. At the far end of the production area stood Mary-Anne, waiting in front of Green Room #3. The clock read 1:27 p.m.

§

Yasmine Dubai

"I let them go early," Mary-Anne said, lighting a cigarette in her office. "After a couple of rounds of this, Yasmine, you become real good at picking winners. It's amazing how soon the genuine talent shines while the ones who only put on a good show fade. Men ... they're fucking transparent, all of them!"

Yasmine sat in Mary-Anne's large office in the building's executive area, a notepad in her hand. Her ostensible job was reporting on the focus group studies of their current on-air talent. But Mary-Anne often liked to have a cigarette and talk about the day with Yasmine. At first, Yasmine enjoyed being privy to the inner workings of TeleShop's management. But, for the last few months, listening to Mary-Anne's constant self-aggrandizement and caustic barbs had become boring.

"Reid McBain's out," Mary-Anne announced. "Asked to see me half-an-hour ago and said he didn't think the job was for him. Pussy! That leaves four."

"Don't you mean five?" asked Yasmine.

"Four. You're under the mistaken impression the training group included six people. There were never more than five. That Bondero kid is *not* going to be a show host. If Billy-Ray thinks we make the operators happy by letting them pretend they can go on-air, he's crazy! That's why they're fucking operators!"

"So what about the rest of them?"

Mary-Anne took a long drag on her cigarette and leaned back in her chair. "MacKenzie is the obvious choice. He has it. You can tell by his eyes he understands the fundamentals. Lowenstein is a whiner; I doubt he'll make it, but hey, shit happens!"

Yasmine suppressed a wince. She didn't mind vulgarity and was not averse to employing it herself. But with Mary-Anne, it was nonstop and without reason. It was one of the many reasons feeding her disillusionment.

The other was Billy-Ray. While she found his hayseed shtick exasperating, Yasmine had to admire his basic intelligence. At heart, Billy-Ray had the soul of a great businessman. Their president played his cowboy folksiness to the hilt. The western suits, the "aw shucks" mannerisms, his airhead secretary, all spoke to a classic stereotype. Yet, when Yasmine had mentioned the famous Persian King, Cyrus the Great, in passing one day, Billy-Ray knew the name. He spoke about Cyrus founding the Achaemenid Empire.

"I didn't get to where I am by being stupid," he said with a small grin before walking back to his office. Yasmine watched him leave, feeling schooled for the first time in years.

She found Mary-Anne's constant undermining of TeleShop's president exasperating. It only distracted the entire management team from their main goal: increasing profits and long-term viability.

"That leaves Terry Pavão and Alan Bennet," continued Mary-Anne on a self-congratulatory roll. "They both have their pros and cons. Pavão's got more experience, but I have to wonder what the hell he's doing here? You saw his résumé; this is a guy who's used to making six figures and he's settling for seven bucks an hour. Bennet is hungry and has talent, but does he have the sophistication we're looking for long-term? His style is more Billy-Ray Newton than Rodeo Drive. Gotta admit though, he is good looking!" Mary-Anne smiled and laughed, inhaling from her cigarette while putting her feet on her desk.

"Any hunches?" asked Yasmine.

"I don't know. Have to see what happens tomorrow. I'll keep Sandy around 'til the end to keep Billy-Ray happy and I'll let Lowenstein stay for safety's sake. I'm going to want them to pair off tomorrow and try some practice-pitching and it's always easier with a spare." Mary-Anne rolled her neck around and glanced at her watch. "It's 4:30, I've got to get out of here. You send that memo off to Billy-Ray?"

"I finished it before coming here and left it in his mail slot."

"What'd it say?"

"Pretty much what you've told me. I didn't have the benefit of seeing the group in action; I based the memo on their résumés and interviews," Yasmine replied.

"Go on."

"I said that Robert MacKenzie was by far the strongest. He could be a real winner. I thought Sandy Bondero was hopeless, as was Saul Lowenstein. I recommended we didn't hire them."

Mary-Anne squinted, annoyed by the last statement. She took her feet from the desk and drew herself up in her chair. "What do you think you're doing? The memo Billy-Ray asked for was to confirm my hiring decisions. Not to throw Sandy Bondero in his face. When you tell him his program to train operators as show hosts is bullshit, you're not exactly going to endear yourself!"

"That's not what I said," replied Yasmine, piqued.

"Sure it is. I know Billy-Ray. He doesn't like junior employees telling him he's wrong. He *told* me it was a good idea to bring Bondero on board. When you say it was a mistake, it doesn't make you look bad, it makes *me* look bad. You're my assistant, for Christ's sake! You're not supposed to question the wisdom of whom I hire."

"Mary-Anne, that's not what I did!"

"In effect, it is. No! Don't say anything," Mary-Anne almost yelled, waving her hands when Yasmine tried to respond. "I'm pissed. And what the Christ is wrong with Lowenstein?"

Yasmine refused to become flustered. Mary-Anne was prone to hyperbole and drama, her frequent outbursts flashing like lightning. When very upset, her practiced diction slurred into a southern drawl. Yasmine knew little about her manager's background. She often wondered about Mary-Anne's rise at Triboro, since Mary-Anne was never forthcoming.

"You said yourself you thought Lowenstein wouldn't make it," Yasmine said. "I told you that *after* his interview!"

"Oh, so now you're hiring the hosts?" replied Mary-Anne, on the defensive. For a smart and strong woman, she could surprise with her brittleness. "Lowenstein has a great TV background *and* a great voice! Besides, he's Jewish. Isn't one of our main goals to attract affluent Californians? Do you know how many wealthy Jews there are in Los Angeles alone? Look, I accept you might not understand; you're from the Middle East."

Yasmine was on the verge of anger, her voice controlled and tight. "I'm from Canada. Yes, my family's from Iran. But I'm *not* an Arab and I'm *not* a Muslim! And anyway, almost half the hosts are Jewish. If we hire people based on race, do we need another Jew? We only have one black host. We don't have any Asian hosts. Do you have any idea how many wealthy Asians there are in Los Angeles alone!"

"Yasmine, I don't like your tone."

Yasmine heard the implicit threat in Mary-Anne's voice and held her temper in check. She hadn't worked sixty-hour weeks for a year to find herself out on the street. Mary-Anne did have a point about presenting a unified front, although Yasmine hated the way she expressed it.

"Mary-Anne, I'm sorry if I've offended you. I should have checked before sending the memo. But the remark about the Middle East hurt me. Fanatics murdered my father in Iran. I don't have time for intolerance against anyone and I hate people accusing me of it based only on my background."

"I apologize for the comment," Mary-Anne said with forced calm. The threat in her voice remained, only masked by a show of humility. "It was inappropriate. But I stand by what I said about the memo."

The two stayed silent, the hostility now subdued but still present.

"Is there anything else I should know?" Mary-Anne asked.

"No. I agreed with your analysis of Pavão and Bennet. I also commented that the résumé's of MacKenzie, Pavão, *and* Bennet all looked to suffer from a degree of fiction about their backgrounds."

"The good ones always do," Mary-Anne replied smiling. "Go back in the files and look up the Dealmaker's application sometime — it's almost a novel!"

Yasmine grinned, as did Mary-Anne.

"I've got to get out of here," Mary-Anne said. "The group is back tomorrow at 9:00 a.m. Sit in on part of the session, will you? And do me a favor, if you're planning on disagreeing with any of my decisions, let me know about it first!"

"Alright, Mary-Anne," Yasmine acknowledged.

"Let's go home. I'll see you tomorrow morning."

"Sure thing. I'll see you then," replied Yasmine walking toward her office.

Despite Mary-Anne's comment, it was nowhere near time for Yasmine to leave. She still had to finish the focus group analysis and complete her monthly customer buying pattern report. With luck, she could leave work by 10:00 p.m.

Oklahoma City was not Yasmine's idea of living in the United States. Ever the snob, picturing America, she thought of Manhattan. Or Chicago. Or Boston. The intellectual stimulation of Wharton versus the glamor of Hollywood. In moments of reflection, she missed Toronto's cozy familiarity and Montreal's French smugness.

After a year, her condo resembled a hotel room more than a home. Boxes lay still packed on the floor, and neither art nor knick-knacks adorned her walls. For someone who worked at a company that had lifted the selling of trinkets to an art form, Yasmine had little to display.

The exception stared at her daily. Atop her TV sat a miniature crystal Santa. TeleShop had given one to every employee last Christmas. With all the anger Yasmine directed toward her adopted town, she never stopped to think if her sadness was, in reality, a comment upon herself.

When the loneliness became overwhelming, Yasmine reacted more out of desperation than genuine desire. On four occasions, she had ventured out alone for a drink, becoming quietly drunk while turning down men. The next morning, an even larger void filled her than the night before.

Two months ago she'd gone out again. There was a man at the bar. Tall and swarthy with piercing eyes who charged her attention. After several drinks, Yasmine struck up a conversation. She loved his eyes — their intensity, their fire. Yasmine felt drawn to him even though it didn't take her long to realize he had a wife.

By 2:00 a.m. he joined Yasmine at her condo, naked, their bodies locked on her mattress. When the mechanics finished, she barely heard him leave. Later, Yasmine noticed the unfamiliar wetness of his semen on the sheets. While she didn't have a problem with the night's morality, sitting up alone in her bed, she felt completely empty and somewhat cheap. Yasmine raised her left hand to rub the sleep from her eyes, and only then noticed she was crying.

CHAPTER SIX

Mary-Anne Warner

"You're quite the stud, aren't you?"

Mary-Anne Warner looked at the ceiling, a cigarette in her hand. Next to her lay Alan Bennet, propped up on a pillow in Mary-Anne's large, oval bed.

"I didn't figure drinks after work meant I'd be spending the night with the boss," he said, smiling.

"Hey, lover. Don't get presumptuous. You got to fuck the boss, but you're not spending the night." Mary-Anne ran her hands through Alan's hair, mussing it. "But don't worry, we can do this again if you'd like."

"I'd like it very much."

Mary-Anne butted her cigarette in an ashtray on the night stand and got to her feet. "I've got to take a shower and you've got an early morning tomorrow."

"It's not that early," Alan protested.

"It's early enough. Get dressed and get out of here. And I don't have to tell you to keep your mouth shut."

"About what?" Alan asked. "That the boss invited me out for drinks at the end of the day to talk about my performance? That she plied me with alcohol, took me back to her place and then fucked my brains out? Is that what you mean?"

Mary-Anne crawled back onto the bed and crouched over Alan, her breasts swaying inches from his face. "That's exactly what I mean," she said while kissing him and grasping his penis. "If you keep this up, among other things, you have a great future at TeleShop." She finished her kiss, got back to her feet, and walked toward her shower. "I'll see you at work tomorrow. You can let yourself out."

Mary-Anne always washed away the smell and sweat of her lovers immediately after sex. Of late, Mary-Anne had only slept with much younger men. Alan Bennet was twenty-five while Mary-Anne was forty-four. She enjoyed the power imbalance and the often-profound Oedipal undertone of sex with a boyish man.

Although she worked out every day, in the last couple of years she had found it harder to keep her body lean and tight. Her small, firm breasts had begun to sag. It was the same with her behind. She compensated by wearing shorter skirts and sheer nylons, bringing attention to her legs, an area she thought in better shape.

She lingered in the shower longer than necessary. She didn't want to catch Alan on the way out because she only had two jobs to fill and from initial impressions, MacKenzie and Pavão looked like the best candidates. She should never have slept with him. In fact, she didn't intend to hire Alan Bennet at all. Taking on Robert MacKenzie filled her demographic need for a younger, male host. But Alan had been her last interview of the day. She liked his blonde, California looks, even if he had a thick New York accent. She also liked his smarminess and wondered about his real reasons for being in Oklahoma City. According to Bennet, he was visiting friends when he noticed the ad in the paper.

She didn't care about his history. As she told Yasmine earlier, the show hosts often came from questionable backgrounds.

When Mary-Anne finally left her bathroom, a towel wrapped around her still-wet body, she lit up a cigarette. Alan had left and the sheets on her bed lay askew. Her immaculately furnished condominium sat in the city's most affluent area. Its impressive view of the darkened skyline highlighted her condo's emptiness.

She liked to think of herself as a modern, urban woman, forgetting about her upbringing in West Virginia, her father a coal miner, her mother a housewife. She had eight brothers and sisters and of the lot she was the only one to finish high school. Studying part time at City College of New York, she left her rural roots far behind. She worked reception at a Manhattan talent agency to finance her studies. After graduation, West Virginia became a distant memory. She didn't speak to her family much anymore and hadn't been home since her father's funeral six years ago.

What am I going to do with you, Alan? Could I get away with hiring three hosts? Then again, Pavão or MacKenzie might not make it. No, forget that, Pavão might not pull it off, but MacKenzie? He's hungry and he's got talent. If he looked at me the way you did Alan …

§

Robert MacKenzie

Robert MacKenzie also lay on his bed, drinking a can of Olde English and watching TV. He'd knocked on the Dealmaker's door earlier that evening, but there wasn't an answer. Unsettled, he strolled about the motel's parking lot, observing the trucks rolling off I40 and watching the sun set over the vast and rolling Oklahoma prairie. He walked back to his room, hoping to catch sight of the Dealmaker's Duster. But other than the odd car pulling up to the office, there was only silence.

From time to time, Robert left his unit to get ice from the cooler. He used the trips as an excuse to walk by the Dealmaker's room and check to see if the older man had come home. He finally resigned himself to an evening alone, wondering why he had such a powerful need for company. It was atypical. Robert had always been a loner.

At eight p.m., he called Delroy.

"Yo' brother, where y'all been?"

"I'm in Oklahoma City. I got the job at TeleShop."

"Shit! You for real?"

"No, I got it. Well, I'm in training, but I'll get by. What's up at the office?"

"Real simple, you don't show up for your shift tomorrow, you're out of work."

"How did they know I'd miss it?" Robert asked.

"Gadberry gave you a call at home on Monday to talk about switching shifts. When you didn't get back to him by today, he called me a few hours ago and asked if I knew where you were. Said you were out of town on family business. Gadberry phoned the office, told 'em you were absent without leave!"

"That asshole! God, he's a prick. Does he think we're in the army?"

"Exactly, my brother," Delroy replied. "If you're gone, I'm going to have to work with that knob more often."

"Jesus," cursed Robert. "It's not like I haven't shown up for work. These are the vacation days I booked. And they accepted them. Why should they expect me to notify them if I leave Phoenix? It's not fucking legal!"

"Yeah, I know. They say if you go out of town you gotta tell them so they can make contingency plans."

"Well, to hell with them! Tell them I quit. They can mail my last check."

"No problem. How's TeleShop? If my old lady sees you on there, she's gonna scream!"

Robert paused, taking a final swig from his beer and tossing the can toward the garbage pail. He let out a belch (only partly covered by his hand over the receiver) and continued. "It's enormous. You've never seen so many telephone order takers in one place. They've got more operators than the phone company."

"No shit," replied Delroy.

"Serious! When one of the products gets selling, the entire building starts to cook. You can feel the energy. People run out of their offices to look at the call monitors. You've never seen anything like it. But the tension … Jesus, it's unreal! During my interview, I saw a guy weeping in his office. People yelling curses—and I mean the worst kinds of curses—at the top of their lungs right up and down the hallways. Nobody bats an eyelash Delroy; it's like nothing else on Earth."

"Y'all think you're gonna like it?"

"I don't know. But I know I have to try."

"Guess you're making some pretty serious money, huh?" There was a clear hint of envy in Delroy's voice.

"Well, in the future. I'm only starting at seven bucks an hour. But I hear if I'm any good, I can make over a hundred thousand dollars a year."

On the other end of the phone there was only silence.

"Delroy you there?" Robert asked.

"Yeah, I'm here. Jesus that's a lot of cash." While it had been Delroy's idea for Robert to try out for TeleShop, the sound of envy became the sound of resentment.

"Yeah, it might be. God knows I can use the money. I've never made big dollars before."

"Ain't that the truth," Delroy answered, a hollowness in his voice. "Shit, what I could do with that sort of coin. Kinda puts you in a whole new snack bracket, don't it."

There was another, now awkward pause in the conversation that Robert tried to fill.

"Well, I'll cross that bridge if or when I get to it, Delroy."

"Good luck," his friend replied. "Hey, man, my kid's screaming. I gotta take care of her before I go to work. Y'all take care."

When he hung up the phone, Robert believed he would phone Delroy again, but the moment passed and he knew the call would never happen. Whenever he moved from city to city, from job to job, Robert closed the book on his prior life. The people, no matter how close, became memories. It always startled Robert when that awareness hit and he knew he'd moved on. As he sat on his bed in Best Value Inn, that same sense of finality overwhelmed. Robert held the emotion, allowing its force to expire before turning his attention back to the television.

§

Robert MacKenzie

"Today, we're going to do some practice-pitching," began Mary-Anne. "I want each of you to pair up, take a product from the table and try selling it to one another. We're going to do this for the next twenty minutes and then each of you is going to select a product and try to sell it to Yasmine and me."

There wasn't even a murmur from the assembled trainees. The five remaining candidates sat at the table in Green Room #3. Mary-Anne occupied her usual position at the head, while Yasmine sat on her left.

Robert enjoyed seeing Yasmine, dressed as always in a sharp business suit. He couldn't tell if the smile she gave him when he said good morning meant more than a simple hello. When Pavão and Bennet walked in the door together minutes before 9:00 a.m., Robert compared the greeting Yasmine gave them to his own.

This is making me nuts. Does she like me or not? And why do I care so much?

He'd driven into TeleShop at 8:30 a.m. As the first to arrive, Robert spent twenty minutes killing time in the cafeteria, waiting for the others. At 8:50 a.m., Mary-Anne entered the cafeteria. She greeted Robert and he followed her back to the green room. By this time, Sandy Bondero and Saul Lowenstein stood outside the door, drinking coffee. Yasmine showed up a minute later.

Mary-Anne began by informing them of Reid McBain's departure. The trainees greeted the news with a mixture of relief and fear.

Looking around the room, Robert considered potential partners. Terry Pavão was his nearest competition in talent. But since the incident at the Excelsior yesterday, Robert found himself disliking the former ad man. As for Alan Bennet, something had changed. Gone was the previous day's raw-edged nervousness.

What's he doing with that shit-eating grin on his face? He's a bit more cocky and a bit less nervous than yesterday.

Robert wouldn't waste his time with Sandy Bondero or Saul Lowenstein. Neither of them had a hope of making it past training.

"Robert, let's get together and practice. Okay?" said Alan, mooting his deliberations.

"Sure," he answered, squaring off in a corner after moving seats and picking a cordless telephone to pitch.

Mary-Anne remained at the table's head. Robert and Alan occupied the corner nearest the door. Sandy Bondero teamed with Saul Lowenstein in the corner opposite. Robert considered them rats on a sinking ship.

If you two had any brains you would try to get as far away from each other as possible and find new partners. Instead, you're making it obvious you're both going to get bumped!

McBain's exit left the group uneven and Terry Pavão without a partner. Mary-Anne whispered in Yasmine's ear and she got up to team with him. Robert cursed Alan's big mouth, loud smile, and his own unluckiness.

"Do you want to start or should I?" Alan asked.

"Go ahead," Robert replied.

The group began the pitching in tones ranging from the subdued mutterings of Bondero and Lowenstein to the staccato ring of Alan Bennet. Terry Pavão tried selling Yasmine a diamond ring. With more interest, he listened to Yasmine try to sell Pavão the same. She sounded good, if a trifle dispassionate.

"Hey, MacKenzie. Your turn," Alan said to Robert.

"Uh, yeah, okay."

Robert took a moment to study the phone and its packaging. With little hesitation, he began his pitch ...

"Have you ever done the thousand-yard, frenzied dash across the carpet when the phone rings? Are you upstairs when the phone rings downstairs, downstairs when the phone rings upstairs, outside when it rings inside? Does it ever make you crazy? It makes me insane. You know you're going to trip and kill yourself one day. Why don't you forget the aggravation and get yourself a cordless?"

The room went quiet as everyone concentrated on Robert, somehow speaking with practiced ease. The trainees' expressions ranged from astonishment to jealousy. Mary-Anne and Yasmine paid careful attention.

"It's not going to bankrupt you; this Sanyo Compander only costs ninety-nine ninety-nine. Look, I know what you're saying. You hate the sound quality on the darn things. Well, forget it. Sanyo has finally licked the problem. This new Compander model uses special circuitry to compress your voice for transmission and expand it at the other end. That's always been the trouble, you know? The silly cordless phone frequencies don't have enough room to broadcast your whole voice. They make you sound like you're talking through a tin can and string."

Robert expressed the technical information with confidence and folksy-sounding wisdom. Years before, he had worked in a Chicago electronics store. Describing product features came naturally. Robert couldn't imagine one day he'd be grateful for his brief moment as a retail salesman.

"I'm telling you, the Sanyo Compander solves that nonsense once and for all. Finito. Hey, it's also a ten-channel model! That means you don't have to put up with poor reception because you've got a bad channel. Has this ever happened to you? You buy a cordless phone, you get it home, and it doesn't work. You go a bit berserk and drive all the way back to the store. The guy there plugs it in and it works like a charm and you feel like a buffoon. You get it back home and *voilá*, it's back on the fritz. It's enough to make you jump off a bridge!"

Robert's careful examination of the phone's packaging now paid off. He rattled on and on, focusing on every feature, explaining every benefit.

"But the problem isn't with the cordless phone; it's where you live! You see, the quality of reception varies by geography. What was a good channel in the store's neighborhood can be a lousy channel around your house. Since the Compander uses every channel allowed by law, what are the odds of all ten of them not working? Hey, if that's the case, I hate to say it, but you don't have a cordless phone in your future! Pick up the Sanyo Compander—it's inexpensive, it's convenient *and* it works! Call now!"

Robert stopped speaking. His sharp focus had blocked out the room.

Alan Bennet scrutinized him in amazement; Sandy and Saul looked angry, while Terry Pavão appeared impressed. Even Yasmine watched with interest.

"Now *that* was a 'pitch!'" Mary-Anne broke the silence. "Gentlemen, don't picture yourself speaking to a television camera. You want to sell exactly the way Robert did. Pretend you're in a friend's living room. Talk to them *like* a friend. Robert, that was very, very good."

The other trainees expressed their admiration in degrees. The Gruesome Twosome (as Robert had begun to think of Sandy and Saul) acknowledged him with some reservation. Terry had respect in his eyes and Robert felt good seeing the grin disappear from Alan's face.

"Let's continue. I want to get in several more practice attempts before we start having you pitch to Yasmine and me," Mary-Anne said, breaking the forced reverie.

"Alan, why don't you try selling me the phone," Robert said.

"Yeah, give me a sec," Bennet replied, a trace of resentment in his voice.

They spent the next three hours pitching back and forth. Sandy and Saul were hopeless. Saul wasn't a salesman. He had a beautiful, deep voice that dictated attention. Unfortunately, without an announcer's script to read, he sounded hapless. Wonderful, dulcet, bordering on profundity, get-your-attention hapless, but hapless nonetheless.

Sandy didn't even have a great voice. He performed as you would expect a nineteen-year-old: stammering, sputtering, and without a clue about how to sell anything to anyone. Unlike Saul, his voice was high and screeching, and by his second practice-pitch it became clear to everyone that Sandy's time was no longer numbered in days, but hours.

Terry Pavão's performance was at times rocky, but he had something to offer. You could detect his advertising background. Terry loved adjectives. He presented a lady's purse to the group. The words, *luxurious*, *soft*, *creamy*, and *dainty* all found their way into his spiel.

Alan Bennet was a borderline case. He had a decent, if forced, voice. At times, he sounded as if he was still barking on a midway, raising his inflection at the end of each sentence. While Alan didn't have Sandy's adolescent whine, he did lack Terry Pavão's descriptive prowess.

Robert viewed Mary-Anne as most likely hiring himself and Pavão. Hiring himself and Bennet was also possible but not as likely. As the day dragged on, Alan's overbearing how's-the-boy cockiness from the morning disappeared.

When 12:30 rolled around, Mary-Anne said they'd break for lunch and have an announcement when the group returned.

The trainees exited the green room with Robert hanging around its door. He wondered if anybody felt like eating in the cafeteria. Terry wanted the pair to head to the Excelsior, but Robert declined. Considering that morning's practice, staying at TeleShop was a better strategy.

Sandy and Saul disappeared through the parking lot exit as did Terry. Alan Bennet sped down the office corridor trying to catch up with Mary-Anne — he had no idea why.

Shrugging it off, he entered the cafeteria. Wherever he walked, people pointed him out. It wasn't rude, but it was obvious and made him self-conscious.

It must be the same for any new show host. I hear we come and go in great numbers. The operators and others must wonder who will make it past training. Yasmine said finding show hosts was ongoing and never-ending. How many people did TeleShop audition before finding a successful candidate? How often did another Dealmaker or Dragon Lady wander into the building?

Robert sat at an empty table with his coffee and a turkey sandwich. His coffee tasted like typical machine brew and his sandwich made him think fondly of the Excelsior's fare.

Like the rest of TeleShop, there were television monitors everywhere. Last night at the motel, he found himself clicking onto TeleShop every ten or so minutes. The Dealmaker had told him that he could never get away from it.

"It's too goddamn easy, that's the problem. Kid, you tell me another occupation where you not only take the job home with you, but it's right there on your fucking TV. Watch yourself, or you'll find you're tuning into the show every goddamn minute of every goddamn hour. When you're having a slow week, seeing another host sell the piss out of something can eat your insides right away. I'm telling you, it's enough to start you drinking!"

Robert laughed out loud, remembering how they had raised their cans of Olde English and toasted each other at the Dealmaker's remark that night.

"Robert?"

He broke from his train of thought and looked up to see Yasmine Dubai. She stood in front of him with a slight smile on her face.

"Would you come with me, please?" she asked.

"Sure," he replied, noticing she'd called him Robert for the first time.

"Oh, I'm sorry, I didn't see your sandwich. We can wait for a few minutes if you'd like"

"It's finished," Robert replied. "Actually, it finished about a week ago. Nobody noticed until now."

Yasmine laughed, her face lighting up like the other day. Robert tossed the sandwich into the trash and downed the rest of his lukewarm coffee with a single gulp.

"Have you seen Mr. Pavão?" Yasmine asked.

"Yeah, he headed off to the Excelsior."

"Oh."

"You go there much yourself?" Robert asked.

"As little as possible."

"I was there yesterday. I don't know which was worse, their Banquet Burger or that sandwich."

"A bit of a Hobson's choice, I'm afraid," Yasmine said, again with a smile.

"Exactly! I always figured it would be pretty difficult finding a bad burger in the Southwest, but I guess I managed."

"Oklahoma City doesn't have a lot of haute cuisine," Yasmine said. "If you like steak and potatoes, you're in heaven, but otherwise … "

"Hey, Phoenix is the same. Except if you like Mexican, they've got great Mexican!"

"Do you like Mexican, Robert?"

"Actually, no. Not much. Don't get me wrong, it's okay, but it's not my favorite."

"So what is your favorite?"

"Indian. I love curry. The hotter, the better!" For a white guy from Massachusetts, this was not a typical response. Robert meant it, but wondered if Yasmine believed him.

As he expected, Yasmine raised her eyebrows. "Is that the truth, Mr. MacKenzie?"

"No, seriously. Madras, Vindaloo, Biryani, I love it all. And hey, what's with the Mr. MacKenzie? I thought we agreed you'd call me Robert."

"We didn't agree on that at all," Yasmine replied. "I said I'd think about it."

"I figured you did," Robert said with a trace of innuendo.

"Well, it will depend upon whether you really do like curry or you're just saying that."

"Now, Yasmine, why would I lie?" he asked with a small grin, trying not to sound flippant.

"Please!"

Robert turned on his best smile and looked into Yasmine's eyes, laughing. "I like curry. Period."

"So where did the young Brahmin from Massachusetts learn to love Eastern food?" Yasmine asked.

"Hard to say. I moved out of the house when I was sixteen. Got a job at a bar in Boston slugging beer into the cooler. Anyway, I lived above the bar for a while. There was an Indian restaurant across the street. I ate most of my meals there. Took an immediate liking to the food. Must be my Scottish heritage. You know, the famous Highland Curry?"

"Highland Curry? Oh, of course. You worked at a bar at sixteen. Wasn't that illegal?"

"I won't tell anyone if you don't."

"Hard to say, Mr. MacKenzie! I looked at your résumé and I don't recall seeing any mention of a bar at sixteen," said Yasmine, a mocking tone in her voice.

The pair walked through production by this time and it became clear Yasmine wasn't taking Robert to the green room. As they entered the long corridor leading toward the offices, they stopped. Robert stared into Yasmine's eyes and noticed, for the first time, she stared back.

"Maybe you got the wrong résumé," he said.

"Maybe I did," she replied.

They continued their stare before breaking it and again moving toward the offices.

"Where are we going?" Robert asked Yasmine.

"To Mary-Anne's office."

"Good news I hope?"

"I should think," replied Yasmine. She led Robert into the executive area and Mary-Anne's office.

Mary-Anne sat behind her desk. A cigarette lay in an ashtray next to her, burning itself to its filter. Rob's new boss gestured for him to sit. Yasmine leaned over to say a few words in Mary-Anne's ear and then left the office, shutting the door behind her.

"Thank you for coming, Robert."

"Oh, no problem. None at all."

"Well, I'm sorry for interrupting your lunch. But we have important news, and we thought you should hear it."

"Please, go ahead."

"We don't have a set schedule for training hosts. As a rule, we plan on three days, but circumstances sometimes dictate change," Mary-Anne began. "In this case, we've decided to cut the training short."

Robert nodded his head while a pit in his stomach throbbed. He hoped he wasn't about to hear bad news. If they didn't plan on keeping him then he was in deep trouble. Regardless of his situation in Phoenix, Robert couldn't go back there now. Not after his conversation with Delroy the night before.

There had been many moments in his life when the time to move on grew legion. They sat in memory, rarely accessed. A job became intolerable, or he became intolerable to a job. Upon reflection, there was far more of the latter than the former. A city waxed desultory, while another, glistening in the light of a new dawn, sparkled in its firmament. As for women, none that mattered. And that was the saddest part.

Robert wanted, and more to the point, *needed* to be a show host—it was but simple fact, this moment a fork in the road. No. That wasn't enough. This moment was *the* fork in *his* road. Make the wrong choice, and wind up in some place, in some town, in some state, at some time, indistinguishable from his decade past. Only it wouldn't be a decade past. It would be decades future.

Make the right choice, and there was a chance for calm. For success. For the expiation of emptiness. And with luck, with Yasmine. Standing by his side. He didn't know why her image coursed through his dreams. It didn't matter. She just did.

The tension in TeleShop's air, its constant and unrelenting intensity, demanded his attention, while Robert's self-respect demanded he finally get a real job. At the same time, there was a piece of his spirit requiring him to stay near Yasmine.

As Mary-Anne continued speaking, he tried not to sit on his chair's edge, but found himself leaning forward anyway.

"We'd like to offer you a position as a show host," Mary-Anne said. "It's a trial position, and its permanence depends upon your on-air performance. Are you interested?"

"Of course," Robert replied, a poorly concealed wave of relief slamming against him. "That's why I'm here."

"Good. The wage for probationary show hosts is nine dollars seventy-five cents per hour. We'll make that effective Thursday. I'm going to have you shadow the Dragon Lady during her jewelry show tomorrow."

"Shadow? The Dragon Lady?"

"Oh, sorry, Dixie Carter. Shadowing means you're going to follow Dixie from the moment she arrives. You'll watch her show prep and meeting the director. When she goes on-air, we'll wire you up with a headset. You'll join the Dragon — er, Dixie — on-air at her discretion. She may or may not let you say anything. It depends upon her mood."

"That sounds good. Is Dixie a senior host?" Robert asked.

"Yes. It's always a contest between her and the Dealmaker as to who brings in the most revenue every month. Dixie specializes in selling jewelry."

"And they call her the Dragon Lady? Why?"

"Don't worry. It's only a nickname," Mary-Anne replied. "It doesn't mean anything."

"Well, thank you for the opportunity. What time should I show up tomorrow?"

"Dixie does our 6:00 to 9:00 p.m. Eastern Time show. As I said in training, we orient all our shows to Eastern Time. Since we're an hour behind, she's on from 5:00 until 8:00 p.m. Dixie is very punctual. Get here at 2:00 p.m. You'll find her in the show host prep room; it's right around the corner from Green Room #3."

"I appreciate the opportunity you've given me, Ms. Warner. I won't let you down," Robert said.

"I know you won't."

"Can I ask about the other guys in the group?"

"Most companies would decline to comment about that information. But, again, this isn't most companies. Besides yourself, we're also taking on Terry Pavão and Alan Bennet. We'll let them practice-pitch to each other for another day or two before having them shadow. However, we're confident they'll do fine."

"That's great," Robert said and then added, "I thought there were only two positions open?"

For a moment, Mary-Anne looked bothered. But she regained her minor loss of composure in an instant. "We're also flexible about how many trainees we hire, Mr. MacKenzie. Sometimes we find it expedient to tell our potential hosts there are less than the actual number of positions available. It helps to focus their attention," Mary-Anne replied.

"What about Sandy and Saul?"

"Mr. Bondero has returned to his duties as a network representative. We offered Mr. Lowenstein some voice-over work but he wasn't very happy at losing the show host position and declined."

"Sorry to hear that," Robert said.

"So were we," Mary-Anne replied.

"Is there anything I have to do before tomorrow?"

"You'll need a headset. Each piece is custom-made, so we'll need an injection cast of your left ear. We send it to Los Angeles. It takes about a week. Do you remember how to find the control room?" she asked.

"Yes."

"Go see our Director of Engineering, his name is Larry Brown. You'll find his office to the left of the control room's entrance. Larry's a black man, mid-thirties, around six feet tall. Ask anyone around that part of the building, and they'll point him out. Tell him you're a new host and you need a headset. He'll give you a temporary unit and do the molding of your ear."

"Ms. Warner, thanks again. I'll get right down to engineering and see to it."

Mary-Anne offered her hand. "Have fun tomorrow, Robert. And don't let Dixie intimidate you."

"I'll try not to." Robert left the office toward the main corridor and his new job, the pain gone from his stomach and a big smile on his face.

CHAPTER SEVEN

Robert MacKenzie

"Anyway, I gotta get there by two o'clock. By the way, why do they call her the Dragon Lady?" Robert asked the Dealmaker. The two men sat on lawn chairs outside the Dealmaker's room, an ice-filled bucket filled with cans of Olde English between them. The early evening sun had begun to set, the day's relentless heat finally abating.

"It's self-explanatory," the Dealmaker replied. "Like Mary-Anne, she's a bitch. Except in these politically correct times you can't call a woman that, so you have to be a touch more subtle."

"C'mon, Dealmaker, she can't be that bad."

"Kid, you ever hear anybody call her Dixie?"

"Not exactly."

"I rest my case. You think Mary-Anne's a piece of work, you should check out Dixie Carter. Seen her show yet?"

"No," replied Robert. "I've heard the name bandied about, and Mary-Anne told me we're working together tomorrow."

"God help you."

"You're a lot of help. What's wrong with her?"

"A better question would be what's *right* with her. Dixie will steal you blind and smile while she's doing it. Remember I told you if you don't bitch and scream you won't get any product?"

"Yeah."

"Well, the Dragon Lady will go behind your back and steal the feature item right out of your goddamn show. She'll tell Billy-Ray she can do a better job, or the timing's wrong, or her show is shit, or whatever the hell else it takes!"

Robert detected a note of sanctimony as he'd watched the older man pull the exact same stunt in the control room on Monday. "Doesn't everybody do the same thing?"

"Sure, to a degree. But that fucking broad will do it *while* you're on the air! She's got no shame. Hey, I'm as big a prick as the next guy, but they call *me* the Dealmaker. We all get the moniker we deserve. Dixie's earned hers in spades!"

Robert finished his beer and reached immediately for another. He had long stopped noticing how drinking became automatic whenever he was with the Dealmaker.

"Any advice for tomorrow?"

"Yeah, keep your mouth shut! The word's out on you, kid. I hear you blew Mary-Anne away during training today. This stuff has a habit of surfacing. Mary-Anne wants it known she's hired a potential heavy-hitter. Our esteemed president needs to impress the Triboro pricks. Hey, I even heard Yasmine mouthing off on the set about how good you were. And she never says anything about anyone. Come to think of it, I shouldn't be speaking to you either. You might be gunning for my job!"

Robert laughed, scratching his hair and raising his head in the fading light. He looked over at the Dealmaker, liking the unrefined curmudgeon and feeling a genuine rapport with him. Robert didn't have friends in the conventional sense. He had situational acquaintances that changed from city to city, place to place. But he felt alone and exposed in Oklahoma and needed to talk. He admired the way the Dealmaker masked his own crushing loneliness with an irascible charm.

"If that's the case, you don't appear worried."

"Kid, while you may appeal to the young professional, whether they know it or not, they're always going to have the old broads as their main audience. For that, they need me. Besides, I'm getting sick of this bullshit. I'm thinking about quitting just to keep the money from my ex. Shit, that would drive her right over the edge!" the Dealmaker said with a large smile.

"To the ex," Robert said, hoisting his beer.

"Fuck her!" the Dealmaker replied.

A minivan pulled up and parked three spaces from the Dealmaker's room. A young man and his wife got out along with three young children. They began unloading luggage from the side door. The father glanced at the Dealmaker and Robert and looked away, unimpressed with the two men drinking beer in the parking lot.

"Screw him," the Dealmaker said. "Kid, remember one thing tomorrow: Nobody loves you. The reps and the crew are jealous of your celebrity and money. Same with the office staff. The other hosts are okay, except for Dixie. But they'd push you into a sewer and climb over your body to get a hot product for their show. It's nothing personal; it's the way it is. Watch your back, take no shit, and you'll be fine."

"For God's sake, Dealmaker. You make it sound like a battle zone."

"Exactly!"

"Could I ask you something else?" Robert ventured. "What did you hear Yasmine say about me?"

The Dealmaker took the beer from his lips and turned, facing Robert with a leer. "Uh oh, me thinks the squire hath interest in a wench." The Dealmaker laughed, throwing his arms in the air and letting go a prodigious fart.

"Christ, Dealmaker!" Robert exclaimed.

"Yup."

"Yeah and fuck you very much too," said Robert. "Please, what did Yasmine say?"

The Dealmaker continued laughing, his face broad with a hearty smile. He liked watching Robert's expectation break through his wall of false confidence. Without drawing out the pain of teasing too much, he finally gave in. "Today, during a break, she was on set talking to Susie."

"The tiny floor director?"

"Yes. Anyway, Susie asked her about the new show hosts. Yasmine gave her standard, non-committal, Director of Talent line. Until she mentioned your name." He changed tack. "Say, that's a mighty fine sunset, isn't it kid?"

"Fuck off. What did she say?"

"Today's youth doesn't understand patience," laughed the Dealmaker, the grin still on his face. "Okay, in a very uncharacteristic manner, Yasmine said she thought you were the best candidate she'd ever seen. Said you were a natural."

"Well, I suppose that's good news," Robert replied, a little let down.

"Jesus, what'd you think she was going to say? That she wanted to blow you?"

"Well, no—"

"You're an imbecile, kid. How old did you say you were? Fourteen?"

"I'm twenty-five."

"No shit! Had a lot of success with women?"

"I've done alright," Robert said.

"That's amazing. Most blind men don't do so well with the ladies!"

"What do you mean blind?"

"I *saw* you on set on Monday, remember? Yasmine escorted you into the control room."

"Of course I remember! So what?"

"I don't know how your generation ever gets itself laid," the Dealmaker declared. He had a smug look on his face that he buried beneath another can of Olde English. "Didn't you look at the woman? Did you check out her eyes?"

"Uh, well, yeah."

"Kid, the eyes tell it all. You stared at her and she stared right back. I like Yasmine, but she's got a reputation as a bit of an ice queen. I don't think she's dated anybody from TeleShop the entire time she's been here. Yasmine hardly ever talks about the hosts, and she *never* stares. She sure as hell doesn't waste her time on the possums!"

"Possums?" Robert asked.

"Oh, sorry—new hosts. You guys come, you guys go and don't usually make much of an impact. What can I say?"

"Great, I'm looked upon as a rodent."

"You'll get over it. Are you hearing what I'm saying?"

"You're saying she's interested."

"Praise be to God! The squire hath a brain, after all. Cheers!"

Robert clicked cans with the Dealmaker, his feelings lifted by his new friend's observations. "So, you figure I have a chance?"

"Shit, are you deaf? Yes, you have a chance."

"Good," Robert replied. "Don't tell anybody I'm interested in Yasmine. Okay?"

"Kid, that won't be a problem. Everybody's interested in Yasmine. She's got a body that won't quit. You're another in a long line of potential suitors. Now, if you get *into* her pants, that's a whole different story! By the way, what are you planning on doing tonight?"

"I don't have any plans," Robert said. "I figured I'd hang around here until I fell asleep. I'm not exactly flush."

"Shit, that reminds me—here's the twenty bucks I borrowed." The Dealmaker pulled a roll from his pocket and peeled off six twenties, handing them to Robert.

"Where'd you get the cash? I thought you couldn't pay me back until Friday?"

"Got lucky at the track, what does it matter?"

"Thanks, you don't have to lend me the extra hundred."

"What's a yard between friends? Hey, I'm meeting some people from TeleShop in about an hour?"

"Who?"

"Some of the crew and a couple of people from the office."

"Where ya goin'?"

"Chuggers. Thought I'd knock back some bourbon and titties. Want to come?"

"Sure," Robert said. "Let me grab a shower."

"Go. Hurry up; I'm almost out of beer!"

Robert got to his feet, finishing his can of Olde English and walking the short distance to his room.

Robert's door shut behind him as the Dealmaker reached for a last can of beer. "If that kid gets any happier, he's going to hurt himself," the Dealmaker said out loud, squeezing off another fart and staring across the parking lot to the highway.

§

Robert MacKenzie

Robert still felt wretched by 2:00 p.m. The only thing that kept him from crawling into a ball and disappearing under his sheets was the knowledge it would end his new career. They'd rolled out of Chuggers at 2:00 a.m., drunk and singing all the way home. In retrospect, it amazed Robert they'd made it back and the police hadn't picked them up for DWI. While it was tough getting to work at 2:00 p.m., Robert could only imagine how the Dealmaker must have felt having to be on-air at 11:00 a.m.

He parked his Civic and walked through the employee entrance. By now, Hank only grunted at him, his feet and pistol rarely budging from the table.

Robert picked up a coffee from the cafeteria before walking through the network door and into the production area. He approached Green Room #3, strolling past it and winding up in front of a modest room marked, "Show Host Preparation Office." Inside was a small desk, some chairs, a TV, a call volume monitor, and a wizened, middle-aged woman. She sat hunched down in a chair, staring at some papers on the desk, sucking on a 120-mm cigarette and tapping her pen.

"Excuse me," Robert said while rapping on the door.

The woman moved her head and scowled at him. It was not a pretty sight. Makeup caked her face, the skin stretched tight across the skull and looking like one face lift too many. She had a near-emaciated frame with intense eyes that burned with concentration.

"It's five after two; you're late. Why?"

"I've been here for a few minutes," Robert answered. "I stopped by the cafeteria for a coffee."

"Not good enough. Do you see that schedule on the wall?" Dixie said, pointing to a piece of paper hanging on the bulletin board opposite.

	Show Airtime *(Eastern)*	Local Time	Shift Begins
#1.	Midnight to 3:00 a.m.	11:00 p.m. to 2:00 a.m.	8:00 p.m.
#2.	3:00 a.m. to 6:00 a.m.	2:00 a.m. to 5:00 a.m.	11:00 p.m.
#3.	6:00 a.m. to 9:00 a.m.	5:00 a.m. to 8:00 a.m.	2:00 a.m.
#4.	9:00 a.m. to Noon	8:00 a.m. to 11:00 a.m.	5:00 a.m.
#5.	Noon to 3:00 p.m.	11:00 a.m. to 2:00 p.m.	8:00 a.m.
#6.	3:00 p.m. to 6:00 p.m.	2:00 p.m. to 5:00 p.m.	11:00 a.m.
#7.	6:00 p.m. to 9:00 p.m.	5:00 p.m. to 8:00 p.m.	2:00 p.m.
#8.	9:00 p.m. to Midnight	8:00 p.m. to 11:00 p.m.	5:00 p.m.

"What time does it say to be here for Show #7?"

"2:00 p.m."

"In this business you've got to be punctual. If we can't rely on you, you're no goddamn good to us! Understand?"

"Yes, ma'am."

"Sit down. Here, look at this," the woman said, throwing a sheaf of papers at him. "This is a product selector. It's a mainframe printout of every single item TeleShop has in stock. It's very important; it gives you a breakdown of our competitor's typical retail price for the same item, our current price, and the last sale price. This is your bible. Memorize it! Do you remember the Scheduling department?"

"The office down the long hall by the lobby?" Robert asked.

"Yes. You pick up your show three hours before airtime from them. You spend the next three hours making it better. Those assholes couldn't build a good show if their lives depended on it. Remember that or you won't last the month."

"Yes, ma'am."

"Don't call me ma'am. My name is Dixie Carter. Call me Dixie to my face and the Dragon Lady behind my back. But I fucking hate *ma'am*. Understand?"

"Yes, Dixie."

"Good, grab me a coffee. The machine at the far back of the cafeteria, extra strong and black."

Robert nodded and left the office. He looked behind himself and saw Dixie Carter again buried in the product selector, another cigarette between her lips, her pen still tapping.

§

Mary-Anne Warner

"Three? You hired three? What the hell for? I told you we're running over budget in the host department. We don't even need two new hosts; we were looking for one, a young male. You know this, Mary-Anne! *Shiiit*, it's one thing to hire a backup, but two backups?"

Billy-Ray Newton didn't look pleased. It had been a trying week. The Triboro Media Group had examined his books and operation in detail, finding fault in both. Billy-Ray always ran his companies his own way and didn't like having to answer to a group of buttoned-up accountants from up North.

"Billy-Ray, I picked MacKenzie for obvious reasons," Mary-Anne began. She shouldn't have hired three new hosts and she knew it. It would have been so easy with MacKenzie and Pavão. But Bennet had caught her in the hallway during the lunch break yesterday and been very insistent in her office later. Mary-Anne enjoyed his nervous energy and fear as he pleaded and half-threatened to expose their affair if she didn't give him a chance.

Mary-Anne hemmed, telling Alan they were over budget and hiring him was impossible. She always savored control and loved toying with people. It made her very aroused.

Locking her door, Mary-Anne had pulled up her skirt and leaned against a wall. "You want to be a show host, Alan? Prove you deserve it," she'd said, mocking him.

Bennet wasted no time, slamming his body against her own, ripping her panties to one side and entering her, his hands and tongue on her breasts and mouth. It was only after their brief but intense, sexual encounter that Mary-Anne said she would hire him. The memory's intensity caused her to lose her train of thought.

"Mary-Anne, go on. I'm listening."

"Sorry, Billy-Ray. I also thought Pavão had a certain way with words and might work out on Show #1 if we later move MacKenzie to prime time. You know that spot is always underperforming. We can't afford to keep a top host in there, but it deserves better than our overnight people! I felt Pavão would fit that show. As for Bennet, he's in the same demographic category as MacKenzie. What if our new potential star doesn't work out? Aren't we better off having a ready-trained backup than going through the whole process all over again?"

"Okay, you got a point, Mary-Anne. But how about you explain it to Triboro when that cocksucker CPA they sent down — what's his name?"

"Rolfberg."

"Yeah, Rolfberg asks me why I'm forty per cent over budget on host salaries and spiffs!"

"No problem. I'll move Pavão and Bennet's costs onto the training ledger."

"That's for new operators," Billy-Ray said.

"De facto, it is. However, *all* training can come under that category. Since we haven't been hiring as many network representatives lately, that department is eighteen per cent *under* budget."

"*Shiiit*! Now that's thinking, Mary-Anne. When did you come up with this idea?"

"In bed the other night. It's good to have some maneuvering room when you need it."

"Damn straight! When are these Triboro people leaving? I hate the lot of them."

"I can't say for sure."

"Cut the shit, Mary-Anne."

The two sat across from each other, allowing an uncomfortable silence to fill the air. Mary-Anne finally broke it.

"I hear they're leaving tomorrow. They want to get back to New York before the weekend."

"Good. It must be awful having to put up with the likes of us. I don't know what you see in those people, Mary-Anne. You'll never be one of them. You didn't go to Princeton and your family doesn't own property in the Hamptons. To them, you'll never be more than poor white trash from West Virginia."

"I am whatever I say I am, Billy-Ray. Isn't that what America is all about?"

"You can lay that crap off around me, Mary-Anne. I grew up in Bumfuck, Tennessee. I know you and your kind and believe it or not, I respect the fact you've made something of yourself."

Mary-Anne either didn't want to recognize or couldn't recognize the basic truth of Billy-Ray's words. She was far too ambitious to let anything get in her way.

"To Triboro, you're a smart, ruthless woman. They'll pay you and promote you; but they won't ever invite you to their tables or their clubs. You aren't their kind of people. And cut the *God Bless America* BS, save it for our Fourth of July special."

Billy-Ray had made a lot of money catering to cities in the South and rural communities all over. Mary-Anne had discussed her ambition in passing before. When it came to success and cash, Billy-Ray didn't care from where it came.

"Christ, I don't know who wants to rise the corporate ranks more, you or your assistant. I figure Yasmine's got another year before she either accepts that Oklahoma City isn't such a bad place or she explodes with her own unfulfilled ambition. You've got some choices to make in the next few months, Mary-Anne."

Mary-Anne knew her cover as a Triboro plant had been long blown. She only hoped he didn't understand the real depth of her loyalties.

Billy-Ray continued, "We both know Triboro wants me out and I don't have a problem with that. The question is, who do they want in?

You—the Southern girl made good, or the Ivy League MBA whose kids go to the same private school as their own? Think about it."

"Billy-Ray, I'll do whatever it takes," Mary-Anne Warner said with frost as she got up to leave.

"Yes, I'm sure you will. Keep me posted on the training."

"Yes, sir," she replied, walking out of the office and back to her own.

§

Robert MacKenzie

"Okay, head down to Scheduling and get me a drop-in for the tanzanite ring." The Dragon Lady didn't ask. She didn't tell. She spoke, expecting her pronouncement to have the weight of biblical truth.

"Which one?" Robert asked.

"There is only one." The word "idiot" came implicit with her speech. "Trust me, they'll know what I mean. Get out of here; we meet with the director in twenty minutes. We have to have the show finalized by then."

"Back in a bit," Robert said as he left the show host prep room, his helpful expression changing to a frown.

I'm a goddamn messenger boy, not a performer, not a salesman. This is humiliating.

The people in Scheduling smiled with feigned politeness, but he knew they didn't want to hear from him. On his last trip to the office, a half-hour ago, he requested one of the schedulers give him a drop-in of an electronics product. The woman asked if the Dragon Lady had okayed it and when Robert said he hadn't run it past her, the scheduler chuckled and said no. He knew he had no experience or reputation but he still couldn't stand his total lack of independence.

"Dixie wants the tanzanite ring," Robert said to the busy office.

Nobody paid him any attention, the chattering the same as before.

"Excuse me," he began again, increasing his tone by a measure. "Dixie would like the tanzanite ring dropped in."

"We heard you the first time. There's no need to shout," replied one of the women sitting at a desk. "Give us a minute. This whole network doesn't revolve around the whims of the Dragon Lady!"

"Give him the fucking ring! I don't need your shit!" a very loud voice screamed from behind him.

Robert spun about to see an enraged Dixie with her head in the doorway.

"I'm off to see Billy-Ray. I want the goddamn ring when I get back!" The Dragon Lady threw her body out of the jam and headed down the long corridor toward the executive area.

"That fucking bitch," the woman who had spoken to Robert said.

"Hey, please don't shoot the messenger; it's my first day." he replied. According to Robert's (abbreviated) training, Scheduling held the keys to the kingdom. Always best to make friends.

"I'm sorry. That woman brings out the worst in people. We all forget because you're forced to work with her doesn't mean you're like her."

"Amen," said a black woman at another table.

"I'm Robert. Robert MacKenzie. This is my first day of shadowing and I could use all the help I can get."

"Hi, Robert. I'm Dawn," the first woman said, offering her hand.

"And I'm Lateesha," said the black woman.

"Hi."

The one man and remaining two women all introduced themselves.

"Is she always this bad?" Robert asked.

"You call that bad? That's nothing compared to where that woman's been," said Lateesha.

"She gets worse?"

Lateesha laughed out loud. "Who here remembers Pierre?"

"Oh that was horrible," Dawn said.

"I've only heard stories," came the reply from the only man in the room, an effeminate male with a tight, clipped mustache.

"Robert, about four years ago, *that* woman was in the running for Mary-Anne's job, can you believe it? She figured she was a lock. Turned out Billy-Ray had other ideas. Brought down this French guy named Pierre. Nice man, kinda quiet, English wasn't that good. Anyway, he was some kind of retail expert, moved here from Paris or something."

"Montreal. He was from Montreal. French-Canadian guy, came here with his new wife and baby," said Dawn interjecting.

"Okay, French-Canadian. What the hell do I know about French anyway?"

Everyone in the room, including Robert, began laughing.

"So, if I may continue. He starts work here on a Monday morning. The shit hits the fan right away. They told the Dragon Lady on Friday night she had a new boss, let her stew about it all weekend. She won't talk to the guy all week. I mean this is her boss and she won't say a damn word to him. Walks past him in the hallway with a sneer on her face. This Pierre guy is real nice, kinda low key. He's not taking the snubbing very well."

"So all she did was snub him?" Robert asked.

"Hold your horses. It gets worse. The next Monday, the Dragon Lady's had it. Pierre's office is up the hall from us, where the buyers are now. Dixie is walking up and down from the prep room to get products as usual. Every time she walks past his office, she sticks her head in and whispers something to him. We don't know exactly what she's sayin', but we can tell by Pierre's reaction it's gotta be filthy. Pierre tries to ignore it. But, she keeps this up non-stop for days. Pierre starts walking in here, swearing in French, all panicky. We all ask him what's wrong, but he won't tell us."

"I remember it like it was yesterday," Dawn said. She looked up and grinned as if remembering a private joke. The entire room smiled with nostalgia as Lateesha continued.

"A week later, she starts letting him have it. Pierre's been here two weeks and the Dragon Lady hasn't said a civil word to him. She's whispering evil stuff every time she walks past his office. And then it happens."

"What?" asked Robert with honest excitement and intrigue. He *had* to know all the details.

"Dawn, you remember?" Lateesha said to her friend.

"Oh, yeah!"

"What?" Robert repeated on the verge of frustration.

"We're all sitting in this office when we hear a wail. And I'm not sayin' a shout, either. I mean a top-of-your-lungs, blood-curdling, run-for-your-life scream. Honey, it could have woken the dead! It's about ten in the morning; Dixie used to have the Dealmaker's time slot. 'Enjoying the chair, you cocksucker!'" Lateesha said in an eerie impression of the Dragon Lady's voice. "Don't get too used to it, motherfucker. You're gone real, real soon!'"

"Get the hell out of here!" said Jack, the only other man in the room besides Robert. "The Dragon Lady screamed that at him?"

"Like watching a horror movie at the drive-in on a Friday night. Scared the shit out of us!"

"She's not kidding," said Dawn. "It was unbelievable."

"What happened?" asked Robert.

"It went on for days. Every time she walked past his office, she let go with another one. You couldn't imagine the stuff that came out of her mouth. Poor Pierre tried leaving his door closed but it didn't work: 'Hey, you French asshole! I know you're in there. Open up the fucking door and face me like a man, you goddamn fruit. I'll kill you, you motherfucker!'"

"No way. This didn't happen," said Robert. "It's too much. Billy-Ray would have fired her!"

"Sugar, you don't know Billy-Ray. He likes things a bit stirred up. Always says nervous people create sales; relaxed people don't. Besides, I hear he got the Frog for a song. He didn't have a Green Card, only a work permit, so he couldn't leave and get another job. Would've had to go back to France first."

"Canada," Dawn said.

"Whatever!"

"So why didn't this Pierre guy file a complaint?" Robert asked. He found it impossible to believe anyone would tolerate such a toxic environment.

The rest of the room held inner smiles, laughing at his naïveté.

"A complaint," Lateesha began. "With who? This was almost four years ago. And besides, this is Oklahoma, not New York. How far you think this guy, a French-speaking foreigner would have got against a woman back then? He didn't have a chance!"

"So what happened?" Robert asked.

"The screaming went on for over two weeks. Afterward, he disappeared."

"He quit?"

"Quit? Hell, he disappeared! Went back to France or Canada or wherever. Didn't show up for work one day and that was that."

"Christ, is she like this with every boss?" Robert asked, shocked.

"Don't sweat it, Robert," Lateesha said. "Only that one. She was expectin' the job herself and didn't take it real well when she didn't get it. Nowadays, she's like what you heard a minute ago."

"I suppose that's good," Robert said.

"Hey," chimed in Jack, "that can be bad enough. I'm glad I didn't have to see poor Pierre."

"Amen, again," said Lateesha.

"Does anybody like her?" Robert asked.

"No," the entire room said at once.

"The devil's own spawn," Lateesha added. "She's going to be back from Billy-Ray's in a minute. Take this drop-in and meet her in the prep room."

"Thanks," Robert replied, a slight smile on his face.

"Don't mention it," Lateesha said. "Y'all come back now, ya hear?"

They all laughed. Robert left the Scheduling office and headed toward the prep room. Hearing the sudden, brisk stride of stiletto heels behind him, he knew it was the Dragon Lady and quickened his pace.

CHAPTER EIGHT

Robert MacKenzie

At 8:00 p.m. Robert dragged himself from the studio, pulling out his earpiece and heading toward the floor director. The Dragon Lady didn't say a word to him; she gathered her notes and walked out of the studio, disappearing behind the "Live Set" sign. Robert planned on saying a quick goodnight but Dixie didn't give him a chance. Instead, he stood next to the floor director with his mouth open.

"Don't sweat it," the small woman said to him. "She's like that with everyone."

"Thanks," Robert replied. "I'm happy I'm not the only one. Your name's Susie, isn't it?"

"That's right."

"Hi, it's good to meet you," Robert said while extending his hand. "I hope I wasn't too tough on the crew."

"No, you were fine. The Dragon Lady didn't let you get in more than five words. And don't worry about that either, she's always like that too. Dixie makes everyone who shadows or co-hosts with her feel like furniture."

"Lovely. Yet people put up with her?"

"Got to, she brings in a ton of money. No way Billy-Ray will ever get rid of her."

"These Triboro people might have a different perspective," Robert said.

"Sure and I'm getting my own sitcom next week. Money talks, bullshit walks. Nobody around here thinks Triboro will be any different than Billy-Ray."

Robert shook his head, saying goodnight and waving to the rest of the floor crew. The crew replied to his wave in a friendly manner. They were already setting up the next host, a medium-sized, wiry man named George. The new host fussed with his papers and appeared uncomfortable with the bright lights of the TV studio. Several beads of sweat ran down his face, cueing the makeup person to refresh his powder. Robert thought the man screamed nervous, but he said nothing, leaving the studio area and walking through the network toward the prep room. He turned and waved to the operators, thanking them and noticed the several startled looks he received.

Jesus, don't any of the other hosts thank the operators? What kind of place is this?

As he continued through the network, he saw the Dragon Lady (now understanding why she deserved the name) skirting through the back rows of operators toward the exit, looking straight ahead and saying nothing. She left through the rear door by the cafeteria and the employee entrance. In the six hours he'd spent with her, the amount of words they'd shared numbered under a hundred. Although he'd spoken little when on-air and during preparation, he felt exhilarated.

He had stood next to Dixie when the floor director cued them and then watched the Dragon Lady's demeanor change as soon as the camera's light turned red. Her face lit up. She smiled and she introduced Robert with real charm. The same electrical charge from his first day pulsed through the studio as the camera went live. It was hard to believe that was only four days ago.

The Dragon Lady warned viewers of the reprise of her amazing deal on TeleShop's fabulous diamond and tanzanite masterpiece: The Celebration Ring. Only this time she'd managed to have a few rings (actually two thousand) crafted in genuine 10K yellow gold with white gold tips for only three hundred ninety-nine dollars ninety-nine cents. Never again would anyone experience this kind of a buy, so please stay tuned at 8:00 p.m. Eastern Time for their debut.

As Dixie predicted, at the appointed hour, the lines erupted. The entire batch of two thousand rings sold out in fifteen minutes. The Dragon Lady hadn't let him do much more than *ooh* and *ah* every so often. Still, he enjoyed the rush of watching the operators try to process the incoming calls. Before the show, the product selector indicated the ring's margin was fifty percent. That meant it cost only two hundred dollars, while they sold it for four hundred dollars. In fifteen minutes Dixie Carter brought in eight hundred thousand dollars in gross revenue. No wonder she could act the way she did.

Robert entered the prep room, dropping into the chair Dixie had been in when he arrived that afternoon. Tired, his neck muscles pulled taught across his back producing one of his chronic headaches. He massaged his temples and leaned back in the chair, putting his feet up on the desk.

"Are you sure you don't want to get a bit more comfortable, Mr. MacKenzie?"

Startled, Robert pulled his feet from the desk. He looked in the direction of the voice and saw Yasmine Dubai laughing while leaning in the door jam. Although she wore another beautiful, tailored suit, she looked worse for wear. Fatigue etched her face.

Yasmine straightened and walked into the prep room, carrying papers. She fed them into the mail slots on the wall opposite the door while continuing to glance at Robert.

"You scared me," Robert said with a big smile. "You always sneak up on people like that?"

"Sometimes," Yasmine replied with a coy tone.

"I guess I'll have to watch myself. What brings you to the prep room this late at night?"

"The prep room?" Yasmine taunted. "Aren't we the casual one. Whatever happened to the "Show Host Preparation Office?" You're getting into the swing of things and it's only been what, four days?"

"I pay careful attention."

"I saw you with Dixie tonight. You did a good job. I know she didn't let you say much, but most people sulk about and look uncomfortable around her. You didn't."

"Thanks," Robert replied. "I appreciate it. I was nervous, but the thrill of it all balanced it out."

"You liked being on-air?"

"Yes. There's a certain amount of glamor in it."

"Glamor? That's like déjà vu to me. I felt the same way when I got here last year."

"I take it you don't see that much glamor anymore?" Robert asked.

"No, not much," Yasmine said, sighing. "I didn't think glamor involved the kind of ridiculous hours I work." Yasmine put down her papers and sat in the chair across from Robert. "I sometimes think I'm the only one who doesn't put their feet on the desk. Mary-Anne does it, Billy-Ray does it, the Dealmaker always does it and Hank the security guard never stops doing it! What about me?"

Robert detected an ounce of desperation in Yasmine's voice. He felt very close to her, unaware why. Her comments were rhetorical, more personal than anything else. He appreciated her frankness and honesty.

Robert got to his feet and moved around the side of the desk. Reaching down, he grasped Yasmine's nylon-clad legs in his hands and raised them, placing her feet on the desk. She looked at him in shock, their eyes locking like they had yesterday afternoon.

"If you're still here at 8:25 p.m., you've more than earned the right to put your feet up," he said, sitting back down in the chair, and raising his eyebrows at Yasmine.

"Thank you," she said.

"You're welcome."

They said nothing for a few moments. Robert picked up one of the papers Yasmine had put in the mail slots. It was a host schedule for the next two weeks. It listed him as shadowing with the Dragon Lady on Friday and then hosting the midnight to 3:00 a.m. slot alone, starting on Monday.

"You've got some confidence in me," he said. "To whom do I owe the thanks?"

"Me," Yasmine replied. "I was finishing the schedule tonight. Mary-Anne said I should watch you and determine how you looked on-air. If I thought you were ready, I should slot you into Show #3."

"That's 6:00 to 9:00 a.m., Eastern Time?"

"Right."

"But you've got me doing midnight to 3:00 a.m.? That's Show #1. Didn't you say in training that's a much more important show?"

"Right again."

"Why?"

"We normally start new hosts in Show #2. Show #3 is where we put people who are better than average in training. You're way better than average. Show #1 is a chronic underperformer. We've always felt it could bring in a great deal more revenue. Although it airs after midnight

111

on the east coast, in California it's only 9:00 p.m. As we increase our West Coast cable penetration it will become the show to watch. You could be one of the reasons for the change."

"I don't know what to say," Robert replied, humbled.

"I know that, too. If you were like the rest of the hosts, you'd either be strutting around like a peacock or winking at me as if you were in the know about how things work around here."

"Not my style," Robert replied.

"Nor mine."

There was another pause in the conversation. Robert liked the sense of intimacy, but worried that Yasmine might find the silence uncomfortable.

"What time do you finish?" Robert asked, interrupting the calm. A wince of panic gripped him. He wanted to work an invitation to dinner into the conversation, but his nerves got the better of him. His question hung about, waiting for an answer.

"I'm done now. Tonight's an early one. I only had to finish the schedule. Usually, I don't get out of here until ten."

"What time do you start?"

"I like to be in for eight."

"You ever come in on the weekend?"

"I'm here most Saturdays. Sundays sometimes."

"Life?"

"None."

"Me neither," Robert said.

They both laughed. Yasmine took her feet from the desk and rolled her neck around. "I guess it's time to go home."

"Do you feel like doing something?" Robert asked, his nerves on overdrive.

"Mr. MacKenzie, that wouldn't be appropriate. Would it?" she replied with a smile.

"I hate appropriate," he said. "It's my total contempt for the appropriate that's got me where I am today. I'd say that in triumph, but I have to wonder if where I am today is a plus or a minus."

Yasmine laughed again, looking beautiful. She had striking features, yet her constant business attitude gave her an undeserved harshness. She projected cool and confidence, but with a certain lack of compassion. It was only when she laughed her face began glowing, and her eyes showed traces of warmth and vulnerability.

"You're quite the card, Robert."

"At last, I'm Robert again—a definite triumph."

"Women are fickle."

"And unpredictable."

"And unpredictable." Yasmine agreed, smiling as her eyes met his. They sparkled in the harsh fluorescent light. Leaning back in the chair, she spun about and faced him, her lithe body an invitation.

"Yasmine, I've been in this city for five days and I haven't done a damn thing except have drinks with the Dealmaker. I'm going out of my mind."

"You've had drinks with the Dealmaker?" Yasmine asked with interest. "Where?"

"We're staying at the same motel. I bumped into him by accident on Monday night. He's a very nice guy. A bit sad, but nice. He took me out last night with some of the crew."

"Where'd you go?" she asked.

"Chuggers. The one downtown."

Yasmine's look changed from amusement to concern. "Is that your idea of entertainment? Are you only attracted to big-busted women who need men fawning over them?"

"No," Robert replied, backpedaling. "It's not my kind of spot at all. I'm more of a foreign film, dance club kind of guy. But you've got to understand my situation. I don't know anyone in this city. The Dealmaker almost runs this place and when he asks me out to meet some members of the production crew, I'm supposed to say *no*?"

Yasmine's features softened. She looked back at him, losing the coldness. "I don't suppose you could. But if you're planning on asking me to Chuggers, you can forget it right now."

"Don't be silly. I was going to ask you if you knew a place we could go. You've lived here a lot longer than me."

Yasmine began laughing again, her eyes crinkling.

"What's so funny?"

"Excuse me, I can't help it." Yasmine kept chuckling. "I've lived here for ten months and I've gone out four times. I'm so damn busy with work, I don't have time to see a movie. At least I rent the odd video. What more do I need?"

"I know what you mean. I'm not exactly the hail-fellow-well-met type myself."

"That's not the way you appear," she replied.

"Appearances can be deceiving. I have a public persona, but keep my private self, private."

Robert's lack of confidence was never more plain than in his relations with the opposite sex, always hit or miss. There were times he asked a woman out, even though it would have been obvious to anyone else that it was hopeless. By the same token, there were occasions when women threw themselves at him, and he couldn't see it for love or money. The manager of the video store in Hollywood was a prime example. If she hadn't finally pulled up her skirt in the peep booths one day, he would never have noticed her interest. Then again, that affair didn't end well. At all. A major reason for his decamping to Phoenix.

§

Yasmine Dubai

Yasmine Dubai didn't know what to do. She liked this man. He projected a diffidence, and at the same time confidence, possessing many of the qualities she admired. Yasmine liked how he looked, and couldn't help but find his nomadic past attractive. It was a sop to the way she grew up; she needed a man with an element of danger about him.

During the interview, her professional side said to investigate his background, while her personal side liked to watch him when he wasn't looking. She enjoyed it when their eyes locked. Yasmine thought of him more than once as she drifted to sleep.

Yesterday, with Robert's stellar performance in training class, she found herself rooting for him, although she made sure she kept her enthusiasm hidden. Showing favoritism was inappropriate. But Mary-Anne noticed the attention; Mary-Anne noticed everything.

Did I see jealousy? Did you catch him looking at me, Mary-Anne? I don't think he's your type. I don't get the feeling he intimidates easily. You'd be better off with Alan Bennet, a handsome man but a lot more controllable.

In the two months since her last night out, she hadn't socialized once, not even with her colleagues. While Yasmine's strong physical desires remained unmet, she could control them. But her emotional needs raged. Several other men at work continued trying to ask her on a date, but she didn't find any of them attractive, with the possible exception of Billy-Ray, and she didn't ever want to delve into the reasons behind her interest.

"Robert," she began, "there's a place called the Silver Rail. It's a quiet bar and restaurant. We could go there. I don't feel like a lot of noise."

"Neither do I."

"Why don't I meet you there in a couple of hours? I want to have a shower and get changed. We can catch a late dinner."

"That would be great. How should I dress?"

"Oh, it's kind of upscale, but casual. I eat there from time to time. Do you like Italian?"

"I love Italian," replied Robert, as the couple locked on each other. "Are you sure the kitchen's open?"

"Positive. They serve food Thursday through Saturday nights until 11:30. Here, let me show you where it is."

Yasmine took some paper from one of the mail slots and wrote down a street address.

"It's 8:30 now, so why don't we make it, 10:30? Is that too late?"

"No, I'm a night person. Besides, I don't have to be back here again until 2:00 p.m. What about yourself?"

"It's time I slept in. I haven't had a morning off for months."

"Great, I'll see you in a couple of hours."

§

Robert MacKenzie

In reply, Robert grasped Yasmine's left hand. She squeezed it softly in return, nodded, then left the prep room.

Robert watched her go, the softness of her skin still tingling on his fingers. Her perfume, with its subtle notes of myrrh and black cherry, danced in the air before quietly evanescing.

When he put his hand on hers, Yasmine yielded. He savored that most of all about women. Not the sex, but that sense of contact. The emotions of need and desire reflecting back toward him with the touch of someone special.

Robert panicked, thinking he might not have enough money for an evening at a high-end restaurant. He could hardly ask Yasmine to go to McDonalds. Reaching into his wallet, Robert pulled out three, twenty-dollar bills. With the change in his pocket that brought his total liquidity to sixty-two dollars and thirty-seven cents. He had another one hundred dollars in the bank and this total had to last him until his next payday. That would be in three weeks from TeleShop, or whenever his old employer mailed him his check, and that could take forever.

I can't afford this. I should put it off for a week or two.

But even as the thought crossed his mind, he ruled it out. He was going, pure and simple.

It's time I saw how the other half lived in this city.

Turning to leave, Robert noticed the next host hadn't arrived yet. According to the schedule, someone named Stefano should have been sitting in the office preparing his show. Either he was late or there was another prep room. Regardless, Robert wasn't going to let anything get in the way of his date with Yasmine. Walking toward the employee entrance and his car, Robert hoped he wouldn't have trouble finding the Silver Rail.

§

Robert MacKenzie

He arrived at Best Value Inn and waved at the Dealmaker, who sat outside on a lawn chair, drinking. Robert raced into his room for a shower and shave. Brushing his teeth and combing his hair, he put on his last clean shirt. Robert had one pair of ironed black pants and a pair of polished black shoes left. After checking himself in the mirror, he exited his room and walked over to the Dealmaker.

"Kid, I'm impressed. You got a date with Yasmine," said the Dealmaker with a hearty smile. "There's going to be a lot of very jealous people around TeleShop when this gets out on Monday. It's a good thing you're a show host or it could affect your career!"

"How did you know?" Robert asked.

"Cause you came running in here like a bat out of hell and now you're all clean and pressed and ready for action."

"So, why does that mean I'm going out with Yasmine?"

"Kid, you may be blind, deaf, and dumb, but I'm not! What else would get you all dolled up? Especially after you talked my ear off about her the other night."

"Okay, I'm going out with Yasmine."

"Where ya takin' her?"

"We're meeting at some place called the Silver Rail."

"La-de-da. Yasmine's idea I assume?"

"Yes, why? What's wrong with the place?"

"Wrong with the place? Nothing." The Dealmaker began speaking in an affected tone. "It's a quaint bistro in an exclusive part of town. The quiet ambiance and continental cuisine help to create the perfect atmosphere." He finished and broke out in laughter. "I bet you never thought you'd hear me say 'quaint,' did ya?"

Robert chuckled with the Dealmaker, who raised his can of Olde English in a toast. "No, I never did. You're a multifaceted man."

"That I am. How's your cash?"

"I'll get by."

"Trust Yasmine to pick one of the most expensive restaurants in the city." The Dealmaker gave him one hundred dollars and swatted away his attempt at saying no. Then after thinking for a moment, he handed over a further hundred dollars and gave Robert directions to the restaurant. "Don't worry about it, pay me back when you can. If you leave now, you should arrive by 10:15. You got reservations?"

"Ah, I don't think so," replied Robert.

"You got reservations; Yasmine doesn't leave anything to chance."

"What does that mean?"

"Never mind, kid. You'll find out."

The Dealmaker didn't explain himself further. Robert thanked him again for the money and jumped into his car. The sun had set as Robert drove up the I40 on-ramp and onto the highway.

Exit 40. Don't forget Exit 40. What kind of car does she drive? What will she wear? Hell, will she show up?

His usual worries and nerves set upon him. The closer he arrived to his cutoff, the more intense they became. Robert left the highway, driving north into an elegant area of Oklahoma City. Expensive shops lined the streets.

Where is her condo? How nice is it? Better, what's the rent?

In the distance, on the left side of the street and past the traffic lights, sat the Silver Rail. Robert pulled to a stop in front of its broad picture window and its chic neon sign, grateful for an available parking space. He checked his appearance in the rear-view mirror, shutting off his engine and climbing out of his car.

One of the things that did catch his eye were the other automobiles parked around the restaurant. Outside the front door was a vintage Ferrari Dino. There were a couple of Mercedes, the odd Cadillac and Lincoln and right next to his Civic stood a beautiful Jaguar XJS HE. Robert always fantasized about owning a Jaguar—something about its twelve-cylinder engine fascinated him.

He wanted to look at it, but his watch said 10:20 p.m. He was about to walk to the restaurant when he caught sight of the Jaguar's license number.

Ontario

ACY ♛ 777

Yours to Discover

God, those are Canadian plates. Yasmine's from Toronto. Jesus, please don't tell me she drives a Jag! What kind of chance do I have with a woman who owns an XJS when I have to borrow money so I can eat after I pay for dinner? Thank you, God, I appreciate it!

If he lacked confidence before, Robert's last remaining reserve made a dash for the exit.

She's in there waiting for me and I show up in a beat-up Honda Civic. Did she see me park? Is she watching me now while I fawn over her car? I don't need this shit.

While he let himself fall apart inside, Robert continued his walk toward the Silver Rail's entrance. The doorman let him in and Robert found himself in front of the maître d'.

"Hi, I'm meeting somebody," Robert said.

The maître d' raised his eyes from his podium in the manner of maître d's everywhere. "And with whom are you meeting?" he asked with more than usual condescension.

"Her name is Yasmine Dubai. Very tall, brunette, brown eyes, quite striking."

"Yes, sir," he said, oozing smugness. "She's over there; please follow me."

The maître d' led Robert to a quiet table in the back. He saw Yasmine from behind, sitting with a menu in her hand, drinking a glass of wine.

"Madame, your party has arrived," said the maître d'.

Yasmine turned and made eye contact with Robert. She looked beautiful, wearing a long floral print dress in shades of rose and cream with matching shoes. The fatigue she exhibited earlier was gone.

"Hi," she said to Robert, her face lighting up, its sincerity taking away every measure of stress he'd felt that week.

"Hi." Robert locked on her, hoping his face didn't give away too much, but accepting it probably did. Robert sat across from Yasmine, making a conscious effort to appear relaxed and unstressed. "Have you been waiting long?"

"No, I got here five minutes ago. I live nearby."

"You look great," Robert said. "I mean that."

"Thank you. You say it with such sincerity."

"That's because I am. You can't tell me other men don't ever tell you you're pretty?"

"They do. But I always get the impression they want something."

"Don't be so sure I don't," Robert said laughing.

"You men, you're all alike," Yasmine responded. "Did you have trouble finding the place?"

"No, the Dealmaker gave me directions."

She raised her eyebrows a touch at the mention of the show host. "It sounds like you two are getting quite close."

"Yes, we are. He likes to sit in the parking lot at night and have a beer or two."

"Or ten or eleven," Yasmine said.

"You do know the man. Anyway, he was there when I came home."

"Did you mention you were meeting me?"

"I didn't have to. He brought it up."

"How did he know?" Yasmine asked, surprised.

"I might have mentioned your name a few times."

"Should I feel touched or offended?"

"C'mon, Yasmine. The Dealmaker's not a bad guy. He's in a bad marriage, and he's lonely, so sue him. We all have to deal with our problems in our own way."

"Alright, I'll let it rest. Do you like the restaurant?" Yasmine turned on a smile that Robert could only describe as mischievous. He hadn't seen that particular look before and liked it immediately.

"Yes," he said with a measured pause. "It's nice. There's quite a selection of hi-end automobiles parked on the street."

"Well, this is Oklahoma City's idea of high culture. If this was a Friday or Saturday night, or if it was even an hour earlier tonight, we would have had to line up. I made a reservation for us before I left TeleShop."

The Dealmaker knows you better than you realize.

"Hey, was that your Jag outside?"

"Yes, how did you know? Did you see me driving it to work?"

"No, my car is next to yours. You still have your Canadian tags. I didn't figure there'd be much chance of seeing a car with Ontario license plates parked outside an Oklahoma City restaurant this time of night that *didn't* belong to you."

"Touché. I should change them. I've been here ten months, but I can't ever seem to get around to it."

"I'll have to do mine; I've got Arizona plates," Robert replied. "If the Oklahoma City DMV is anything like Phoenix, it won't be a treat."

"Toronto's the same way. That's something all people have in common, standing in line at the Motor Vehicle Office."

They both laughed and Robert began to relax.

"I didn't think you made so much money you could afford a Jaguar — an XJS no less."

"I can't complain; I'm actually doing okay, especially as a recent grad. But the car was a gift from my mother when I finished Wharton. She owns a very successful clothing boutique back home."

"It's a nice car."

"It is. You might drive it someday," Yasmine said while looking into his eyes.

"That would be very nice. Should we order?"

The couple picked up their menus and studied them for a few minutes. When their waiter appeared, Yasmine ordered the veal scallopine with Madeira sauce and another glass of house white. Robert had the veal parmesan, also with the house white. After twenty minutes of conversation, their food appeared.

"I'm starved," Yasmine said while cutting a piece of veal. "I haven't eaten more than a sandwich all day."

"I'm the same way. But I have to wonder if you're trying to overwhelm me?" Robert replied in a conspiratorial tone.

"Overwhelm you, how?" Yasmine asked, putting down her fork.

"Well, I'm tired of the new vegetarianism. I can't remember the last time I was out with a woman who ordered a meat dish, other than boneless, skinless, air-cooked chicken. It makes me a little crazy. What the hell's wrong with a steak?"

"Nothing. I love steak," Yasmine said.

"You're not concerned about the horrible way they treat the cows to make veal?" Robert asked.

"Fuck them," Yasmine replied.

Robert laughed, his body shaking. He put his wine glass down to avoid spilling it all over his pants. Yasmine paused, staring into Robert's eyes and then joined him in laughter.

"I hate that politically correct bullshit," Yasmine said, still giggling. "Humans are at the top of the food chain and I refuse to feel guilty about it."

"Amen. It's good to know a female carnivore. And it's also good to hear you swear."

"I swear from time to time, I'm just not a zealot about it, like Mary-Anne," replied Yasmine.

The meal proceeded with a light-hearted intimacy. Robert enjoyed the food, although he dreaded what it would cost. He spoke about his travels in detail, while Yasmine talked about grad school and her future. She had a sharp focus on career and an eventual move to Manhattan.

They finished their main course and ordered cheesecake for dessert.

"To New York," Yasmine said, while slicing her fork through the cake. "This cheesecake is the closest taste of the Big Apple I'm going to get for a while."

"Cheers," Robert replied. "Why do you want to go to New York so bad?"

"Where else should I go? If you aspire to a career in top management, everybody's head office is in Manhattan."

"What about Los Angeles? There's always the entertainment industry."

"Fine. To Los Angeles, or Boston, or Chicago, or Toronto, or anywhere, but Oklahoma City!"

"You're ambitious," Robert said.

"Is that a problem?" Yasmine replied. "Isn't a woman allowed to have a career? God, I'm tired of the put-downs and the comments; I hear the ice queen jokes at work. Didn't any of those assholes ever think that maybe I just don't find them attractive? It wasn't anything personal. There's a rumor circulating now I'm a lesbian. So what if I am! Should that be anyone's business?"

Robert saw the tears well in Yasmine's eyes. Her outburst was so sudden, it took him off guard. He put down his own fork and reached over with his right hand, placing it against the side of her face.

"No, it isn't anyone's business. And you're right, a woman's overt ambition still isn't accepted. There's not much you can do about it except fight."

Yasmine grasped Robert's hand and held it. With her other, she picked up her napkin and dabbed at her cheek, staring at him. In that instant, with her pain and hope displayed so naked, Robert could have loved her.

"I'm not, you know," Yasmine said.

"Not what?"

"A lesbian."

"Good," replied Robert. "Neither am I."

They chuckled again. Robert would ask himself later how often they had laughed over the course of the evening. For now, it was a pleasure simply being with Yasmine.

Over coffee and dessert, Yasmine told Robert about her life in Tehran, the months in London and growing up in Canada. Robert spoke about his own estrangement from his family and the coldness he found in New England. He even filled in some of the missing details from his résumé. Yasmine liked hearing about the bar and the adult video store he worked at in particular. Robert wondered why.

The waiter coughed behind Robert and handed him the check. Yasmine made a motion to pick it up.

"Please, I asked *you* out," he said.

"But, you need your money, what with your upcoming move and all?"

Robert winced at the notion of his move. He still hadn't made plans to pick up his belongings in Phoenix. He also hadn't opened a local bank account yet.

"Don't worry about it," Robert said with confidence. "I insist."

Yasmine dropped her hand.

"Thank you for dinner, Robert. It was lovely." She reached across the table and took Robert's hand in her own, squeezing it and melting his heart. "I have to use the restroom. I'll be back in a minute."

Yasmine moved with grace from the table; he watched her leave and noted again the simple, elegance of her dress.

She was born with a sense of style.

The bill came to ninety-eight dollars and fifty-six cents.

Thank God the Dealmaker lent me money!

125

Robert counted out one hundred fifteen dollars and placed it in the leather sleeve. He finished his glass of wine and waited for Yasmine's return. She appeared a minute later.

"Shall we, Mr. MacKenzie?"

"We shall, Ms. Dubai."

Their hands found each other as they strolled through the restaurant toward the front door. There was only one other couple left. He glanced at his watch.

"Did you know it's 1:00 a.m.?" Robert said.

"Yes, I looked at my watch in the ladies room. Time flies."

"It does. Yasmine, I had a great time tonight. I'd love to do it again."

The couple stopped in front of Yasmine's Jaguar. Yasmine leaned against the front door and placed her hand on Robert's face. "I'd like that too."

It was always this moment that caused him the most trouble. He never knew what he should do. Kiss her? Shake her hand? Try to score an invite back to her place? He wanted more than sex from Yasmine and almost hoped she didn't ask him back. Instead, he wrapped his arm around her waist, drawing her to him and kissing her. He invited Yasmine's tongue into his mouth, feeling her interest as she pressed her body tight against his. Through his thin shirt, he became conscious of Yasmine's firm breasts. His hand moved down across her behind, feeling the outline of her panties.

As his own passion mounted, he pulled away to stare into Yasmine's eyes.

"I thought I'd stop before you asked me to," he said.

"How do you know that's what I wanted?" she replied, making it clear he could proceed.

"I don't. There's a lot of time for this. Let's think about it. I've got to make arrangements to move my stuff from Phoenix this weekend, but would you like to get together on Sunday?"

"I'd like that," Yasmine said, surprised at his actions, her curiosity piqued.

Robert let her words hang, then he kissed her on the lips and stepped back.

"Where's your car, Robert?"

"Right here," he replied, kicking the tire of his Civic. He pulled his keys from his pocket and reached toward the lock.

Yasmine opened the door to her Jaguar and turned to step inside. She paused. "Thanks, Robert."

"You're welcome," he replied, climbing into his car and putting the key in the ignition. He waited for Yasmine to pull away before he turned over his engine. As the Jag pulled out and headed down the street, Robert found he lacked the will to start his car. He sat for several minutes, his thoughts broken only by the sudden darkness when the Silver Rail turned off its neon sign. With a sigh and a smile, he started the motor, made a U-turn, and headed back for the motel.

CHAPTER NINE

Yasmine Dubai

The drive back to her building took twenty minutes. Yasmine parked her XJS in the underground lot, surveying its quiet as she locked the car's door and headed to the elevator. The garage's muted darkness served as metaphor; Yasmine's heels clicked and echoed against the concrete, their sound empty and soulless.

Entering her condo, she dropped the keys on the hallway table. She slipped off her shoes, removed her jacket, and proceeded to strip, walking to her bedroom and reaching for her pajamas. She considered taking a shower but elected to pass. While pulling up her pajama bottoms, Yasmine felt cramps and realized she was getting her period.

Wonderful. Is there anything else I need to deal with?

She told Robert she'd arrive at the office late, but knew it was a fantasy. The clock ran to 1:30 a.m. While TeleShop was only twenty minutes away, Yasmine would still need to get up by 6:30 a.m. to arrive by 8:00 a.m. That meant five hours of sleep if she was lucky (and she was rarely lucky of late).

Yasmine climbed into bed, letting the room's darkness envelope her, its silence near total. The dim lights of surrounding buildings displayed against the bedroom windows while the muffled sounds of the Interstate pulsed in the background.

Yasmine liked Robert, pure and simple. The physical side of her attraction was obvious. The issue with her being his nominal boss not so clear.

He didn't finish high school. He's had no career to speak of. His last job was security guard and he can't stay in one place for any length of time.

If this was Toronto, her mother would forbid any sort of liaison. She may have given up on Yasmine marrying a nice Bahá'í boy, but there was no way she would countenance an itinerant without education or prospects. Neither would Yasmine. Her boyfriend at Wharton, Daryush, was an Iranian Christian from a good Tehrani family, wealthy bazaaris involved in the export of saffron. For the length of their three-year relationship, she entertained the notion of returning to Iran. Finally accepting the truth of her (lack of) feelings, she broke up with him in the month before graduation.

But this wasn't Wharton or Toronto; this was Oklahoma City. Yasmine found the men at work antiseptic. Bland. Without color. A lot like Daryush. The irony was not lost on her. Robert wasn't like that one bit. If all he had to offer was his looks, she would never have bothered. But he had more than looks.

In her career at TeleShop, Yasmine watched a series of men and women try out for show host. A few remained, though no one of significance. None of them had Robert's gift; he sparkled on camera. He may not have gone to college, but he knew how to speak — his vocabulary complex, and his spiel effortless. Yasmine liked smart, confident men.

She'd endured so much bravado from potential show hosts during her brief time in Oklahoma City, and she knew the job could be terrifying. Fear wasn't the issue. Facing fear and overcoming it was what separated the wheat from the chaff.

Yasmine read the worry in Robert's eyes during training and his resolution to meet it straight on. It's what she always needed in a partner, but never allowed herself to have. Her former boyfriends were handsome, intelligent men who let her dominate. They never understood that was fatal. Yasmine demanded they submit and then hated them for doing so. When Robert broke off his kiss in the parking lot of the Silver Rail, Yasmine made it clear he didn't have to stop. That he did anyway produced warmth. And safety. And fear.

The rest of the staff had only seen Robert shadow Dixie and walk around with other trainees. They hadn't heard him pitch. That would soon change, and with it their perception. Women liked successful men; they would forgive all sorts of physical and moral shortcomings for the right degree of prestige. And money. And if Robert did make it, he'd make a lot of money. It was only a matter of time before women noticed.

Yasmine's hand slipped into her pajama bottoms. It wasn't thinking about Robert that made her seek relief; it was everything, the sum total of the last ten months. The stress, the loneliness, and the sudden thought she may have competition for Robert's affection. This moment was opportune; her upcoming cycle made everything inconvenient.

With closed eyes, Yasmine explored herself as idealized images of men flitted about. All of them abstract. All of them speaking with confidence. All of them holding her tight.

§

Mary-Anne Warner

"Cliff, what do you mean I shouldn't have hired MacKenzie? You've been telling me for two years to get the numbers up, and now you're not happy about it?" Frustration oozed from Mary-Anne's voice and tension swarmed her chest as she spoke on the telephone to Cliff Johnson, her division head at Triboro Media in Manhattan.

It was 8:37 a.m. in Oklahoma City and 9:37 a.m. in New York. As always, there was no rest for the wicked.

Her boss's full sobriquet was Clifford Mark Joseph Johnson III. He ran Triboro's *International Cable & Satellite Television Group* in the collegial manner befitting a graduate of Andover and Harvard. Triboro's current CEO, William Graves Simcoe, pegged Johnson as his successor upon Simcoe's retirement, early next year.

Active in society and charities, Johnson typified (at least on the surface) the Eastern monied elite Mary-Anne wanted so desperately to join. Beneath Johnson's avuncular exterior dwelled a tyrant, willing to flame-throw any group or individual in his path. His professed love for the downtrodden a pose. Mary-Anne hitched her career to Johnson and would rise or fall with him.

Last night, she joined the Triboro group for goodbye drinks and dinner at the Skirvin Hotel. By now, they'd be on the corporate jet back to New York. Mary-Anne wouldn't miss them. Billy-Ray had a point in saying they would never let her join their group.

Let those Ivy League types flee to Manhattan. If they find Oklahoma City parochial, try where I grew up. This place is Paris compared to Welch, West Virginia.

On the phone, Johnson now dictated TeleShop's numbers tank. With the buyout approved, Triboro didn't want to pay Billy-Ray Newton market rate for his stake. Instead, they ordered Mary-Anne (not in so many words, that would have been illegal) to keep sales impaired by whatever means necessary. If TeleShop's valuation hit the agreed-upon strike price, it would cost Triboro two hundred million dollars. If not, it would cost fifty million. As Billy-Ray said, "That's a lot of goddamn money."

Jesus, I should have hired Lowenstein and Bondero. What does Triboro expect me to do? I don't run this place. There's no way Billy-Ray will let me mess with the Dealmaker or the Dragon Lady. And he's going to pay particular attention to Robert MacKenzie.

"I have an idea how to proceed. You'll have to do the actual dirty work; I can't be too obvious," warned Mary-Anne. "Here's my plan ... "

It came down to vendors. TeleShop was a small fish in a very large pond, and Triboro a colossus that owned its own sea. A sotto voce hint that manufacturers should pass supplying hot products to the shopping channel would prove TeleShop's undoing.

"That's an excellent plan, Mary-Anne," Cliff said in a warm and convivial tone, his affected "Mid-Atlantic" accent superficial. "Keep us apprised of anything that has sales potential. Make sure you identify the original vendor and any alternate suppliers. We'll take it from there."

"Yes, Cliff," replied Mary-Anne.

"Oh and Mary-Anne? I know how much you want a seat at the table. When I take over from Bill Simcoe, you'll take over from me. If anything happens that stops my ascension ... let's say I hear the weather's lovely in West Virginia in summer."

"I understand, Cliff."

"Good. We'll talk again soon." Her boss hung up without another word.

Mary-Anne leaned against her desk, considering the challenge. She'd faced obstacles before; she'd face obstacles again. Nothing was going to stop her from getting back to Manhattan. Nothing.

§

Robert MacKenzie

Robert awakened late on Friday morning, the memory of yesterday's date with Yasmine fresh on his mind and in his spirit. He'd returned to the motel after 1:30 a.m. The Dealmaker's chair sat empty, cans of Olde English littering the pavement. Robert paused outside his door, listening if his new friend was still up. But all he heard was snoring. With a sigh, Robert entered his own room, stripping down and climbing into bed.

The next morning Robert slid off his mattress wearing a sly grin. He walked around his room singing "A White Sports Coat" by Marty Robbins. For some inexplicable reason that was his go-to song when feeling happy.

Today was his second and last day shadowing the Dragon Lady. He didn't want to hear more criticism for being in the cafeteria rather than the prep room at 2:05 p.m. Instead, Robert got ready early. He shaved, showered, and dressed before strolling to the Dealmaker's room. It was a few minutes before 10:00 a.m. when he knocked.

"Hey, kid," said the Dealmaker as he opened the door. A stench of cigarettes, beer and ennui poured out of the motel unit. "How'd it go with Yasmine last night?"

Robert walked inside and gave the Dealmaker a rundown of his date. He held back his honest excitement and minimized his open emotions.

"So, you didn't fuck her?"

"No, I didn't fuck her! We kissed by our cars. It was nice. I suggested we do something on Sunday."

"Ya shoulda fucked her, kid." He held up his hand to stop Robert's interruption. "No, don't say anything. You want a beer?"

"Dealmaker, I'm shadowing Dixie at 2:00 p.m. I can't drink."

"Shadowing again? You're at the studio at 8:00 p.m. on Sunday for your first show, right?"

"No, I'm working Show #1 on Monday."

"Yeah … And what time do you think ya gotta get in for Show #1 on Monday?"

Robert paused, imagining the show time bulletin on the prep room's wall. *Shit! I screwed up my date with Yasmine. I'm such a cretin.*

"I asked Yasmine out on Sunday."

"Well, you better close the sale in the afternoon."

"Close how? I can't drink before my first show. Besides, I'm going to be crazy nervous all day!"

"You'll live," began the Dealmaker. "To hell with shadowing. Co-host with me today. I'll actually let you talk!"

"Won't that upset the Dragon Lady?"

"Yes and no. She won't miss you one bit. But the idea I grabbed you out of her show will make her nuts."

"Do I want to upset her?" asked Robert. "I don't need her hating me."

"Kid, she already hates you! She hates everybody. Don't sweat it."

"I see your point. If I go for it, will you please not show up late?" pleaded Robert. "Between the Dragon Lady and Yasmine, I don't need more stress in my life."

"Kid, I'll be there with bells on. Jump in your car and head over to TeleShop; I gotta take a dump. I'll follow behind in a bit."

"Thanks for sharing. I'll see you there."

Robert went back to his room, grabbed his car keys and drove off to TeleShop thinking, *Dealmaker, please be there on-time. Help a buddy out, please ...*

It was the same traffic and the same weather. The same nerves and the same circumscribed optimism weighing on his soul. Within twenty minutes, Robert pulled his Civic into TeleShop's parking lot. Although only four days since his first appearance, Hank didn't even grunt as he walked past. The rotund guard's revolver remained on the table as TeleShop's first line of defense smoked and read a copy of *People Magazine.*

The studio remained buzzing, although not at the same frenetic level as during the Dragon Lady's show. On the TV, Kirk smiled at the camera, selling a cubic zirconia ring in gold plate with red rhinestone accents. The graphic gave his full name as Kirk Glazer.

"It's a great look, ladies," said Kirk with a big smile, pausing for a second before directing his stare into the camera. Robert thought him a bit disingenuous. Although, what could he say about cheap costume jewelry that countless others hadn't said before?

The Dragon Lady would know. The Dealmaker would create a conspiracy of mystery over the ring's origin and price and make it into a game.

That was the difference in show hosts. Drama. Story. Enthusiasm. Kirk didn't have it. His spiel was serviceable, but lackluster.

"Pick up the phone and call now; don't miss out on the deal. We'll be right back." The feed cut to a promo for the Dragon Lady's show later that day.

"What brings you here so early, Mr. MacKenzie?" Mary-Anne Warner stopped by his side, walking out of the production area toward the office. Her sudden appearance startled Robert, who'd hoped to ask Yasmine about co-hosting.

"Good morning, Ms. Warner. I'm supposed to shadow Dixie tonight, but the Dealmaker said he'd like to co-host with me today. We're staying at the same motel. I was coming to see either you or Yasmine about it."

Mary-Anne's general air of inscrutability disappeared for a second. She looked at Robert, a small grin appearing on her face. He didn't know what it meant but didn't have time for consideration.

"That's a great idea, Robert. Go for it. I'll tell Dixie." Mary-Anne turned and toured away, heading down the corridor to the offices.

Robert didn't know what to make of what had just occurred. He stood outside production and the prep room, hesitating. Some of the operators gave him a casual glance but, for the most part, his presence drew minimal notice. That was the way of the possum. Robert didn't like it. He wanted to command attention like the Dealmaker or the Dragon Lady.

After reflecting, Robert walked toward Scheduling. He entered the busy room, where three women and one man typed away at their data terminals. Robert recognized Dawn and Jack. He didn't see Lateesha.

"Good morning, all," he said. "How is everybody?"

Dawn looked up puzzled. "Why are you in so early, Robert? Aren't you shadowing the Dragon Lady in Show #7?"

"I was, but the Dealmaker suggested we co-host today. Mary-Anne said it was okay. He's not here yet; could I look over his show?"

The rest of the room stopped. They peered up from their terminals, staring at him.

"Tell me you're kidding," said Dawn. "I'm serious; say it's a joke."

The Scheduling department continued focusing on Robert. Behind him, Lateesha walked in, a revised product selector in her hands.

"Hi, Robert. How are you?" she said, placing the printout on her desk and pulling out her chair.

"The Dealmaker took Robert out of the Dragon Lady's show," said Dawn to Lateesha. "He's going to co-host instead of shadow. Mary-Anne's said it's okay."

Lateesha stopped pulling out her chair. Instead, she straightened up and faced Robert, a look of utter shock on her face.

"Jesus, the Dragon Lady's gonna lose her shit!"

"What's the problem?" Robert asked. "I don't get it. She didn't want me on her show last night. Why should she care?"

"Because she will," said Dawn. "The Dealmaker and the Dragon Lady are always fighting for the top slot. Shadowing is casual. We don't assign your name to the statistics. When you co-host, your name appears in the totals and you're expected to help with selling. There's some buzz behind you, Robert. The Dragon Lady will figure this is the Dealmaker trying to outflank her by building an alliance."

"But she never wanted me in the first place?" Robert said, frustrated.

"It doesn't matter," replied Lateesha. "It's the principle. The Dealmaker's fuckin' with her. She won't take it well!"

The entire affair was petty. He told them the Dealmaker should be in soon and said goodbye. Picking up the Dealmaker's show, he walked back to the prep room.

Scheduling gossiped among themselves for the next few minutes, speculating about the affair. They weren't upset; rather, it was excitement. The brightening of their dull week with tiff and scandal. TeleShop's pressure cooker environment encouraged all manner of diversion, if only to relieve its unremitting fierceness.

§

Yasmine Dubai

Yasmine arrived at the office at her usual time of 8:00 a.m., managing to grab her predicted five hours of sleep.

On the brief drive to TeleShop she ran through last night's dinner with Robert. There wasn't much to say; she enjoyed herself, more than she cared to admit. She found him charming and attractive and earnest and … dangerous. Not in a physical way, but in the manner of her career. She could get around being his boss. What she couldn't square was that success at TeleShop would bind him to Oklahoma City. The greater his gain, the more money he made, the less chance he would leave. And in the end, Manhattan was her destiny.

She spent the morning running last night's numbers and preparing reports. After two hours, Yasmine grabbed a sheaf of host memos and headed to the prep room. Production had already placed an embossed tape strip with Robert's name on Rick Furfaro's old slot. Rick had worked at TeleShop for eight months. While well-liked by the office staff and crew, his sales were at best average. Yasmine fired him two weeks ago and now found it difficult to remember his face.

While distributing the host memos, Robert walked into the prep room. Yasmine turned to face him, and began smiling, before stopping herself.

"Hey," he said, reaching for her hand.

Yasmine moved to reciprocate but pulled back. A puzzled look overtook Robert.

"It's okay, we're alone," he said, stating the obvious.

"I'm sorry; I know we're alone," began Yasmine, an unnatural pause hovering as Robert waited for an explanation. "This is awkward. I had a lovely time last night, I did. But technically I'm your boss and it's a problem. We shouldn't have gone out."

"Is it that big a deal?"

"It's more than that," replied Yasmine, struggling to maintain tact. "I know you're going to be very successful at TeleShop. It's obvious. People who have a natural gift for selling on home shopping channels are rare, impossible to quantify. Every now and then somebody just rolls in. That's how we found the Dealmaker and the Dragon Lady. They showed up out of the blue one day, both nomads. Coming here was like finding their destiny. They'll never leave. You're like that too."

Robert stood motionless, hoping he displayed the correct degree of seriousness and sadness.

"Robert, I'm not staying in Oklahoma City. I can't. At some point soon, I'm moving to Manhattan. And you're going to remain here. Between being your boss and knowing we don't have a future, it doesn't make sense to get involved. I could rationalize myself around it. That's what I did with my boyfriend at Wharton. But I really like you and I can't put both of us through the drama when it's time for me to leave."

"I like you too, Yasmine ... " Robert's words trailed off.

Like most women, Yasmine never respected begging and hoped Robert wouldn't try. He didn't. Instead, Robert stood in front of her trying to look stoic (with limited success). He said he understood, turning away while sitting down at the desk and looking over the Dealmaker's show.

Yasmine wanted to touch his arm, but resisted the urge. An emptiness sat in her stomach as she walked out of the prep room.

It's the right decision. If this affects me so much now, how would it affect me in a year or two?

Heading back toward her office, Yasmine looked up as the Dealmaker passed her in the corridor. He nodded on his way to the prep room.

If someone as abrasive as the Dealmaker can meet new people, why can't I?

§

The Dealmaker

Regardless of her manner, the Dealmaker liked Yasmine. She was as buttoned-down as a closeted gay man on a football team. As he told Robert earlier, if something didn't give—and give soon—she'd detonate. Rather than find her disdain troubling, he thought it funny. The Dealmaker admired her pluck. And "pluck" was not a word he used easily or often.

He passed by Scheduling, made a couple of perfunctory greetings and walked into the prep room. Robert sat at the lone table, reading the show's printout.

"Hey, Dealmaker. Thank Christ you're here. I was getting worried."

"Jesus, take a fucking pill! I've never missed a show yet." The Dealmaker waxed indignant, his bluster loud and self-righteous. He looked about and saw again the room lay empty except for himself and Robert. "Okay, I've missed the odd show, but it hasn't happened for a while and never for anything major."

The Dealmaker reached for the show's printout. He checked it in detail, huffing and puffing the entire time.

"We got nothin,'" he said. "Fuck all! Those dumb Scheduling fucks don't understand you got to have a hit at the top and bottom of every hour. And you need your major grease at the top of your third hour. What am I supposed to build a show around? We got a couple of collectibles. Some Capodimonte. A ring that ain't worth a pinch of shit ..."

"Mary-Anne said Scheduling knew their stuff. But you and the Dragon Lady always want to move things around and add extra products. Why?"

"Why?" The Dealmaker gawked at Robert as if he had asked where babies came from or if Santa Claus was real. "Why? Kid, I told you, you're judged by every show, every day. There's a reason the Dragon Lady and I are on top. We know what sells, when it sells, and how to sell it. Scheduling looks at the updated product selector, picks whatever shit they hope might work and throws it on the air. If you rely on them, you're dead!"

The Dealmaker paused, shaking his head. He made some noises, appeared to weigh his options, scratched his chin, and otherwise looked contemplative. Raising an eyebrow, a sardonic beam worked onto his face as the Dealmaker smiled. If this had been a cartoon, a lightbulb would have appeared over his head. Instead, the Dealmaker stood up and headed for the door.

"I'm going down to Scheduling for two drop-ins. When John gets here, tell him I've gone for a smoke and I'll be back in a bit."

"John?"

"Our director. We're meeting with him to discuss the flow. Tell him we're adding drop-in #1 to our 12:30 p.m. slot and drop-in #2 goes at 2:00 p.m."

"What drop-ins? Besides, Dealmaker, the show's over at 2:00 p.m."

"Christ, kid. Didn't you pay any attention in training? Eastern Time — we go by Eastern Time! Leave the drop-ins to me. Tell John what I said. I'll be back in a bit."

The Dealmaker noted this was the second occasion Robert had forgotten about the time shift. The first occurrence only derailed his date with Yasmine. In TeleShop's unforgiving environment, a third mishap could be fatal.

§

Robert MacKenzie

The meeting with John took five minutes. They discussed the show and strategy. The experience stood in stark contrast to his time with the Dragon Lady. She tolerated him at best. The Dealmaker included him fully in the preparation.

Their director, John Duguay, played bass in a local band, the Nomadic Cowboys. They'd finished recording their debut album, *Pool Here Good* and had a live release show on Saturday night at Lucky Charm Saloon, a nearby club.

"Johnny-man, of course I'll come. Put me on the guest list. And put Robert on it as well," said the Dealmaker, always ready for a night of drinking.

"You sure, Dealmaker?" replied John with expectation. "Would you mind if we added your name to our posters?"

"Johnny-man, of course. Knock yourself out!"

John's excitement at the prospect of the Dealmaker's name on the posters gave Robert an indication of his local prominence — or notoriety.

"Thanks, Dealmaker. I'll see you tomorrow night. I gotta get back to the control room. Good luck with the show. The drop-ins are genius."

John left the prep room for the set as the Dealmaker turned to him. "Don't sweat paying for drinks; I'm flush until payday. Got lucky at the track."

"Dealmaker, you're assuming I can make it on Saturday. How do you know I'm free? And what does he mean your drop-ins are 'genius'? You've slotted a record at 12:30 p.m. and a baby doll at two o'clock. How's that special?"

"Kid, ya told me Yasmine doesn't want to see you anymore. What else ya gonna do? It's time ya stopped playin' with yourself and started playin' with a girl. There's always lots of broads at that club. Guaranteed some skirt from the office will be there too. As for the drop-ins, trust me, they'll be great. It's all in the presentation, kid. It's always the presentation!"

§

The Dealmaker

They were on the air twenty minutes later. The Dealmaker was effusive in his praise of Robert, calling him, "Big Mack."

"Friends, I've kidded you in the past and I'll kid you again in the future. But today I'm not kidding you at all. This is one of my greatest shows ever! In twenty-five minutes, at 12:30 p.m. Eastern Time, Big Mack and I have a few copies of my favorite album of all time. When I need to unwind, this is the music I listen to at my palatial digs here in mighty Oklahoma City. No, I'm not going to tell you the title. You'll have to wait. Oh, and at 2:00 p.m. Eastern Time, get ready. We have a rare appearance of our anatomically correct infant dolls. Boys and girls both. All I'm sayin' is they have all their parts. That's all I'm sayin'! Let's go shopping … "

The Dealmaker kibitzed with Robert, back and forth, to and fro. They had a natural repartee. The show began with the blue-blocking sunglasses, guaranteed to eliminate eye strain and only nineteen dollars ninety-nine cents.

The B-L-U-U-U-U-U-E BLOCKERS, as the Dealmaker called them, lit up the lines as thousands called in.

"If you're down in the dumps, start up the pumps. Cut out the blue and live your life true!" sang the Dealmaker with the cadence of a preacher.

The Dealmaker operated in a manner polar opposite of the Dragon Lady. When the camera was on, she sparkled. When the camera was off she didn't. The Dragon Lady's crew skulked about on tenterhooks. The only thing she had in common with the Dealmaker was her ability to sell. But when said and done, that's all that mattered.

"Let's go to a call," announced the Dealmaker. "We got Josie from Pella, Iowa on the line. Josie, ya there?"

"I'm here, Dealmaker. How are you? Hi, Big Mack!"

Robert said his first hello to a live caller on-air. She swooned over the Dealmaker and was very polite and kind to Robert.

"Dealmaker, can I say hi to my husband, Dave, and my son, Smitty? My husband's a trucker and my son just joined the army."

"Josie, go right ahead. Nothing's too good for America's working men and women and we always honor our service members."

"Thanks so much, Dealmaker. But I have to ask, what's the record at 12:30?" The caller's piercing curiosity boded well.

"Josie, I can't tell ya. I want to so bad, it hurts. But I'm going to hold off. Ya gotta forgive me," the Dealmaker replied with a smile so large the camera almost caught fire.

"Big Mack, do you know the name of the record?" she pleaded to Robert.

"Josie, I do. But if I told you I'd have to kill you," Robert said in his deepest voice.

The Dealmaker broke out in genuine laughter as Robert's intercom cut in with the shrieking of the production crew. Off to the right, Susie — the floor director — shook with bemusement. This power to create laughter was heady; Robert was going to get used to it in a big way.

The Blue Blockers sold well and ran long forcing a rethink of their original plan. They meant to air four products before their 12:30 p.m. special. Instead, the Dealmaker told John to cut items two and three. They'd segue to item four, the 8K Electronic Pocket Directory, for a few minutes before going to break and returning at 12:30 p.m. for their feature.

During the break, Robert noticed an East Indian woman smiling at him. She stood near the control room dressed in a black pantsuit with a whisper blue silk blouse. The woman was in her late twenties, standing about five feet eight inches, and was slim, with long black hair and piercing slate eyes. Like Yasmine, her appearance contrasted sharply with the majority of TeleShop's staff.

"Dealmaker, who's the woman over there?"

The Dealmaker glanced over. They had less than a minute before their break ended. "That's Sandiya King. She's the assistant corporate counsel, works with Nat in the legal department. Been here about a year. Why?"

"Just wondering," Robert replied.

"Just wondering my ass!" chuckled the Dealmaker. "We've got exactly two Middle-Eastern dames working here and you've managed to notice both of them."

John broke in over the intercom. "Dealmaker, we're back in thirty. We're already getting calls about the album. I don't know how you do it."

"It's my charm and good looks," said the Dealmaker as Susie began the countdown. She pointed to them as the tally light turned red.

"Well, *arby-dar*, it's the Dealmaker with my good buddy, Robert 'Big Mack' MacKenzie back and ready for something that's personal to me. Big Mack, what kind of music do you like?"

Taken aback, Robert looked flustered for a second before blurting out the first band that came to mind.

"U2. They released their new album, *The Joshua Tree*, a few months back. It's great." Robert looked to the Dealmaker hoping he'd given the correct answer to a question that had none.

"They American?" asked the Dealmaker.

Is the Dealmaker serious or was he playing around?

"No, they're Irish."

"Well, my favorite album's also foreign. By the way, my favorite American band is a local outfit. Big Mack and I are going to be at Lucky Charm Saloon tomorrow night to see the Nomadic Cowboys. Feel free to drop in and buy either of us a beer. Or five!"

In the control room, John stood up and bowed low in appreciation.

"If you're like me, ya get stressed. God knows we all need a break. I want you to get ready. Because Big Mack and I are offering my absolute favorite album of all time right now for only nine dollars ninety-nine cents. I want ya'll to kick back. Imagine a little peace and quiet in your life. John, let me hear my album."

A haunting melody played through their headsets bringing back vague memories of an old, direct-response TV commercial.

At their meeting earlier, Robert didn't understand the Dealmaker's idea at all.

"Dealmaker, it's a ten-dollar album. The product selector says it hasn't aired in over two years." John had watched the pair with interest, the *senpai* with his *kohai*.

"Look at the cost," replied the Dealmaker. "It's two bucks net. We're gonna retail it for ten bucks. The other hosts couldn't give it away; they never figured out a hook. Our old smallgoods buyer screwed up and bought ten thousand of them by accident. That's why he's our old smallgoods buyer. It doesn't matter; it's my favorite album of all time."

"Are you serious?" asked Robert.

"Fuck no! I like Chuck Berry and Jerry Lee Lewis."

"Then how are we going to sell it?"

"With mystery and a lot of bullshit. Trust me."

As 12:30 p.m. struck, the Dealmaker looked at the camera dead on. He appeared to tear up.

"Friends, I give you *Zamfir, Master of the Pan Flute!* It's taken two years to get this back in stock. Don't ask me why; I don't know. But it's here. We got ten thousand copies, and it's going to sell out. I'm serious. It is going to sell out. Don't miss out on this less than half-price buy on the most relaxing music ever."

In the background, every sad song ever recorded played at low volume. Robert looked at the inbound call monitors and watched the numbers rise.

"This is for when you've had a bad day, and God knows I've had a lot of bad days lately. Without this album I swear I'd be dead! I've been fighting with our smallgoods buyer for over a year to get this back in stock and at a great price."

The Dealmaker stood up from his chair, rising like a missionary at the anchor desk and pointing to the camera.

"When it came in this morning, I told our Scheduling department to make sure I got it before Dixie. She's gonna kill me when she hears I sold it out. Whatever you do, don't call Dixie tonight and tell her you got Zamfir on my show. Don't do that to her. She loves Zamfir and this is going to destroy her."

With unbelievable animation, the Dealmaker gesticulated like a madman; he related stories — whether true or not — from his past about drinking too much and needing comfort the next morning. About missing his family when away on sales trips. About getting old and looking to his past with regret.

An exponential surge of inbound calls overwhelmed the network reassigning customer service agents to sales as their current calls ended. The emergency light flashed in the cafeteria, directing all operators to return to their stations at once. A counter appeared on their feed starting at nine hundred sixty-two units sold and shooting up like a missile.

"Friends, I told you this would happen. Don't miss out. Don't hear my sad lament, *Too late, too late will be the cry, Dealmaker Dave and the deal have passed you by!* It's going to disappear soon. Please, I'm not joking. Call now for Z-A-M-F-I-R, M-A-S-T-E-R--O-F--T-H-E--P-A-N--F-L-U-T-E!"

The Dealmaker cut their mics as the screen faded to a video of Zamfir playing his soulful flute. He hit the intercom.

"Of course he's the master of the pan flute. Nobody else knows how to play the goddamn thing!"

The crew, Robert and assorted hangers-on burst into laughter, their guffaws lasting minutes. If his mic had been hot or the feed not showing Zamfir, all hell would have broken loose. But it didn't. The incoming calls reached maximum. There were far more customers than operators to process them. In quick fashion, Zamfir sold out. At eight dollars gross margin that was a profit of eighty thousand dollars in the near blink of an eye.

"Friends, I told you. I know we're going to try and get Zamfir back in stock. I hope we can. Big Mack and I will be back after this quick message. Don't forget, we have the anatomically correct dolls coming up at 2:00 p.m. Eastern Time. Remember, all I'm sayin' is, they have all their parts. That's all I'm sayin'. We'll be right back."

§

Robert MacKenzie

As it turned out, the dolls did have "all their parts." For the life of him, Robert couldn't understand how the Dealmaker knew they would sell. The anatomically correct dolls had aired several times in the past with uninspiring results. The Zamfir records hadn't aired in two years and didn't sell when they did. Before today, they were a complete flop.

When 2:00 p.m. hit, after a slow initial burn, the dolls began flying. TeleShop offered both white and black dolls, male and female. Ten minutes of pitching, with a constant refrain of "they have all their parts, that's all I'm sayin'," ignited the flame.

It turned out he worked well with the Dealmaker.

"Dealmaker, let me clarify this, please," Robert would ask. "Are they complete?"

"Big Mack, as complete as the Good Lord allows!"

"So you're sayin' — "

"I'm sayin' they got all their parts; that's all I'm sayin'!"

Every caller they took to air laughed, with some making off-color comments.

"Big Mack," said a woman with a thick, Southern accent. Robert didn't want to trade in stereotypes, but she sounded black. Her first name was Shanice. "I'm buying a boy and a girl for my sister's youngest, Deja. Now, Big Mack, welcome to TeleShop. Y'all tellin' me they got all their parts?"

"Shanice, thank you for the kind words," answered Robert with a big voice and a bigger smile. "My best to your sister and Deja. I checked out those dolls before we went to air. The Dealmaker's right, they got all their parts. As for the boy, it looked to me like he was packin'!"

The set went dead quiet. The operators, listening to the feed as they worked their terminals, became still. No sound came from Shanice. The Dealmaker, with a look of complete shock, turned to Robert at the anchor desk, staring wide-eyed.

Without notice, Shanice began laughing hysterically. In the background, others in her home joined in. One of the operators started giggling causing her colleagues to laugh as well. The crew lost it. The Dealmaker howled, as did Robert. This went on for several minutes.

Robert felt like a stand-up comic slaying the crowd at a nightclub. The call screens maxed out yet again. The dolls cost TeleShop fifteen dollars but retailed for thirty-nine ninety-nine and there were sixty-five hundred in-stock. The product selector indicated they were a closeout with no more available.

Robert watched their sales monitor. Every ten seconds the screen updated with an average of forty-six hundred dollars per minute. In the thirty-five minutes they spent selling the dolls TeleShop made a gross profit of over one hundred sixty thousand dollars.

Yasmine was right. He would never leave.

CHAPTER TEN

Sandiya King

Sandiya King didn't like Yasmine Dubai at all; not one bit, not from the day they first met almost a year ago. Sandiya found Yasmine, arrogant, self-righteous, and condescending. If she ever thought about looking inward (she didn't), Sandiya would have recognized the parallels with herself.

"Did you send out the regulatory filings?" Sandiya tried not to snap at Nat Fluxgold, TeleShop's corporate counsel and her ostensible boss.

At best, she just about tolerated Nat. He was fiftyish, Jewish, married with two teenage kids, and a lousy attorney. While Nat's grasp of the law was often tenuous, his real problem was laziness. Intellectual laziness, work laziness, physical laziness — Nat embraced them all. Plus, his avarice was the reason Sandiya was at TeleShop. Nat had a fondness for Las Vegas and was as effective at gambling as he was at law. Triboro owned several casinos and was happy to forgive his debt for a favor. Or two.

"Yes, I FedExed it to Washington last night," Nat replied.

Sandiya had only worked for TeleShop a year, it being her first job since graduating from the University of Chicago School of Law, but in reality she already ran the department.

Her family were Hindus from Dhaka, Bangladesh who moved to Buffalo, New York where Sandiya was born.

That was one of her problems with Yasmine. Buffalo lay opposite Toronto on Lake Ontario. The two cities were a study in contrast. Toronto was vibrant and growing, and only a two-hour drive away. Buffalo was a city in long decline with even worse weather than its northern neighbor. Sandiya watched Toronto TV and its constant reporting of that city's hosting international conferences. Buffalo stations aired footage of fires and municipal budget cuts.

Yasmine's so full of herself it makes me sick. She thinks she's the only one with ambition? Fuck her. She's out, along with Mary-Anne. They just don't know it yet.

Like Yasmine, Sandiya would never have considered employment at a low-rent home shopping channel in Oklahoma. While Mary-Anne scouted Yasmine, Cliff Johnson scouted Sandiya.

"You'll be my shadow," Cliff told Sandiya in Manhattan after recruiting her surreptitiously at the University of Chicago. "Get yourself called to the Oklahoma Bar and then get hired at TeleShop. Their counsel, Nat Fluxgold, is a halfwit, but he's *our* halfwit."

Mary-Anne Warner's aggressive furthering of Triboro's agenda before the takeover would taint her, making Mary-Anne expendable. Yasmine didn't even figure into the equation.

"Since you'll be Triboro's lawyer, we'll have attorney-client privilege. Here's the bottom line: Mary-Anne won't know you work for us, and it has to stay that way. Will that be a problem?"

"No, sir. Not at all."

"Good. You'll get your regular salary from TeleShop as well as your salary from Triboro." Clifford Johnson dangled the lucre in front of

Sandiya, watching her react. For a woman who grew up lower middle class in a Rust Belt city, the offer was impossible to turn down. "After the acquisition, we'll move you to our legal department in Manhattan. How does that sound, Sandiya?"

"It's a wonderful opportunity, sir. Thank you very much."

"Good. Let us know everything that goes on at TeleShop and you have a bright future with us."

A month later she was assistant corporate counsel. At twenty-seven years old and as a newly minted lawyer, Sandiya began her surveillance of Mary-Anne. Nat Fluxgold had some idea of her true purpose, but chose to remain as oblivious as possible. Whoever handled Nat made it clear that, appearances to the contrary, Nat worked for Sandiya.

By chance, she'd caught the looks Yasmine gave Robert. He returned the attention, something only an idiot wouldn't have noticed. That didn't sit well with Sandiya. None of the hiring decisions or vendor deals escaped her attention. Sandiya reported everything back to Triboro.

She dropped by the set when Robert co-hosted with the Dealmaker. It wasn't Yasmine's interest alone or the rumors of his ability on-air that piqued her attention. Robert was a good-looking man, slightly younger than herself. Sandiya read his employment application in her capacity as assistant corporate counsel, noting its style. He knew how to write. Glibness was an essential element of a good show host. And Robert was glib. The question was, how much of what she read was truth and how much was fiction? This only added to her interest.

He's confident and speaks like an English major. What the hell has he been doing with his life? The Dealmaker's taken him under his wing and he knows talent. Yasmine likes him and that's reason enough to pursue the matter.

Like Yasmine, Sandiya lived alone in a shiny, anonymous condo, by chance a five-minute drive from her nemesis. Unlike Yasmine, Sandiya had no trouble picking up locals for casual liaisons.

For the last four months, she'd been seeing a man named Grayson Palmer. He was the scion of a prominent family who'd lived in Oklahoma since it was a territory. The Palmers controlled Sooner Oil and Energy, their corporate offices located in Liberty Tower, the tallest building in the city.

Despite his protestations about marriage, Sandiya knew it would never happen. Their kind did *not* marry dark-skinned women from Bangladesh. Sandiya didn't care. She would never marry stuffy, local bigwigs who thought their provincial worldview urbane.

Grayson wanted to get together on Saturday, but she begged off after hearing the Dealmaker and Robert would be at Lucky Charm Saloon for John Duguay's band.

As a tactic, she'd taken to ingratiating herself with many of the office and production staff. Her friendship may have been facile, but was effective nonetheless. Yasmine's icy aloofness and Mary-Anne's caustic indifference couldn't compete.

"Susie," she'd said to the floor director, bumping into her accidentally-on-purpose in the cafeteria, "Is anybody going to see John's band tomorrow?"

"Everyone's going. John's band is great. They're alt-country, like Meat Puppets or Jason & The Scorchers."

Sandiya hated country music, "alt" or otherwise.

"Fabulous," Sandiya replied with counterfeit sincerity. "Where are they playing?"

"Lucky Charm Saloon, in Bricktown. We're all going around eight. Their show starts at ten."

"Tell John I'll go. I'll meet you there."

"Super. The cover charge is seven dollars."

Sandiya said goodbye, leaving the cafeteria with a cup of insipid coffee from their generic machine.

Would it kill Billy-Ray to invest in a goddamn percolator? Please let this merger happen so I can get to Manhattan. Oklahoma City makes Buffalo look exciting.

§

Robert MacKenzie

As he walked off the set with the Dealmaker they received a round of applause. The crew and operators smiled in congratulations. Robert beamed, thanking everyone and waving. The strong opening with the Blue Blockers, the sellout of the Zamfir records, and the doll's absolute smash energized the atmosphere.

Heading past the prep room, the Dragon Lady stuck her head out and glared at him, wanting him dead. Her face bore a look of total evil, piercing malevolence, and rage.

"Hey, Dixie," said the Dealmaker. "Sorry, we sold out the Zamfir records. I told everybody they shouldn't call you tonight and let you know."

"Fuck you, Dave!" she replied. A match tossed in her direction would have ignited the very air itself, burning TeleShop to its foundations. "And don't get too full of yourself, you prick," she said to Robert. "The show was down to the Dealmaker. Your contribution was sweet fuck all!"

She pulled herself back into the prep room. Robert thanked God he hadn't left anything there so he could head straight home.

"Robert! Congratulations, son. You and Dave had a hell of a show. You work great together." Billy-Ray Newton appeared with his secretary standing in front of him. She still had that same blank face and heaving bosom as the time in the control room. "Here's a little token of my appreciation."

His secretary handed Robert an envelope. Billy-Ray shook his hand and looked to the Dealmaker.

"The co-hosting was a great idea, Dave. Keep it up. I owe you." Billy-Ray smiled, turned and headed back to his office, his secretary following behind.

A loud and guttural scream of "Fuck!" spewed out of the prep room as its door slammed shut. The Dealmaker grinned and clapped Robert on his back as the pair walked toward the parking lot exit.

"Hey, Dealmaker; hey, Big Mack," said Hank as they walked past the security office.

Robert liked his new nickname. With the Dealmaker's approbation, his days as a possum now lay in the past.

§

Robert MacKenzie

Before leaving TeleShop, Robert opened the envelope in the parking lot. The Dealmaker looked on with a knowing grin. It contained five, crisp one-hundred-dollar bills; Robert ogled the money, stunned.

"Kid, you're in like Flynn," said the Dealmaker, clapping Robert on the back. "Looks like Billy-Ray's considering you for the 'A' team now, mon frère!"

Robert focused on the Dealmaker, then back to the money, then back to the Dealmaker, and then back to the money.

"Dealmaker, Mary-Anne already told me she's bumping my pay to nine dollars and seventy-five cents per hour. But this is over a week's salary. And in cash, without deductions."

"Yeah," replied the Dealmaker, for whatever reason, enjoying the moment. "And also off the books. Billy-Ray doesn't say shit to the IRS about cash envelopes."

"Isn't that illegal?" Robert asked with enormous naïveté.

"Yes, it is," whispered the Dealmaker like he was speaking to a complete pinhead. "Do you think we should say something?"

For a moment, Robert considered the idea before getting the sarcasm.

"Right, sorry about that," he replied embarrassed. Robert grabbed two of the bills and handed them to the Dealmaker. "I really appreciate your helping me out; you've been more than kind. Thank you. Let me pick up the tab tomorrow night at John's show."

For the first time since they'd met, the Dealmaker said nothing. He looked solemn, his perpetually flushed face a shade darker than usual.

"Thanks, kid," he mumbled, pocketing the money, turning away and walking toward his car. "I'll see you back at the motel."

Robert shared several cans of Olde English with the Dealmaker upon their return. The cash, his co-hosting, the Dragon Lady, and the alcohol served to wear him out. Announcing he needed rest, Robert walked to his room.

His nerves remained fraught, and the knowledge he still had to deal with his apartment in Phoenix nagged. His Civic had made the fifteen-hour drive to Oklahoma City, gasping all the way like a nightmare riff of *Jingle Bells*. Robert's hyperbolic sense of drama, while draining, also contributed to his success at telling stories on-air.

Lying on his bed, the raw exhaustion and stress of the past few days emptied his last reserves. Robert fell asleep in the late afternoon and didn't wake until 6:00 a.m. on Saturday.

The weekends were always the major sales days at TeleShop, with Sunday edging out Saturday by a fraction. Show #5 at noon and Shows #6 & #7 from 3:00 until 9:00 p.m. grossed the week's biggest revenue. If you were a show host who wasn't scheduled every weekend, then you were a show host who didn't matter.

The Dealmaker always hosted Show #5 and the Dragon Lady

always hosted Show #7 from Wednesday to Sunday. Between them was Alexandra McMurdo, who hosted Show #6 from Friday to Sunday and Show #5 on Monday and Tuesday. The contrast between Alexandra and the Dragon Lady went far beyond their name.

Alexandra was a fifty-year-old Southern Belle from Charleston, South Carolina and a graduate of Mount Holyoke. Married with twin daughters, her husband Mitchum was an oil executive who attended Amherst College. They had met at a mixer.

Alexandra was gracious to a fault, elegant in style—which made sense since she focused on selling fashion—and told salty jokes like a Borscht Belt comic. Robert met her with the other trainees on their second day and liked her immediately.

But he didn't have a shift until 8:00 p.m. on Sunday, his accidental scheduling problem with Yasmine now moot. Instead, he read while sitting outside his motel room door.

The Dealmaker left his room around 9:30 a.m. They spoke for a few minutes. He griped some more about his soon-to-be ex-wife and complained again about his daughters not speaking to him. Then, throwing a six pack of Olde English onto the passenger seat, the Dealmaker sped off to TeleShop (Though with his Dodge Duster, *sped* was a relative term).

A branch of OKC Sooner Oil State Bank that operated on Saturdays was a five-minute drive from the motel. Robert opened an account, receiving an ATM card. The clerk asked him if he wanted to apply for a credit card, pointing to a sign on her desk, "Quick Credit Decisions on all VISA & MasterCard applications."

Robert would have loved a credit card, but knew his credit rating was a disaster. To save embarrassment, he declined, wearing a knowing grin that suggested he already had far too much credit and didn't need any more.

The Dealmaker got back to the motel at 3:00 p.m. with tales of glory and big sales.

"I saw the Dragon Lady this afternoon. She wants me dead. And you too!" He laughed with his typical bonhomie and bluster. "Last night she kept gettin' call after call apologizing for having Zamfir sold out from under her. I watched the tape. Looked like she was gonna shit herself."

Robert chuckled with the Dealmaker but also worried about getting the Dragon Lady too angry. He had way too much on his plate and didn't need to add desert.

"Ya call a cab?"

They would take a taxi to Lucky Charm Saloon at 8:00 p.m. Even the Dealmaker knew driving home afterward was an object lesson in stupidity and suicide.

"Yes, it's getting here at 8:00 p.m., Dealmaker."

"Good. I'm gonna get some shuteye. Wake me around 7:30. if I'm not already up." The Dealmaker cracked open a can of Olde English and slipped into his room, loud snoring shaking the windows a few minutes later.

As 8:00 p.m. rolled around, their cab arrived. They climbed into its back and reached Lucky Charm Saloon twenty minutes later.

A long line waited at the club's entrance. Robert followed the Dealmaker who strolled with confidence bordering on certitude toward the doorman. He didn't even have to announce his name. The bouncer smiled, recognizing the Dealmaker and opened the door for them both.

A mass of people packed the room. Music blared through the house PA as they walked to the bar.

Robert was about to order drinks when John Duguay ran up and interrupted him.

"Don't worry about paying, Big Mack. When I told the manager we could use the Dealmaker's name he comped your booze. Look at the place—it's packed!" The director and bass player beamed as he approached the Dealmaker. "Dealmaker, we really appreciate your helping us out. Thanks so much."

"Johnny-man, don't worry about it. Happy to oblige. Where we sittin'?"

"I've reserved the big table in the first row, stage right."

"Who's there now?" asked the Dealmaker as Robert handed him a large glass of draft beer.

"A bunch of people from production. Susie's here, also Mark and his girlfriend. Oh, Sandiya King came as well."

The Dealmaker clapped John on the back. Robert tagged behind as they made their way to the front, people staring, some pointing. The Dealmaker was in his element, returning their attention, chortling while hoisting his beer to the crowd. Robert had known, in an abstract sort of way, of the Dealmaker's celebrity, but this reception made it obvious.

Jesus, what would these people do if they knew he lived in a broken-down motel off the highway?

"Hi Dealmaker; hi, Big Mack." Susie greeted them with infectious enthusiasm. She wore fitted jeans and an Oklahoma Sooners football T-shirt.

While five feet tall on a good day, Susie had a taut figure and sunny disposition. Combined with her girl-next-door features, she sparkled. Susie was the sort of person people liked as soon as they met, a complete contrast with Yasmine's icy exterior and distance.

Sitting next to Susie was Sandiya King. She wore tight black lycra pants and a beautiful, black silk blouse, the disparity between vulgarity and elegance striking. A black Movado watch lay on her left wrist while a black bangle bracelet wrapped around her right. Dressy, black, medium-rise sandals adorned her feet.

To be frank, she looked sensational.

Susie moved one seat to the left, opening a chair between them for

Robert while the Dealmaker thumped down next to Mark, the director from the day of his interview. Robert sat with them, their side of the table having a clear, unobstructed view of the stage.

"Hi, Robert, I'm Sandiya King," the lawyer said with a gracious smile, her eyes locking on his. "I saw you with the Dealmaker yesterday on-set. You worked great together."

Robert felt an instant attraction to Sandiya and also instant guilt, which surprised him. Yasmine's shutdown earlier hurt, even though they'd only had a single date. Still, it was her admission that he might break her heart if he didn't move to Manhattan that resonated.

"I noticed you too. Thanks for saying I did well. I've never worked on-air before; it's very stressful."

"Well, if it helps, I couldn't tell you were new at all. When you made that joke about the baby doll packin', the whole office laughed!"

Robert's face lit up, happy his comment went over so well. The pair angled their knees toward each other and talked. She told him about Buffalo, school in Chicago and moving to Oklahoma City, but didn't say a word about her *real* job. He told her an edited version of his own life that differed somewhat from the truth and markedly from his résumé.

They spoke for over an hour. Other than greetings and early pleasantries, Robert hadn't paid attention to anyone other than Sandiya since his arrival.

The rest of their group paid close attention to them. The Dealmaker made the odd comment that, while funny to their party, sailed over Robert, unnoticed.

As the clock struck ten, the band started its set …

§

Sandiya King

Hidden knowledge and power aroused Sandiya. That she found Robert handsome didn't hurt either. As a show host (and one to watch), involvement with Robert, meant a direct pipeline to Mary-Anne. She'd also piss off Yasmine, and that was pure gravy.

She listened to Robert talk about himself, smiling inside. He didn't know Sandiya had already combed through his history. She had carte blanche to inquire about all TeleShop vendors and employees. Sandiya had used a skip tracer, provided by Cliff Johnson, to glean details about Robert he didn't even know himself.

Robert soft-pedaled any talk of Yasmine and still hadn't mentioned their date. Sandiya remained blissfully unaware of his real interest in her bête noire. Her bliss would turn into explosive rage if she ever learned of their sojourn. It didn't matter if her potential relationship was real, strategic or both. Sandiya lived by the adage *Hell hath no fury like a woman scorned.*

She flirted, moving her hand onto his. Unlike Robert, Sandiya noticed the looks and comments from the others, but didn't care. Although she was careful not to be too aggressive that first night.

The sudden echo of John Duguay's voice through the house PA ended her scheming, at least until the end of the set.

"I want to thank y'all for coming. We appreciate it. Thanks to our friends at TeleShop for being here tonight and especially to Dealmaker Dave Leonard for his support. We're going to start our show with the second track from our new album, *Pool Here Good.* This is 'Small Ground' ... "

§

Yasmine Dubai

Yasmine left TeleShop at 8:00 p.m., stopping at a nearby restaurant for takeout, then driving the short distance to her condo. Whether Philadelphia, Toronto, or here, locals often bragged of their greasy spoon of greatness; hidden gems with delicious, honest fare. The place near her home served dull, phoned-in food of no particular distinction. Wearing a Wharton hoodie with matching sweats, Yasmine sat at her kitchen table finishing her cheeseburger.

She heard the crew plan their trip to Lucky Charm Saloon. As was typical, nobody invited her. It wasn't an active attempt at rebuffing Yasmine, rather it was her own self-imposed apartness.

At some point during the afternoon, Susie mentioned Robert would attend with the Dealmaker. The news caused a pang that swept through Yasmine, weakening her resolve, if only for a second.

I can't go on spending Saturday evenings alone, watching TV or reading. But I can't go to the club tonight either. After what I said to Robert, I'd look pathetic.

Earlier, Yasmine walked through production toward the sample room. TeleShop received a shipment of gray market Rolex watches and she needed to count the inventory. As Yasmine moved behind camera #1, another female crew member spoke to Susie.

"Is anybody from the office going?"

"Some of the Scheduling people said they would," replied Susie, arranging the next product, an amethyst ring, on its display stand. "I also bumped into Sandiya in the cafeteria. She's going as well."

As Sandiya didn't like Yasmine, Yasmine didn't like Sandiya. Like her bugbear, Yasmine didn't see their similarities, also oblivious to the irony.

"Hey, Susie-Q, I caught Sandiya checking out Big Mack during the show."

"Wow," Susie responded with glee, breaking into a smile and wanting more information. Like all offices, gossip was TeleShop's currency and intrigue its fuel. "What happened?"

"Sandiya was standing off camera by the anchor desk. She observed Robert the whole time he pitched the Blue Blockers with the Dealmaker."

"So ... "

"So what was she doing in production?" asked the crew member. "She's a lawyer. Besides, you should have seen her eyes. She was staring. You know what I mean?"

The women broke into laughter. Susie finished hanging the ring, telling the director the item was ready for preview.

That fucking bitch! She likes country music as much as I do. Christ, I'm a mess. I've got my goddamned period and no goddamned life!

§

Robert MacKenzie

Robert wasn't a big fan of country music, but enjoyed listening to John's band. Their lead singer was a red-headed woman wearing a low-cut top and tight jeans. She belted out song after song with a powerful, contralto voice. Regardless of the genre, the band was very tight. John's solid bass playing impressed Robert.

While he liked Sandiya and found her attractive, she didn't captivate Robert as Yasmine did. It wasn't anything specific; Sandiya was very pretty and had a great figure. Like Yasmine, she knew how to dress and exuded intelligence. Nonetheless, there was an element missing.

He didn't want to sound recondite, but Yasmine possessed something unquantifiable. He felt it the minute he first saw her, and Yasmine sensed it as well. Looking back, their casual body language spoke volumes, as did their immediate and tight occupation of each other's personal space.

Why am I so stuck? Yasmine's made it quite clear we're not an item. I need to find an apartment and settle here for the long term. I'm not moving to Manhattan. And I want more from a girlfriend than a casual fling in the back of an adult video store.

If he hadn't met Yasmine, none of this would matter. Robert would have welcomed a successful and attractive woman showing interest — witness the harsh disappointment at Seagull Inlet. But he had met Yasmine. And that changed matters, or so he thought.

They'd had a date. A single date. It was hardly Robert's first, neither was it Yasmine's. What mattered a single date? What mattered a chance encounter? What mattered was nothing — what mattered was everything. Carly Simon said she'd marry James Taylor the first time she saw him on television. Sting claimed he fell in love with Trudie Styler the moment they met.

Robert had traversed the US from the East Coast to the West. Alone. From the north to the south. From one temporary home to another place of impermanence. He was okay by himself. Sure, there were women. But in the end, they mattered not.

And then he saw Yasmine. In the lobby at TeleShop. In exordium. In the beginning. What lay before was now meaningless past.

John announced the end of their show to hearty applause and an ovation. After a brief recess, the band returned with two more songs for their encore. When they finished, John thanked the Dealmaker one more time before leaving the stage.

"Robert, did you enjoy the show?" Sandiya asked. She spoke with a breathy tone, smiling while her eyes glowed.

"Yes, they're very good. I'm not a country guy but I liked them." Robert looked back at Sandiya, returning her smile and focus.

The couple leaned in toward each other. Sandiya's perfume wafted around her. She placed her hand in his, their knees touching. Robert took this as his cue, lowering his face toward hers, their lips meeting in the faintest whisper. The merest soupçon of a kiss ended finally with a tiny caress of their tongues against each other's open mouth.

"Christ, would you two get a room!" boomed the Dealmaker as the rest of the table laughed. He drained a large mug of beer and ordered another.

Sandiya pulled back, looking first at Robert and then to their colleagues. She dipped her head, bowing to their audience with a smile. But behind the friendly acknowledgment, her eyes flashed a quick look of steel. There was more to this woman than what lay on the surface. It should have given Robert pause, but the intoxicating atmosphere of their kiss masked deeper analysis, at least for the moment.

A while later, John Duguay joined their table. He brought the band's singer, introducing her as Sára Mender, a friend he'd met while attending the University of Oklahoma.

It was after midnight when the Nomadic Cowboys finished their performance. It was now past 1:00 a.m. and their table's numbers had diminished with time. Mark and his girlfriend had left with Susie ten minutes before, and only a few people from Scheduling lingered.

The Dealmaker was very drunk; it was down to Robert to get him home without incident. While Robert didn't have to go on-air until late Sunday night, the Dealmaker needed to at least appear fresh for noon.

"Sandiya, I need to help the Dealmaker back to our motel," he said. "Would you like to get together sometime? I'm working Show #1 all next week."

"I'd like that, Robert," she replied. "Let me give you my number in case I don't see you at the office."

The pair stood and turned away from the table. Without hesitation, Sandiya kissed Robert, moving against him, biting his lip as their

165

tongues snaked together. He pulled into her tighter than planned, Robert's drinking having lowered his inhibitions. Sandiya didn't resist and he enjoyed feeling her press against him. He wanted to grasp her backside against the lycra pants, but resisted. There would be time for that later.

Sandiya broke away, brushing his cheek, then left the bar, disappearing through the door.

Robert moved to John and the two men pulled the Dealmaker up, slipping their shoulders under his arms, helping him to the club's exit. A couple of taxis waited outside Lucky Charm Saloon and they poured the Dealmaker into the back of one.

"You going to be okay?" asked John. Sára stood behind him, her hand resting on his shoulder. It only struck Robert then they were a couple. Clearly he'd been paying a lot of attention to Sandiya.

"Yeah, we'll be fine. I'll get him to his room. Thanks for the help. By the way, you sounded great. Congratulations on your new album. Sára, you're a hell of a singer."

John and Sára thanked him for the praise. Robert climbed into the rear passenger seat next to the Dealmaker and rolled down the taxi's window for a final goodnight.

"Take care of him, Robert," said John, his arm around Sára. "I've worked at TeleShop for three years. The Dealmaker's always liked to party, but he's starting to go overboard. He never used to get this drunk. And he's looking a bit pale."

Thanking John once again, Robert rolled up the window and told the driver to hit the Interstate. The Dealmaker snored next to him as the taxi slipped with little notice down the highway toward Best Value Inn. As they turned into the parking lot, the motel's tawdry, end-of-the-line appearance managed to announce itself through the cold glow of sodium vapor lamps and broken down, flickering neon.

"Come on, Dealmaker, we have to get you to your room."

Robert paid the driver and manhandled his friend from the back of the cab toward his unit. The harsh lighting cast a dramatic shadow on the Dealmaker's face like some old German silent movie. If that had actually been the case, an intertitle would have announced, "Foreshadowing here."

§

Sandiya King

Sandiya drove her RX-7 XT from the club to her home. The Mazda was her first new car and while she didn't care about its rotary engine, she did like its turbocharged performance and sporty design. With her two hefty salaries, buying what used to be a dream, was now within easy reach.

Unlike the rest of the TeleShop crew, Sandiya had paced her drinking. Returning from the bathroom, she'd picked up a straight cola at the bar, nursing it like a mixed drink. If the others thought she liked highballs, so much the better. People lowered their defenses when drinking, especially if they believed you were as lubricated as them.

She liked Robert. Not really *liked*, just regular liked. He was a bit too earnest for her. His physicality checked the right boxes and his on-air skill impressed Sandiya. But she tended to date bad boys. Robert, with his peripatetic lifestyle, came across as a renegade. Yet speaking with him at the club brought out his basic kindness. Sandiya found it disappointing.

Her actions made no rational sense. Greg, her boyfriend from law school, was a bad boy. He cheated on her whenever he could (as she cheated on him) and when it came to sex, he was very aggressive. Sandiya liked Greg pulling her hair and calling her vulgar names, often slapping her hard on the butt while inside her.

When Greg appeared to lose interest, Sandiya's volcanic temper reared. At the very end, with graduation looming and their relationship hanging by a thread, Sandiya had sex with Greg's best friend and his girlfriend. She didn't much enjoy having sex with a woman but very much enjoyed Greg's reaction.

As she stripped and climbed into bed, Sandiya gamed out her plan.

Robert, I'm going to fuck your brains out. At the office, in my car, here or wherever. If you have a kink, I'll do it — I don't care if it's twisted or sick. I'm going to Manhattan and joining Triboro's legal department. You're a back channel of information. One of several. Nothing's going to stop me. Not you. Not Mary-Anne. And especially not that cunt, Yasmine Dubai.

CHAPTER ELEVEN

The Dealmaker

The Dealmaker arrived hung over like a fart for his Sunday program. Show #5 and Show #7 on Sunday competed to be the biggest revenue generator of the week. As always, the Dealmaker arrived late — although not as late as he'd been on Robert's first day. Since his wife kicked him to the curb, his punctuality had been getting worse and worse. As usual, he hadn't examined his show and it needed tweaking in a big way. Somehow, the Dealmaker managed to pull yet another rabbit out of his hat (or out of his ass, depending upon whom you asked).

The Dealmaker "discovered" the provenance of an obscure garnet ring that hadn't aired in a very long time. When it had aired, it didn't sell.

Before his sudden epiphany, the ring's graphic reflected its simplicity.

Garnet Ring in Beautiful 10K Gold
Only $79.99

After his "discovery," the Dealmaker changed its onscreen description.

Tibetan Shangri-La Garnet Ring
Set in the Silky Majesty of 10K Gold from the Himalayas
Insane Price and Crazy Rare!
$129.99!!!
Do NOT Miss this Incredible Bargain
A Dealmaker Select Buy

After its initial assignment, changing an item's price required special entry by the data priests (or computer guys, as they were also known). One single terminal, located next to their Burroughs A15 mainframe computer, accepted these changes. Only the respective buyer with approval from the Director of Purchasing could alter the price. For graphics, modifying the onscreen display of any item needed the direct sign-off of the legal department. There were no exceptions. None!

"Hey, Mark," said the Dealmaker to his director before the show. "I need you to get the Chyron guy to change the graphics for my two o'clock."

"Sure thing, Dealmaker."

"Lenny, I need a favor," the Dealmaker asked the on-duty data priest. "Increase the retail on Item #108992 from seventy-nine ninety-nine to one twenty-nine ninety-nine."

"No problem Dealmaker."

And so it goes …

The Dealmaker added the "Dealmaker Select Buy" line on a whim, figuring he'd use it again if it worked. As for the price, the ring had a cost of fifty-four dollars ninety-nine cents. There were six thousand in stock and the product selector listed it for remaindering to a distressed goods vendor for its gold value next month.

At its new retail of one hundred twenty-nine dollars ninety-nine cents the gross profit was seventy-five dollars per ring. The Dealmaker blew out all six thousand with many, many more he could have sold. It took almost an hour and brought in four hundred fifty thousand dollars in gross profit.

On his way out the door he walked past the Dragon Lady. She maintained her composure, but her greener-than-usual complexion said it all.

§

Robert MacKenzie

Later, at the motel, the Dealmaker told Robert all about his success with the ring. He offered Robert a drink — well, several — knowing he would decline and understanding the reason.

The thought of seeing the Dragon Lady that evening already made him nervous, and the Dealmaker talked about her beyond foul mood with a broad smile. Robert didn't need any more aggravation before his first show. The Dragon Lady got off at 8:00 p.m. while he arrived at the same time. He considered showing up late, but thought it would look weak and not bode well.

As it turned out, he caught the Dragon Lady in passing, him entering, her exiting. Enraged. Vituperative. Inflamed. All those words described her appearance yet none of them quite captured the dense, dark bitterness she displayed. Water splashing against her face would have turned to steam in a fraction of a second.

Robert found out later she had a very successful show, although not an out-of-the-park home run like the Dealmaker.

What does this job do to people? They fire you if you don't sell. The Dealmaker is in meltdown. The Dragon Lady ... I don't know what to say about the Dragon Lady. Yasmine hates the place and Sandiya ... What the hell's up with her? I get why Yasmine's here. What made Sandiya choose TeleShop? She graduated at the top of her class from one of the best law schools in the country. She made Law Review. Why here? What's going on?

After checking the prep room, Robert walked to Scheduling. A lone woman named Linda waited for him. Her job was to give Robert his print-out and check if he wanted drop-ins. He didn't. Linda left at 8:30 p.m., leaving Robert alone with his show, his nerves and his thoughts.

As the minutes ticked down to airtime, Robert sat in the prep room, thinking and analyzing his time with the Dealmaker and the Dragon Lady. The Dragon Lady may have been a miserable human being, but she knew how to sell. Although she didn't let him say much while shadowing, Robert paid careful attention to her product selection, placement and pitch.

Like the Dealmaker, she had a story for every item. The Dragon Lady held to a steady rhythm. Compared to other hosts, she stood apart. Her on-air geniality sounded natural, even if it wasn't. The Dragon Lady knew her audience and how to bond with them.

Robert met with Helen Cunningham, that night's director, and went over his show and its features. She was very supportive and accommodating. Robert didn't foresee any trouble ahead other than conquering his nerves. As long as he maintained his confidence, what could go wrong?

At 10:38 p.m., Terry Pavão walked into the prep room. He wore another expensive, bespoke suit. His well-coiffed hair appeared fresh cut. His left wrist bore a Breitling watch, and a diamond pinky ring glistened on his right hand. Terry stepped about in crocodile shoes while removing a gray fedora from his head, hanging it on the coat rack in the room's corner. He was also drunk as shit.

"If it isn't the prodigy," Terry announced. While he didn't slur his words, his phrasing sounded forced. The odor of whiskey hovered about his person.

"Hey, Terry," replied Robert, concerned. "You okay?"

"Yes, I'm fucking okay. I'm going to kick ass tonight. Why wouldn't I be okay? I've got twenty years of advertising under my belt. You think this place is tough? Try pitching to Fortune 100 execs when you got nothing. I mean fucking *nothing*! Your creative is dogshit and you're there standing alone with your dick in your hand. And your fucking wife doesn't give a sweet goddamn regardless!"

Terry walked over to the mail slots and removed the show Linda had dropped off earlier. The fact he managed not to stagger was either a testament to luck or experience.

Robert eyed him warily, considering his options. He should have called Yasmine. That's assuming she was home and awake. But it was the director's call about on-air issues. Besides, Robert didn't want to inform on Terry. He still had to work with the guy.

"I've got to hit the set, Terry. Good luck with the show." Robert stood up and made his way to the door.

"Yeah, whatever. What makes you so fucking good?" Terry said with obvious derision. "You didn't finish high school. I've got an English degree from fucking Duke!"

Robert didn't wait for an answer, considering the question rhetorical. He made his way to the set. Behind him, Terry's mutterings of impotence one second and crowing the next followed him from the prep room.

§

Yasmine Dubai

I hate this place! I fucking hate this fucking, fucking place!

Helen Cunningham called Yasmine in the dead of night, waking her from a sound sleep. Since moving to Oklahoma City, a solid night's rest was an unusual occurrence.

Terry Pavão had passed out. He began his show at 3:00 a.m. Eastern Time already "under the weather" and things deteriorated from there. At first, Terry wasn't so bad that Helen thought it necessary to cut to a pre-recorded segment. But something was going on. The longer he spoke, the more disjointed and weird his musings became.

The last product Terry aired before collapsing was the Crystal of the Month, the same item the Dealmaker had debuted a few days before. This month's crystal was a multicolored fairy sitting atop a faceted rock. Terry started referring to himself as the "Fairy Prince," spinning a bizarre yarn about the Brothers Grimm, Goldilocks, and Gandalf conspiring to create this magical sprite for only nineteen dollars ninety-nine cents. His jabbering sounded like bad ad copy.

That pushed Helen over the edge. She planned to keep Terry on-air until 4:00 a.m. Eastern Time. Then, she'd either find the next host or go to tape. As they went into break, Angela, the floor director, asked Terry how long he wanted to stay on the next item. Terry began ranting in response, an incoherent mess of an answer that bore no resemblance to the question.

"Watch me!" he said, standing up and moving his arms about. "Watch me … "

Nobody had any idea what he was talking about. Halfway through the promo he sat back in his chair, looked quizzical, dropped his head down hard, and keeled over.

When the crew ran to check on Terry, they found a half-empty bottle of Canadian Club on the floor, its cap off, amber liquid spreading like an oil spill. He'd managed forty-two minutes on-air for his first (and now last) show. Helen aired a prerecorded infomercial for the Scandinavian Recipe hair tonic and called Yasmine. She had dressed in a hurry and driven to TeleShop in a semi-panic, arriving thirty minutes later.

"Don't worry about your show, Alan. Drop everything and get your ass on-air now!" she barked at Alan Bennet in the prep room. He'd been girding himself for his own first show at 6:00 a.m. Eastern Time.

Alan stared at her in a panic, looking like a boy caught jerking off by his mother. The cockiness he exhibited during training had packed its bag and headed west.

"But, Ms. Dubai, I haven't prepped. I don't know the products," he protested in a desperate attempt to stave off the inevitable.

"Alan, we're a television network; we don't do dead air. Helen Cunningham will make sure you're okay. Get to the set, now!"

"How long will I be on?"

"Now!"

Alan sprinted from the prep room toward production. Yasmine stood alone, exhausted watching him flee like a villager running from Frankenstein. Whatever savoir faire he claimed from his years as a carny left with him.

"Yasmine?" called Angela. She stood at the prep room's entrance eying a very bedraggled Yasmine Dubai.

"Don't tell me," Yasmine said. "Helen's wondering what we're going to do with Terry Pavão?" She spoke with supreme resignation. The soon-to-be-former show host slept on a prop couch off to the side of the set. "Get our security guard and have him babysit. When he wakes up, get the guard to escort him off the premises. I took his pass already. I'll deal with the paperwork later."

Yasmine stared with flat affect, tired in a profound way. After dealing with Pavão, she'd catch some sleep in her office and then start her "regular" job.

Angela nodded and turned to go. Before the floor director left, Yasmine asked about Show #1

"It went well. Robert's a very nice guy—polite and friendly, great sense of humor. Did a super job on-air."

Yasmine nodded in response, feeling a slight grip of sadness while thinking about Robert, that is until Angela continued:

"We saw John's band at Lucky Charm Saloon last night. You should have come. Lots of people from production and the office showed up. Robert was there too. He sat at the front table with Sandiya King. They paid a lot of attention to one another. We all had a laugh about it."

A lead weight kicked Yasmine in the gut as she struggled to remain calm. In response, Yasmine offered a sincere-looking, but mechanical smile.

"Are they already a couple?" asked Yasmine, managing an insouciant glow, all the while attempting to keep it together.

"I don't know about that. But they talked to each other all night. And they kissed a couple of times too. I swear if there weren't so many people around Robert would have felt Sandiya up. And Sandiya would have let him."

With heroic effort, Yasmine laughed along with Angela. Then as the latter turned to head back to production, Yasmine said she'd take care of the host situation and commended the crew on a good job.

Angela gone, Yasmine closed the door to the prep room, standing alone in its quiet.

That fucking prick. And you wanted to take it slow, Robert? I bared my heart to you and now you go off whoring the first chance you get. Well, fuck you! And fuck you too, Sandiya. Fuck you too …

Later, in her office, Yasmine meant to rest. Between interrupted sleep and emotional tumult, physical and mental exhaustion strangled her.

Why now? Why does Robert affect me this way? He's just a man; I've had boyfriends before. Breaking it off wasn't just the right decision. It was the only decision.

At least she maintained her composure for Angela and hoped the floor director hadn't detected the true state of her upset. Yasmine only had herself to blame. She was the one who didn't want to proceed. Still, it didn't quell her anger.

Why Sandiya King? Of everyone at TeleShop or even in Oklahoma City, why her? What have I done to deserve this shit? I'm only aspiring for a career. Is that so bad?

Yasmine tried lying to herself, saying her mood was no more than conventional loneliness. Any man could answer her need for intimacy. But it wasn't true, and she couldn't maintain the fiction. It wasn't physical intimacy she needed. Not really. It was emotional intimacy.

When Robert picked up her legs and put them on the prep room table, she had melted. There was a kindness and decency in his eyes, a strength both of body and character. Yasmine longed for masculine strength. None of her past boyfriends had it. She'd seen to that.

The quiet and early hour brought back memories of London. After her father's murder, London represented darkness and rain. Her mother was unable to explain the reasons for his death. Yasmine loved her dad. His absence built a hole she couldn't fill.

For romantic partners, Yasmine always selected handsome men who displayed confidence on the surface. But inside, they were malleable, their thinking anodyne. She wouldn't engage with anyone of genuine independence. Instead, she flirted with the showy, humoring their caprice. Daryush was a perfect example.

Yasmine pulled the logger tapes for Terry Pavão's show. It was standard procedure in the event of trouble. She would examine his single and only hour of glory to ensure TeleShop faced no difficulty.

The network backed up their broadcast on VHS cassettes, each tape recording six hours of programming. When Yasmine entered engineering at 5:07 a.m., the logger VCR had just finished the midnight to 6:00 a.m. Eastern Time segment. She pulled the tape, signed the log, and headed back to her office.

Yasmine shut her door and locked it. She planned on sleeping for a couple of hours and didn't want interruption. Popping the tape into her VCR, Yasmine leaned back in her chair with a notebook and pen.

The lies Yasmine told herself stopped the second she hit play. She planned to fast forward the tape and watch Terry. But that's not what happened. Instead, Yasmine pushed back further in the chair, placed her feet on the desk and started from the beginning at midnight—Robert's first show.

"Friends, thanks for joining me," began Robert, a big smile on his face and a twinkle in his eyes. He sat at the anchor desk with confidence—to the manor born. "This is my first show, and I'm super excited to be here. I want to thank Dixie Carter who was so kind to help me out the night before last. Also, I need to thank my friend, Dealmaker Dave Leonard, for letting me co-host with him yesterday. That was a lot of fun. I noticed we still have a few hundred of the Blue Blocker sunglasses in stock, so we're going to have them on at 12:30 a.m. Eastern Time."

Robert's a natural. He has "it" and Billy-Ray is going to start paying him big money very soon. Robert won't leave now. Not for a long time.

The thought should have made her sad, but it didn't. Yasmine couldn't say why. For some reason, she felt proud. Watching Robert speak and smile, gesticulating with a hearty laugh, took away some of her pain. It didn't make sense; if anything, it should have made it worse.

Yasmine spent a solid forty-five minutes watching Robert's first show. She laughed along with him, admiring his stories and volubility.

Her floral sun dress had risen up her legs at this point, and she thought about masturbating. While TeleShop created countless emotions for Yasmine, sexy was not one of them. If only this once, Robert changed the mood.

A year working in this damn office and the only time I've ever felt like relieving myself, I have my period. I can't deal with any potential mess, either physical or spiritual.

Frustrated, Yasmine fast forwarded to Terry Pavão. While he didn't say anything of concern, neither did he have "it." Even if Terry had been sober, for all his bespoke suits and Ivy League credentials, it would have made no difference. He couldn't compete with Robert.

Again, and counterintuitively, the notion made Yasmine happy. At some point, she finished reviewing the tape and fell asleep. Afterward, she'd go and talk to Mary-Anne. But first, she needed to dream …

§

Mary-Anne Warner

Mary-Anne arrived at TeleShop on Monday morning. Her assistant and Director of Talent walked into Mary-Anne's office with mussed hair and casual clothing. That meant trouble.

"What?" Mary-Anne asked with trepidation and weariness. She had a remote terminal tied to TeleShop's mainframe in her condo that delivered real-time sales data. The Dealmaker's huge numbers on Sunday should have made her happy. But with Cliff's demands, big sales became a source of big concern. The Dragon Lady pulled off a minor miracle as well, blowing out a lot of older-stock jewelry. What should have been a great week instead turned into one of worry.

"I fired Pavão," began Yasmine. "He got drunk before the show and passed out during a break."

Mary-Anne listened to the dreary details, though Yasmine remained unaware she actually lightened her boss's mood. Pavão's dismissal made hiring Alan Bennet appear prescient.

"And … ?"

"I brought Alan Bennet on two hours early at 4:00 a.m. and had him finish at 8:00 a.m. Then I had Stan Hormel go on at 8:00 a.m. instead of 9:00 a.m. to make up the difference. He's on-air now, finishes at noon. Alexandra McMurdo takes over and we're back to normal."

Mary-Anne mulled over the news, happy on the one hand and troubled on the other. She needed to throw a spanner into TeleShop's well-oiled works. Stan Hormel — aka Stale Chili — was a case in point TeleShop's nicknames while often brutal were also accurate. Not only was Stan an average host at best, but he was also eccentric, to say the least. Most of the hosts were. Something about the job attracted unusual personalities. With Stan, Mary-Anne wondered how he got hired in the first place; many thought his extreme social cluelessness autistic.

Mary-Anne planned on firing Hormel as soon as they found a new host, preferably female. Stan's numbers fluctuated from slightly above bad to slightly below acceptable. He'd occupied the 9:00 a.m. to noon, Monday to Friday, slot for a bit less than eighteen months. Now, with Cliff Johnson's voice ringing in her head, Mary-Anne decided to hold off.

"How was MacKenzie and how was Bennet?"

"Robert MacKenzie did a thorough and professional job. His numbers were average but his products were average as well." Yasmine struggled to hold down her metaphorical bile. If Sandiya departed TeleShop for another job or left this world for a higher plane, Yasmine would have welcomed either.

"And Bennet?"

"Okay. He struggled with his nerves and maintaining a coherent sales pitch. We need to watch him."

Mary-Anne listened to the recap and offered meager thanks, her mind distracted. She ran through her options while sitting alone in her office. Saturday, July 4th was three weeks away. After Thanksgiving and Labor Day, Independence Day was TeleShop's biggest event. This year, it fell on a Saturday. Huge sales were crucial. Billy-Ray's cash-out based itself on TeleShop's valuation at the end of July. They'd know the truth early on August 1st when their mainframe produced the monthly sales total. For official purposes, Arthur Andersen would certify the results at noon on Friday, August 7th. The next few weeks would determine the fate of many.

Forcing the issue from her mind, Mary-Anne reached for her phone and called the data priests.

"I need the print-out for all our jewelry products for our Fourth special."

"Do you mean July 4th?" asked the nerd who answered the phone.

"No, idiot. I mean the special we're having on August 4th."

"We're having a special on August 4th?" replied the computer guy with guileless innocence that bordered on raging stupidity.

"Of course, July Fourth. Get it to me ASAP!"

"Only senior management has access to that report," continued the fool on the other end.

I hate these computer losers. They have the same social skills as Stale Chili. Is Stan gay? Is the nerd? If so, I should fix them up; they're made for each other.

"It's Mary-Anne-Fucking-Warner, Vice President, you imbecile. Unless you want to be saying, 'Would you like fries with that?' I'd print the goddamn report!"

Mary-Anne hung up before he answered. She had the germ of an idea and needed to confirm the vendors to make it happen.

§

Mary-Anne Warner

"They're our biggest supplier of jewelry. Actually, they're the biggest manufacturer in North America," said Mary-Anne to Cliff Johnson, feeling paranoid and very conspiratorial.

"'Choice Work Jewelry?' And they're in Montreal? Okay. How does that help us?" asked Cliff, his voice expressing a modicum of curiosity. His carrot of amiability could disappear in an instant, replaced with a stick of menace.

"Since last year, we've changed the way we stock jewelry," began Mary-Anne maintaining a clear focus. "We get stuck with non-performing rings and chains all the time. With the price of gold varying it makes keeping our books accurate a nightmare. Plus, it ties up our purchasing department's capital. That's why we're always selling our excess gold at distressed prices for smelting."

"Go on," said Cliff. "Get to the point."

"Now, we establish a limit on the quantity we'll buy and bring in ten percent of that amount. The balance is fiction; it's based on the maximum amount Choice Work can supply. So, if we want ten thousand rings, we only land one thousand. If they don't sell, the balance of nine thousand disappears. If they do sell, we have them shipped."

"I still don't quite get where you're going, Mary-Anne. Your weekend sales were great, and that is not helpful. Not helpful at all."

"Cliff, if we don't land the initial ten percent of our order, we can't air the product. Our mainframe won't allow it. We had to have Burroughs rewrite our system code to accept our new stocking policy. It took them almost a year."

"Mary-Anne, I'm busy," said a testy Cliff Johnson.

"Our July Fourth special is always ring-based. Our shipment for the Fourth arrives by truck express from Canada next week. Four years ago, Triboro's TV competitor in Los Angeles had to delay their very expensive, high profile signal increase party. Somehow their new German TV transmitter got 'stuck' in Customs ... "

The absolute silence on the phone said it all. Mary-Anne could almost see Cliff Johnson's glowing smile beam through the phone from

Manhattan.

"I'll have someone contact you. Give them the details. Good work, Mary-Anne."

As was typical, he hung up without saying goodbye. That no longer bothered Mary-Anne. Sitting alone at her desk, considering her options professionally and personally, Mary-Anne hoped Alan Bennet was still in the building.

§

Robert MacKenzie

Robert's debut show went well, and he thanked God he'd left before Terry Pavão passed out. He had quickly picked up TeleShop's groove without trouble: arrive on-time, hustle for drop-ins, choose his features, and develop his pitch. Meet with the director. Be nice to the crew. And *always* be nice to the operators.

Few realized they were the last stage of the purchase. With a simple change in tone, an operator could help close a sale or scuttle it. This was especially true when it came to expensive jewelry. There was a reason certain operators completed more high-end ring orders than others. If it was up to Robert, he would have paid then commission.

His schedule on Show #1 would prevent his drinking with the Dealmaker. Robert found the situation conflicting. On the one hand, it would save him money and constant hangovers. On the other, he would miss bonding with the Dealmaker. And the crew. He knew he would look back fondly on that night at Lucky Charm Saloon.

Robert wondered how Yasmine would react to his kissing Sandiya. At some point, she'd find out what had happened. It didn't matter that calling off their nascent romance was her idea. Ascribing logic to a relationship was like putting your faith in a "system" when playing the ponies. It may have the patina of rigor, but in the end, it amounted to no more than wishful thinking.

It turned out he didn't have to wonder for long. Angela told him Yasmine showed up incensed over the early-morning human resources crisis. The floor director relayed the story to Robert with a smile, telling how she informed her of Robert's tête-a-tête with Sandiya. Like his almost-erstwhile partner, Robert pretended to grin and laugh, although the tale squeezed his soul.

He didn't see Yasmine that Monday evening. Sandiya left a note in his mail slot saying he should call when he arrived, which he did. Their conversation, as brief as it was, didn't actually state he should drop by Sandiya's condo and fuck her brains out. But that was its clear, unspoken message.

Like most men, Robert did much of his thinking with his dick. And like most men, his dick didn't ever consider the long term. Sandiya was a very pretty woman. She was forthright, without Yasmine's air of ambiguity. Although Sandiya didn't articulate her goals with the same zeal as Yasmine, her time in Oklahoma City was also an obvious prelude to a greater tomorrow. That left Robert in the same predicament as before. And while he liked Sandiya, she didn't quite gut punch him the same way as Yasmine.

This remained true even after Robert dropped by her condo on Tuesday around 6:00 p.m. Their ensuing rendezvous put a special spring in his step when he departed for TeleShop a few hours later.

§

Robert MacKenzie

"I need a smoke, kid," said the Dealmaker, leaning against his car in the parking lot while lighting up a Camel. "I'll meet you inside."

It was 3:00 p.m. on Thursday, and Robert had followed the Dealmaker down the highway from the motel to the office, both heading for the show host's weekly meeting in TeleShop's boardroom.

He found it ironic how his tiny world kept getting smaller. Best Value Inn was a short drive to TeleShop. TeleShop was a short drive to Sandiya's condo. Sandiya's condo was a short drive to Yasmine's condo (which he wondered if he'd ever actually see). And Yasmine's condo was a short drive to TeleShop. The word of the day and increasingly his life was "circularity."

Am I really in Oklahoma City? Perhaps I'm still in Phoenix? I'm not in Los Angeles and I'm certainly not in Massachusetts. When your entire life is a drive of twenty minutes in all directions are you really anywhere?

Saying hello to Hank and no longer noticing his stray revolver, Robert walked past security and up the stairs toward the prep room. Stan Hormel stood inside making pained conversation with Alan Bennet. Kirk Glazer moped about drinking coffee. Joe Giannini (he of the chicken soup/chicken shit maxim) lay on the sofa reading a magazine. Other hosts he'd only seen on-air lolled about the room. The Dragon Lady sat at the desk, examining her show.

"Robert," said Alexandra McMurdo, looking elegant in a draped linen suit. "It's a pleasure seeing you again. I watched part of your midnight show on Tuesday; you did a great job."

"Thank you so much," replied Robert, happy for normal courtesy. Alexandra extended her hand and he shook it in reply as they made small talk.

Robert's eyes looked about the room, landing for a second on the Dragon Lady.

"Fuck you," she said, glaring for the briefest of moments before returning to her show

"That's what I love about you, Dixie. Class. You're all about class," drawled Alexandra, smiling at Robert. He didn't know about the women's relationship, but Robert didn't imagine the Dragon Lady had friends anywhere, certainly not at TeleShop.

"Fuck you too, Alexandra. And mind your own goddamn business!"

At that moment, Yasmine walked into the prep room, her dark hair pulled into a bun, her form striking with its tall angularity. She wore a severe, navy blue pantsuit over a cream silk blouse. Medium-heeled, jet-black pumps bedecked her feet.

He hadn't seen Yasmine that Tuesday, nor did he see her on Wednesday. He had known she would be in attendance that day, but the sight of her wrecked him all the same.

Yasmine observed the room. Her eyes met Robert's, passing them without so much as a flicker.

"People, please follow me to the boardroom. We need to discuss our weekly operations and our strategies for the Fourth," she called. Then, noting his absence, "Where's Dave?"

"Here," the Dealmaker replied, turning up at the prep room's entrance looking (as always these days) the worse for wear.

"Let's go," Yasmine stated, turning about and heading toward the office. She used her security badge to access the executive area and enter the boardroom. The other hosts — a motley collection of aging hipsters, past their prime rebels, the young guard of up and comers and the elegant Alexandra McMurdo — followed behind.

Sandiya King already sat at the large boardroom table, surprising Robert with her presence. Unlike Yasmine, Sandiya flashed a droll look, hinting a follow up to their Tuesday assignation. She nested to the right of Billy-Ray Newton's usual chair. Today, Mary-Anne would conduct the meeting in his place.

Yasmine sat opposite Sandiya. Looking first at Yasmine and then at Sandiya, their separate, yet intense, stares fascinated Robert. Sandiya appeared triumphant while Yasmine looked wary, and he had no idea of the reason.

§

Mary-Anne Warner

A moment later Mary-Anne walked in taking position at the table's head. Since her call with Cliff Johnson on Tuesday, Mary-Anne had forwarded several product selectors for the upcoming special to Triboro. They contained confidential pricing, delivery times, available quantities, and Customs information.

Other than a brief and anonymous call from somebody (supposedly) at Triboro, Mary-Anne heard nothing. While she didn't care about Cliff's rude behavior on the phone, Mary-Anne did find this sudden lack of access troubling. It was as if she was being compartmentalized with all its attendant dangers. Mary-Anne's own ruthlessness put her on guard, aware of any potential setup that might impact her future and career.

"You'll notice Sandiya King joins us today. From now on, Sandiya will attend all sales meetings. It's a regulatory issue; with the upcoming buyout, Mr. Newton wants legal on board at all times. Are we good?"

The assembly exchanged nothing more than a few nods and grunts. Yasmine managed a small smile and acknowledged Sandiya, who smiled back in return.

Mary-Anne spoke about the week's sales. The group listened, save for Stan Hormel who went on at length about inconsistent merchandising during morning shows.

"If we want to drive numbers," Stan mumbled in his weird cadence. "We need to have Scheduling provide a live body for drop-ins. It's gonna be win-win. Better merchandising for the overnight and early morning shows means more revenue for everybody."

Stan was not known for speaking in sales meetings, so his announcement grabbed attention, albeit of the wrong sort. Everyone knew overnights lost money, and the only reason they stayed on-air past Show #1 was for the network's image.

"Stan," said Mary-Anne with frustration borne of repetition, "we've had this conversation. Scheduling operates between 7:30 a.m. and 8:30 p.m. to cover shows five through eight. There's no budget for extending the hours. Even if we had the money, finding someone to staff the office overnight would be very difficult. I'm sorry."

"But what about the numbers?" Stan asked with put-on alacrity.

"Come to me with a promotion that doesn't cost money, and I'll consider it," Mary-Anne replied. "Now let's move on — "

"But that's not fair!" Stan sat up in his chair and leaned forward into the table. His face, childlike at the best of times, wore a pattern of red. The room stared in uncomfortable silence. Mary-Anne rolled her eyes.

"Why are we always so focused on sales?" asked Stan, halfway between rhetorical and literal. "Maybe our viewers aren't having fun. If they don't have fun, they won't watch our shows. What do you think about that? If we have more fun, the sales will follow."

The boardroom maintained its stony silence. Mary-Anne shook her head, percolating with frustration. The Dealmaker stared. Others shifted around unsure about what to say. Was Stan's gambit an exercise in genius or lunacy?

The Dragon Lady provided the answer.

"Who is this ass clown? Hey, Stale Chili, are you fucking high? Do you work for the same company as the rest of us?"

Stan's face turned from red to scarlet, his eyes opening wide.

"You can't talk to me like that!" stammered Hormel. "I'm trying to help."

"Then please help all of us and fuck off, you fucking moron!" yelled the Dragon Lady. "No wonder our overnight's in the shitter. Jesus, Mary-Anne, get this dick out of here."

"If I'm not appreciated, I'll leave," said Stan, grabbing his notes while fleeing. Mary-Anne watched him escape. She would have fired his worthless ass on the spot, but with the new mandate from Cliff, Mary-Anne needed Hormel. Terry Pavão's flame-out left her short of hosts in general and of bad hosts in particular.

"Let's continue with the Fourth," said Mary-Anne ignoring the distraction, Stan's absence a welcome relief. Mary-Anne found it surprising how little the minor hosts mattered. Then again, that's why they were "minor" hosts — even if they now possessed a relevance of which they were unaware. "Dixie, we have ten thousand units of your Celebration Ring in ten-carat gold arriving on Monday."

"Did you get them numbered with a certificate of authenticity like I asked?"

"It's done," replied Mary-Anne with assurance, though knowing that wasn't the whole story. While the rings had already shipped from Montreal with their new "certificates" in every box, trouble loomed. Cliff Johnson would see to it. "You'll need to cut a promo next week for the rings. We're going to advertise them like crazy all week."

"Dave," began Mary-Anne shifting to the Dealmaker, "we managed to find ten thousand more of your 'Tibetan' garnet rings."

"Don't you mean Tibetan Shangri-La garnet rings?"

"Sure, whatever you say, Dave," answered Mary-Anne, trying not to sound cynical and failing in the process. "Funny thing, Choice Work Jewelry said they've never heard of Shangri-La garnets."

"They're very rare," responded the Dealmaker.

"They must be if the biggest jewelry manufacturer in North America doesn't know of them. I wonder how their description got onscreen?"

Mary-Anne looked to Sandiya, who said nothing. Billy-Ray

Newton loved the sales and the story and insisted they feature during Independence Weekend. TeleShop's assistant counsel kept hers and declined to comment.

"They're a bit darker than regular garnets," said the Dealmaker with a humorous edge.

"Right," replied Mary-Anne. "Choice Work figured it out and they've shipped them together with the Celebration Ring. They'll be here by Monday."

Mary-Anne went over weekly revenue at length. She needed to give the appearance of caring about sales while actually caring about their lack.

Jesus, Cliff, please tell me the fix is in. If we blow out these two rings alone that's upwards of three million dollars in gross profit.

Before finishing, Mary-Anne watched Sandiya give Robert the eye time and again. Their new "star" affected casual indifference, but it was an obvious feint.

Christ, MacKenzie, what's up with you? Sandiya and Yasmine both like you and you've only worked four shows? What am I doing stuck with Bennet?

"We're moving up next week's meeting to Wednesday at 3:00 p.m. for our Fourth kickoff. Starting from Show #4 on Saturday, we're double-hosting and extending shows to four hours between noon to midnight Eastern Time. Yasmine will get your updated schedules early next week. Please be creative; we need big sales. I'll see you Wednesday."

The room emptied. The show hosts walked back to production and the prep room like gunslingers. Yasmine eyed Sandiya with barely-concealed contempt. The two women mouthed saccharine platitudes that fooled no one as they left, their inner voices so malignant, they sounded into the air …

Bitch, thought Yasmine.

Cunt, thought Sandiya.

CHAPTER TWELVE

Mary-Anne Warner

When the trouble happened, it hit with a fury. Choice Work Jewelry shipped TeleShop's massive July Fourth order on June 26th. The goods traveled Freight on Board Montreal via Geoff Griffin Truck Logistics. The transport company delivered all TeleShop's orders from Choice Work and had done so for years. Delivery took three to four days on average.

When the order didn't arrive on Monday, nobody worried. On Tuesday, their shipment was still nowhere in sight. TeleShop's purchasing department should have called Choice Work. In turn, Choice Work should have confirmed their order's arrival. Neither occurred. It was Wednesday, July 1st before the shit hit the fan.

"Where's Champlain, New York?" yelled Kellie Yull, TeleShop's jewelry buyer, running into the boardroom. Like all buyers, Kellie ate stress for a living. A buyer's career averaged three years before they cracked. Kellie pushed five and wore the strain all over her face. She entered the room panicked, her eyes ablaze, veins popping on her skull.

"It's south of Montreal, right on the border." The Dealmaker answered as his face, gleaning disaster, turned ashen.

"Are you sure?" responded Kellie. "Is there a Customs facility there?"

"Trust me, I'm sure; if you sell yearbooks to high schools in the Northeast you know every half-assed town in the region." The Dealmaker focused on Kellie, looked over to the Dragon Lady and turned to Mary-Anne. She ran the meeting again in place of Billy-Ray, who was seldom out of his office of late. "Of course it has Customs; I told you it's on the border. Why?"

"I got a fax from someone named Howard Murray, Port Director of Champlain Station, US Customs. They've seized our shipment from Choice Work."

The Dragon Lady, sitting across from Robert, gasped. Her pallor turned an even darker shade of green and she almost swallowed her cigarette.

"The whole shipment?" The Dealmaker watched as a ponderous anvil of doom descended upon the room. "Why?"

Mary-Anne's eyes opened wide in pure astonishment. She couldn't stop a small and inappropriate smile from stealing across her lips.

Jesus, Cliff, you don't fuck around.

"The fax says: *Shangri-La garnets of undocumented origin. Certificates of authenticity for tanzanite rings not accompanied by notarized proof.*"

"Kellie, is the rest of the shipment okay?" asked Mary-Anne with quiet intensity. While this Customs issue solved her problem with Cliff, she had split loyalties. Her burning ambition directed Mary-Anne to Manhattan. But she hated the albatross of a failed Independence Weekend sitting on her shoulder.

"The fax says: *Entire shipment seized for improper documentation. Goods subject to disposal. Consignee must provide appeal documents within thirty days.*" Kellie Yull trembled, the paper shaking in her hand. This had never happened to any of her shipments in the past. In fact, it had never happened to any shipment of jewelry from Choice Work before.

"I assume we're covered?" questioned Alexandra McMurdo. "We have to have insurance." A hopeful air appeared for a moment before Yasmine shot it down.

"Insurance doesn't cover Customs seizures," Yasmine stated with minimal emotion. "Also, Choice Work ships everything FOB Montreal. That means the moment they stick it on the truck, it's our problem."

"You and your fucking Shangri-La garnets," seethed the Dragon Lady to the Dealmaker. "You've fucked my show on Saturday. If they've grabbed the whole shipment, I can't air my Bismarck platinum chain either. There goes my fucking Sunday!"

"Yeah, well fuck you too, Dixie," answered the Dealmaker, on the defensive. "Whoever heard of a goddamn certificate of authenticity for a ring, anyway? You fucked me as well!"

"At least we can fix the certificate issue. How're you supposed to fix the Shangri-La rings? Why don't you call the High Fucking Lama and get him to help you out—you prick!"

Panic clutched the two hosts as they hurled recriminations at each other. Those not scheduled for the special displayed overt concern combined with secret relief. Alexandra maintained a poker face while Robert didn't know what to think. Mary-Anne noted the small sardonic smile on Sandiya's face. directed toward Yasmine. She wondered why.

§

Robert MacKenzie

It was a shit meeting that turned into a shit day. Mary-Anne (or Yasmine) changed his schedule that weekend. He no longer worked Show #1. Instead, Robert double-hosted with the Dealmaker for Show

#5 on Saturday and Sunday. The extended four-hour program ran from noon to 4:00 p.m. Eastern Time, packed with all manner of bargains. Or would have if Choice Work's shipment wasn't consigned to the bowels of Customs hell.

It was a quiet, hot Thursday afternoon. The pair sat outside their rooms at Best Value Inn, trying to put together a show.

"What about the anatomically correct dolls?" suggested Robert, grasping at straws.

"Gone. Fare thee well. Hasta-la-fucking-Vista," The Dealmaker nursed his Olde English Malt Liquor. Nursing a drink was not the Dealmaker's way. His slow consumption reflected the situation's gravity.

"The Blue Blockers?"

"Kid, don't be an ass. They're twenty bucks and almost sold out. Our target's seven hundred fifty thousand dollars per day. You don't make scratch like that with low-rent teasers."

Robert recognized his own naïveté the moment he made the suggestion. Earlier, the Dealmaker "borrowed" two product selectors from the Scheduling department. He brought them back to the motel to knock around ideas.

"Zamfir?"

"What part of sold-out don't you understand?" The Dealmaker, his voice steeped in frustration, opened yet another pack of Camels.

"Jewelry?"

"We got dogshit. Customs seized all the hot stuff, and Dixie's grabbed what's left."

Focusing on the product selector, Robert noticed a late addition, buried at the bottom of a page near the end. The item had never aired even though it arrived three weeks before.

"Dealmaker, what's this? The Quasar Force Gauntlet video game controller? We have the Quasar Force Gauntlet? How? Quasar meant to scrap them."

"Kid, what the hell are you talking about? What the Christ is a Force Gauntlet?"

"Quasar Electronic Games introduced it eighteen months ago. You wear it like a glove. It looks super-cool and allows you to control most games from all major video game companies."

"So?"

"So, it flopped. Nobody understood how to operate it. Plus, the Force Gauntlet retailed for four hundred dollars. Quasar spent a fortune developing it and almost went bankrupt when it didn't sell. We bought ten thousand as a closeout. Jesus, our cost is only thirty dollars. We're selling it for sixty."

"Your point?" said the Dealmaker, his curiosity aroused.

"If there's one thing I've learned in my very brief tenure at TeleShop, it's that we tell stories. That's how we sell it. We'll explain how the Force Gauntlet works, shoot a product demo and run it as a promo. Then, we'll take a page from your Shangri-La playbook and up the retail to ninety-nine ninety-nine. That's still a seventy-five percent discount off its introductory price. Trust me, Dealmaker; we can sell it. I know we can!"

"Kid, if you're serious tell me now and I'll call Billy-Ray. We'll feature it as our main item on Sunday."

"I'm serious."

"Give me a minute." The Dealmaker walked into his room and closed the door. A muffled conversation bled through the motel's thin walls. Letting out one of his trademarked guffaws, the Dealmaker farted with joy. He slammed down the telephone, and relieved himself with enormous gusto. The Dealmaker emerged from his lair, laughing. The flushing toilet served as the soundtrack.

"Kid, we're off to TeleShop. Have to shoot a promo. Billy-Ray was very impressed. I told him this was your idea."

"Thanks, Dealmaker. You didn't have to."

"Sure I did. Do you know Dixie's problem?"

"She's miserable?" replied Robert. His answer didn't require a great deal of introspection.

"No. She's too obvious with her misery. That woman's a born salesman—she's great. I'll deny I ever said that even though it's true, but she has no allies. Nobody at the office would piss on her if she was on fire. Kid, you gotta have friends. When you're gracious, you get favors. And everybody needs favors. Besides, who would believe I knew anything about a Force Gauntlet?"

"Is this going to take long?" Robert asked.

"Yup."

"Then we have to hurry, I need to prep for Show #1 tonight," said Robert as they walked to their cars.

"Don't worry about it. Billy-Ray's getting you a replacement. Concentrate on the promo. That's what's important."

"This isn't a joke?" asked Robert, surprised.

"Nope. Oh, one more thing. Billy-Ray's a touch desperate—he's going to up the retail like you asked. And if we sell all ten thousand, and only if we sell them all, he'll spiff us a buck fifty each per unit. Do you know what that means?"

"Ah ... "

"That means if we sell them out we get fifteen grand. In cash!"

"What the hell? Are you serious?" Leonardo, the leader of the Teenage Mutant Ninja Turtles appeared without warning. He fist-bumped Robert and offered his congratulations. Demi Moore walked past. She raised her right hand in a telephone gesture and whispered he should call. Other celebrities clapped him on the back. A photographer from the National Enquirer took pics.

Robert stood impassive and wide-eyed, a frozen grin stamped on his face.

"Christ, kid, are you okay?" asked the Dealmaker, staring at his partner's statue-like pose.

"How … "

"On occasion, Dixie and I get an extra bonus on certain items if we sell large volumes at high margins. It doesn't happen often, but when it does, that's how they keep us motivated."

"Jesus, Dealmaker, do the other hosts know about this?"

"Yes and no. Everybody gets spiffed. Certain products have promotions a few times per year. They're open to all hosts. But Dixie and I get "special" spiffs from time to time. Yes, the other hosts know. And no, they won't admit it because doing so would make them nuts. Now you're involved. Don't say a word to anybody. Dixie's gonna find out regardless. She'll hate you so much you might want to check your Honda for a bomb."

"Fifteen grand? That's more than I made all last year. I'll catch a flight to Phoenix with the money *and* I'll buy a new car!"

"What about me?" asked the Dealmaker wearing the widest grin Robert had ever seen. "That writ of garnishment doesn't cover spiffs. I made sure my wife never knew about them. Always took my haul and kept it quiet. Thank you, Jesus!"

"Praise be to God!" laughed Robert, a mountain of naked bills dancing in front of him.

"Remember, kid, we only get the money if we sell out the Force Gauntlet. By the way, who came up with the name? It sounds like a brand of French ticklers."

Chuckling, the Dealmaker stepped into his Dodge Duster and headed off to TeleShop. Robert followed close behind in his Civic as dreams of luxury and new digs sat next to him in the passenger seat.

§

Robert MacKenzie

Robert had an idea of what he wanted to say and spent hours fleshing out his concept. The Dealmaker didn't need to stay for Robert's explanation segment; he could have gone home. Instead, he watched as the team filmed Robert speaking at the anchor desk.

Billy-Ray had Stefano Verde, one of the standby hosts, take over Show #1 that evening. Stefano's name belied his origins. People expected him to speak with an exotic, foreign accent. But Stefano hailed from Biloxi, Mississippi and had a strong Southern drawl.

It was midnight by the time they finished shooting the promo. Billy-Ray asked the production guys to cut the ad together and get it to air ASAP.

"Thanks, guys. I appreciate your time." Robert said to the production staff as he walked with the Dealmaker toward the exit. "When will you cut the promo?"

"We have to pull an all-nighter," answered Helen Cunningham.

Susie, who had taken over as director for Shows #7 and #8 that evening also spoke up. "This must be important, we're actually getting overtime. Oh, I like your concept for the promo; we should do more of them."

Thanking the crew again the two hosts headed to the exit and their cars.

"You did a good job, kid. Serious. If this promo hits and you continue doing what you're doing, you may find yourself getting a call from AVN," the Dealmaker said.

"You mean, American Value Network?" asked Robert.

"No, you simpleton, I mean Adult Video News. Of course, American Value Network. They're four times our size. TeleShop is the bush league; AVN is the show."

Before starting at TeleShop, Robert had never heard of any home shopping network. Now, the vagaries of television retail occupied his thoughts day in and out.

AVN was the largest and oldest network. They'd started as a local channel in Cleveland in 1980. Two years ago, they moved into their massive new headquarters in Connecticut. Every cable network in the country carried their signal.

The second biggest retailer was Pacific Discount Channel. PDC began the year after TeleShop. Based in Seattle, ComArc, the country's dominant cable provider, owned them. Many of ComArc's competitors declined to add PDC to their lineups. In answer, their parent company placed PDC on a low channel on all their systems. Low channel placement was a significant factor in ratings. PDC had grown past TeleShop and was now double their size.

TeleShop USA was the fourth player in a three-player race. Billy-Ray had muscled his network onto more and more cable systems through raw will. Due to their size disparity, ComArc couldn't deny carrying TeleShop for monopoly reasons. But they didn't make it easy. Most of TeleShop's carriers were secondary providers in smaller markets. They were lucky if sixteen percent of California cable systems broadcast their signal.

This meant TeleShop had enormous potential for growth, hence Triboro's interest. It also meant the clock ticked on their success. As they burned through viewers, their appeal to other cable systems diminished. At some point, their numbers would go negative.

"Have they ever contacted you?" Robert asked, wondering why the subject had never come up before.

"Hell, no. I'm not what they're looking for. I appeal to the old ladies they don't want. I also look like shit. You don't have to tell me otherwise; I'm not blind. Besides, I like it here. I'm the king. I don't want to start over again."

"I see what you mean. What about the Dragon Lady?" The Dealmaker smiled, his eyes lighting up as they reached their cars. Pulling his keys from his pocket, the Dealmaker opened the door to his Dodge Duster.

"Kid, they already called Dixie two years ago." The Dealmaker climbed down into his car and glanced back at Robert. "Nobody's supposed to know. She interviewed at AVN when they moved from Cleveland to Connecticut. The interview went okay, a bit of a culture shock, but okay."

"So, what happened?"

"Do you remember what I said about needing allies?"

"Sure."

"We used to have a director, DeShawn Davis, colored guy from Oklahoma City. Smart as nails and a good director. AVN poached him the year before they called Dixie. He bumped into her in the hallway during the interview."

"How did you find out?" asked Robert, fascinated.

"Kid, everything gets back. This is a very small industry. Anyway, DeShawn didn't like Dixie one bit and she didn't like him. They'd promoted DeShawn to management and he had some words with their HR people. Needless to say, AVN didn't offer Dixie the job."

"How did she take it?"

"How do you think? The great part is she couldn't say anything because the whole interview was on the Q.T. If you ever get to AVN, I swear to God she'll set herself on fire!"

Robert laughed while climbing into his Civic. The late-night air still held much of the day's heat. Turning over his engine, Robert followed the Dealmaker out of the parking lot and into the street, wondering if his gambit with the Force Gauntlet would succeed.

§

Mary-Anne Warner

Mary-Anne labored in her office at noon on Friday, mulling over the upcoming weekend. Friday was the technical start of the long weekend. Regardless, all production and logistics staff had to work. Scheduling and every host had scrambled to find anything that might generate revenue. In TV home shopping, sales beget sales. Counters and sell outs were like a contagion. If enough people missed out on bargains, they'd often buy the next item as a fallback.

The needed gross for the weekend was three million dollars per day. The extended Shows #5, #6 & #7 had targets of seven hundred and fifty thousand dollars each. The remaining twelve hours had a cumulative budget of the same amount.

The Dragon Lady was going with a scorched Earth policy. She'd found every chain, ring, and bangle in gold and silver that hadn't sold. Her plan was to slash prices to the bone, creating a tidal wave of sell outs on both days.

"Mary-Anne, I know there's no margin, but what are our options? We can remainder these items for smelt value and get fuck all *and* have a disastrous weekend. Or, we can blow them out, clear out our dead inventory, and start afresh when we clear up the Customs imbroglio."

Mary-Anne should have forbidden the price cuts. But if she did, the Dragon Lady would only go to Billy-Ray and have her overruled. She wasn't a miracle worker; Mary-Anne had given the vendor suppression idea to Cliff in the first place. There were more inventory "disasters" to come—she knew it for a fact. Besides, she could always blame Billy-Ray for the discounts. Mary-Anne hated sabotaging her own show.

The Dealmaker co-hosted with Robert MacKenzie on both days. Alexandra McMurdo co-hosted with Sandi Olver. The schedule called for the Dragon Lady to co-host with Joe Giannini. But—as always—that didn't happen. Closing out both Saturday and Sunday, the Dragon Lady hosted alone.

On Saturday, the Dealmaker would use the same strategy as the Dragon Lady. They'd lined up every cut-price closeout they could find. It would be four hours of non-stop sellouts, God willing.

On Sunday, the Dealmaker and Robert decided to roll the dice and go all-in on their two feature items. They had a brand-new portable carpet cleaner, the Houdini Carpet Magician. Its wholesale cost was fifty dollars and it retailed for ninety-nine ninety-nine. Six thousand units waited in their warehouse for its (hopeful) blow-out on Sunday at 2:00 p.m. If both it and the Force Gauntlet hit, they'd be heroes. If not ...

Houdini was a brand-new company and had slipped under Triboro's radar. Mary-Anne looked at the scarlet red and yellow plastic device and remained unimpressed. She didn't see it as a winner and neither did the other hosts. Its cheap packaging and lightweight appearance made it look like a toy. Like junk. Nobody wanted to debut it. That is until the Dealmaker selected it as their feature. In that moment, it became hot. But the Dealmaker locked it in to his show with Robert, and that's where it stayed.

The excuses and delays from vendors unable to supply products had begun to trickle in. Billy-Ray didn't need to be a genius to figure out Triboro's game plan. His withering looks whenever he saw Mary-Anne actually made her feel guilty.

Glancing up from her desk, Mary-Anne looked at the network feed. Alexandra McMurdo was going to break when the Dealmaker appeared onscreen.

"Well *arby-dar*, it's the Dealmaker; I'm here to talk to ya about our Independence Weekend special. First off, I'm sorry, we're still having trouble finding more Shangri-La garnets. Those few of you who managed to grab that ring should consider yourselves lucky. We're tryin' to get some more, friends. We're tryin'. But it won't happen this weekend."

Mary-Anne grimaced at the mention of the ring, but watched as the promo unfolded. In the background, dressed as Luke Skywalker, appeared Robert. He wore the Quasar Force Gauntlet on his left hand and approached the Dealmaker from behind.

"So friends, forgive us. We've loaded our four-hour Saturday and Sunday specials with lots of quick sell-out items. Don't say I didn't warn you; if you snooze, you lose! I'm co-hosting with my buddy, Robert 'Big Mack' MacKenzie—"

"Dealmaker! Dealmaker! I've got to talk to you."

The Dealmaker turned and looked at Robert, pretending to do a double-take. "Who the heck are you supposed to be, Big Mack? This ain't Halloween."

Intrigued, Mary-Anne continued watching. She liked the way the Dealmaker and Robert worked together. They had natural chemistry.

"Dealmaker! We have an insane bargain on the Quasar Force Gauntlet video game controller. It's the buy of the century. The normal retail price is four hundred dollars and we have exactly ten thousand units. We're selling them at 3:00 p.m. Eastern Time on Sunday for only ninety-nine ninety-nine."

"Hey, that's a heck of a price. But what does it do?" asked the Dealmaker, playing up his innocence for all it was worth.

"Watch this," said Robert as the scene cut away. Robert appeared again without the Luke Skywalker costume. He leaned against the anchor desk, surrounded by cameras and props. Looking into the camera, Robert went on in great detail about the Force Gauntlet. He explained its operation. Its advanced technology. Why it made a great gift. And why everyone needed to do their Christmas shopping early.

Mary-Anne stared at the screen. She didn't own a video game console and knew nothing about the Force Gauntlet. But if only as an object lesson in marketing, the promo was impressive.

"Wow," said the Dealmaker when the explanation ended. "That's incredible! You say we have ten thousand and we're airing it on Sunday at 3:00 p.m. Eastern Time?"

"Yup."

"And it's only ninety-nine ninety-nine?"

"Yup."

"And you're sure we're going to sell out all ten thousand?"

"Yup."

"Anything else, Big Mack?"

"Dealmaker, make sure people don't watch Sunday at 2:00 p.m. Eastern Time. We're going to clean their carpets and we don't have enough units."

"Clean their carpets? Is that a metaphor?"

"Nope, it's literal, but we messed up the quantity. We got the last of the Force Gauntlets but we couldn't get enough machines to clean everybody's carpets. We're embarrassed."

"Okay, Big Mac. I don't know what you're talking about but I'll tell everybody."

"Thanks, Dealmaker."

"Friends, join Big Mack and me on Saturday for our quick sell-out special, noon until 4:00 p.m. Eastern Time. Then, make sure to be here for our Sunday extravaganza, also beginning at noon Eastern Time. We'll surprise you with scads of deals. Please don't watch at 2:00 p.m. because we can't clean enough carpets. You'll find out what Big Mack is talking about then. But the amazing Quasar Force Gauntlet airs at 3:00 p.m. We have ten thousand only. That's it. No more. Please don't hear my sad lament: *'Too late, too late!' will be the cry. Dealmaker Dave and the deal have passed you by!'* We'll see you this weekend."

§

Sandiya King

"Mary-Anne kept her cool and appeared surprised by the Customs seizure." Sandiya King whispered with an air of conspiracy.

She sat alone in the legal office, her hand shielding the telephone's mouthpiece. At the other end, Cliff Johnson listened and said nothing. The office may have been empty, but Sandiya still embraced discretion. She didn't need her idiot "boss" overhearing any part of the conversation. The less Nat knew, the better.

"I've gotten to know Mary-Anne in the last year. She has mixed feelings about the seizure, I can tell."

Cliff responded with affected calm. An amused smirk strode atop his ostensibly warm voice. "That's Mary-Anne being Mary-Anne. She's competitive. We've had her in place for two years working at building sales. Ironically, she's done too good a job. Since we've decided to buy TeleShop, we need Mary-Anne to dial it down — in a big way. I don't know if she can and that's another reason she's expendable. You recall why I brought you in, Sandiya?"

"Yes, sir." While Sandiya sat by herself in the well-lit office, it felt as if she whispered in the dark.

"Plans within plans, Sandiya. Plans within plans ... I like you a lot, Sandiya. Is that a problem?"

"No, sir. It's not a problem at all."

An apparition of Sandiya's father, Abhoy, stared from the room's corner. An angry man, in Dhaka he worked as an engineer; in Buffalo, he drove a bus. Her father's cold mien reflected his inner winter. Pleasing him was never possible, although Sandiya tried. Like Cliff, he smiled when necessary and spit frost when it wasn't. Unlike Cliff, and very much like his daughter, he didn't understand subtlety.

"I'm happy to hear that, Sandiya. I may bring you to Manhattan on our jet so you can report face-to-face. We'll have dinner at Balthazar. Their dry-aged côte de boeuf is outstanding. Interested?"

"Yes, sir. Very much."

"Good. Keep me informed. We'll talk again soon."

"Yes, sir. I look forward to it."

The line went dead. Sandiya replaced the receiver in its cradle and looked about the shabby office. Nat's desk lay empty to her right. It was Friday afternoon and Sandiya hoped he'd already left for the weekend. She hated his obsequious mincing.

Gathering herself, she prepared to leave the office and head to Scheduling. She'd study the weekend's inventory stats and look for anomalies. That might provide a legitimate excuse to call Cliff. She found their discussion intoxicating. Its subtext was obvious and not a problem in any way.

Robert, you're okay, but you're not Cliff Johnson. You're a means; he's an end, and I like the attention. Let's see how it plays out. As for you Yasmine …

Instead of exiting the office, Sandiya drew the bolt across the doorjamb. She walked back to her desk, pulling up her skirt and sitting back in her chair. Smiling, Sandiya removed her panties.

§

Yasmine Dubai

For the first time since her arrival in Oklahoma City, Yasmine left work on Friday at a normal hour—5:00 pm. She'd be back at TeleShop all day Saturday and Sunday for Independence Weekend. Tonight, she needed the break.

Yasmine whipped down the highway in her Jaguar. The night before, she bought a frozen shepherd's pie from the McCartney's Grocery near her condo. That was her dinner. Still, it beat the insipid fare from the hamburger restaurant around the corner. And she was sick to death of pizza. And Chinese food. Yasmine missed her mother's ghormeh sabzi, with its rich gravy, herbs, and succulent cubes of lamb.

As a Bahá'í, she wasn't supposed to drink, but Yasmine enjoyed wine, as did her mother. Her younger sister, Farrah, worked part time at a Toronto café to help defray tuition. Unlike her mother and sister, she didn't drink. Not even a little.

Regardless, the sisters were very close and spoke on the telephone often. Farrah had started dating Jagdish—a "nice Bahá'í boy," as her mother put it. Yasmine knew they were in love and marriage inevitable.

Farrah, I'm happy for you. And Mom sounds like she's in heaven. Why do I make my life so difficult? I have these ridiculous standards I can't surmount. I'm going to be at work all weekend and I'll see Robert. Please don't let Sandiya drop by. Please.

Yasmine proceeded from her car to the elevator and from there to her condo. As always, she dropped the keys on the hallway table and walked into her kitchen. Unlike Robert, Yasmine didn't play "A White Sport Coat" in her head. The only music she might have heard was her mother's favorite, "Hungarian Rhapsody No. 2" by Liszt. Hardly the same thing.

Yasmine put the shepherd's pie into the oven and poured a glass of wine. Her evening uniform was sweats and a Wharton hoodie, a far cry from her daily business attire.

Besides shepherd's pie, McCartney's sold copies of *Top Gun* on

VHS. Yasmine bought one on impulse. She'd meant to see the film with Daryush in Philadelphia last year, but missed it.

Yasmine turned on her massive thirty-five-inch television. Popping the tape into the VCR, she sat down and relaxed. The large TV had been one of the few items she had splurged on since moving into her condo. Incessant television watching now occupied way too much of her free time.

Top Gun's overt machismo was not supposed to appeal to Yasmine. She should have rejected its "alpha" male caricatures. Then again, she'd also had enough of her "beta" male boyfriends. Daryush was the latest and best example.

Where is Robert in all this? He's a bit like Tom Cruise's character. Sweet inside with a hard shell. He's not Val Kilmer. Not at all. If he was older, he'd be more like Tom Skerritt, quiet and confident in his command.

Again, she fixated on Robert. It wasn't supposed to be this way. Yasmine was good at moving on and accepting the necessity of change. She implemented it immediately and, if necessary, with cold dispassion. In this, she was a mirror of her fixation, even if she didn't know it.

The oven timer beeped. Yasmine put down her glass and stopped the movie. Getting up, she walked to the kitchen and refilled her wine.

When Yasmine turned off the VCR, TeleShop appeared on the screen. As much as she should have chosen another station as her default channel, she kept TeleShop. Like so many employees at TeleShop, they ended up tuning into their jobs, every hour of every day.

As Yasmine sat down, the Dragon Lady went to break. TeleShop ran the Force Gauntlet promo they'd been airing constantly. The Dealmaker's well-worn visage appeared. He spoke about the Shangri-La garnet, now infamous and unavailable. From behind, Robert walked onscreen and in costume, interrupting the Dealmaker.

"Who the heck are you supposed to be, Big Mack? This ain't Halloween … "

Even after many viewings, Yasmine watched the rest with great interest. Robert was a natural. And he did work well with the Dealmaker. Their styles contrasted, the Dealmaker gruff and earthy, Robert earnest and upbeat.

This is even more confirmation that Robert's going to make a lot of money. I see his fingerprints all over this promo. I bet it was his idea.

Last month, Foster Hyde, TeleShop's electronics buyer, introduced the Force Gauntlet. It happened at the weekly new products meeting that Yasmine always attended, bored. Nobody thought much about the game controller. Foster only bought it because of its extraordinary wholesale price. Quasar's offer hinged on purchasing all ten thousand units.

The Force Gauntlet sat in inventory for weeks. It was too much of a financial commitment to debut overnight. And none of the prime-time hosts understood how it worked.

This is genius. We should do more promos like this. We'll explain difficult products and set them up as introductory specials. And what are they airing at 2:00 p.m.? It's not that toy carpet cleaner, is it? If it is, I've gotta give them both credit; they've got balls.

The promo finished and the Dragon Lady reappeared on the set. Yasmine muted the volume. She ate some more of the shepherd's pie, noting her mood flattened its taste. Taking another sip of wine, Yasmine turned the sound back on and resumed watching *Top Gun*.

CHAPTER THIRTEEN

Robert MacKenzie

Saturday did not go well. Try as they might, they lacked product variety and quantity. Seven hundred fifty thousand dollars in sales was a fantasy. Robert and the Dealmaker had fun (or at least they made it look like they had fun). But, when 4:00 p.m. rolled around, their total stood at one hundred ninety-eight thousand dollars.

They sold out lots of items: The remaining Blue Blockers. The duck decoy telephone. The pig slippers. The Mountain Breeze air purifier. The Big Ear spy microphone and the Juicy Smoke food dehydrator. Still, it wasn't enough.

"Lookin' good there, *Dave*," said the Dragon Lady as she walked past the anchor desk, an evil smirk plastered on her face. She had arrived early and was preparing her Saturday show with great attention. "Oh and Big Mack—go fuck yourself!" The Dragon lady cackled like a witch from a fairy tale.

Stage left, the production staff had set up a giant display of closeout rings and chains for her show. The prices were amazing. The Dealmaker looked at Robert. Robert looked at the Dealmaker, and they both looked at the Dragon Lady. She lit up with a mug that could burn down forests.

Recognizing futility, they gave up. Halfway through their Saturday debacle, the pair started pushing their Sunday special. "Big Mack, why can't people tune in at 2:00 p.m. tomorrow?"

"I told you, Dealmaker. We messed up and don't have enough units. We can't clean enough carpets. Our friends should take a break. Make sure they're in line for the Force Gauntlet at 3:00 p.m."

"Who needs a clean carpet if you've got the Force Gauntlet?"

"Dealmaker, you do. I've been to your place. Your carpets are terrible. If you got the Force Gauntlet and had folks over to play games, how would it all look with dirty carpets?"

"Not great, I guess, Big Mack."

"Exactly. Folks, don't join us at 2:00 p.m. tomorrow unless you're prepared to lose out. But make sure you're around at 3:00 for the Force Gauntlet."

As they left the anchor desk, Alexandra McMurdo and Sandi Olver began hooking up. Sandi was a very tall brunette in her early thirties and known for her biting wit.

"What's it like out there, Dave?" Sandi asked.

Alexandra said a quick hello to Robert as the audio tech checked her wireless microphone.

"I've seen better," replied the Dealmaker. "There's an audience out there and they're prepared to buy, but we don't have a lot to sell. How's your show?"

Alexandra and Sandi glanced at each other and shrugged. "We're doing an hour of closeout fashion as our main feature at 7:00 p.m. What does that tell you?" asked Alexandra, her voice quiet and filled with frustration.

"Ouch," the Dealmaker replied. "Good luck."

The team left the production area, waving to the operators and headed to the prep room. In the meantime, the Dragon Lady zipped through the set. She adjusted her displays, gleeful with anticipated victory. Cordiality and modesty were not concepts she understood.

§

Robert MacKenzie

The Dragon Lady had a spectacular show. There was no margin in it, but everything sold like wildfire. Chain after chain and ring after ring blew out the door. The Dragon Lady milked the excitement like a skilled auctioneer. As one bangle went down, another popped up. The Dealmaker and Robert watched from the motel.

They didn't know Alexandra and Sandi's total. But the team would have been lucky to have hit one hundred thousand dollars.

"Mark, what's she at?" the Dealmaker asked, on the phone to the director. It was a few minutes before 11:00 p.m. and the Dragon Lady was in the last moments of her show. "Good God! Fuck me, but I'm impressed. Don't tell her that; I couldn't bear eating that much shit."

Turning, the Dealmaker hung up the phone and stared at Robert. "She's hit one million dollars."

"How good is that?"

"With what she had available and the quantities in stock, it's amazing. It's beyond amazing—it's remarkable. They were sending all that crap she got rid of for smelting. Billy-Ray will be in heaven."

"Do you think she'll get spiffed?" asked Robert, continuing his streak of naïve and uninformed questions.

The Dealmaker replied by shaking his head. His expression suggested Robert was a complete nitwit. Cracking a fresh can of Olde English, he lit up yet another Camel. "The moment Billy-Ray spiffed us, he spiffed the Dragon Lady. It would get ugly otherwise."

"Honest? Then why did Billy-Ray add me to the special spiff list?"

"Kid," the Dealmaker replied, looking frustrated, "for somebody so smart, you are so goddamn stupid!"

"I don't understand—"

"Shut up for a second. You're great on-air—a natural. I knew that after five minutes of co-hosting. You get that everything's a journey. Our customers don't buy products, they buy us. Your Force Gauntlet promo's outstanding. Your reverse-psychology ploy with the Houdini might not work, but it's a great idea regardless."

Robert listened to the Dealmaker, not expecting to feel so humbled. The day's revenue disappointment weighed him down. He wanted the fifteen-thousand-dollar spiff. Still, achieving the weekend's top sales motivated him almost as much.

"But when it comes to everything else, you're a blind man. Billy-Ray looks after his money the way Colonel Parker looked after Elvis. Yasmine and Sandiya both want you? Kid, you're a good-looking guy, but you're not Richard Gere. Why do you think they're all paying attention?"

Robert would have stammered an answer, but ended up looking doleful.

"Success! Women love success. Billy-Ray needs to meet our sales goal to get his full payout. You think he's going to let a few grand here and there stop him? Kid, you're in the right place at the right time. Go with it. Take the money and run."

Robert didn't say much in reply. The two hosts sat outside their rooms, finishing the evening's drinking. The Dealmaker consumed much less beer than usual (although he still smoked like a chimney). He wanted to beat the Dragon Lady's weekend sales and that desire kept his alcohol consumption in check.

By midnight, they gave up and each headed to bed. Robert lay under the sheets for a short while before drifting off into a troubled sleep.

§

Yasmine Dubai

With the Dragon Lady's show the great exception, Saturday was a bust. Yasmine arrived at TeleShop around 10:00 a.m. and spent most of the day running around, putting out fires. Much of the trouble was well beyond her control. Mary-Anne didn't make it in and Yasmine thought that strange. Very strange.

Carrie Hall co-hosted with Diamond Jim RamJet in the 9:00 a.m. to noon slot.

Carrie was a former TV weather girl from Fort Myers, Florida. Sunny and optimistic, like her home state, she was always a bright presence on-air. Her co-host, Diamond Jim, was neither. If forced to choose, Yasmine would have elected to spend time with Stan Hormel any day. Stan was eccentric. Diamond Jim was weird—the kind of guy women avoided, not knowing the exact reason why.

In the TeleShop sales hierarchy, the Dealmaker and the Dragon Lady were the King and Queen. Alexandra McMurdo was the Crown Princess. Carrie, Diamond Jim and a few others occupied space at the royal family's periphery. Everyone else fought for the crumbs left by their betters.

TeleShop functioned like some Ruritanian melodrama. Robert was the "pretender," threatening the old order. In reply, cliques and factions, gossip and plotting abounded. Snide comments and worried adulations reached Yasmine in the hallway. The production area. The executive offices. And even the toilet.

Last week, Cyd Steinberg had approached Yasmine while she was washing her hands in the ladies' room. "Hi, Yasmine."

Yasmine smiled, not wanting a lengthy conversation. It was the day after Robert's afternoon co-hosting.

"Robert sounded good. Will he be co-hosting more shows with the Dealmaker?" Cyd had asked.

Cyd was in her late thirties and had worked at TeleShop as a show host for three years. She was a local girl, married to a doctor who played drums part-time in Legend, an Alice Cooper tribute band. A better host than many, Cyd had nothing to fear from Robert MacKenzie. But, like most performers, there was always a lack of confidence buried deep within.

Frustrated and tired, Yasmine knew this and took cheap advantage.

"Hard to say, Cyd. We'll see how it goes," replied Yasmine. "Robert's definitely a man on the go. I'm happy to hear you thought he did a good job. I'll be sure to give your comments to Billy-Ray."

Cyd had forced a smile, dried her hands and left the lavatory. Yasmine turned away, entering the stall and shutting the door. She felt guilty about her offhand comment.

I shouldn't take my frustration out on Cyd. She's only curious about her position in the pecking order. The constant gossip is unyielding and exhausting, even if Cyd is one of the easier hosts. But making fatuous barbs isn't cool. I'm better than that.

She saw Robert from a distance, an hour before he went to air. He stood in production, next to the Dealmaker, talking to some crew members. The Dealmaker made a remark and the people around him lit up with laughter. Robert chuckled and turned toward the prep room, his eyes locking with Yasmine's.

He dipped his head. She offered a small smile in reply. As Robert raised his left hand, Yasmine responded with a quiet nod of her own. They held their gaze longer than necessary, both wanting to look away, but holding fast.

That is until Sandiya jumped in.

"Hey, Robert," said the lawyer, dressed with immaculate style. Sandiya wore a flowing black, pleated skirt with matching patent leather shoes. Her bishop-sleeved, forest-green blouse was satin, and open at the collar.

Great. What a lovely Saturday. I show up in jeans and a sweatshirt while Sandiya comes in like she just stepped out of a photo shoot.

Sandiya entered the production area and said hello to the crew. Pretending to see Yasmine for the first time, she affected a quick smile before moving to Robert and kissing him on the lips. The crew took immediate notice, as did Yasmine. She broke eye contact, turned and walked toward her office.

Entering, Yasmine sat down at her desk. She knew Billy-Ray was under no illusions about the weekend's challenges. The Customs seizure and inventory difficulties created intractable problems. Yasmine's presence that weekend was more symbolic than anything else.

Lounging in her office, Yasmine placed her feet on the desk. She remembered, with a nostalgic tinge, the night with Robert in the prep room.

Yasmine turned her TV to the live production feed. On screen, a crew member set up a display while speaking to the director over headset. Yasmine didn't pay a lot of attention. She looked over inventory reports and planned to leave around 2:00 p.m.

In the background, at the set's far corner, Robert conversed with Sandiya. Yasmine couldn't hear what they said. The only sound came from crew chatter and production directions. But it didn't matter. She didn't need to be a lip reader to recognize the couple's body language.

Sandiya put her hand in Robert's and spoke into his ear. At the same moment, Susie walked past, carrying an upcoming product.

"Susie, tell Big Mack we need him at the anchor desk," said John.

"Got it," she replied, approaching the couple. Susie passed the message and walked back toward the display, a big smile etched on her face.

"Susie-Q," asked Angela over the headset. "What's up?"

"I shouldn't say. It's dirty," Susie announced. She waited for the inevitable pleading.

"So, spill!" insisted Angela.

"Go to Channel B," Susie responded.

There were two wireless channels for production staff. Channel A was for general talk with Channel B restricted to floor crew. Yasmine had access to both and switched over at the same time.

"Remember how Big Mack and Sandiya were at Lucky Charm last week?"

"Of course, how could anyone forget?"

"Well, they didn't see me approach at first. Sandiya said in Robert's ear, and I quote: 'Drop by my office after you get off-air and I'll suck your cock.'"

"What the fuck!" said Angela. "Serious?"

"Serious. Sandiya knew I heard but didn't care. I don't think Big Mack knows."

The two crew members tittered away, but Yasmine had stopped listening. She turned off the TV, grabbed her wallet, and left the office. Enough was enough. She may well have made her own bed, but wallowing in it was another matter.

Mary-Anne directed Yasmine to work on Sunday. But if problems did appear at this stage, there was nothing to do. All Yasmine could hope for was the best possible income with the least possible trouble.

She couldn't fathom why Mary-Anne chose not to come in. With all the issues of late it should have been a no brainer. Something was up. Mary-Anne was as devious as always and Sandiya was making a big play. Its nature wasn't clear, but it wasn't nothing.

While Yasmine was not one to cut and run, between Oklahoma City, Mary-Anne, Robert, and Sandiya, she was at her limit. Yasmine might answer Manhattan's call sooner rather than later. If not with TeleShop, then with somebody else.

§

Robert MacKenzie

Robert had never had a problem with women speaking their truth. And what man ever said no to oral sex? He should have looked forward to dropping by Sandiya's office after the show.

He had been to her condo twice and they'd had aggressive sex both times. Subtlety was not Sandiya's strength. When he'd arrived at her condo, she offered Robert a drink. He parked himself on the living room sofa and Sandiya handed over a beer and collapsed into the couch opposite. Within seconds, she had hiked up her skirt, displaying her fuchsia thong.

"Would it be better if I took off my panties?" she had asked, before removing them and throwing them on the carpet. "That's better. I hope you don't mind."

He hadn't. Sandiya was animalistic when it came to — fucking. He was going to say "making love" but that wasn't accurate. A mixture of raw fury with undertones of real violence was more apropos. Rage sat beneath her exterior that threatened to erupt at any time. Sandiya was very pretty, very smart, very trim, and very, very angry. Robert found it all disquieting. For a man to even consider rejecting the rapacity of a beautiful woman was beyond the pale. Yet, the thought always hovered about whenever they were together.

He made yet another comparison between Yasmine and Sandiya.

They each possessed lithe, taut bodies with electric eyes. Formidable intellect and driving ambition. Both women were as out of place in Oklahoma City as possible. Yet, in spite of Yasmine's icy demeanor, it was Yasmine who sparkled. At least to him.

As much as he liked the lawyer's attention—and as much as he realized it was over before it began with Yasmine—he wasn't going to take advantage of Sandiya's offer. And it was going to get ugly. Robert didn't realize how ugly it was going to get.

Besides, it was time to stop thinking with his dick and start thinking with his heart.

Nice words, but dangerous ones. Robert had more than an inkling of Sandiya's fiery temperament. It was an intrinsic component of her personality. In any case, what woman ever took rejection well? None did. Ever.

There was no time to reflect upon life's existential crises. Not when you were on-air, behind the eight ball and desperate to pull a rabbit out of a hat. Sandi and Alexandra's total from yesterday was one hundred seven thousand dollars. Against their massive target it was a major embarrassment. Robert stood next to the Dealmaker, pitching like crazy during their first hour.

"Big Mack, did you hear Dixie blew out all the jewelry last night?" the Dealmaker announced on-air. He said running away from a competitor's great sales made you look weak. Instead, embrace them and make yourself part of their success.

"I did, Dealmaker. Is there anything left?" asked Robert.

"Not much. Look at what we did Saturday. Sell out after sell out. This weekend is nuts. Are you ready for the Force Gauntlet?"

"I'm ready. We've been getting calls since last week. It's going to sell out," said Robert with the air of a practiced professional. He may have only worked at TeleShop since June, but had picked up the swagger without trouble.

"When I saw you demo the product," continued the Dealmaker, "I couldn't believe it. How'd we get such a great deal?"

"Dealmaker, I don't know. Somebody upstairs likes us."

His partner let off a huge laugh, smiling with glee and looking into the camera. He clapped Robert on the back. "Hey, I heard the carpet guys were in here last night. We got more stock?"

"Dealmaker, you shouldn't tell everybody. We now have every last unit available in the entire country and it's still not enough."

"Big Mack, ya gotta tell me how many we got and how much? Friends, you think I'm kidding. I'm not. Big Mack has kept this item close to his chest. I'm as in the dark as you."

Robert made a knowing smile. He looked left and then right, holding up a single finger to the camera and whispering into the Dealmaker's ears.

"Wow! That's half price. We got six thousand? Thank God. We're going to be okay."

"Dealmaker, we're not okay. The calls for our carpet cleaner have been insane. Everybody wants to know the model and price. It's so inexpensive, Billy-Ray is limiting our time on it."

"What! Why is Billy-Ray doing that?" asked the Dealmaker, playing the role like he was on Broadway.

"It's too cheap. Let's say we ruffled some feathers when we bought up the entire country's inventory and then cut the price in half."

The Dealmaker and Robert kept plugging away at their carpet cleaner without relent. During every break they'd show the Force Gauntlet promo and comment afterward. At this point, their sales stalled. Nobody bought regular merchandise. Even callers to air only wanted to talk about their upcoming featured specials.

As they moved into the 2:00 p.m. break, their total stood at a meager eighty-five thousand dollars.

"Friends," said the Dealmaker, "we'll be right back with some magic. Don't miss it."

The tally light over the camera turned off. "We're out. Guys, you have two minutes. I hope this works," John Duguay said through the intercom.

Robert prayed for a miracle.

§

The Dealmaker

"Listen up, everyone," the Dealmaker announced, speaking to the entire crew. "If Robert and I blow out the Houdini and the Force Gauntlet, drinks are on us. We'll buy all the booze and food you want at Lucky Charm next weekend. What do you say?"

The crew cheered and applauded. While the Dragon Lady may have been a great salesman, she never had the backing of the crew or the operators. It made a difference. Not always an obvious one, but a real one nonetheless.

The camera went live. Robert sat next to the Dealmaker at the anchor desk. A crew member had placed the Houdini Carpet Magician in front of them. Its garish yellow and red plastic shell didn't impress.

"Big Mack, I gotta tell ya, this magician contraption looks like a toy." In the background, several of the crew suppressed a laugh.

"Dealmaker, you're right. When I first looked at the darn thing, it did not blow me away, either. But when I watched Houdini's live demonstration, I couldn't believe what I saw." In fact, the live demo had never happened. Robert hadn't worked at TeleShop long enough to have seen it.

"John, roll the video," said the Dealmaker.

An image appeared of a woman standing on a carpet encrusted with all manner of filth. The "toy" gurgled and beeped, ground and groaned as it cleaned. Steam popped out of its top. Lights flashed along its sides. It resembled something out of an old folk song by Peter, Paul and Mary. If nothing else, the promo captured a sense of drama. In the background, carnival music played as the woman danced about on the now clean carpet.

Standing without warning, the Dealmaker jumped from the anchor desk. "John, play my theme music," he told the director. "Angela, Susie, follow me. Big Mack, what the heck are you doin'? It's time for a conga line. Everybody R-H-U-M-B-A!"

The audio tech brought up some Caribbean-style dance music. Robert didn't know what was happening but followed along, joining the Dealmaker. They bounced around the set with assorted crew members and operators.

John pulled a camera off its tripod and followed the dancers. They moved out of production and into the operator area.

The Dealmaker began singing. *"It cleans your carpets one by one (Hey)! It cleans your carpets with such fun (Hey)! If you don't buy what's on your screen (Hey)! You'll never get your carpets clean (Hey)!"*

Within a few minutes, he had all the operators joining in. When it came time for the "Hey!" the whole building shook. Robert looked toward the incoming call monitors. They shot upward.

"Friends," said the Dealmaker at the head of the conga line, "this is half the normal retail price and we have the entire nation's inventory. Six thousand units, only a hundred bucks a pop. Don't say Big Mack and I didn't warn you. See the calls? It's blowing up. You know what I always say, 'You snooze, you lose!'"

The Dealmaker went back to singing and dancing. He bumped about with half the studio joining him at the hip. *"It cleans your carpets one by one (Hey)! It cleans your carpets with such fun (Hey)! If you don't buy what's on your screen (Hey)! You'll never get your carpets clean (Hey)!"*

At fifteen minutes before 3:00 p.m., the Houdini sold out, and TeleShop went to break.

§

Robert MacKenzie

"Dealmaker, why didn't you tell me about the conga line?" asked Robert, breathless and excited.

Before the Houdini, their show stood at eighty-five thousand dollars. Now, with the blow out, they were at six hundred eighty-five thousand dollars in gross revenue. The fifteen-thousand-dollar spiff with its new digs, new car, and new life beckoned.

"Had to keep you on your toes, kid. With that kind of loot on the line, did ya think I didn't know what was goin' on?" They walked back to the anchor desk. The conga crowd dispersed after everyone gave each other a big round of applause. "I guarantee Dixie is shitting herself. She knows we're going to destroy this Force Gauntlet. We are going to sell it out, right, kid? I *need* the cash!"

"Dealmaker, no *bout adout it.*"

Robert sat down with the Dealmaker at the anchor desk as he howled in reply. Susie counted them in.

"Big Mack, it's time for our main feature. I gotta tell ya, in my five years here, I have *never* seen this kind of interest before in a product we're offering. We've been getting people trying to pre-order it all week. Folks, I am *not* kidding. Our competition in the TV shopping game isn't happy. Everybody wants a piece of the Force Gauntlet. What are we going to do?"

Robert looked at the incoming call monitors and gasped. The screen displayed an error message. He turned to the Dealmaker with confusion, who stared back, shocked. He looked at the camera and spoke in a very subdued way.

"If you're wondering why Big Mack looks so amazed, it's because our incoming call screen is down. I've only seen that happen once before. It was two years ago when Dixie and I did back-to-back jewelry extravaganzas over Christmas. Big Mack, we're getting so many inbound calls it's knocked out our system."

The Dealmaker gave the information, flat, without any bluster. Robert stared as the Dealmaker nodded. He looked over at their dollars per minute. It climbed like a rocket.

Five thousand dollars per minute.

Eight thousand dollars per minute.

Twelve thousand dollars per minute.

Fifteen thousand dollars per minute.

"Jesus," the Dealmaker said on-air. Cursing wasn't allowed, ever. Nobody noticed. Robert stared beyond the cameras at the operators. Everyone typed away at their order consoles, the air crackling with pure energy.

The crew had set up the Force Gauntlet's display. But they now stood around it, staring in wonder. The operators were so busy there was nothing else to do. They didn't need extra shots or hype.

On screen, Robert and the Dealmaker occupied a window in the upper left corner. A closeup of the controller filled the rest of the screen. In the lower right corner appeared a counter. It started at one thousand and raced up higher and higher and higher.

Robert looked to their sales screen. It had maxed out at twenty-two thousand dollars per minute. Tapping the Dealmaker's shoulder, he pointed. His partner glanced over and shook his head, their actions visible to all viewers. It was this reaction of pure honesty that fueled their sales even higher. TeleShop's customers knew that constant hype was part of the game. This complete lack of hype sold the product. It wasn't something they'd seen before.

"Big Mack, ya gotta watch this because you won't see it again. Friends, this product is as gone as gone can be. It's now a formality. We're taking orders as fast as we can. If you're in the queue you have a chance. But only if you're already on the phone. I'm going to say something you've never heard me say before, but I mean it. Don't bother calling us. You won't get a Force Gauntlet. I'm sorry. There is no way. Robert, any chance for more of these?" The Dealmaker asked in earnest for what may have been the only time in history.

"No, Dealmaker," Robert answered with calm measure. "They're a closeout. The Force Gauntlet was so ahead of its time Quasar didn't know how to sell it. Its original retail price was too high. This deal we have today is extraordinary. Ladies and gentlemen, I'm sorry if you miss out. I am. We're going to go to a promo. When we come back we'll finish the show with our remaining Independence Day specials."

John cut to their Force Gauntlet video. It was 3:17 p.m. Eastern Time and there was nothing more to do. At some point within the next twenty minutes, the Force Gauntlet would sell out. Robert and the Dealmaker would go through the formality of ending their show.

Their weekend's revenue came to one million eight hundred eighty-three thousand dollars. "The Dragon Lady?" asked Robert, suggesting their success may have affected her mood.

"The strain might be too much for her," chuckled the Dealmaker in reply.

They both laughed and waited for an opportune time to go back on air.

"Johnny-man," said the Dealmaker through the intercom. "How much does your band charge for a private concert? Tell your friends at

Lucky Charm that Big Mack and I will pay your appearance fee and buy all the drinks for the crew. Choose a night!"

The crew applauded as the Dealmaker smiled. Looking at him, Robert thought it the most genuine and peaceful look he'd seen on his friend since they had met.

CHAPTER FOURTEEN

Sandiya King

When the show ended, Sandiya waited in her office, watching the production monitor. It showed the Dealmaker and Robert leaving the set as the operators applauded. Both hosts smiled and thanked everyone for their hard work. The Dragon Lady's absence brought home their triumph. The Queen of Home Shopping couldn't even bring herself to swear at them.

Sandiya watched Robert say something to his partner. With a knowing smile, the Dealmaker walked toward the parking lot. Robert headed to the legal department.

For much of the afternoon, Sandiya had spied on their show and masturbated. Her panties sat on top of her desk. She didn't consider Robert so much as her new career and what she'd do to Cliff Johnson when they got together. Sandiya couldn't comprehend any problem with her thinking.

When the show ended, she got up and unbolted the door. Leaning back in the chair, her legs on her desk, she waited for Robert. After a few minutes, there was a knock.

"Come in," Sandiya said with practiced innocence. Robert entered, shutting the door behind him and looking at Sandiya. She touched herself, her skirt hiked up, her blouse open. "How can I be of help?"

From his initial expression, Sandiya knew something was up. He wore a small, apologetic smile. Robert didn't stare between Sandiya's legs. Moments after his arrival, she pulled down her skirt and sat up in the chair.

"What the fuck is wrong?" she asked, holding down her anger as best she could.

"Sandiya," he replied with artificial calm. The buzz coming off the show, knowing they'd destroyed their target and earned their spiff, was hard to hold down. "I don't think we should continue. I like you and you're very smart and pretty —"

"Shouldn't fucking continue?" she yelled. "How dare you, you broken-down high school dropout. I made law review at the University of Chicago. *You* want to stop seeing *me*? Go fuck yourself. You're lucky I even considered fucking you!"

"Sandiya, that's the trouble. You're very sexy and pretty. And yes, you're very smart. But you're also the angriest woman I've ever met. No, make that the angriest person I've ever met. There's always this torrent of violence beneath your surface. It's off-putting."

"You think you can throw me over for that cunt, Yasmine Dubai? Fuck you and your whore!"

"I'm not involved with Yasmine," said Robert. "What gave you that idea?"

"Do you think I'm a goddamn fool? I see the way you look at her. And I see the way she looks at you. You're not involved now, but you want to be. You're not getting rid of me to bang that slut."

Her face burned crimson. She stood up, her eyes narrowed and focused on Robert.

"Get out of my office," she fumed, her syllables clipped and stressed.

"Mr. MacKenzie, we'll readdress the issue of your employment after I've had time to investigate your résumé further. I found elements of it 'off-putting.'"

With cold and malignant wrath, Sandiya stared him down as Robert said nothing. He turned about and left the office with as much self-assurance as he could muster. Sandiya remained standing, ire holding her in its grip.

She saw her father again in the corner of the room. He bore his constant look of disappointment. The only time he ever smiled was at night, when her mother was asleep. When he would enter her bedroom to talk and relate stories. And more. Much more.

§

Mary-Anne Warner

"Cliff, what do you want me to do? We had the Force Gauntlet in stock *before* you told me to tank sales."

It was Sunday evening and Mary-Anne was at home watching TeleShop. The Dragon Lady was on-air trying to repeat her Saturday success. While she wasn't going to hit those extreme numbers, products still flew out the door. It was more a quantity issue than anything else. The lack of inventory was the limiting factor.

"Mary-Anne, I have no idea what you're talking about. I *never* said you should 'tank' sales." Cliff Johnson paused for a moment allowing his words to sink in. Mary-Anne understood his meaning. "Pardon me, Cliff. I misspoke."

"Thank you," he replied, his unemotional flatness imbued, as always, with a hint of the sinister.

"But you need to help me out. I can't *unschedule* products. Billy-Ray wouldn't allow it, and besides, it would give away my hand."

"What about the carpet cleaner?"

"It's the identical problem. Houdini shipped it at the same time as your—I mean *my*—product boycott. They're an independent company and came direct, without a distributor. You don't have a lot leverage over them."

"Does the product have legs?" asked Cliff. "Will TeleShop buy more, and is there inventory available?"

"I don't know; the host spiels are all about hyperbole. Both the Force Gauntlet and the Houdini were Robert MacKenzie's idea. I hired him. He's displayed more native talent than anyone else I've seen," boasted Mary-Anne. Until last month improving sales was her job. This new role left her troubled.

"Perhaps his future at TeleShop isn't as bright as appearances suggest," said Cliff with his typical quiet tension. He didn't mention receiving a call from Sandiya a few hours before.

"What do you mean?" asked Mary-Anne, shocked.

"*Please*, Mary-Anne, stop pretending! As for Houdini, something tells me they might become a part of the Triboro family soon. Remember, deal with MacKenzie. His success is now a liability. I know you understand. Goodbye, Mary-Anne."

The line went dead. While hanging up was typical Cliff, his use of "Goodbye" versus "Goodnight" did not augur well.

Am I going to be the fall guy? Christ, what the hell am I supposed to do? He wants me to fire Robert? Why? Billy-Ray would never allow it. Cliff possessed information he shouldn't have had. Am I their only plant?

Mary-Anne wouldn't put anything past the Triboro boss. Nothing at all.

§

Robert MacKenzie

"Y'all know how much I appreciate what you did for us over the weekend," said a gleeful Billy-Ray. He stood in his office, next to Robert and the Dealmaker. Billy-Ray's blank-eyed secretary chewed gum while holding two, small bags. "You two work great together. A conga line? Jesus, I damn near thought I was gonna shit myself, I laughed so hard. Dave, that was your idea?"

"It might have been," replied the Dealmaker. A gigantic grin spread across his Monday morning face. "But the whole carpet cleaning thing was Robert. As was the Force Gauntlet. I gotta say, Billy-Ray, the kid's a natural."

"Thanks, Dealmaker. I appreciate your support."

Robert couldn't believe how much his life had changed over the course of a month. Knowing they'd get their spiff, he had called Delroy in Phoenix and offered him five hundred dollars if he cleaned out his apartment. Delroy could keep whatever he wanted and dispose of what he didn't. Robert would courier the keys to his former colleague later today or tomorrow.

"Honest, keep whatever you want. Throw the rest in the trash and give the landlord his keys. Oh and tell Gadberry and the guys at the office to go fuck themselves. I'll include a money order for the five hundred with the courier," Robert had told Delroy.

He'd meant to go back to Phoenix himself and take care of his apartment, but nothing he owned was worth anything. Any keepsakes from his childhood were with his mother. Best to make a clean start.

"Boys," said Billy-Ray, pulling Robert back to the present. "As promised, here's another token of my appreciation." He nodded at his secretary, who handed each host a bag. Robert didn't know if it was polite to look inside. The Dealmaker didn't care and opened his right away.

"Billy-Ray, this is twenty grand, not fifteen."

"Dave, I spiffed you and Robert on the Force Gauntlet. But that damn idea with the carpet thing was genius. It brought in six hundred thousand dollars at fifty points margin." TeleShop's president looked at Robert. "Go ahead son. Open the bag."

Robert peered inside. It contained two stacks of one-hundred-dollar bills. Ten thousand dollars per stack, twenty thousand dollars in total. He felt faint.

"I may be tight with money when it comes to operational costs, but I've always paid my talent well. Y'all know I'm up near the end of my ownership. I won't give you a specific number now, but if you help me hit the strike price, I plan to be generous. Very generous. Say nothing to nobody. Dixie will be part of this as well, but don't say nothin' to her neither."

"Dixie, who?" said Robert with faux innocence.

Billy-Ray and the Dealmaker broke out in laughter. The secretary remained motionless, standing in place, chewing gum.

"Go see Yasmine after you leave," Billy-Ray said to Robert. "She's going to talk to you about some schedule changes."

"Yes, sir," he replied. Robert looked toward the Dealmaker, who smiled.

"Robert, I'll see you in a bit. I've got to talk with Billy-Ray and grab my show."

"No problem, Dealmaker; thanks again, Billy-Ray." Robert walked out of the office and headed toward Yasmine's. He hoped she would be in and at the same time hoped that she wouldn't.

Mary-Anne walked past on the way to her own office. "Great job on the weekend, Robert," she said with a certain flatness and lack of passion.

Robert thanked her, noting her manner and speech.

At the risk of sounding arrogant, I did help save the weekend. What's up?

Arriving at Yasmine's open door, he knocked on the wall. She sat at her desk, dressed in a tailored, pleated silk blouse in cream. Her jacket hung on the coat rack next to her desk. He couldn't see if she wore slacks or a skirt, but found it interesting how much he cared.

"Come in, Mr. MacKenzie. Please close the door behind you." Yasmine spoke with little emotion, flat with an undercurrent of anger. He would have sloughed off the "Mr. MacKenzie" comment, thinking she was making a joke. But she wasn't.

"Yasmine, what's going on?" he asked, confused.

"Let's stick to Ms. Dubai, shall we?" Again, that same murmur of resentment leavened her words.

Robert sat down at her desk. He carried the bag of money in his hands, but resisted the impulse to let her see.

"Billy-Ray has asked you move to Show #8 on Mondays, Tuesdays and Wednesdays right away. As today is Monday, you can take the day off and show up at 5:00 p.m. tomorrow for your first shift's prep. You'll also be co-hosting with the Dealmaker every Saturday and Sunday on Show #5 in July. We've promoted you from probationary show host to regular show host. Effective today, you are no longer an hourly employee. You're on salary at thirty-five thousand dollars per year. You will also become eligible for TeleShop's executive health plan."

A month ago, he labored overnight in a condominium's security office. He made six dollars and seventy-five cents per hour and had no real health insurance to speak of. His new salary was two and a half times his old. Plus, he carried a bag with twenty grand in cash. It was as if he lived another's life.

Regardless, Yasmine's cool exterior gave him pause.

"Thank you, so much," he said. His words were formal, not reflecting his feelings toward Yasmine.

"Don't thank me. Thank Billy-Ray. We're done. I appreciate your dropping by."

The abruptness of his dismissal hung in the air. Yasmine sat at her desk, looking at him. She either couldn't or didn't care to hide the hostility in her eyes.

"Yasmine. What the hell is wrong?"

"Nothing's wrong, Mr. MacKenzie. Whatever gives you that idea?"

"Don't play coy. Something's wrong and you damn well know it. Please, tell me. What have I done?"

"You haven't done anything. I'm your boss and we've had a meeting. Did you expect that something else might happen?"

"Excuse me?"

"We're in my office alone with the door shut. What exactly were you hoping for? That I'd offer to suck your cock?"

Robert didn't know how Yasmine knew about Sandiya's proposition. Besides her anger, her face displayed hurt. It didn't matter if their non-starting romance was her idea, he drew no satisfaction from Yasmine's pain.

"Well, this is quite the moment. I'm moving up in my career and have also managed to upset two women at the same time."

§

Yasmine Dubai

Yasmine's face changed with a momentary flash of indecision. She asked what he meant without actually saying anything.

"Yes, I was in Sandiya's office after I got off-air yesterday," he began without actual prodding. "And yes, she wanted to 'suck my cock,' if I'm to be blunt. But I declined."

Yasmine stared at him, her expression telling him to continue.

"I meant what I said on our date. But what did you expect I was going to do when you said we couldn't see each other? Become a monk?

Was I supposed to tell Sandiya I wasn't interested?"

Yasmine knew that jealousy, not logic, drove her reaction. She couldn't help herself.

"Did you have to move on so quickly?" she asked. "And of all the women in the world, why date the only other Middle Eastern executive at TeleShop?"

"Yasmine, it's not like women are knocking down my door all the time. Sandiya is very pretty and she's a lawyer. It was flattering."

"So why did you tell her no?"

"I don't think she likes me that much. I mean, yes, she likes me to some degree. But it's more of what I represent than who I am. Look, I'm not trying to sound supercilious. I told you, I want something more than sex. I want to fall in love."

Yasmine felt foolish. Jealousy was never pretty. She couldn't blame Robert; he hadn't done anything wrong. She was the one who stopped their burgeoning relationship. If relationships were all about logic, life would be a lot easier.

"You told her you didn't want a blowjob?"

"Yes. I also said we should stop seeing each other."

Yasmine looked at Robert with shocked curiosity, unbelieving. His comment was not at all expected. Instead, Yasmine figured Robert would do what men always did—dissemble. His directness and earnestness caught her off-guard.

"How did she react?" she asked, sounding confused, verging on the defensive.

"Were you here when the guy went nuts at the post office in Edmond last year?"

"I was in the process of moving."

"Kinda like that except she didn't have a gun."

Yasmine couldn't help but laugh, which was a welcome change to her mood of late. She loved his wit — very much. In any man it was sexy. With Robert, it was a key part of his charm.

"I'm sorry. I *do* like you a lot. You already know that's the problem. I'm jealous and shouldn't be. But your weekend success reinforces my reasons for not wanting to get involved," Yasmine said.

"So, we're back where we started?" Robert asked, his voice ending on an up-note.

"More or less," she replied, standing up and walking out from behind her desk. "We'll see," she continued, approaching Robert with a seductive gait. Yasmine wore black, pleated slacks that moved with grace against her legs.

Standing in front of Robert, she looked up. Robert brought his lips to hers and kissed her, drawing Yasmine's tongue into his mouth. She felt for his right hand and placed it onto her breast, squeezing his hand against hers. He felt her bosom's plush and hardening nipple.

Robert pulled into Yasmine into him, allowing his left hand to slide down her backside. She raised her leg against his and moved her body in concert.

This time, Yasmine broke it off.

"We'll talk later. Not in my office," stated Yasmine.

Robert inhaled her perfume and kissed the side of her face. "Will you call me tonight?" His intonation made the question more of a demand.

"Yes."

"Good," Robert said with satisfaction. Turning, he adjusted himself and went to open the door. Yasmine broke out with a playful chuckle at watching him straighten his pants.

"Because of me?" she asked, the rancor finally gone from her voice.

Robert raised his eyebrow and said nothing. He opened the door and left the office.

§

Yasmine Dubai

Hours later, Sandiya walked past Yasmine's office and poked her head in. "Yasmine, we need to see Mary-Anne, right away."

Sitting at her desk, Yasmine still felt the warmth of her brief time with Robert. She had no idea what the lawyer wanted. They'd never had a joint meeting with Mary-Anne before.

"What's going on?" she asked, perplexed. An air of foreboding surrounded the question.

"A HR issue has come up that requires immediate addressing."

Yasmine got up from her desk and followed Sandiya the short distance to Mary-Anne's office. The coincidence of Robert and Sandiya's clash from yesterday could not be accidental.

Mary-Anne looked up as Sandiya knocked. Yasmine followed inside. From her expression, it was clear Mary-Anne knew what was about to happen. The room's atmosphere reflected an unspecific tension. She indicated the pair should sit. Yasmine did so while Sandiya closed the door.

"Yasmine, Sandiya asked to meet right away. She called a few minutes ago and needs to go over a recent discovery." Mary-Anne nodded toward the lawyer.

"You've changed Robert MacKenzie's status. He's no longer a probationary, hourly employee. He's a regular, salaried employee. I tried to confirm his references, and they don't exist. I need to understand what happened during the hiring process. As Mr. MacKenzie is a public face of our organization, we're required to confirm his background."

Mary-Anne looked at Yasmine to explain the omission. As it was Mary-Anne who said the Dealmaker's résumé was almost a "novel," the hypocrisy made her want to wretch.

"The Triboro people were here during the interview. We also had an urgent need for new hosts; we must have forgotten," said Yasmine with a clear and unapologetic tone.

"Forgotten?" asked Mary-Anne. "How could that have happened?"

"You didn't know?" Sandiya questioned. "You're vice president; talent is your responsibility."

Sandiya's endgame was obvious and Mary-Anne knew it. Her boss was about to throw her under the bus in favor of her own career. Whether Robert had a future was still up in the air. Yasmine could have claimed Mary-Anne knew all about hiring exigencies. But that would only have served to embarrass Mary-Anne. Yasmine would still require a reference if she needed a new job.

"No, I assumed Yasmine took care of it. She's the Director of Talent and responsible for HR issues related to the show hosts."

"Yasmine," said Sandiya, holding back her malevolence and triumph, "you've admitted you didn't check references as required. This is a direct endangerment of our buyout agreement with Triboro. Do you have anything else to say?"

"No," Yasmine stated her point with restraint. If today was to be her Waterloo, she would meet her fate with dignity.

Mary-Anne looked to Sandiya and then to Yasmine. "Yasmine, please give Sandiya and me the room. Wait for us in your office."

Yasmine left and walked back to her own. She'd had enough of the job—and Mary-Anne—a long time ago, but she couldn't abide failure, and getting fired for something she didn't do was inconceivable.

She walked into her office and sat down behind her desk. Then she grabbed a banker's box and started packing.

§

Billy-Ray Newton

Mary-Anne sat with Sandiya in Billy-Ray's office. He'd told his secretary to leave them alone as he stared with fury at the pair.

"Y'all fired Yasmine?" he stated with utter contempt and disbelief.

"Yes, sir," said Mary-Anne. "Sandiya brought to my attention a serious breach of protocol on Yasmine's part. It was our only option."

Sandiya sat in the chair next to the vice president as Mary-Anne related the details. Billy-Ray found it difficult to imagine the degree of their naïve, unbridled stupidity.

"Sir," said Sandiya. "As corporate counsel—"

"Assistant corporate counsel," interjected Billy-Ray. "Where the hell is Fluxgold?"

"He's not feeling well today," said Sandiya, beginning to understand her actual position.

"No, I don't imagine he is. Tell me, is that asshole in Oklahoma or is he still in Vegas?"

"Sir, I don't know."

"Did you run this past him?" asked Billy-Ray, his fiery eyes burning into the lawyer.

"No, sir."

"Mary-Anne, are you telling me Yasmine's already gone?"

"Yes, Billy-Ray. Hank escorted her from the building an hour ago. Sandiya drew up the paperwork. In exchange for three months' severance and a good reference, Yasmine resigned."

"And all this because she didn't check MacKenzie's references?"

"Yes, Billy-Ray," said Mary-Anne.

"Do you two idiots understand that none of the host's references check out? Especially the good ones? Mary-Anne, I know you get it. What in the name of Christ is going on? The truth, please."

Mary-Anne appeared uncomfortable. She squirmed in her chair, unable or unwilling to answer.

Sandiya took over, speaking with her best lawyer's voice. "Sir, our buyout agreement with Triboro has an exit clause. Discrepancies in the background of key personnel are grounds for its termination. As hosts are de facto public representatives of the company, they're considered 'key.'"

Billy-Ray sat at his desk, shaking his head, unable to comprehend this level of imbecility. "You two are as crazy as a sprayed roach. I assume we can't get Yasmine back?"

"No, sir," said Sandiya. "It would expose us to liability."

"Billy-Ray, this is only one half of our problem." Mary-Anne interrupted her boss. She understood what she'd done by throwing in her lot with Sandiya. Since Mary-Anne came as part of the buyout agreement, Billy-Ray couldn't fire her. But he could make her job disappear, leaving her with nothing to do.

"Come again?" asked the very disgruntled president.

"Robert MacKenzie ...," said Mary-Anne.

"What about him?"

"Since we've asked for Ms. Dubai's resignation, we need to look at dismissing Mr. MacKenzie as well. He lied on his application." Mary-Anne looked to Sandiya, who nodded in agreement.

Billy-Ray's mouth opened agape. His color turned dark and he began speaking with a distinctive and dangerous cadence.

"You two fools listen to me," he began. "Yasmine's a done deal. While I'm very unhappy, it's over. But under *no* circumstances will we fire Robert MacKenzie."

"But, sir," interrupted Sandiya, "this exposes us to liability."

"Miss King, don't interrupt me. Not ever! I don't give a flying fuck about liability. Don't think I didn't notice the way you parachuted into your job and took over the legal department. Nat's a lazy fool, but he bent over for a reason. Y'all understand you're TeleShop's corporate counsel?"

"Yes, sir."

"You admitted to any other bar than Oklahoma?"

"No, sir."

"Do you two think I'm stupid? I mean what I say. Do you believe I managed to get financing for this network by accident?"

The two women sat in front of Billy-Ray, chastened. Sandiya recognized her hot-blooded play was not going as planned.

"Miss King, you graduated at the top of your class from the University of Chicago. I know why Mary-Anne's here. What the hell brought you to our low-rent operation?"

Sandiya had no answer.

"When you showed up, I asked our outside counsel about you."

"Outside counsel, sir? I didn't know we had outside counsel."

"I know. Y'all want to know what he told me?" Billy-Ray proceeded without waiting. He reached into his desk's lower right drawer and removed a single sheet of paper. "Section 1.8(b) of our state bar's 'Rules of Professional Conduct' says: 'A lawyer shall not use information relating to the representation of a client to the disadvantage of the client."

Sandiya's face turned red. It took all her effort not to lose her composure. Looking at Billy-Ray, she knew no bribe, either sexual or monetary, would stop whatever plans he had.

"Mary-Anne, please get out of here and go back to doing whatever it is you do. And I don't want Triboro getting wind of this meeting. Y'all get what I'm sayin'?"

"Yes, sir, I reckon I do," said Mary-Anne, her upset visible, but thankful she could leave. She didn't notice the Southern twang that slipped into her speech. Without even a quick glance at Sandiya, she fled the office in a hurry.

Afterward, Billy-Ray stared at the lawyer with controlled anger. "Now, listen to me. As of this moment, you're going to relate whatever bullshit you hear from Triboro to me. I don't care how you do it; that's your problem. If you don't, consider yourself fired. I'll have our outside counsel file an ethics complaint with the Oklahoma Bar Association. Miss King, y'all get yourself disbarred in Oklahoma. You'll never get called to any other state bar in this US of A. Ya feel me?"

"Yes, sir," replied Sandiya. Billy-Ray got the idea that for the first time in a long while, she knew legitimate fear. Not fright born of paranoia or existential rage, but honest distress over her actions.

"You're done here. Continue with your boilerplate legal stuff and don't make any waves. If you play ball until this buyout's complete, you can do whatever you want. Stay. Leave. Change careers. I don't give a damn. As long as you do, I'll take my cash and retire. If you don't … Do we have an understanding?"

"Yes, sir."

"Good. Now get the hell out of my office and don't darken it again."

Sandiya stood up and hustled out. Billy-Ray leaned back in his chair, an indignant scowl carved on his face.

§

Robert MacKenzie

Robert sat outside his room drinking beer with the Dealmaker. It was late afternoon. For reasons unknown to either, they'd moderated their consumption.

"Dixie's going to push a mighty log when she hears we're co-hosting on weekends this month," said the Dealmaker. He raised his eyebrows in a sly arch while farting into the breeze. "And we won the weekend's sales!"

"Was it close?"

"Yup. You already know we hit one million eight hundred eighty-three thousand dollars. Dixie did one million seven hundred ninety-seven thousand dollars. Also, our margin was sixty percent. Dixie may have done an incredible job, but most of her products had negative margins. She finished off at five percent."

"Who's gonna co-host with the Dragon Lady?"

"Co-host? Are you kidding? Dixie hates co-hosts. Besides, nobody wants to co-host with her anyway. She resents that we get to do something she can't. And don't go on about the logic. There ain't none."

They sat outside in the heat, consuming Olde English Malt Liquor. At some point, Robert would order delivery. He talked about his time with Yasmine earlier. Then he added an abbreviated version of his showdown with Sandiya. His friend listened without interruption, nodding in response.

"Dealmaker, are you going to move? Or buy a better car?"

"Kid, are you nuts? The moment I upgrade my accommodation or get new wheels, my wife will figure it out. It'd be like walking around with a sign saying, 'Got brass in pocket.' What about you?"

Robert considered moving, but it wasn't an urgent matter. He liked living close to the office and enjoyed spending time with the Dealmaker. A better set of wheels was a different matter altogether.

"I'm not in a hurry to move, but I need a new car. My Civic is on its last legs. Plus, I want air conditioning. I can't take it any longer. I'd like to buy something with monthly payments, but my credit rating is garbage."

"Billy-Ray knows everybody. Say the word and he'll take care of it. You'll have something in no time. He'll get ya to put down a chunk of cash and the rest will be on the cuff."

Before Robert could answer, the phone rang in his room. He excused himself, placed his beer on the table, and walked inside.

"Hello."

"Hi, Robert." It was Yasmine. He loved that she called. Shutting the door, he crashed onto the bed. "Hey, it's good to hear your voice. Are you at the office?"

"No. I'm at home, packing. I got fired."

"Excuse me? Did you say you got fired?"

"Yes."

"What the Christ for? This isn't a joke?"

"It's not a joke; it was Sandiya. She 'discovered' I didn't check your references. It's a rule when you become a salaried employee. My omission 'jeopardized the buyout.'"

"Serious? That's ridiculous. Jesus, I'm sorry, Yasmine. I don't know what to say."

"Don't say anything. It's complete bullshit. We never check references if we like a potential show host. Mary-Anne knows this but she declined to help. Something's up. I'd say they're working together, but Mary-Anne appeared as clueless about the matter as me."

Guilt swept over Robert. He never considered Sandiya would be so upset she'd make a move on Yasmine. He still didn't know how she planned to come after him.

Do I tell her what happened? Fuck, no! That would only make it worse. Christ, what the hell am I supposed to do? I was finally getting somewhere with Yasmine and then this. What the fuck!

"Give me directions and I'll come by. I'm so sorry." Robert tried salvaging his planned phone call for later that evening. His earlier triumph turned to tragedy and slipped away into the dustbin.

"Robert, no. I have almost nothing to pack. I called Susie and told her the crew members could have my furniture and TV. I'm going to start my drive to Toronto in the morning."

"Yasmine ... " Robert's voice trailed away. He thought about confronting Sandiya, but didn't know how it would go. If he didn't work at TeleShop, the relationship with Yasmine was moot. If she left for home, there was no relationship to end. Or even begin.

"Something is going on. I'm sure Sandiya wants your head on a pike far more than mine. I'm a first strike. You need to be careful."

Yasmine expanded on what had transpired. At one point she teared up, bringing Robert to the edge. He wanted to hold her in the worst way, but she wouldn't give in.

"Robert, I'm not upset with you in any way. I like you. A lot. We'll work something out. I have to get back home and regroup. You didn't know, but I was at the end of my rope anyway. I like Billy-Ray, even if he ignores my suggestions. I like the crew and the staff. But I can't stand Mary-Anne and I fucking hate Sandiya. I always have. Your being with her was more than I could take. It might be my own goddamn fault, but that's the truth."

"I didn't mean to hurt you, Yasmine. I'm sorry."

"You didn't try to hurt me. I hurt myself. You're a very good guy, Robert. Give me some time and I'll be in touch. I'll give you my mother's number."

The conversation went on for several minutes, more out of inertia than anything else. As promised, Yasmine gave her mother's phone number and hung up, her voice tight and controlled.

Robert sat on his bed, running back their talk, expecting to feel rage toward Sandiya. Instead, he felt only pity. And contempt for Mary-Anne. Her expression in the office earlier now made sense.

Robert thought of quitting TeleShop out of solidarity. But it wasn't even bluster. His status as show host was part and parcel of his appeal. A retail clerk or security guard had zero chance of enticing Yasmine.

What's going to happen to me? Jesus, I should be more concerned with

Yasmine. What does that say?

He needed to speak to the Dealmaker. Robert got up from his bed and walked back to the patio outside their room. His beer, now warm, sat undisturbed on the table.

The Dealmaker looked at Robert, noting his blank expression. "Kid, what's up? Who was that on the phone?"

Robert explained the situation in detail, speaking with urgency. For the first time, he gave all the fine points of his relationship with Yasmine and Sandiya. His friend nodded, prodding Robert to go on while again saying nothing. He'd seen glimpses of the Dealmaker's empathy before. It was an oft-hidden part of his true self. Without bravado. Without arrogance.

"And what happens if they fire me?" Robert asked. "I can't move to Canada. I can't make real money other than here. Dealmaker, I've gotten used to having cash in a hell of a hurry. I can't go back to being broke."

"Kid, I don't know how it went down, but I guarantee Yasmine getting the boot happened without Billy-Ray's knowledge. This will piss him off beyond words. He liked Yasmine and respected her ideas and work ethic. This little incident does not portend well for them — especially Sandiya."

"Is that the truth?"

"Hell, yeah. I don't see anything happening to Mary-Anne other than Billy-Ray pushing her to the sidelines. But Sandiya? Dumb. Very, very dumb. She acted without thinking. Women do that. The feminazis can scream all they want about chauvinism. Nothing brings down shit like a woman betrayed."

The Dealmaker had stopped drinking when Robert left and didn't resume when he returned. He did continue chain smoking, lighting each cigarette from the remnants of the last.

"Will I be okay?"

"Jesus, do I have to say it all the goddamn time? You are the stupidest smart guy I've ever met. Do you think Billy-Ray handed you twenty large in cash and promised more to come because he wants to fire you?"

"I don't imagine so."

"You don't imagine so? Kid, you ain't goin' nowhere. Get it through your head."

"What should I do about Yasmine?

"Nothing. Don't do a damn thing. True love has a habit of working itself out."

"What do you mean *true love*? We had a single date and we've only kissed twice."

"So what. I told you before: Watch the eyes. It's always the eyes. You two locked on each other the moment you met. She was here going on a year and didn't have the time of day for anyone. You went out with her late at night after your first time on-air. Kid, I'm telling you, it'll be okay."

CHAPTER FIFTEEN

Mary-Anne Warner

It was time to look for a new job. With hindsight, she should have realized Sandiya was a Triboro plant. She was a striking woman with impeccable credentials. What possible circumstance would have brought her to TeleShop?

Mary-Anne, you're a goddamn fool! Your own hubris blinded you. You've always known Cliff Johnson was an amoral prick. You were never his only chess piece.

She had to act fast; God knows Billy-Ray would. When Cliff discovered TeleShop had blown Mary-Anne's cover, he'd disavow her. Once that happened, Billy-Ray would get rid of her that same day. The question was: What to do about Sandiya?

I don't know what Billy-Ray said to her after I left, but it couldn't have been good. I need to meet with Sandiya ASAP and make plans. We have common cause, even if she doesn't know it yet.

Mary-Anne kicked herself for going along with the lawyer's idea. She "found" a reason to fire Robert the day after Cliff's admonition? It was a ridiculous coincidence too precious to be true.

But I bought it hook, line, and sinker. Idiot!

Gathering her thoughts, Mary-Anne left her office and walked to the legal department. Nat Fluxgold wasn't in (not an unusual occurrence) and neither was Sandiya.

Mary-Anne went back to her office. She looked at the host schedule to see if Alan Bennet was around, but he'd gone home hours prior. Regardless, the bloom was off the rose. Alan dropping by her condo had become more trouble than it was worth.

While Mary-Anne enjoyed the mechanics, she didn't like getting rid of him after they'd finished. These days, their sex was ending quicker and his exit was taking longer. Besides, he was a lousy show host. Alan would be lucky to get promoted from Show #2 to Show #3. He didn't have "it." Average hosts who didn't sparkle on-air could always keep their jobs as long as they could sell. Alan didn't sparkle and he didn't sell either. Were it not for Terry Pavão's implosion in June, Alan would have been gone before the Fourth of July.

There was a knock on her door. "Come in," said Mary-Anne.

It was Sandiya. She entered and sat down, a somber look on her face.

"Cliff Johnson hired me out of law school as a spy," Sandiya announced without preface or apology. "He never trusted you."

Mary-Anne stared at the young lawyer. She would have been angry, but at this stage felt only detachment. "You were never going to join him in Manhattan," continued Sandiya. "Your role in the inventory affair made you unsuitable."

Mary-Anne listened in silence, unmoving. Reviewing her options. Sandiya droned on, not bothering to justify her actions, but having some need to explain what she'd done.

"What did Billy-Ray say to you after I left?" Mary-Anne asked. "Tell me everything. Believe it or not, we need each other, and now is *not* the time to be cute."

In fact, Sandiya did tell her everything, including the details of her trysts with Robert. Mary-Anne raised an eyebrow in reaction to the lawyer's conspiratorial admission.

"You knew about Robert?" questioned Sandiya.

"Everybody knew about Robert. This is a small company. Let me guess, his spurning made you want to get even?" Sandiya remained motionless. "So you figured you'd get him fired. I can't believe I went along with your plan. Cliff demanded I get rid of Robert on Sunday night. When you came in to speak about Yasmine, I figured I'd found an excuse. Robert would appear as collateral damage."

For a moment, the two women sat across from each other in odious quiet.

Mary-Anne broke the silence. "I've seen the way Robert looks at Yasmine and how she returns the attention. You thought he wanted to dump you for her?"

"Yes," Sandiya replied.

"Believe it or not, I understand getting even. Men have fucked me over before and it hurts. I'm sure you've heard the adage: 'Revenge is a dish best served cold.'"

"I have," said Sandiya. Her face clouded as she recognized common cause in Mary-Anne.

"That was your mistake. You should have made a plan to destroy the prick."

"Coulda. Shoulda. Woulda," said Sandiya in a voice just above a whisper, devoid of expression.

"And I was a fool to listen. Now we're both screwed."

"I thought TeleShop couldn't fire you?"

"No, they can't. That is until Cliff gets word of what's gone down. Then I'm history. I stopped working for Triboro when I transferred here.

Until the merger closes, I work for TeleShop. Part of the agreement says they can't dismiss me without permission. Trust me, that permission is now days away."

"So, what should we do?" asked a defeated Sandiya, the wind blown out of her sails. On the rare occasions she felt this empty, Sandiya never let anyone see. Never. Certainly not her father. Or her mother, the perpetual victim. That she hated her father was obvious. For her mother, she felt only contempt. And for herself only disgust.

Mary-Anne noted the use of "we" right away. Something inside her soul made Mary-Anne reach out.

"You need to eat your vengeance. It's over and you've lost. TeleShop won't fire Robert. Your days are like mine—numbered. Forget about Triboro and Manhattan. Have you ever thought about entertainment law?"

"No. Why?" asked Sandiya.

"I have a contact at Crane Studios in LA. Disappear in a hurry with minimal fuss and I'll recommend you for an in-house counsel position. Will you have any trouble passing the California bar?"

"No," Sandiya replied with some of her former confidence. "Why would you want to help?"

"Two reasons. Your immediate disappearance bides me time. You also remind me of myself in my twenties. I have a hot temper and can act without thinking too. Plus, I have issues with my family and so do you."

"What makes you think I have issues with my family?"

Mary-Anne stared back at Sandiya, her face a mask. Unenumerated pain peeked out from behind her not-quite-placid face. Sandiya nodded in mutual recognition and said no more.

"Give Cliff a call and make up some story about getting found out. Say you had Yasmine fired on your own as a precursor for getting rid of Robert. Leave me out of it, but tell him about the potential ethics complaint. That will motivate Cliff to let you go without trouble. He won't want any of this inventory tampering and spying coming up during a tribunal."

"How do I know I can trust you?" asked Sandiya.

"You don't. No matter what happens, I'm gone. Your leaving first gives me an extra week or two. My friend at Crane owes me. She'll hire you if I call in my favor. Sandiya, I don't gain anything from screwing you over. You'll find this out at some point. It's always better having allies and people who owe you than always standing alone. Call Cliff, draft your resignation, give it to Nat—Christ, there's fucking irony—and head to LA. I'll phone Crane and arrange an interview. Here's my home number. Let me know when you're set up in California."

"Billy-Ray wants me to be a double-agent. How do I square that circle?" asked Sandiya.

"Leave it with me. I'll go see Billy-Ray and tell him I'll fix everything to his advantage. I know Billy-Ray; I'll make sure he understands this new arrangement is his best option."

"And here I was looking forward to dinner with Cliff in Manhattan." Sandiya grinned with an obvious and plastic sincerity.

"At Balthazar?" Mary-Anne replied. "Try their dry-aged côte de boeuf. It's outstanding."

For a moment the two women stared at each other before breaking into howls of laughter. "Jesus, I'm so naïve," Sandiya exclaimed. "How was it?"

"The beef. Great, Cliff? Not so much. Triboro keeps a suite at the Plaza that I visited on several occasions. Cliff never quite understood that I wanted to leave afterward every bit as much as him."

The admission created more laughter. They spoke for an hour before parting. Sandiya agreed to hand her resignation to Nat by tomorrow afternoon. Mary-Anne would meet with Billy-Ray that morning.

Fuck me, Cliff? No. Fuck you! I'll get your former agent provocateur set up in LA and I'll see to it you pay through the nose for TeleShop. I fucking swear it!

§

Mary-Anne Warner

"I'm not even going to try and ask for my job back. I may have way overplayed my hand, but I'm not stupid." Mary-Anne sat across from TeleShop's president on Tuesday morning, arguing her position with precise calm. "Sandiya will resign and leave today. I'm going to get her a job in LA. I know you wanted her to spy on Triboro, but I have a better plan ... "

Before seeing Billy-Ray, Mary-Anne had phoned Cliff Johnson. As Sandiya admitted her real purpose at TeleShop, so Mary-Anne expressed her bile with great passion and exquisite detail.

"Sandiya was about to call you and say she needed to come back to Manhattan. She's freaked out by the potential ethics complaint and admitted everything to me. As I'm not a lawyer, there's no attorney-client privilege. If this hits the press, it will get nasty in a hurry."

Mary-Anne listened to the ruffled feathers of a panicked Cliff Johnson for the first time. "You can't let that happen, Mary-Anne. It would be a blow to our reputation and our share price."

More like a blow to you succeeding William Graves Simcoe as CEO, you fucking prick. It's time you danced for your supper.

"Cliff, if you want this covered it's going to cost you." Mary-Anne played her card of publicity with fervor and precision.

"Go on," he replied, not enjoying the turning of the tables.

"I'll get Sandiya to resign today and leave without fuss. I know a corporate counsel in Los Angeles who owes me a favor and will give her a job. You'll need to ensure there's no issue with her departure. Plus, she's going to need one year of severance pay."

"One year? Why?" asked a perturbed Cliff.

"I haven't finished yet," Mary-Anne continued. "It's one year to get her to leave without causing trouble. And it's *another* one year's pay to *me* for taking care of everything. Cliff, I don't need your bullshit. One year's severance to Sandiya and a one-year bonus to me. I want the cash in our respective accounts by tomorrow or you can deal with the fallout yourself."

"Mary-Anne, is that a threat?"

"Why, yes, Cliff. It is. TeleShop is a TV network in Oklahoma City and Billy-Ray *owns* this town. Triboro is a listed company. Market manipulation — I can already smell the steaming pile of shit!"

"This blackmail does not help your career, Mary-Anne." Cliff spoke with a slow and affected menace attached to his words, laying as much venom as possible into his speech. But, this time, his implicit warning carried no sting.

"Career? Fuck off, Cliff. Please, fuck off! My career with Triboro was over the moment you had me tank the sales. Billy-Ray will get wind of this soon enough and fire me. And don't say you won't give permission. You will. Let's leave it at that. In return for getting Sandiya to quit, you need to pay up. I'll also leave in a few weeks. I want a great, effusive reference — a real tearjerker. Billy-Ray is going to have an honest shot at hitting his strike price. And if he does, you're going to pay up. Also, the inventory mess stops now. Cash by tomorrow or shit by the day after. Your choice, Cliff. Your choice!" Mary-Anne hung up on her "boss" with enormous satisfaction.

Now, sitting in Billy-Ray's office, she finished relaying her "plan". The TeleShop president had an expression of amusement fixed on his face.

"Billy-Ray, I spoke to my friend in LA. It's done. Sandiya will be on her way by tomorrow. She's already drawn up her letter of resignation. She couldn't believe I got her a year's severance."

"Y'all say they're going to stop messing with the inventory?"

"Yes, Billy-Ray."

"I'd let you keep your job and give you a bonus for this, but too much has gone down. Y'all understand?"

"I reckon I do, Billy-Ray. Keep me on 'til the deal closes and I'll leave that same day. I never liked squashing sales; it didn't sit proper with me." Mary-Anne's West Virginia accent made its second appearance in as many days. Billy-Ray noticed right away as a droll grin spread across his face.

"I appreciate your making amends, Mary-Anne. I'm also sorry about being right when I said they'd never invite you to their table. Those self-righteous pricks never do. Where y'all going to go after Triboro takes over?"

"I'm not sure. I'm leaving my options open. Probably something on either the West Coast or the East."

Billy-Ray chuckled. Mary-Anne smiled in return and left his office. His secretary sat at her desk, reading a Harlequin Romance. She sounded out the words with her lips, oblivious to all. Everyone had their part to play in life's great drama, in spite of the clichés. The absurdity of it all made Mary-Anne laugh even more. She left the executive area and walked to the cafeteria. A dead chicken sandwich and a watery cup of coffee awaited.

CHAPTER SIXTEEN

Robert MacKenzie

It had been two weeks since their Fourth of July special and the need for sales had now reached obscene levels. TeleShop was shy of its revenue target by a few million dollars. Their typical solution was to throw negative margin items on-air to make up for the shortfall. But they also had an issue with profitability. Without hitting both requirements, Billy-Ray would lose a huge amount of money.

At the Dealmaker's urging, Robert went to see Billy-Ray about a new car.

"Son," said the president with a smile, projecting his typical aura of affability. "Y'all know I'm going to take care of you."

"Thanks, Billy-Ray. My credit isn't great."

"Yeah, and the sky is blue. You're a show host. Any host who's ever been worth a damn has bad credit. Go see Honest Phil on Thirty-Third street. I'll give him a call. He'll let you put down half in cash and the rest on easy monthly payments. Don't let him get too easy. Friend or not, the interest will kill you."

§

Robert MacKenzie

Robert grabbed his sack of cash he had hidden behind the refrigerator and jumped in his Civic. When he arrived at the car lot, Honest Phil had finished shooting his latest TV spot. "Check out the competition, then y'all come back to Phil's. He'll make it right!"

"You're Robert," said Honest Phil, offering his hand. The car salesman was a tall, thin man in his late thirties. He sported long, chestnut hair and a Simon Legree mustache. He wore a bolo tie and a western shirt with metal collar tips.

Robert shook his hand. Phil went on about his long and close relationship with Billy-Ray and the Dealmaker.

"I've got the perfect car for you. It's the best of the best and I've been saving it for a special customer. Now, it's not cheap, but trust Phil—I always make it right!"

They walked to a bright, red sports car. It glistened in the sun, exuding sex appeal from every angle.

"Y'all are lookin' at a 1986 Alfa Romeo Spider Quadrifoglio. It's got a five-speed shift, fuel injection and alloy wheels with all power disc brakes. Power windows. Power steering. Stereo sound system with real leather bucket seats. And … air conditioning!"

Robert stared in love (or at least lust) at the sexy, Italian beast.

"This beauty is in magnificent shape, no more than a year old and listed for twenty thousand dollars new. As a friend of Billy-Ray's you're a friend of mine. I'm going to write it up for fifteen grand on the nose, all in. Give me eight large down and I'll make your payments two hundred sixty per month for thirty-six months. You don't have to thank me. Any friend of Billy-Ray gets my best deal!"

Robert wanted to say something but couldn't. The seductive European stallion slung low to the ground, beckoning. Benjamin Braddock peered out from behind the steering wheel. He gave Robert an encouraging dip of his forehead. In the distance, Candace Fedoruk, from Seagull Inlet, winked in seductive splendor.

"I'll take it," Robert said. "You can keep the Civic."

§

Robert MacKenzie

The Dealmaker stared, impressed, as Robert drove the Alfa Romeo into the parking lot of Best Value Inn. Instead of beer, Robert bought an iced tea from the vending machine and sat with the Dealmaker. It was Thursday, July 23ʳᵈ.

"Dealmaker, why so jumpy?" Robert asked his friend. The Dealmaker's pallor had gone from pale to bleached in the last two weeks.

"It's gotta be the coke, kid. All this money and nothing to spend it on is killing me." The Dealmaker guffawed again. Robert noticed the strain required to pull off his usual humor. The Dealmaker looked even worse for wear than normal, if that was possible.

"Coke, Dealmaker? Honest? You're not in great shape. Are you sure you can take it?"

"Ah, fuck off. What are you, my mother? Let it lie. Hey, did I ever tell you my three rules of snorting cocaine?"

"No, but I know you're about to … "

"Don't be smart. Before I begin, what does the word cocaine actually mean?"

"It has a meaning?" asked Robert, unsure. "What?"

"More!" The Dealmaker laughed with a crazed frenzy. Robert joined in, admitting his friend had a point. "Okay, here we go. The first rule of using cocaine is it must be good cocaine. There's nothing worse than bad cocaine. You get a bit of the taste, but none of the punch. It's like near-beer. What's the fucking point?"

In spite of himself, Robert smiled and laughed in reply. The Dealmaker took it as a sign he was winning the argument.

"Rule number two is, if you have good coke, you must also have lots of it. Running out of good cocaine is a goddamn crime. It's a tragedy Shakespeare might have turned into a play. Don't go there."

Robert listened, amused and impressed. What made a great show host was their ability to tell stories. The Dealmaker was a king in that regard and should have written a novel.

"Now, Robert, rule number three is by far the most important. Never ignore rule number three. Do you hear me, never!" The Dealmaker stared at Robert, expecting a reply.

"I hear you, Dealmaker. Never ignore rule number three."

"Thank you. When you're snorting cocaine, one, it must be good cocaine. Two, you must have lots of it. And three, pay close attention to this one ... Somebody else must pay for it!"

The Dealmaker almost choked himself to death he laughed so hard at his own punchline. Robert joined him. He'd done cocaine on several occasions but didn't care for it. For all the humor, its second name, "More!" was apropos.

"I worry about you, Dealmaker. Please take it easy."

"Jesus, kid. I'm almost a monk as it is. I live in this shithole. I drive a shitmobile. My life is a shitshow. What should I do? I'm living off the cash Billy-Ray did us up with and it's burnin' a hole in my pocket."

Last Friday, they'd treated the crew to drinks and food at Lucky Charm Saloon. The Dealmaker paid the Nomadic Cowboys twelve hundred dollars to perform at the club. Robert picked up the tab for everything else which came to another thousand dollars. He couldn't complain; even after buying his car he still had ten thousand dollars in cash left. Never before had Robert made that kind of money. It would have been great except for one thing. Yasmine was in Toronto.

"How's it going" he asked her later. Robert lay in bed at the motel while calling Yasmine at her mother's house. Her mom had answered and while she wasn't hostile, neither was she enthusiastic. Mrs. Dubai thought her daughter could do a lot better. It didn't matter that Robert gave the traditional Bahá'í greeting of *Alláh-u-Abhá* when saying hello. Yasmine's mother considered it flip.

"It's okay. We can talk for a bit." said a conflicted Yasmine. "Mom's busy at work. The weather is lovely. And my sister is crazy in love and getting married."

"When's the wedding?"

"Next spring. Mom's booked the ballroom at the Royal Canadian Yacht Club for the ceremony and reception."

They spoke several times per week, but the conversation never ventured beyond platitudes. When he injected romantic language into their talks, Yasmine would shoot it down. She knew of his ongoing success at TeleShop and the cash he received from Billy-Ray. He even mentioned his new car. Nothing added warmth; it always lay steaming beneath the surface, struggling to escape.

"I have an interview next week in New York," Yasmine stated. She announced it out of the blue, sandwiched between talk of the weather and business. "It's at Chase Manhattan's headquarters on Liberty Street. A Bahá'í friend of my mother's arranged it."

"What's the job?"

"It's in their compliance office. Assistant to the department's head. Good money and a great future."

Robert hoped she got the job. But it didn't solve their fundamental issue. Whether Yasmine stayed in Toronto or New York, she was nowhere near Oklahoma City. She'd identified the problem after their first date, and that was never going to change.

They continued their conversation for a few minutes more before saying goodnight. Insoluble problems caused desolate moods. Robert got off his bed and headed outside to speak with the Dealmaker.

§

Yasmine Dubai

Yasmine hung up and lay in bed. Alone. In the dark. In the quiet of her room and the tumult of her heart. At college, convincing herself she was in love didn't take a great deal of effort. Whether it was McGill or Wharton, Yasmine told herself what she needed to hear. She played her feelings in a circular manner, reinforcing them with repetition. At some point, she believed black was white and up was down. Or so she claimed. But, in her soul — the only place that really mattered, she knew she didn't love Daryush. Or Mohammed, her Algerian boyfriend from McGill.

And at that same moment and in that same place, Yasmine admitted she was in love with Robert. It didn't make any sense. They could never be together. That which made him special, his ability on TV, prevented their union. Yasmine could try her old technique of self-deception, but with supreme irony, the truth of her love wouldn't allow it.

I can't live in rural America. I can't. Robert is a unicorn. He has a singular and lucrative talent for one thing. And that thing only works in that one place.

It was especially cruel watching her sister's excitement. Her fiancé, Jagdish, was a good man, a management consultant born and raised in Toronto. He was the modern, western face of Bahá'í.

Farrah graduated with honors from the University of Toronto.

Their Faculty of Medicine had accepted her for the fall term. Walking on clouds, Safia helped her daughter make wedding preparations. She counted down the years to becoming a grandmother.

In the interim, Yasmine tried not to brood. She was happy for her sister, but wanted more than anything to escape her mother's house and head back to the States. Even talking to Robert was difficult. Holding down her feelings hemmed in their conversation. There was only so much to say about the weather, the wedding, and the past. And TeleShop and Oklahoma was becoming the past in a hurry.

§

Mary-Anne Warner

Mary-Anne had a two-fold strategy. The first was finding a new job. She'd sent out feelers and called in favors. With her mea culpa and amends to Billy-Ray, she thought he might give her a decent recommendation. That led to the second part of her plan. Mary-Anne needed Billy-Ray to hit his strike price. It would help with her reference and strengthen her résumé.

The problem was they were sailing under the target by a few million dollars. Projections showed they didn't have enough time to recover, and throwing sale priced merchandise on-air would only make things worse since they needed the margin. The end of July was eight days away. It was time for a Hail Mary.

Mary-Anne walked to the president's office. As always, his blank-faced secretary looked on in dullness. She made a gesture to speak. Mary-Anne brushed her off saying she needed to talk to Billy-Ray.

He looked up as Mary-Anne entered, raising his right eyebrow.

"Billy-Ray, I'm not going to sugarcoat this," she began. "We're not going to make it. Hitting our top line is possible, but we can't do the bottom line as well. We don't have the inventory depth and time. I need your help."

"Go on."

"We need to spiff all the hosts. As much as you can afford. They have to accept significant limitations on airing low-margin products. We also have to get the Dealmaker, the Dragon Lady, and Big Mack in a room and make a plan. You'll need to spiff them extra. I can't see any other option."

Billy-Ray took note of Mary-Anne referring to Robert as Big Mack. It underscored her changing teams. "How much?" he asked. Mary-Anne didn't know of his plan to spread cash around to his main hosts anyway.

"I want to hold a meeting and tell every host they'll get ten thousand dollars in cash if we hit your strike price. The money will have to come from your personal account. If it comes from TeleShop you'll be open to a manipulation charge."

Mary-Anne saw the interest in Billy-Ray's eyes.

"And rent Lucky Charm Saloon for a party if we make target. You'll also make a one time payment to each crew member of one thousand dollars.

Motivate them. Let me tell them it will be the biggest blast in the history of TV shopping. But nothing happens unless we hit target."

"It's going to be expensive."

"Billy-Ray. I haven't finished yet. I know the details of the buyout agreement. It's nothing compared to what you'll make if we hit target. Talk to the Dealmaker, the Dragon Lady, and Big Mack. Tell them they'll get an extra fifty thousand dollars in cash on top of the ten if they co-host next Friday. Let them put aside their histrionic horseshit and pull together. We need a big close. Friday, July 31st is only eight days away."

"And you think we can do it? Won't this extra spiff paid to the three of them upset the other hosts?"

"This is not a time for bullshit. I know all about the cash you give them on the down low. They'll say nothing. I'll say nothing. You'll say nothing. The other hosts will pretend not to know and everything will be Jake."

Billy-Ray laughed as a cynical smirk played across his face. He shook his head and stared at Mary-Anne. "Y'all have plans, don't you?"

"Let's say I have some irons in the fire. Don't worry. If we hit target, you'll be gone and they won't affect you one bit."

"You don't want anything for yourself?"

"A reference, Billy-Ray. A glowing reference will do fine."

"Done. Let the cat out of the bag. And tell the whole company about the party at Lucky Charm Saloon. Everyone can come as long as we hit target."

"I'll get started on it now." She grinned and left the office. Billy-Ray's secretary didn't pay much attention; she played a handheld video game at her desk. Mary-Anne walked with vigor toward production, thinking about next week's logistics.

CHAPTER SEVENTEEN

Mary-Anne Warner

At the special show host meeting on Friday, the spiff came as a sensation. The hosts glowed with avaricious zeal, counting their payday before earning it.

Joe Giannini tried to hide the bloom on his face, fantasizing about spending his newfound wealth. Ten thousand dollars of excitement would shut up his mistress and stop her from talking to his wife. He needed another divorce like he needed syphilis.

Kirk Glazer required the cash. Nothing more; nothing less. He lived beyond his means and had since his teenage years. Ten grand would go a long way toward stopping debt collectors from phoning.

Alexandra McMurdo would buy her husband a new watch for his birthday.

Cyd Steinberg would take her family on vacation.

Nobody had a clue what the Dragon Lady planned, but everyone wondered regardless.

As for the Dealmaker, he would do what the Dealmaker always did — live larger than life.

If certain other hosts knew of the extra spiff planned for Robert, the Dealmaker, and the Dragon Lady they would have screamed bloody murder! And then folded like cheap suits the moment Billy-Ray threatened to shitcan it all.

News of the party and the crew payment furthered the mania. Everyone had an idea, an angle to sell existing product at existing prices. Mary-Anne hammered at the profit consideration. There would be no unauthorized drop-ins. Scheduling, for the first time, would be in charge of sales and profitability. Yasmine would have felt vindicated.

Later, Mary-Anne gathered the Dealmaker, the Dragon Lady, and Robert in the boardroom. She staggered everyone's arrival. The meeting's actual purpose needed to remain secret.

"Fifty large plus the ten?" asked the Dealmaker.

"Fifty large plus the ten," responded Mary-Anne. "Only if we make target. And it's *not* going to be easy. We don't have a lot of depth with merchandise. Billy-Ray will give us a free hand with products as long as we can prove they'll get us to the strike price."

The Dragon Lady grinned in an evil and suggestive manner.

"You three are going to work together," said Mary-Anne. "You're going to co-host on Friday. All day. You'll jump on-air in everyone's show. You'll bring specials, new products, and enthusiasm to all you see. I don't give a damn if it's bullshit. If we don't hit the target by midnight on Friday, you get fuck all."

"What's our theme?" asked the Dragon Lady. She didn't mince words. Her tone and directness expected an immediate answer.

Robert provided one.

"Christmas in July," he said with finality, rising to the challenge. "Some of the stores back home use it. Madman Muntz, Crazy Eddy, Spag's. I've an idea. Let me go and talk to Foster Hyde. You guys," Robert went on, pointing to the Dealmaker and the Dragon Lady, "I need you to pick and blowout one ring each. We have to maintain margin, but we'll bring down the price for this single airing."

"Which ring?" asked the Dragon Lady.

"Yeah, which one?" the Dealmaker added.

"Get Kellie Yull on the phone to Montreal. We need the Celebration Ring and the Shangri-La garnet air-expressed."

"They're seized, idiot!" the Dragon Lady said with her typical spite.

"Mary-Anne told us that's over. Also, they're seized at Champlain, New York. An air shipment will go through a different office. We have to try."

"So what are you saying?" asked Mary-Anne.

"I'm saying we need hot products. The Celebration Ring retails for three hundred ninety-nine dollars ninety-nine cents. Let's do a one-off airing on Friday for two hundred ninety-nine dollars ninety-nine cents. That's still a thirty-three-point margin. We've already boosted the Shangri-La ring to a fifty-seven-point margin. I have three electronic products in mind. We sold two of them during the Independence Day special."

"Which two?" the Dealmaker asked, impressed with the depth of Robert's thinking.

"The Big Ear spy microphone and the Mountain Breeze air filter. The Big Ear is seventy-five points margin and the Mountain Breeze is fifty. Both items took off, but they sold out before we had a real chance to start a wave because we had no quantity to speak of. I know we can do it."

Mary-Anne, the Dragon Lady, and the Dealmaker stared at Robert. That he'd managed to master the job's complexities was one thing; his intuitive grasp of marketing was another.

"Tell Kellie Yull it's time to squeeze Choice Work," continued Robert. He spoke with passion, taking immediate charge. "We need this done yesterday. I'll speak to Foster."

"What's the third item?" Mary-Anne asked.

"That's the game changer—the one that will create frenzy. We have four thousand five hundred South Korean VCRs in stock. Our cost is two hundred dollars. The cheapest VCR across America retails at two hundred forty-nine dollars ninety-nine cents. We'll sell out the lot of them for ninety-nine ninety-nine."

"Are you crazy?" yelled Mary-Anne. We'd lose a hundred dollars per unit."

"Yes, but if we sell out everything else we'll still gross a bit under three and a half million with a profit of over one million. That's a twenty-nine-point margin. We need to finish at twenty-five. Look, this is a long shot, but this promo gets us over the top for both sales and profit. We just need to maintain our current daily sales. That's why we need more hype than ever. Selling way below cost on the VCR will prime the pump for the rest of the products. If anyone has a better idea, let me know!"

Nobody said a word. If nothing else Robert had clearly thought it through. The Dealmaker and the Dragon Lady were famous for tactical thinking, but this was strategic. Yasmine had said many times TeleShop's lack of strategy was their Achilles' heel.

There was a lull in the conversation before Mary-Anne broke it.

"Both of you," she said, indicating the Dealmaker and the Dragon Lady. "Go see Kellie Yull right this moment and call Montreal. I don't give a shit if those fuckers are already heading out for the weekend. Tell them if they want our business, they need to get this done. Robert, this is Foster's moment to shine and I don't want him to fuck it up. If he does, we're going to have a new electronics buyer by next week. Go!"

The trio left the room in a hurry as Mary-Anne thought about one of her options after leaving TeleShop. Robert might make a strong addition to it.

§

Robert MacKenzie

Robert tried speaking to Yasmine several times after their last conversation. He wanted to share his promotional ideas and give her strategic insight its due. But either her mother said she was unavailable or Yasmine was too tired for a lengthy talk. In due course he recognized the futility and finality of saving the unsavable. Neither could change their geographies. In the end, that's what mattered. Robert wasn't one to obsess over women. Nonetheless, there was a pit in his heart.

He'd always sequestered his relationships. With friends. With companions. With anyone, as he moved in aimless fashion across the country—lost. Robert had never been in love before. Not really. He hadn't faced the black hole of emptiness he stared at now.

Don't tell me I've fallen in love with her. That's a nonstarter. If she felt the same way we could talk about it. But she hasn't. Yasmine's off to New York. While she might not get this job, she will get a job. In Manhattan, not Oklahoma. And soon.

TeleShop hadn't left much of their customer's money on the table after their Independence Weekend sale. Their demographic skewed toward blue collar and lower middle-class families. Stay-at-home moms and shut-ins who didn't have a lot of disposable income. Triboro's interference with their inventory had also suppressed their monthly total—hard. It was Wednesday, July 29th and TeleShop was behind.

Robert and the Dealmaker finished Show #5. They walked off-air and headed to the prep room, hearing they'd met their target by a whisker. Yesterday, Choice Work confirmed they could fulfill the jewelry orders. The manufacturer had loaded the rings with innocuous descriptions on Dumbarton Air Cargo. The plane had pre-cleared US

Customs in Montreal and landed in Oklahoma City that morning.

"I can't believe we pulled it off, kid," the Dealmaker announced with a self-congratulatory air, leaning back in his chair. "We've got the goddamn rings. Those French fucks won't work overtime for nothing. Kellie Yull must have put the fear of God into them."

Since the Friday meeting, Robert, the Dealmaker and the Dragon Lady had had no downtime. While other hosts stepped up their game, the three principals went into overdrive.

Every day, the Dragon Lady jumped into daytime shows. She'd bring very low quantity jewelry designed for immediate sellout. Each item was stage managed to look great, but not damage that month's profitability.

After the Dealmaker and Robert left production, the Dragon Lady ran onto Alexandra's show with a ruby ring in her hand. "Alexandra! Alexandra! Quick, quick — I've got one hundred ruby and cubic zirconia rings. They're in sterling silver and only twenty-four ninety-nine."

"Dixie, how? That's impossible," said Alexandra McMurdo. It was remarkable watching the two women, who detested each other, act as friends.

"It's straight from Billy-Ray. He's watching as we speak. One hundred only and that's it!" The Dragon Lady appeared to have run the quarter-mile from the president's office to the set.

"Billy-Ray, thanks so much. You know this won't last," Alexandra said into the camera. "Call now! Reserve your place in line!"

"That's a smart idea, Alexandra. And Billy-Ray, how do you do it?" asked the Dragon Lady. She was neither truthful nor rhetorical. Only mendacious.

Robert had a brilliant idea and leapt to his feet. The Dealmaker stared at him as he ran from the prep room to the live set.

"Alexandra! Dixie!" he shouted entering production. "We got

the word five minutes ago." The director swung a camera over to a disheveled Robert 'Big Mack' MacKenzie. He huffed and puffed as he approached the anchor desk.

"Are you okay, Robert?" asked Alexandra.

"Yes and no, Alexandra. Yes and no. Ladies, we have the Celebration Ring, but no extra supply. What they shipped is all we're going to get. And we only received half the Shangri-La rings we ordered. Nothing we can do."

"Half?" cried the Dragon Lady in obvious (and completely fake) distress. "Please tell me there's more. What about the VCR?"

"Dixie, we can't talk too much about the VCR. We've got every retailer in the country angry at us. And no, we may never see the Shangri-La ring again."

The phone lines exploded. The ruby ring sold out in less than three minutes.

"Mark," Alexandra said live on-air to the director, "run the 'Christmas in July' promo. This ring is gone!" A "Sold Out" stamp appeared on screen. The view faded to a scene of the Dealmaker, dressed as Santa Claus. He sat on a beach set, sipping a cocktail, next to a Christmas tree.

"Well, *arby-dar* friends. It's Dealmaker Santa comin' at ya from our secret beach location. This Friday is our very special one-day 'Christmas in July' extravaganza! Santa Robert and Santa Dixie will host throughout with unbelievable specials. We have the lowest priced VCR available anywhere in the US. We have the greatest buy ever on the Celebration Ring. We have two items that you don't even know how much you need. Do you ever wonder what your neighbors are saying? Then check out the Big Ear spy microphone. Does your house sometimes smell like dead fish? Then you have to get the Mountain Breeze air purifier. Trust me, they're amazing."

"Dealmaker, Dealmaker, you forgot about the Shangri-La garnet."

The Dragon Lady walked on-set dressed as Santa's helper. She smiled with pixyish delight. The fact she pulled off the innocent glow both intrigued and terrified Robert.

"Dixie, my gosh, you're right! We have what may be the last appearance ever of the Shangri-La garnet. We're airing it sometime on Friday." The two hosts laughed with a secret wink and smile. "Hey, Dixie, where's Big Mack?"

"He's taking a nap in the warehouse, Dealmaker. Santa Robert carried in so many great buys he collapsed under the strain." The Dealmaker and the Dragon Lady howled together as the camera cut to Robert, also dressed as Santa, sleeping on a packing crate in the warehouse.

When the promo ended, Alexandra and the Dragon Lady stood about, giggling.

"Dixie, this is big. Have we ever done a sale like this before?" Alexandra spoke with feigned incredulity, selling the moment with perfect ease.

"Alexandra, I've been here five years," replied the Dragon Lady, "and I've never seen anything quite this monumental."

"Amen, Dixie. Amen!" said Alexandra. The Dragon Lady grinned from ear to ear and walked off-set. Alexandra waved goodbye and went back to her regular show. "Friends, take a look at our beautiful Cinderella doll with her magical glass slippers. She's a fabulous buy at only thirty-nine dollars ninety-nine cents ... "

The Dealmaker and the Dragon Lady's phony amiability impressed Robert no end. He looked over to Alexandra who made a discreet sour face and winked at him. He smiled in return.

Even the crew moved about with maximum energy. There had been nothing but non-stop talk about the one-thousand-dollar spiff. The average crew member made six dollars fifty cents per hour; the bonus worked out shy of a month's salary.

How has this happened? A few months back I was a security guard making six bucks an hour. Now, I have more cash than I know what to do with. I've got more status. More respect. I've found a real friend in the Dealmaker. But without Yasmine, it all feels empty. Jesus, does anything ever work out like it's supposed to?

§

Yasmine Dubai

Yasmine left Chase's office on Liberty Street about 2:00 p.m. The sun glowed, cooking Manhattan in its urban heat island glory. The bright sky reflected her mood; the interview had gone well.

She walked to her hotel on Washington Street with a sense of triumph. Her business suit and jacket gave Yasmine the appearance of cool and calm. But, in reality, Manhattan's July fire baked her like a pretzel.

The interview, obtained via a personal connection, hit every note. Yasmine had excellent credentials and always presented well to employers. Her H-1B work visa was still valid. Eric Parker, her presumed new boss, said transferring it from TeleShop to Chase would be no big deal.

The job is mine — I know it. Eric was direct but not coarse; the opposite of Mary-Anne. He would never have brought up the visa issue if he wasn't interested. I liked him and he liked me. Please make this happen. I need to be here — not Oklahoma City.

Even as the thought occurred, Yasmine knew she was being disingenuous. She missed Robert all the time. His smile. His laugh. The way he held her in the office that last day. Especially that last day.

Arriving at her hotel, Yasmine walked to the elevator. She had a 6:30 a.m. flight from LaGuardia to Pearson on Air Canada. Her mother would be anxious to hear about the job.

Her mom was not at all upset that Robert remained in Oklahoma City. Yasmine's dalliance with Daryush didn't bother Safia. Neither did her daughter's affair with Mohammed. Although Yasmine would never admit it, the men in her life were always acts of rebellion. Gestures of accommodation. Trials of will.

Of the sisters, Farrah was the easy one. Yasmine pushed limits in a constant test and struggle. Her boyfriends were never more than a show. She couldn't supplicate herself for anyone, least of all a man. Yasmine had physical desires to sate, and she liked handsome men hanging on her arm. But, most of the time, she enjoyed her own company.

When she met Robert, something clicked. That click remained, stirring up emotions best left unstirred. She would *not* let any man dictate her happiness. Not after losing her father.

The elevator door opened. Yasmine reached for her key and entered the room. She'd watch HBO and get an early rest before heading to the airport in the morning.

§

The Dealmaker

The Dealmaker hadn't felt healthy for years. He'd smoked since he was thirteen and started drinking around the same time. He often wondered how he would have made a living if he wasn't good at selling. The Dealmaker was never one for physical labor.

Crawling out of bed had become a chore in and of itself. With his newfound cash, he started paying Ahmed to do his laundry. That is, he'd pay Ahmed, who made his wife or son perform the actual washing. That reminded the Dealmaker of his own father, an army cook. He was always happy to delegate, not so happy to do.

The Dealmaker was born at Fort Lewis, Washington in 1944. His father had joined the service during the depths of the depression. It was almost impossible to enlist back then. The army was small and its manpower requirements minimal. But his father had worked in diners since leaving school at fourteen and was an excellent cook.

The Detroit recruiter happened to need a chef when his father walked into his office. It was a late afternoon in January. Snow covered Woodward Avenue as the temperature slipped down into the teens. Eleven years later and now married, his dad had spent the war years at Fort Lewis.

The Dealmaker didn't like reflecting on his youth. After the war, he'd bounced around the country with his sister and parents, traveling from base to base. He tried enlisting in the Air Force when he was eighteen. They rejected him because of a heart murmur. His father looked on the affair with amusement, saying his son had lucked out and could now avoid the draft. His father felt he had also lucked out. He was a World War II veteran who'd never left the US.

After the air force refused his services, the Dealmaker moved out. His dad was about to retire and had spent the last three years working at the Pentagon dining room. It was a plum job.

The Dealmaker moved to Philadelphia. He was selling appliances when his father died of a heart attack, a month before retirement. His mother died of cancer two years later and he lost touch with his older sister around the same time.

He married Eve in 1965 and had two kids before the end of the decade. The Dealmaker worked in traveling sales, enjoying its itinerant life. It didn't matter so much what he sold. He needed the constant movement.

Divorce was always his fate. The Dealmaker never got down with the idea of fidelity. Eve could ignore rumors, but humping their basement apartment tenant was too much. Ergo, his current situation.

Last week, he'd pissed blood in the shower. A rational man would have gone to see a doctor immediately. But rational people rarely made good show hosts. The Dealmaker opted to towel off, light up a cigarette, and drink a beer. Then he headed to work.

CHAPTER EIGHTEEN

Mary-Anne Warner

Here's the inventory chart," said Mary-Anne to the show hosts in their 9:30 a.m. meeting. It was Friday, July 31st and the day of the Christmas in July special. "These products are the ones that will take us over the top. Study them." Her face bore a look even more intense than usual. Many considered that an impossibility, but they were wrong.

Product	Cost	Retail	Qty	EX Cost	Profit
Big Ear	$20	$79.99	6,000	$120,000	$359,940
Celebration Ring	$200	$299.99	4,000	$800,000	$399,960
Mountain Breeze	$50	$99.99	5,500	$275,000	$274,945
Shangri-La Ring	$55	$129.99	6,000	$330,000	$449,940
VCR	$200	$99.99	4,500	$900,000	**-$450,045**

Totals:			
	Gross Revenue:	$3,459,740
	Cost of Goods:	$2,425,000
	Gross Profit:	$1,034,740
	Retail Margin:	29%

Scheduling would waste nothing of note on the overnight shows. They'd seed the odd special for appearance's sake, but no more. Joe Giannini had long finished Show #1 and gone home. Alan Bennet hung around after the end of Show #2, resembling a lost puppy. He looked at Mary-Anne, expecting recognition that he didn't receive. Like all the hosts, Alan was unaware of Mary-Anne's upcoming departure.

For God's sake Bennet. Fuck off. Do I have to write you a goddamn note? It's over! How many times do I need to say "I'm not in the mood" for you to get the message?

"Diamond Jim and Carrie are on-air now," Mary-Anne began. "Dixie, drop in one ring special at their 11:00 a.m. break. Make sure they promote the Dealmaker and Big Mack at noon. Hint that the Celebration Ring airs on your show at an undetermined time."

The Dragon Lady didn't even grunt. Instead, she shook her head with a half-sneer and went back to looking at her printout.

"Remember, as of Show #5, we're doing four-hour shows. The Dealmaker and Big Mack are on from noon until 4:00 p.m. Eastern Time. Dixie, you and Alexandra are doing 4:00 to 8:00. And I don't want to hear about any trouble. When will you air the Celebration Ring?"

"7:00 p.m." said both hosts together. For enough money, even the Scorpion and the Frog could be friends. At least in theory.

"8:00 to midnight is a free-for-all. Dave, Dixie, Robert and Alexandra, you'll be moving back and forth the entire time. Everybody, listen up. I don't care who does what. No fuck ups! I swear to Christ if anybody costs us the target they can kiss both the spiff and their job goodbye."

The group nodded as a collective. While their greed trumped most things, show hosts knew they'd lucked into the only job most of them could ever do.

"If you're not on-air, you can leave. But if you hang around and help in any way I will appreciate it. That's it."

Mary-Anne left the boardroom. The other hosts departed, all watching each other, wondering whether to stay or go home. Most remained. Even Stale Chili wandered about with his usual hangdog expression. Mary-Anne would have preferred he disappear, but had no such luck.

"Mary-Anne?" said an urgent voice behind her. She didn't need to turn to know it was Alan Bennet. "Can we talk?"

Mary-Anne looked to the young man and made a gesture for him to follow. They walked to her office where Mary-Anne shut the door.

Alan made a clumsy move to embrace her, but she pushed him away.

"What's going on, Mary-Ann?" he asked, wounded. "I thought we were good together?"

"Alan, we had fun. But you had to have known it was never going to last."

"No, I didn't know."

"Then you should have." While Mary-Anne wasn't cruel, she was brusque. And she'd had enough of Alan Bennet. "Alan, let's get down to it. You and me were never a thing to begin with. Now, we're not even that. I'd like to say you're going places at TeleShop, but you're not. You'll never get off Show #2 except for relief on Show #3."

"I can live with that," Alan replied, looking like a kicked dog. Need and hurt beamed from his eyes. Mary-Anne had never found that look attractive.

I should have fucked Robert MacKenzie. He would never beg like this.

"No, you can't. Don't you understand? If you're stuck on overnights, you're a placeholder. We keep you around until we find somebody stronger. Then, you're gone. This buyout has interrupted our hiring schedule. In normal times we bring in training groups around once a month. You might stay for a bit if you hosted Show #3 on a regular basis, although even that would be temporary. But, Show #2? Forget it. The hour glass is already emptying. Do you get what I mean?"

"You're saying I should look for another job?"

"Alan, go home. It's over. I'll give you two months severance."

Mary-Anne might have respected a bit of anger on Alan's part instead of the look of hurt and petulance he displayed.

"What if I tell Billy-Ray about our relationship?" he said with a pathetic whine.

"You do that," replied Mary-Anne with more frustration than disgust. "Be sure to say hi to his secretary while you're at it. This current one is his dimmest bulb yet. When you drop by Billy-Ray's office, knock. You wouldn't want to catch her blowing him when you walk in."

Mary-Anne reached out her hand, staring at the pass around his neck. Alan looked down, removed it, and gave it over.

"I'll have your severance check mailed to you on Monday. Goodbye, Alan."

There was an awkward pause before Alan Bennet turned and left the office. Mary-Anne gathered some papers and headed out a moment later. 1987 had not been her year. Not by a mile. 1988 needed to turn out better. It was time to accept that much younger men did not make good companions. That was something she needed to remember when transitioning to a new job. Mary-Anne had already heard back from her number one pick. Now, she needed Billy-Ray to hit his strike price more than ever.

Fuck, Mary-Anne. Alan Bennet from his first day in training? What the fuck were you thinking?

§

The Dealmaker

"Big Mack," said the Dealmaker, filled with bright light and a twinkle in his eye. The fact he felt like shit and was on the verge of throwing up didn't matter. While he wanted the spiff, he hated the idea of failure even more. Causing the day to miss target or letting the Dragon Lady beat him was not an option.

"What's up, Dealmaker?"

"Big Mack, do you remember the Quasar Force Gauntlet?" They'd been on the air for less than five minutes. The Dealmaker was already pushing their features, working himself into a lather.

"Remember it?" Robert answered with complete (if not genuine) astonishment. "How could I ever forget? We're still getting calls asking us to bring it back. Missing that deal upset a lot of people. Why?"

"Well, you weren't with me when I sold out the Shangri-La garnet ring. That night was even crazier than the Force Gauntlet. It's been torture trying to get more. We have the final quantity available and we're going to air it later today!"

"When, Dealmaker?"

"Later. Hey, Dixie has the bargain of the century on the Celebration Ring!"

"I know, Dealmaker. We were talking back in the prep room and she's very excited."

"We both have the same problem — very limited quantity."

"So I heard. What do you think about our show?"

"Big Mack, at 1:00 p.m. Eastern Time we're going to air the Big Ear spy microphone. At 2:00 we have the Mountain Breeze air purifier. At 3:00 we have the best single deal you will ever see! If you need a VCR, stop everything. Be here for 3:00 and get ready for a bargain beyond belief."

"Are you sure you can't tell me when we air the Shangri-La garnet?" Robert asked with as much innocence as he could produce.

"Later," the Dealmaker replied. "Sometime tonight. I'm sorry, Big Mack. We've got to let our West Coast audience have a chance."

"I understand, Dealmaker. I watched your show with the Shangri-La garnet. That ring is amazing."

"You're not kidding, Big Mack. Let's go shopping. Here is one of my—"

The Dragon Lady ran onto the set in a panic, her face electric red. The Dealmaker stopped talking and glanced at Robert with a knowing smile.

"Emergency drop-in, Dealmaker, Big Mack. Right from Billy-Ray," she declared.

The camera cut to the Dragon Lady, her breathing labored, holding something in her hand. She handed it to Susie who rushed to the display camera with one-thousand-dollars of motivation.

The entire scene appeared ad hoc. But if anyone was paying attention, they may have wondered why the Dragon Lady already wore a wireless mic. Or why the display case was already lit. Or why crew members were stood in strategic positions, looking shocked.

"What is it, Dixie?" asked the Dealmaker. They'd announced their next item would be the Sexy Secret satin sheets. A special sale for thirty-nine ninety-nine. The reality was they were never going to air the bedding.

"Dealmaker, Big Mack—Billy-Ray is going to let us sell last year's employee Christmas gift."

"The crystal Santa, Dixie? Is this a joke?"

"No joke, Dealmaker!"

Their collectibles buyer had over-ordered the employee gift to reap better pricing. She figured to air it during their next Christmas special. In a miraculous twist, Christmas happened five months early.

"Friends," the Dealmaker said. "Every year, at TeleShop's annual Christmas party, every employee gets a surprise gift. Last year, we all received a wonderful crystal Santa Claus figurine." The feed cut to the multi-colored Santa Claus. It sat against a beautiful snow-draped background, its winter wonderland already prepared. Coincidence?

"I have mine on my desk, right next to pictures of my family," said the Dragon Lady.

"That's great, Dixie. Mine is on my collectible shelf in my living room," the Dealmaker answered.

The truth was neither host had any idea where they'd put their figurine, except as a rude metaphor.

"Dealmaker, we have two thousand only. One thousand now and one thousand for later this evening. We both know it's going to sell out. I have to run. Oh, we've been getting calls for the Big Ear since you went on-air." The Dragon Lady fled the set as fast as she entered. The camera cut for a moment to her dashing back to the office.

Before the Dealmaker or Robert could even talk, the lines blew up. With Christmas music saturating the air, Santa sparkled in the display case. A counter appeared on screen. It moved with speed to its one thousand unit sell out.

§

Mary-Anne Warner

In her office, Mary-Anne watched the show with feverish interest. She'd hung up fifteen minutes earlier with her possible new employer. Early next week, Mary-Anne would catch a flight for an interview. Meanwhile, she hoped (and prayed) for the best. Today's success would mean a great deal for her prospects.

The crystal Santa blew out in minutes. Airing it was Dixie's idea and a good one. Their cost was eight dollars while they bumped the retail to thirty-nine ninety-nine. Although claiming only two thousand in stock, the fact was they had four thousand. Somebody made a mistake. Or not.

TeleShop went to break as the time approached 1:00 p.m. Mary-Anne glanced at the incoming call monitor. Its high numbers reflected the crystal Santa and not the Big Ear spy microphone. For the life of her, she didn't see the Big Ear's appeal. In reality, it was a child's toy.

The Big Ear's construction was wholly of plastic. A microphone stood in the center of a transparent parabola. The cone-like shape measured eighteen inches in diameter. A blue handle attached itself to the body with cheap headphones plugged into the side.

I don't get it. This is for kids and it's shit. Who would buy it?

Managers and sales people often possessed different skill sets. This was especially true for home shopping hosts. A great host not only recognized the right product, but they saw the angle necessary to sell it. Mary-Anne was an effective manager. She would never have made a show host.

The Dealmaker and Robert began hyping the Big Ear the moment it appeared onscreen. Mary-Anne looked at the call monitor. The inbound numbers remained unmoving, and her chest tightened. The Big Ear's success represented almost a half million dollars in sales. And seventy-five points margin.

"Gossip?" bellowed the Dealmaker. "Who wants to overhear gossip?" He winked with a cynical shake of his head. Robert laughed in response.

"Dealmaker, that wouldn't be right, would it?" Robert mimicked the Dealmaker's expression. The pair looked like something out of *Monty Python*.

Mary-Anne kept staring at the call monitor. The inbound numbers remained low, but managed to eke upwards in small measures.

"Dealmaker," said Robert. "Do you see Dixie?"

"Where?"

"Way at the back of the studio, by the exit to the cafeteria."

The Dealmaker made a great show of peering off in the distance. Mary-Anne noticed, fascinated by their pitch. The camera focused on a very long shot of the Dragon Lady. She stood talking to Susie, the floor director, in covert conversation.

"I see her, Big Mack. What the heck is she sayin'?"

Robert picked up the Big Ear and pointed it at the Dragon Lady. He fiddled with the gain control, making a face and shaking his head in excitement. "Dealmaker, call John on the intercom. He's got to get this headphone output plugged into our audio console."

Mary-Anne knew it had to be a setup. Regardless, she focused on the screen, immersed in the story.

Frank, the audio tech, walked to the anchor desk with some sort of adapter. He disconnected the headphones and plugged it in.

"Dealmaker, Big Mack, give me a minute. This should work," Frank said as he hurried back to the control room." The number of calls remained flat. Mary-Anne held back her panic and prayed for deliverance.

"There, do you hear it?" asked Robert, speaking with a hushed tone. "Quiet … "

"Dixie, my mom really wants the Celebration Ring," Susie whispered to the Dragon Lady. "I know Billy-Ray says employees can't jump the line, but it's her birthday. Please, when is it airing?"

The Dragon Lady placed her hand on Susie's shoulder and moved down to her ear. "It's at the 7:00 p.m. Eastern Time break. We'll open the lines up during the promos before we come back live."

"Thanks, Dixie. I appreciate it. By the way, is it true about the Shangri-La garnet? Is this our last airing?"

"It looks like it, Susie. The Dealmaker tried and tried to get a large quantity, but he couldn't do it. We have six thousand rings — no more."

"Dixie, that's a huge number," replied Susie, playing her part like an experienced ingénue. In her two years at TeleShop, she'd made the odd appearance in the background. This was her first starring role.

"Susie, that's nothing. We abandoned more calls than that when it aired last time."

The women continued speaking for a few more minutes. After finishing, the Dragon Lady headed to the cafeteria while Susie returned to the set.

The fact was the Dragon Lady wore a concealed wireless microphone. Frank processed the signal, stripping out much of its quality while adding a bit of echo. The resulting sound approximated a surveillance recording.

"Big Mack, no! Billy-Ray's going to kill us!" cried the Dealmaker with phony distress.

"You're right, Dealmaker. We shouldn't have aired that bit," Robert added, maintaining a look of stony concern.

"Folks, the cat's out of the bag. You heard what Dixie said. If you've ever wondered what's going on around you that you shouldn't know, pick up the Big Ear. Dixie was at least two hundred feet away and talking in a whisper. You saw all the operators yammering. This Big Ear is phenomenal. Call us before it's gone."

Mary-Anne found herself involved in the drama. She didn't know the specifics, but understood what she saw wasn't spontaneous. It didn't matter. Incoming calls exploded.

§

Robert MacKenzie

Never underestimate anyone's capacity for voyeurism. Robert had seen the Big Ear's potential with its quick sellout on Independence Weekend. They had less than one hundred units that Saturday, but it flew out the door in minutes. Foster Hyde brought in as many as possible for "Christmas in July."

The Dealmaker came up with the idea of the phony demonstration. The Dragon Lady bought into it right away.

Robert didn't think twice about the deception. He was no longer the same person he'd been when he started. Money and status had a way of changing people. Often in a big way.

The Big Ear sold out with many potential orders left abandoned. Robert grinned with a manic glow as if struck by lightning. He acknowledged the warm smiles and recognition of the crew and hosts. Part of it was actual admiration; much of it was raw greed. Everyone wanted their spiff.

The Mountain Breeze took a lot more time to get going than expected. The Dealmaker did most of the work, telling a tale of remote cabins and fresh, forest air. He should have been a writer.

"Big Mack," the Dealmaker said at the anchor desk. He looked pained. "I don't mean to be negative, but do you recall the comment I made earlier about dead fish?"

"Sure thing, Dealmaker," Robert replied. He didn't know the conversation's direction.

"Well, when I dropped by your apartment two weeks ago, I gotta say it smelled a bit ripe."

Robert stood next to the Dealmaker, flabbergasted. His room at Best Value Inn may not have always smelled of lilacs and daisies, but compared to the Dealmaker, he was freshness incarnate. The Dealmaker's place stunk like a flophouse.

In the background, the crew laughed. John cut to floor staff, cackling away as the Dealmaker bellowed with them.

"Big Mack, ya gotta watch it. You don't want to end up with a new nickname: 'Filet-O-Mack' is *not* a good handle."

As the good-natured ribbing continued, sales began to creep up. But they still fell short of target, managing about three thousand units. The time approached 3:00 p.m. and they needed to get to the VCR.

A quick calculation told Robert they were trending short of the strike price target. The crystal Santa had helped both their gross sales and margin. But at this rate, they weren't going to make it.

When 3:00 p.m. hit it was do or die. Both hosts knew if they got a wave going, nothing would stop the VCR's sellout. With the below-cost price, its negative margin was a real concern.

"Big Mack, do you know you're the only person I've met who had a color TV in the early sixties.?"

At some point, Robert had told the Dealmaker about his father's love for *Bonanza*, a show NBC had broadcast in color since the fifties. In the summer of 1964, his father had spent five hundred dollars on a twenty-five-inch, RCA color television. It was the only color set in their neighborhood. People would often make an excuse to drop by to see it. For years, local shows were still in black and white. Only the various network feeds broadcast color and even then not every show. *Batman* — a show Robert had loved as a kid for its bright, primary colors — was one of them. In fact, Robert often felt like he was Robin to the Dealmaker's Batman.

The Dealmaker relayed this tale to the audience as Robert looked on.

"When did you buy your first VCR, Big Mack?"

"I had one when I lived in Los Angeles about two years ago. I got it used for three hundred dollars."

"Big Mack, do you remember I said I used to work selling yearbook services to high schools?"

"Sure thing, Dealmaker. You had some great stories."

"That I did, Big Mack. Well, 1978 was a great year for yearbook sales. As a gift to my family, I bought a VHS VCR. Do you know what I paid?"

"I have no idea what a VCR cost in the seventies."

"Thirteen hundred bucks, Big Mack. Thirteen hundred bucks. My two girls fell in love with it. My wife and they loved seeing *The Love Boat*. They used to tape it all the time."

Robert tried to appear impressed.

The Dealmaker, oozing gravitas, stared into the camera. "Friends, will you trust me? Will you call now to reserve your place in line? We've done the research. The cheapest VCR in the United States at present retails for two hundred fifty dollars. There's the odd door crasher special for one hundred seventy dollars."

The camera cut from the anchor desk to the display cabinet. A dark silver and brown machine sat inside. The graphics popped on screen:

Park Lee VCR

HQ Circuitry, VHS Hi Fi Stereo

The Bargain of the Year!

$99.99!!!

A Dealmaker Select Buy

"Dealmaker, this is beyond belief! How do we do it? I'm not kidding. This can't be happening."

"Big Mack, it's happening. Friends, you can thank Billy-Ray Newton and our electronics buyer, Foster Hyde. I'm not going to bore you with a long song and dance. You either recognize this deal for what it is or you don't. The bell is tolling as we speak. Is it tolling for you?"

Their incoming call monitors had crashed during the Quasar Force Gauntlet's run. In response, Burroughs came and upgraded their system. This time the call screen froze, but didn't shut down.

Robert looked across the studio to Nancy Chang, their call center manager. She rushed about in a frantic blur, dealing with the sudden influx of calls. Turning to the anchor desk, she raised her hand to her ear in a telephone gesture. Nancy mouthed the words "busy signals" to Robert and the Dealmaker. They'd managed to overload their computers — again.

§

The Dragon Lady

The Dragon Lady and Alexandra McMurdo took over at 4:00 p.m. Now that everyone knew the Celebration Ring's airtime, their show was prologue. Still, both hosts played up the Christmas theme with high spirits. The Dragon Lady remained costumed as Santa's helper. Alexandra dressed as a frumpy housewife, referring to herself as Mrs. Alexandra Claus.

The smell of money created strange bedfellows, and "Christmas in July" reeked of cash. Hosts who would never have been anywhere near TeleShop when not working hung around the set. They popped in and out of shots wearing wide grins and clapping with simulated joy.

Viewers would have sworn the Dragon Lady and Alexandra were old friends. Big smiles and mirth combined with easy body language. Ho, ho, ho, and away they'd go, from one stellar bargain to another. Scheduling repeated the strategy from Independence Weekend. Lots of rings with cut-down margins. For safety's sake, the Dragon Lady and Alexandra needed to maintain thirty-five points. Regardless, they remained behind target.

"Alexandra, where did you put your crystal Santa?" the Dragon Lady asked with even more put-on congeniality than usual.

"It's in my kitchen, on the ledge by the window. The morning sun makes it sparkle," replied Alexandra. Unlike her colleagues, Alexandra remembered where she'd put her crystal Santa — in the garage toolshed.

For the sake of appearance, TeleShop had stopped selling the crystal Santa earlier. They claimed to have only two thousand in stock, even

The Dragon Lady walked on-set dressed as Santa's helper. She smiled with pixyish delight. The fact she pulled off the innocent glow both intrigued and terrified Robert.

"Dixie, my gosh, you're right! We have what may be the last appearance ever of the Shangri-La garnet. We're airing it sometime on Friday." The two hosts laughed with a secret wink and smile. "Hey, Dixie, where's Big Mack?"

"He's taking a nap in the warehouse, Dealmaker. Santa Robert carried in so many great buys he collapsed under the strain." The Dealmaker and the Dragon Lady howled together as the camera cut to Robert, also dressed as Santa, sleeping on a packing crate in the warehouse.

When the promo ended, Alexandra and the Dragon Lady stood about, giggling.

"Dixie, this is big. Have we ever done a sale like this before?" Alexandra spoke with feigned incredulity, selling the moment with perfect ease.

"Alexandra, I've been here five years," replied the Dragon Lady, "and I've never seen anything quite this monumental."

"Amen, Dixie. Amen!" said Alexandra. The Dragon Lady grinned from ear to ear and walked off-set. Alexandra waved goodbye and went back to her regular show. "Friends, take a look at our beautiful Cinderella doll with her magical glass slippers. She's a fabulous buy at only thirty-nine dollars ninety-nine cents … "

The Dealmaker and the Dragon Lady's phony amiability impressed Robert no end. He looked over to Alexandra who made a discreet sour face and winked at him. He smiled in return.

Even the crew moved about with maximum energy. There had been nothing but non-stop talk about the one-thousand-dollar spiff. The average crew member made six dollars fifty cents per hour; the bonus worked out shy of a month's salary.

"Shoppers, today and today only, Mrs. Claus and I are offering an impossible buy. We give you the Celebration Ring in ten carat gold with a princess cut diamond. It's bookended with tanzanites. The price?"

Frank, the audio tech (working a double-shift), hit the drum roll cart …

"Two hundred ninety-nine dollars ninety-nine cents. Never before. Never again. The Rolls Royce version of the largest selling ring in TeleShop's history! A discount on a discount. Now is the time! Pick up the phone and call."

Nobody could accuse the Dragon Lady of either naïveté or ignorance. She knew her audience like no other. She knew their need. She knew their greed. She knew them up. She knew them down. She knew them forward. She knew them backward. She knew what they would buy. She knew what they wouldn't.

§

Mary-Anne Warner

Mary-Anne listened from her office. She needed a sellout on both the Celebration Ring and the Shangri-La garnet to hit target. Even then it would be close. Their current trend left them short by over one hundred thousand dollars.

Selling all the high-priced jewelry items worried Mary-Anne. She didn't know the hidden desires of the Dragon Lady's audience, but she did know TeleShop's demographics.

Are they tapped out? Do they have more money to spend? We're still short, even if we sell out the Celebration Ring and the Shangri-La garnet. Close, but not close enough. And this isn't Horseshoes.

If there was one thing the Dragon Lady did well, it was sell jewelry. God only knew what she did in her life away from the office. Was she married? Did she have kids? Was she gay? A Republican? A

Democrat? Nothing? The Dragon Lady was a cipher. Even her accent was nondescript.

But, regardless of her actual background or personality, when she fired up, it was a sight to behold.

The Dragon Lady glowed with a passion that demanded your immediate attention. Her singsong rose from the anchor desk to the back wall and everywhere between. The inbound calls obeyed her command, climbing in reply.

"Dixie," whooped the Dealmaker, standing twenty feet away. Mary-Anne watched as John cut to another camera showing the Dealmaker and Robert applauding. "It's happening. My gosh, Dixie, it's happening! Two airings only. Two sellouts."

Noticing the glowing tally light, the Dealmaker looked into the camera. "Friends, I have to say, I'm impressed. Big Mack and I spoke a few hours back. It's obvious why the Celebration Ring is TeleShop's biggest seller. It's gorgeous."

"Did you hear back from Montreal?" asked the Dragon Lady. Good sales people always prepared their customers for the next sale.

"Yes, Dixie we did," said the Dealmaker with enormous weight. "It's a no go. We got what we got and that's all she wrote."

The Dragon Lady nodded in reply. "Shoppers, we're talking about one of our jewelry suppliers. We've tried everything to source more of the Shangri-La garnets. Our last hope was Canada and it looks like that's gone too."

"Dixie, we're going to sell out the Celebration Ring this hour. It's obvious." It wasn't actually obvious at all. The ring performed like the Mountain Breeze. Not enough sales taking too much time.

§

Robert MacKenzie

Robert reacted to the Dealmaker as Alexandra worked with the Dragon Lady. He would look serious and nod his head as if his life depended on it. This was the Dealmaker and the Dragon Lady's show.

At the entrance to production stood Mary-Anne. A grave and worried expression hung on her face. Robert had already done the math, figuratively and literally. At this rate they would now be short of target by well over one hundred thousand dollars.

"John," said the Dealmaker to the director on the intercom. "It's time we goosed the counter." Of the four thousand rings available, they'd sold around twenty-eight hundred.

"How much?" John asked without a hint of concern. Counters at TeleShop were more of a guide than a fact.

"I don't know, John. Something tells me there's a surge of sales coming. I see it driving the counter up to thirty-four hundred within the next ten minutes."

"Got it," replied the director. To his right sat Maria Tissot, the Chyron tech. She ran graphics. "Ramming speed, Maria." She clicked a button. The massive surge appeared, propelling the counter to greater heights. In reply, genuine orders increased as well.

"Dealmaker, do we have enough time?" asked Robert, well aware of the truth. There wasn't enough time before midnight and there weren't enough products to make target.

"I don't think so, Big Mack. We don't have the quantity. 'Christmas in July' *must* end at midnight Eastern Time. Let me go talk to Dixie and our merchandisers. We have to figure something out; we can't let our customers down!"

When John switched cameras, the Dealmaker signaled Mary-Anne. Looking to the anchor desk he motioned with his head for the Dragon Lady to follow. Robert rushed on-air and joined Alexandra. This was the first time they'd hosted together. Unlike her erstwhile partner, the rapport between them was genuine.

§

Mary-Anne Warner

Mary-Anne huddled with the Dealmaker and the Dragon Lady. It felt like a Super Bowl championship even if they didn't have the audience.

"We're short. That's it. We're short," said Mary-Anne. "The Celebration Ring is not going to sell out. It will be very close, but not enough. If we assume we do sell out the Shangri-La garnet, we're still off by one hundred thirty thousand dollars."

There wasn't much to say or do. They'd exhausted their inventory and the clock continued ticking. The Dealmaker said nothing. The Dragon Lady looked like she would self-ignite at any moment, but also said nothing. Mary-Anne, for the first time in years, looked and felt defeated.

"I have an idea."

All three looked up and stared. It was Robert. He'd left Alexandra alone at the anchor desk as TeleShop went into a promo.

As was often the case, the Dragon Lady broke the silence. "So, stop holding onto your cock and fucking tell us!"

"Your Bismarck chain," Robert said with all the strength he could muster.

"It's thirteen hundred dollars, you cretin," replied the Dragon Lady. "You think we're going to sell one hundred and thirty grand worth tonight? You're fucking high. I use it as a hi-end closer. A fucking grace note, not a main feature."

Robert looked at Mary-Anne, ready to make himself into the Dragon Lady's peer or die in the attempt. "I checked the initial purchase order.

We made the buy from Choice Work in January of this year. We ordered one hundred units with an option for one hundred fifty more. Dixie, you aired it twice. Once in February and once in May. You sold eighty-three units total. Customs seized the second order of one hundred fifty. We have seventeen units left in stock."

"Do you want a fucking cookie?" asked the Dragon Lady. "Who gives a fuck? How does that help us?"

"Dixie, I am tired of your fucking shit!" yelled Robert. The Dragon Lady, the Dealmaker, and Mary-Anne stared on in shock.

Robert continued, "Now shut the fuck up and listen and I'll make us our spiff. Our software requires we have ten percent of an order on hand to execute purchases. The seventeen chains qualify. Choice Work has committed to selling us one hundred fifty chains. Customs is about to ship the goods back to Montreal anyway."

"Robert, that's very nice," said Mary-Anne, "but how does that help us today? I have to agree with Dixie. There's no way we can sell that many chains at that price. We don't have the demographics."

"Mary-Anne, please let me finish. In January, the price of platinum was four hundred seventy-eight dollars per troy ounce. It now stands at six hundred forty-one dollars per troy ounce. Yes, Kellie Yull looked it up for me. We ordered the chains when platinum was cheap. Now it's expensive. Around forty percent more expensive. Our retail for that Bismarck chain was thirteen hundred dollars. But we've never aired this *new* Bismarck chain before." Robert's face glowed and his eyebrows raised. "Don't *you* remember, Dixie? This is that special *Bismarck Satin* wedding bracelet. The one with the customized finish *you've* been waiting to sell for months … "

The Dragon Lady picked up on Robert's import, her interest piqued. "I'm beginning to get an idea of what you're talking about."

"Our cost was six hundred dollars," continued Robert. "That's based on the platinum price in January. The retail was twelve hundred ninety-nine dollars ninety-nine cents. The margin was fifty-three points. Remember, this special Bismarck Satin 'wedding bracelet' has *never* aired. Its cost is still six hundred dollars. But based on the new platinum price, its retail should be eighteen hundred nineteen dollars ninety-nine cents."

"That's even worse, Robert. We can't sell any bracelet for that much money," Mary-Anne said with irritation.

"It's 'Christmas in July.' Let the kid finish." said the Dealmaker.

Mary-Anne looked closely at the seasoned veteran and then glanced at his protégé. There was an idea afoot — by hook or by crook …

"Again, this 'unique' Bismarck Satin 'Wedding Bracelet' has *never aired*," said Robert to the group. "Understand? It's the first ever combined 'Christmas in July Special from Dixie Carter *and* a Dealmaker Select Buy'. It's for all the couples in love. Tonight and tonight only. The regular price is one thousand eight hundred nineteen dollars ninety-nine cents. It's on sale for only eight hundred ninety-nine dollars ninety-nine cents. We need to sell one hundred forty-five units. That will push us over our shortfall."

"What's the margin?" asked Mary-Anne with sudden interest. She thought about next week's interview and how Robert needed to be a part of it. Even if he wasn't aware of it yet.

"Thirty-three points," replied Robert.

Mary-Anne didn't even need time for consideration. "Do it."

The Dealmaker, Robert and the Dragon Lady ran back to the set. And ran was not hyperbole. Mary-Anne hurried to see the on-duty data priest.

§

Robert MacKenzie

Midnight reared its head quicker than expected, its finality total. Most of the hosts had stayed at TeleShop all day, doing what they could to generate buzz. The crew knew sales were behind. Even the operators felt the negativity. Lower than expected income opened them to profit issues. The VCR's negative margin dragged their totals down far more than expected. Scheduling played catchup, inserting higher-value items into shows as needed. It was a constant game of Whack-A-Mole. They hung on by a fraying thread.

10:00 p.m. came and went. Slow sales of the Mountain Breeze and the Celebration Ring made the show run late. Scheduling's drop-ins compounded the problem. By the time the Shangri-La garnet aired, it was 11:10 p.m.

All four hosts stood at the anchor desk. On the production floor were Stale Chili, Cyd Steinberg, Kirk Glazer, and a cast of thousands. Joe Giannini had come back because he hosted Show #1. He leaned against Kirk, his arm around his shoulder. Robert noticed Alan Bennet's absence but didn't have time to wonder why. The Ghost of Christmas Past, Terry Pavão, hovered unseen in the air, offering his benediction.

"Friends," began the Dealmaker. "The entire TeleShop crew stands here today for our final airing of the Shangri-La garnet. You heard Dixie earlier. This is it. *Ç'est finis*, as the French would say."

"Dave, I am so excited to be a part of this final airing. Thank you for including me," said a beaming Dragon Lady.

"Me too," added Alexandra.

Robert smiled and nodded, making a thumbs-up sign. John cut to a shot of the assembled show hosts cheering with desperate excitement.

"Hit it, guys!" the Dealmaker announced. Maria Tissot brought up the graphics.

Tibetan Shangri-La Garnet Ring
Set in the Silky Majesty of 10K Gold from the Himalayas
Insane Price and Final Airing!
$129.99!!!
A Dealmaker Select Buy

§

Mary-Anne Warner

Everyone from Billy-Ray to Mary-Anne to Kellie Yull had given Nancy Chang the word of God. Tonight was *not* the night for a shortage of operators. Mary-Anne had offered a one-hundred-dollar bonus to every operator who worked a full shift. One hundred fifty dollars went to those who worked a double. She didn't consult anyone about the spiff. What could they do, fire her?

Operators packed every desk. Full-timers, part-timers, trainees, and managers staffed the phones. There were double the regular number. With the software upgrade from Burroughs, TeleShop had prepared for every event. Slower than expected sales did not figure into the equation.

But they needn't have worried. The lines maxed out moments after the graphics appeared. Call after call poured in. The dollars per minute kept climbing. The mania became maniacal. The assembled hosts laughed as they counted their bonuses. Some wanted a new car, others had debts and one owed money to the Mob.

However only Mary-Anne paid close attention to the numbers. They were going to miss their target. Even a total sellout would leave them short. TeleShop needed the Bismarck Satin bracelet and the intercession of the Almighty.

"God bless you, Dealmaker," said Gabrielle from Derby Line,

Vermont. "I missed this ring on its last airing and it's been killing me ever since."

"Gabrielle, I'm happy you finally got in on the deal. Did you wait long?" the Dealmaker asked.

"Not too long, Dealmaker. About five minutes. I phoned right away. Why, is it crazy right now?"

"Gabrielle, it's Dixie Carter. I spoke to our call center manager, Nancy Chang, a few minutes ago. She says some people are getting busy signals."

"Oh my gosh, I'm so sorry to hear that!" Gabrielle sounded like she actually meant it. "Can I say a quick hello to Alexandra and Big Mack?"

"Go right ahead," interjected the Dealmaker.

"Alexandra, I love your sense of style. I mean not tonight—not as Mrs. Claus," Gabrielle said, chuckling. "You always look elegant. And Big Mack, you are so cute. I bought the Big Ear earlier. Have a great night everyone. This is the best sale ever!"

Robert and Alexandra thanked Gabrielle. The hosts who gathered off-camera hooted and hollered in reply. As the time hit 11:24 p.m., John spoke in their headsets. "Mary-Anne says we have to switch to the Bismarck Satin bracelet right now. We're going to break in one minute."

"Friends," said the Dealmaker. "This ring will be gone very soon. If it hasn't sold out by midnight, we have to cut off sales anyway. We're all sad, but there's nothing we can do. However, get ready for a surprise. We're ending our 'Christmas in July' sale with an unannounced special. Stay tuned … "

§

Robert MacKenzie

The feed cut to a promo. Robert had convinced the Dealmaker and the

Dragon Lady to make a joint appearance. "You two *never* work together; tonight's the night. This is our best shot to hit target. Alexandra and I will leave and join the other hosts on the production floor. It's a wedding bracelet. You need to make it look like you were once in love."

Robert expected to hear objections. He prepared for salty language telling him what to do with his love. Instead, both hosts remained mute. Their cordiality was always tenuous, extended in passing. And even then only in front of the camera. They wanted their spiff and understood Robert's idea was the only one that might work.

"What's up?" asked Kirk as he joined the group along with Alexandra. "Why are the Dealmaker and the Dragon Lady up there on their own?"

"Yeah, for Christ's sake. Are you fucking nuts? Why'd you get off the Shangri-La garnet?" asked Joe Giannini, irate. Robert had said almost nothing to the man since he joined TeleShop. Some people you didn't care for from the moment you met. Joe Giannini was one of those people.

"Because we're going to miss the fucking target, that's why, you idiots!" It was Mary-Anne. She had her take-charge face on. The one that said *do not fuck with me*. "Do you think we're changing items in the middle of a rush because we want to? No! We have to! Now keep a lid on it and hope to God we pull a rabbit out of a hat."

Joe Giannini shut up, as did Kirk. Stale Chili appeared out of it, but then for him, that was par for the course. Cyd Steinberg looked like she wanted to laugh. Robert hadn't said much to Cyd either since he joined TeleShop. But, unlike Joe, he liked her. Cyd had a sense of humor. And humor always went a long, long way.

TeleShop came out of break. The Dealmaker and the Dragon Lady stood upright together, each holding the other's hand.

"What the hell?" said Alexandra, astonished.

301

Their on-screen near-intimacy startled every host. The faux-couple even impressed Mary-Anne. In for a penny, in for a pound.

"Shoppers," began the Dragon Lady. She glanced to her left and looked at the Dealmaker, squeezing his hand. The Dealmaker placed his other hand over hers, nodding in appreciation. "Dave and I have seen a lot of great products over the years. Lots of them. Tonight, we close what may be the most successful one-day sale in our history. Dave, do you want to do the honors?"

The unlikely became the unbelievable. The Dragon Lady did *not* hand off a product announcement. Especially a massive sale. Never.

"Thanks, Dixie. We wanted to end with something special for anyone who's ever been in love. Don't ask us how, but we managed to convince Billy-Ray to allow a massive price reduction on a debut product. He wouldn't let us air it before 11:30 p.m. or to promote it at all. Dixie, take it away. This is your baby. You've been waiting for it for months."

"Thanks, Dave. We have twenty minutes left. The lines are still jammed with shoppers trying to buy the Shangri-La garnet. If you get to an operator, take a look at the screen and tell them you want this beautiful bracelet as well. Do you know somebody getting married? Have you tied the knot this year? Ladies and Gentlemen, Dealmaker Dave Leonard and I give you enchantment ... "

§

Maria Tissot

Maria Tissot sat at her console, exhausted. She'd been working since noon. With the thousand-dollar spiff, Maria planned on taking her girlfriend to Acapulco. She needed the break and the romance.

Graphics were usually pre-programmed into the Chyron character generator. Today, Maria needed to improvise and do a lot of work on the fly. She changed descriptions, prices, ran the counter and was also the assistant director.

She glanced and smiled at Frank, the audio tech, who'd started at ten that morning. Like John, he was a musician—a drummer. With his spiff, he was going to buy a new Ludwig Rocker II drum kit. Everything hinged on the next twenty minutes.

With the click of a button, Maria's new graphics appeared on screen.

Bismarck Satin Platinum Wedding Bracelet
Seven Inches, Lobster Clasp
Debut Sale Ends at Midnight!
Regular Price: $1,819.99
Tonight Only: $899.99!!!
A Christmas in July Special from Dixie Carter and a Dealmaker Select Buy

Susie had set the display with enormous care. Three different pinlights illuminated the chain. It glistened and glowed as if alive.

§

The Dragon Lady

"Shoppers," said the Dragon Lady with quiet yet forceful confidence. "The Dealmaker and I know this is a lot of money. Billy-Ray will let us sell this unbelievable deal until midnight, Eastern Time. After midnight, you can still buy it, but the price reverts to its original."

That wasn't true. Only a data priest could switch the price and nobody had any interest in closing the floodgates.

"Dixie, I know your niece is getting married in six months. Do you think she'd like this gift from her aunt?" The Dealmaker joined his tone with the Dragon Lady, oozing sincerity from every pore. The fact was nobody at TeleShop even knew if she had a niece.

"Dave, you know Billy-Ray won't let employees take advantage of this price. It's for shoppers only." There was a wonderful, fake-genuine note in the way the Dragon Lady spoke. If there was an Emmy for "Best Bullshit Uttered During a Home Shopping Appearance," she would have won.

The Dealmaker put his hand on Dixie's shoulder and squeezed. Maria knew it must be fake because it looked so real. "I'd like to get one for each of my daughters." The Dealmaker was not usually good at sounding wistful. Today he was a master.

Off camera, Mary-Anne glared at the dollars per minute and daily total sales monitor. She looked like somebody watching the roulette wheel spin at a casino. She was all in.

The other hosts, the crew, and the operators knew they were close. The clock ticked to 11:53 p.m. The incoming calls rose and the dollars per minute remained high. Time was the keeper.

Their mainframe wouldn't calculate a daily total until 12:15 a.m. As the hour hit midnight, the Dealmaker and the Dragon Lady embraced and said goodbye. John cut to the assembled hosts and crew applauding, cheering on their customer's great buys. Nobody knew they were, in reality, a pack of wolves. But they pulled off the appearance of genuineness, probity notwithstanding.

The old crew surrendered their positions to their fellows, but didn't leave. The operators changed shifts and did. The hosts milled around like movie extras. Everybody looked to Mary-Anne, who stared at the sales monitor with crazy zeal.

12:11 a.m., begat 12:12, then 12:13 and 12:14 until finally the monitor refreshed at 12:15 a.m.

CHAPTER NINETEEN

Robert MacKenzie

"We hit it! We fucking hit it!" screamed Mary-Anne from the live set's periphery. There was a good chance the swearing and cheering made it to air, but nobody cared. She jumped up and down by the data terminal, ebullient. "We needed to sell one hundred forty-five chains and we sold one hundred sixty-one!

Robert grinned with pure and raw elation; he had no idea what he'd do with all the money.

Can I put this in the bank? Won't they ask where I got sixty grand in cash? They'll think I'm a drug dealer.

These were problems for another time. What was worse, having no cash at all, or worrying about where to store your surplus?

From out of the product production storeroom, known with affection as "The Zoo," appeared cases of champagne. Well, not champagne — cheap Chilean sparkling wine. But the sentiment remained. Everyone pulled bottles from the cases. They popped the plastic corks and let the wash spray into the air.

Helen Cunningham, had replaced John as director. She had some of her new crew members shoo away the celebrators. Besides the obvious distraction, the noise bled on-air. The new operators coming on shift didn't know what to think. They'd heard word of the crew spiff, but were unaware of the details. A crowd of hosts drank with the now off-duty crew, joined by Mary-Anne.

The Dealmaker swilled down wine, an entire bottle in his hand. He walked toward the executive area. The Dragon Lady looked to have disappeared. Robert didn't know if she even drank.

"Great job, Robert," said Mary-Anne. She appeared breathless, an enormous weight lifted from her shoulders. She also had a bottle of sparkling wine in her hand. Robert hadn't seen Mary-Anne smile much before, let alone pour wine down her throat. Tonight, she glowed. "You don't know it, but there are going to be massive changes once Triboro takes over. Massive changes."

"How will it affect me? I'll still be a host," he said, beginning to feel the effects of his own drinking. Robert had almost finished his own bottle of wine, his head beginning to swirl.

"Trust me, it will. The party at Lucky Charm Saloon is one week tomorrow. It'll be gigantic. Billy-Ray has given me a blank check for the night. We're renting out the entire club and hiring John's band to perform. You already know all employees and their family members can attend."

"How did you get the club on a Saturday night? There's no way they would have slotted you in based on a chance we'd make target."

"I booked it anyway. It's called faith," replied Mary-Anne.

"Christ, that was a risk. Weren't you worried about Billy-Ray?"

"No, I wasn't. Like I said, there are going to be big changes. And soon. This deal should close by the end of September. We *need* to talk. You're doing Show #8 next Friday. How about we have lunch? Say, 12:30 p.m.? There's a nice bistro called the Silver Rail. I can write down directions."

"It's okay. I know where it is."

Mary-Anne appeared surprised. "Then it's a date." She walked away, the half-empty wine bottle in her hand.

Most of the off-duty crew members stumbled about, intoxicated. Susie embraced Frank; he had his hand over her breast. The sound of hosts singing (badly) poured out of the prep room.

Robert needed to relieve himself. He passed on the general office toilet and used his host badge to access the executive area.

The sound of mayhem disappeared as he entered the executive offices. They stood empty and quiet. Robert walked toward the toilet, located between Billy-Ray and Mary-Anne's offices. The sign on the doorknob read, "Unoccupied." He opened it and moved to go inside.

Instead, he stopped short. The Dragon Lady lay bent over the counter with her skirt pushed up and her panties and nylons hugging her shoes. Behind her was the Dealmaker. He had his pants and underwear around his ankles and was smacking back and forth against the Dragon Lady's ass.

"Fuck me, Dave. Fuck me! Shove your big cock in my wet hole. Eve never let you fuck her like this, did she?"

The Dealmaker grunted and slapped the Dragon Lady's butt, leaving a red hand print. "No, Dixie, she never did. You're a fucking animal. You fuck like a horny bitch. Take my cock. Take it!"

Robert tried to exit without a sound. It didn't work. The Dragon Lady looked over and saw him gaping.

"Get the fuck out of here, you fucking prick! Fuck the fuck off!" she screamed.

The Dealmaker looked over for a moment, a big shit-eating grin splayed across his face.

Robert shut the door as fast as he could. Amazed, he hurried to the regular office toilet. Between the money and the celebration, the cryptic talk with Mary-Anne, and watching the Dealmaker with the Dragon

Lady … It was going to be an interesting week.

§

Mary-Anne Warner

Mary-Anne flew back into Rogers airport late on Sunday night. She'd had an in-person interview that afternoon. It took place over a weekend after repeated phone conversations. That fact alone tipped her potential employer's hand.

Yesterday morning, she had awakened feeling both victorious and hung over. It had been eight days of unbelievable stress. The adrenaline that drove her was gone, leaving her exhausted. It was the first of August. The heat and grime of summer's dog days shimmered like a mirage in the Oklahoma sky.

Since the showdown with Billy-Ray, she'd worked her contacts without a whit of mercy. Always the self-promoter, she created a list of potential employers. She ranked them by career growth potential, salary, and stability. This clear-headed analysis marked her as an efficient manager. A show host would have thrown a dart at a board and said, "Ah, what the fuck!"

She drove back to her condo, knowing she'd get the job. The body language of the interviewers was too positive. Listing her condo and moving her furniture was her next major project. Also dealing with Billy-Ray and speaking with Robert MacKenzie. She couldn't forget either of them.

That night, she slept untroubled. Cliff Johnson had done her a favor, even if he didn't know it. Billy-Ray had a point when he likened the firm to a blue-blooded club. Mary-Anne's time there was on sufferance and sufferance alone. Triboro would tolerate her as long as she performed and no more.

Remember the night at the Skirvin? Those pompous fucks stunk of privilege. They viewed their jobs as their due for graduating from the right schools. And for knowing the right people. They wouldn't have lasted a month in Welch. Coal miners? I don't think so!

On Monday morning she walked past Billy-Ray's vapid secretary and into the president's office. He looked up from his desk, smiling.

"Good morning, I see we scraped by the target price by the skin of our … Oh, you know what I mean."

"Good morning to you too, Billy-Ray. Yes, I understand. But we made it. That's all that counts," Mary-Anne replied, trying to keep an air of smugness off her face. But her smile gave away the game.

Billy-Ray smiled back, leaning against his chair. "You cost me a lot of money. I heard from payroll that I owe the operators bonus cash. They also told me you booked that nightclub and paid for entertainment."

"That I did, Billy-Ray. Go big or go home."

"So, when did you want to announce your exit and make your grand departure?"

"If you want, I can leave today. However, it would be kind if you'd let me stay until the end of August."

"Y'all have plans?" Billy-Ray asked, knowing she did.

"I do."

"Then how about we announce your departure at the party and make your official exit the thirty-first. But once you've made the announcement, you can come back to the office or not. Wind it all down at your own pace or leave. You decide. That okay?"

"That would be great, Billy-Ray. Thank you for the courtesy. I'm sorry for the trouble and mistrust I caused."

Billy-Ray Newton scrunched his eyes. He looked at Mary-Anne with a smile and nodded. "You're welcome. I'm sorry for the situation too. I'm fixin' to get out of town by the close date in September. I bought an old-style, Bahamian house in Key West last year. I need to relax. I'm too old to deal with any more of this broadcast bullshit."

Mary-Anne made a slight bow in return and left his office. She wondered what would become of Billy-Ray's "secretary," but walked past her and said nothing.

When does Billy-Ray disburse the cash? Does he do it in a group or as individuals? Did he use his own funds? No. Of course he didn't.

It was 11:17 a.m. Mary-Anne sat at her desk going through the motions of work. She couldn't finish anything until receiving a formal job confirmation. It was fortunate that fate picked that moment to intervene. Her phone rang.

§

Robert MacKenzie

On Wednesday morning, every host got called into Billy-Ray's office. He handed each a satchel containing ten thousand dollars in one-hundred-dollar bills. Mary-Anne told the crews they would receive their one-thousand-dollar spiff in cash at the party. Payroll announced the operators would get their bonus on their next check.

On Thursday afternoon, Robert met with the Dealmaker and the Dragon Lady in Billy-Ray's office. On the floor, next to his desk, were three black attaché cases. Since the incident in the toilet, the Dragon Lady could only shoot him daggers of death. She avoided his gaze and said even less than usual. That, in and of itself, was quite a feat.

The Dealmaker hadn't been around Best Value Inn since the special. Robert missed his friend and wondered where he'd gone. It was obvious he wanted to ask about the Dragon Lady. The sight of the Dealmaker grinning while slapping her ass in the toilet, remained burned in his memory.

In the interim, there was the issue of the fifty grand. This final spiff scorched through their attaché case's cheap, imitation leather exterior. Its aroma filled the office with an incense of avidity and madness. Nobody had ever received anything close to this amount before. For Robert, it was beyond comprehension.

"I want to thank y'all for your work. Dave, Dixie, that was some amazing salesmanship."

The Dealmaker and the Dragon Lady both beamed in recognition. Other than on-air, Robert couldn't remember ever seeing her smile. She even appeared humble. This entire week became weirder and weirder as it went by.

Whatever could be going on between the Dealmaker and the Dragon Lady? For God's sake, I caught them in flagrante delicto. They must have history. That might explain part of her anger. And she spoke about the Dealmaker's wife too. What the hell is up?

"Robert," said Billy-Ray, "you really saved the day with that platinum chain. I owe you, son. Now, take your money and leave one by one. I don't want none of the other hosts noticing you're carrying identical cases. They ain't stupid. Dumb for the most part. But not stupid."

The Dragon Lady left first. Robert tried to see if there was some interplay between her and the Dealmaker, but caught nothing.

"Dealmaker," he said, "I'm off to Best Value Inn. What about you?"

"Kid, I got some stuff to do. I know what you want to know. I'll tell you at the party. You doin' Show #8 today and tomorrow, right?"

"Yes, Dealmaker."

"Then we won't see each other until Saturday night. We'll talk then. You hide that loot like it's loot. That fucker Ahmed would steal it in a heartbeat if he knew where you stashed it. You get my drift?"

"I got it, Dealmaker. I'll see you later."

"Okay, kid. I'll let you know how to deal with your cash problem on Saturday too. Bye."

The Dealmaker carried his attaché case with perfect nonchalance and ease. Robert watched him waltz through the exit and disappear. He grabbed his own case, thanked Billy-Ray and left as well.

This new absence of stress felt alien. It had been such a high voltage month that the calm was unsettling. He'd put his new cash with the old cash, stuffed behind his refrigerator. The maid service at Best Value Inn was spotty. Move the refrigerator? Never.

Robert nipped back to the motel and dropped off the case. Two months ago he drove a battered wreck to his low-status job. Now, he worried about where to hide sixty-plus thousand dollars.

While his show that night performed to expectation, in reality, it was a come down. Nothing could compare to the raw frenzy of the last week. He should have enjoyed the relaxation. Instead, he found the lack of stress induced listlessness. He was born for this job, his instincts on the day of his interview correct.

He saw the Dragon Lady again in the hall as he prepared his show. She didn't so much as grunt or roll her eyes as they passed. The Dragon Lady fled, as was her want, the moment she left air.

Robert finished his own show, thanked the crew and headed to Best Value Inn. When he arrived, the Dealmaker's Duster was nowhere in the parking lot. His own new car now looked out of place in the motel's low rent digs.

At some point, sooner rather than later, he'd need to rent a condo. Robert thought about Yasmine. He never did get her address. He could always move where Sandiya used to live. Her sudden and abrupt disappearance remained unexplained. There'd been no contact. No word. Nothing. Then again, considering the situation, that wasn't necessarily a bad thing.

§

Robert MacKenzie, Mary-Anne Warner

While it was daytime and lunch, not late night and supper, the Silver Rail looked the same. Robert pulled his new car into the parking lot, recalling the date with Yasmine. Unlike that evening, he felt only curiosity and not an acute fissure of nerves. That was a moment he could have used the confidence brought by his Alfa Romeo.

Robert entered the restaurant and stood again in front of the maître d'. He was different from the man that evening, but had the same imperious air. The maître d' raised his eyebrow.

"Hi, I'm meeting someone — Mary-Anne Warner."

Glancing down to his reservation book, he made a quick checkmark and looked back at Robert. "She's this way. Please, follow me."

Like his date with Yasmine, Robert walked behind the maître d' through the restaurant. They strolled across the front section to tables looking out the bay window. Mary-Anne sat with a glass of white wine, eating hors d'oeuvres. She wore a simple yet elegant, business suit.

Mary-Anne noticed Robert and motioned with her hand to sit down. "Thank you so much for coming, Robert," she said with near-affection.

In the two months he'd worked at TeleShop, he'd come to appreciate her tenacity and ability, if not her warmth.

"Thank you for having me," he replied, sitting down in the chair opposite. He ordered a Heineken from the waitress who handed him a large, fold-out menu.

The pair made small talk, commenting on the food and atmosphere while reminiscing about Robert's job interview. Mary-Anne ordered a tenderloin steak, medium, with a baked potato and dollops of sour cream. Robert again had the veal parmesan.

They sat across from each other for the better part of an hour. Neither said anything of consequence. Robert had no idea why Mary-Anne wanted to meet and found the foreplay trying. When the waitress cleared their entrée for dessert, the real discussion began in earnest.

"Of course you've wondered why I asked you here today … " Mary-Anne began her pitch after their plates disappeared.

"The thought crossed my mind," Robert answered, stating the obvious. Mary-Anne grinned in a manner no longer atypical.

"Have you wondered where Sandiya disappeared?" Mary-Anne fixed on him. Her expression made it obvious she knew all about their relationship.

"I have."

"She's in Los Angeles working as counsel for Crane Studios. I got her the job. It was a sop to Billy-Ray so he didn't get her disbarred."

Robert looked askance, making it clear he wanted more.

"You didn't know? Of course you didn't. She tried to get you fired. And I went along with it like an idiot."

"You went along with it? What the hell are you talking about?"

With all the gory details left in, Mary-Anne related the story. The entire story. Her real job at TeleShop. The inventory sabotage. Spying for Cliff Johnson. Getting rid of Yasmine. Everything. Including her assignation with Alan Bennet. The tale took thirty minutes. They finished dessert and were on a second cup of coffee when she finished.

"Triboro wanted me fired? And now what? Am I still okay?" Robert had become very used to his newfound money and status. He couldn't ever go back to his past ignominy. Not ever. Not at all.

"You're fine," said Mary-Anne. "At least for a while. Since Triboro must now pay the full buyout price, your absence no longer saves them money."

Robert wanted to relax, but there was something in her tone and the words "for a while" that made him uneasy. He looked at Mary-Anne to continue.

"The problem is the cash spiffs, Robert. They're going to bite you in the ass."

"You know about the spiffs?"

"I know about all the spiffs," Mary-Anne replied. "Billy-Ray pays them with corporate funds. Accounting assigns them to advertising or promotion. As long as Billy-Ray is in charge, there aren't any problems. That will change very soon. Robert, I assume you've declared the money to the IRS?"

In reply, Robert sat impassive, answering with his silence.

"No, you didn't. You're also wondering how to get the money into your bank without the Feds taking note?"

"The Dealmaker said he'd help me."

"That's very kind of him," Mary-Anne replied without the sarcasm Robert expected. "When Triboro does its first, full audit after the takeover, they're going to want to know where the cash went."

"Why should they care?"

"Because, at that time, they were minority owners. Billy-Ray had a fiduciary responsibility to be transparent. I should have told Triboro about the spiffs, but I chose to withhold that information. Future leverage, you know? Spending that money to make his strike price was *not* in the interests of the minority investors. It drove up their cost in a material way and was to their prejudice."

Robert sat and listened. This was a very impressive woman. After dealing with his bank issue, he needed to declare the money. While he liked and admired the Dealmaker, Robert didn't want to end up alone in a broken-down motel. That was for sure.

"Someone will get sacrificed," continued Mary-Anne. She noted

Robert's reaction and modulated her story and pitch for its greatest effect. "It won't be the minor hosts. None of them received enough money. Also, they can't fire everybody. No, it's going to be you, the Dealmaker, or the Dragon Lady. I doubt it will be all three of you, although it might."

"So, what are you going to do?" he asked. "You've already said you're announcing your departure at the party."

"That's why we're here. First off, declare the money. The Dealmaker will help get it into your account with minimal attention. Resign yourself to never getting another cash spiff like these again. No regular corporation does that sort of thing. For all their bullshit, Triboro is a regular corporation; TeleShop is the Wild West. Once Billy-Ray departs, the days of the gunslinger are over."

Robert understood she played him like a fiddle. And she was very good at it. Mary-Anne was Jimmy Page and Eric Clapton rolled into one. But everything she said made sense. Perfect sense.

"How's Yasmine?" asked Mary-Anne, another broad grin spreading across her face.

"She's in Toronto. She had an interview with an investment bank in Manhattan. She thinks she's going to get the job."

"She'll get the job. Yasmine is very smart and capable. I need to work on my own temper when it comes to subordinates. Yasmine taught me that. Do you miss her?"

Robert said nothing.

"How would you like a new job? The starting salary is one hundred thousand dollars per year. And there's a signing bonus of twenty-five thousand dollars. That's a legitimate spiff, by the way."

"I owe Billy-Ray," Robert said in reply. "I can't up and leave after what he's done for me."

"That's a laudable notion, but Billy-Ray will no longer give a damn if you leave. Do you have any idea how much more money he's made now that TeleShop hit its strike price? Think of the total value of the spiffs as chicken feed by comparison."

"Why are they offering so much money?"

"Because, Robert, you understand promotion on an intuitive level. That Quasar Force Gauntlet idea was gold. So was the Houdini Carpet Magician. Nobody saw the value in the Big Ear spy microphone. I took one look at that plastic piece of shit and thought you were nuts. I was wrong. Still, the pièce de résistance was the Bismarck Satin chain. You saved the day. Literally."

"Thank you, I appreciate your compliments. But the Dealmaker and the Dragon Lady are also experts."

"Dave and Dixie will never leave Oklahoma. They'll always play to flyover country. East Coast, West Coast corporate culture? Chicago? Not a hope. You are a well-spoken, attractive young man. You're different."

With a pause, Mary-Anne pulled out a contract and went into detail.

§

Robert MacKenzie

Hosts that mattered always worked weekends, but Billy-Ray suspended that rule for the grand party at Lucky Charm Saloon. He changed show times, brought in second tier hosts and added more taped programming. Regular shows didn't resume until midnight on Monday.

TeleShop was not a big company, but everyone wanted to attend the party. All the operators and their families. The crews and their friends. Assorted hangers-on and viewers from the Oklahoma City area who managed to sneak in. By Saturday night, hundreds of people jammed Lucky Charm Saloon.

For the party's budget, Mary-Anne opened TeleShop's checkbook.

What did it matter, if it was actually Billy-Ray's checkbook? When Mary-Anne realized it was now Cliff Johnson's checkbook, she spared no expense.

"As for the food," she had told the bar last week, "Barbeque and lots of it. I also want a large buffet. And I mean *large*! Filled with the best of the best. Don't skimp on the quantity or the quality. Oh and booze, whatever anybody wants. No limit. Top shelf if they ask for it."

At first, the bar's management hesitated. They didn't want to give up a lucrative Saturday night for a company party. But when the bar's owner heard it was TeleShop and learned the party's huge budget, they overruled their managers. You didn't mess with Billy-Ray. Not in Oklahoma City.

There was a grand total of forty-two crew members, full and part time. Mary-Anne saw to it they all got the one-thousand-dollar spiff. Two armed guards from L.A. McIntyre Armored Car Services brought in the cash. They stood guard over the money, wearing looks of grim determination.

The shorter of the two held a clipboard in his right hand. At the appointed time, he'd have a crew member sign next to their name. Then, with a tip of his head toward the president, Billy-Ray would hand over an envelope of cash. It would have made for great drama. They were, after all, a television network. But this part of the show would never play on-air.

Otherwise, TeleShop taped the entire affair. They'd purchased three new Betacam SP camcorders the month before. The party would be their baptism by fire.

Robert arrived shortly after 8:00 p.m. Lucky Charm Saloon already buzzed. It would get a lot crazier in the hours ahead. Every crew member he knew was there. Operators he recognized only by sight waved. Several wanted him to meet their family. Robert posed for pictures, noticing many women glancing at him with interest.

"Big Mack!" It was John Duguay, standing with his girlfriend and the Nomadic Cowboy's lead singer, Sára Mender.

"Hey, John," he replied. "What's up? Hi Sára, it's good to see you again."

John was on the verge of intoxication upsetting Sára. Regardless, she greeted Robert with warmth. He responded with a smile of his own and turned to John. "What are your plans for the spiff?"

"He's going to quit drinking tonight so he doesn't fuck up his playing," Sára announced. "If he pulls it off then he can consider buying that vintage Fender Bass VI he wants." Sára's eyes locked hard on her boyfriend. She displayed a rictus grin and gripped his arm. "I'm going to head backstage. We're on in a bit. Join me in ten minutes, John. *Don't* be late!"

Sára left, threading through the crowd to backstage. Robert and John talked about TeleShop before hearing a hearty bellow.

"Well *arby-fucking-dar* everybody. You can relax, the Dealmaker's here. Let the party begin!" The Dealmaker rolled in, owning the soirée in his wake. People cheered. The Dealmaker walked about shaking hands, smiling, posing for pictures. He carried a bottle of wine, swinging it about. "Big Mack, Johnny-man, we need to hit next-level intoxication this evening!"

For all his amiability, he looked like hell. While heavy air conditioning kept the bar cool, the Dealmaker managed to sweat like a lapping dog. His face glowed red, and his nose had a nervous tic all its own.

"It's great to see you, Dealmaker," said John. "Thanks for booking the band again."

"Johnny-man, thank Mary-Anne, if you can believe it. She asked me if I knew of a group and I suggested you guys. Hey, have you seen the spread by the stage? Holy fuck, they slaughtered half of Texas there.

Now that's my idea of a feast. It's transcended mere buffet and entered the realm of the smorgasbord."

"Dealmaker, it looks great. I'm hungry, but I have to go. We're on in a few minutes. Sára will kill me if I'm late. Bye." John left and walked in the direction Sára had earlier.

Robert turned to look at the Dealmaker, who began speaking at the same time.

"Okay, I know. Where in the Christ have I been and why was I banging Dixie in the executive shitter? Does that about sum it up?"

"Not to put too fine a point on it, but *yes*."

"Alright, let me start from the beginning and make a short story long … "

§

The Dealmaker, Robert MacKenzie

The Dealmaker loved his kids. Liked his job. Accepted his wife. That didn't mean he wasn't a master of self-destruction, only that he knew what he did to himself. The Dealmaker was a serial cheater. Away for long stretches of time, he would meet women in bars and hotels and have fun. If regular women weren't around, a hooker would always do. Eve knew but pretended not to. It made life easier.

Five years ago, the Dealmaker started work at TeleShop. The prior twelve months had been very tough. His laser art business was no longer viable and the yearbook job was long ago. Unlike Robert, the Dealmaker was already in Oklahoma City when he responded to TeleShop's want ad.

"Eve loved me getting off the road," said the Dealmaker. "She didn't want to leave Los Angeles, but we moved anyway. And things got better. For a while."

Robert already knew part of the story told over countless cans of Olde English. The Dealmaker had spoken about moving to Oklahoma City and his job's early days. The situation between the Dealmaker and his wife went south again after a few months. He had never said why.

"Big Mack, you know I like to party a bit." The Dealmaker liked to party like Frank Sinatra liked to sing. "I went back to my old ways a few months after starting at TeleShop."

Robert listened with careful attention, hearing the revelation of buried truth. "That's when Dixie got hired. We hit it off right away."

At the words "right away," Robert thought he would choke "You *hit it off*?" he asked, allowing his tone to dictate his amazement.

"Yeah, we hit it off. Why is that such a big fucking deal?"

"Because you fucking hate each other, that's why!"

"Well, spurned love does that to people, you know?"

"Spurned love?" Robert had lived through an endless series of shocks since starting at TeleShop. Last week's lunch with Mary-Anne was the latest. This news topped them all.

"Jesus did we hit it off! We were fuckin' like rabid dogs weeks after we met. Christ, can that broad fuck. Like a demon. I swear to sweet Jesus, we'd bang everywhere. That time in the toilet was *not* the first time we got caught. Kellie Yull found us playing hide-the-sausage in the high-value jewelry lockup. It was great. And we fell in love."

"You fell in love?"

"That we did, my son. That we did." The Dealmaker affected a rare, wistful grin.

"So, what happened? Why did it end?"

"It was Eve. She got wind of it and hit the fucking roof. She kinda knew about all the skank I had on the road. But out of sight, out of mind — you know what I mean?"

Robert sailed back to the near-past and a not-forgotten conversation.

He heard the Dealmaker defend himself against having sex with their tenant. Reality distortion was always strong with this one.

"She gave me an ultimatum. Either Dixie went or she did. That meant taking the girls back to LA. I couldn't face it, so I caved. Dixie did not take it well."

And America didn't take bombing Pearl Harbor well either. What had once been a relationship of love turned into a relationship of hate. Pure and unbridled. Robert thought for a moment about Sandiya's face in her office that day. The Dragon Lady must have found the Dealmaker's announcement "off-putting" as well.

Since the incident in the washroom, the Dealmaker had been living with the Dragon Lady. It turned out her condo was very near Sandiya's old place. Somehow, Eve heard about the newly-energized affair and went full-on ballistic.

"Talked to her on the phone yesterday," the Dealmaker said with a big smile. "Threatened to divorce me, said she'd already served papers. Laughed myself shitless. Told me the kids wouldn't talk to me; I said they already didn't. Claimed she'd take me for everything I had, and told her to fuck off. I was gonna quit and live off Dixie. She hung up. Thank you, Jesus. She fucking hung up!"

"Are you living with the Dragon Lady?"

"Yup."

"For real? Well, congratulations I guess. This means you're leaving the motel?"

"Yup. If it doesn't work out, Ahmed or someone like him will still be there when it's over. Those types always are."

In the background, Billy-Ray climbed to the stage. The two armed guards walked behind him, carrying the cash envelopes. An older, well-dressed woman he didn't recognize stood on the stage.

"Who's the lady next to Mary-Anne?" Robert asked the Dealmaker.

She was in her late sixties. Her clothes fit with perfection and she wore expensive yet tasteful jewelry.

"That's Elizabeth Newton, Billy-Ray's wife. She was quite a looker in her day."

"I can see that. Where's his secretary?"

The Dealmaker looked over to Robert with a sigh and shook his head. The old *Batman* show had text balloons appear during fight sequences. "Biff!" "Kapow!" Smash!" If this moment had been that kind of scene, the text balloon would have said, "Moron!"

"Oh, about your spiff. Let me tell you how to take care of it before Billy-Ray gets going. By the time he and the band finish I'll be semi-conscious."

"Thanks, Dealmaker. Isn't the Dragon Lady coming tonight?"

"Jesus, kid. Did you grow up in a goddamn kennel? If she showed up it'd be like tattooing the relationship across our faces. These drunken fucks would want me to schtup her up the ass right on stage. Although, with enough bingo, she'd go for it."

"Bingo?"

"Wine, you schlemiel. Christ, how do you even get fucking dressed in the morning? Now, listen, I'm doing you a solid. *Another* solid. You don't need to thank me. You need the cash in your bank, right?"

"Right."

"Okay, take whatever amount you want moved to Honest Phil. Like his name says, he ain't so honest."

"Are you kidding?"

"No, I'm not kidding. Give him the cash in cash. He's going to take ten percent off the top. You'll find the balance appearing in whatever account you want in a couple of days. Any account at all as long as it's with OKC Sooner Oil State Bank."

"That's my bank."

"There you go; it's like you're walkin' with God."

"But, ten percent. That's a lot of goddamn money."

"So? You got another idea?"

"No."

"Then we're done and you're welcome. I gotta take a shit. And get a drink. I'll see you in a bit." The Dealmaker walked toward the toilets and the bar in an order not determined. Robert watched him leave and then heard Billy-Ray asking for everyone's attention. It was time to give out the spiffs.

§

Robert MacKenzie

The bar quieted somewhat as everybody looked to the stage. As instructed, the cameramen put down their camcorders the moment the ceremony began. Billy-Ray started by making a short speech. He reminded the operators their bonus would appear on their next paycheck. With a gigantic grin, he thanked everyone for all their hard work and asked for a round of applause.

The crowd, many of whom already felt no pain, responded with an enthusiastic cheer. Several employees shouted out Billy-Ray's name over and over. He placed his hand over his heart and made a slight bow.

Robert glanced at Mary-Anne. She stared at him from the stage, shaking her head. He'd made his decision and hoped it was the right one. Regardless, it was too late to change his mind.

Each crew member walked onto the stage, thanked Billy-Ray, and walked away with their money. Those not present would get their cash later. Tiny Susie shook Billy-Ray's hand and kissed her envelope. She let out a whoop and danced off stage.

Susie's dulled her inhibitions again with too much booze. I wonder if

Frank's around?

As the ceremony ended, Billy-Ray said he had two important messages. He first introduced Mary-Anne. She took the microphone and announced her departure at the end of the month. Even though Robert knew all about it, he still felt shock. The production crew gossiped in disbelief.

Billy-Ray thanked Mary-Anne with what sounded like honest appreciation. He asked for a round of applause in her honor. When the clapping died down, he smiled at his wife. She walked toward him, taking his hand and raising it in the air.

"Friends, this buyout concludes my involvement at TeleShop. I want to say how proud I am of everybody I've worked with over the years. I could never have done anything without y'all."

Employees knew on some level Billy-Ray had to leave. That was the way of all buyouts. Still, change affected everyone. Combining high emotion with drink, food, and fun made the gossip take off.

"I want to make a very public and honest thank you to my wife of over forty years. I met Elizabeth in London when the US Army Signal Corps stationed me there during the war. Elizabeth, thank you for sticking around all these years. I wouldn't have amounted to nothin' without your patience, strength, and belief. I love you, Elizabeth!"

The couple embraced as the crowd cheered with abandon. Billy-Ray and Elizabeth bowed low, hand in hand, and left the stage. Mary-Anne followed behind with the armed guards and cash bringing up the rear. After a few minutes, Sára Mender walked to the microphone and introduced the band who lit into a song right away. John wailed away on his bass while singing backup. Never underestimate the power of a woman.

CHAPTER TWENTY

Robert MacKenzie

There was an old black-and-white movie that used to play on television all the time. Robert had seen it on innumerable occasions. The film was *A Night to Remember*. Most regarded it as the definitive motion picture to recount the Titanic's final hours.

Other than the title's fun play-on-words, the film's subject matter didn't resemble the party at all. People were having fun. Lots of fun. The "smorgasbord" was a major hit. The Nomadic Cowboys were on fire. There was dancing and drinking—a lot of drinking. The smell of weed floated through the air. Several of the hosts looked high as Christ.

The Dealmaker romped about, always a drink in hand. With a Camel in his lips, his nose twitched in time. So total was his sweating, his shirt changed color in reply.

Robert spent much of the night speaking to people he didn't know. Crew members hoisted their glass when seeing Robert from across the bar. He hoisted his own glass in return. Many of the attractive, part time operators were college students. A lot of them said hello, making Seagull Inlet a distant memory.

As time passed, Robert needed to relieve himself. Heading to the men's room, he approached Maria Tissot. Robert was about to say hi, but didn't. A young woman, about the same height as Susie, had pushed her against the wall. She'd unzipped Maria's jeans and had shoved her right hand down her pants. The woman had also pulled Maria's right breast from her bra and was making a concerted effort to suck it.

Maria noticed Robert and shrugged with intoxication and arousal. He smiled in return, shrugged as well, and laughed. Feet from the entrance to the toilet, Frank leaned against the cigarette machine. Robert was again about to say hello when Frank's eyes warned him off. It was only then he noticed the real Susie on her knees in front of the audio tech.

Now this is a shindig. If I wasn't so worried about my future and about Yasmine, I could let go. But I can't. My career and that Canadian woman occupy all my time.

He entered the men's toilet, packed with both genders smoking marijuana and snorting coke. The cocaine users were crew members who clearly didn't understand the Dealmaker's rule number three. At this rate, their thousand-dollar spiff would disappear up their nose before night's end. The partying crew members offered a line of coke but he passed. Robert entered, finished and left in a hurry.

As the time approached 11:00 p.m., the Nomadic Cowboys prepared for their second set.

"Big Mack," slurred a very inebriated Dealmaker. "I'm fucking drunk!" His friend swayed in front of him. Not quite slack-jawed, but almost.

"Dealmaker, are you okay? Yes, you're drunk and you look like shit. You ought to lay off the sauce"

"I feel like shit. This party's great. My future—not so much."

A bolt of raw current hit Robert with the Dealmaker's admission.

"What do you mean? You said everything's going your way. You're back with the Dragon Lady. That's what you want, right?"

Beyond the physical, the Dealmaker didn't look good on any level. A cry of desperation sat on his reddened face, pleading escape. That he showed it to Robert and no one else made no difference.

"Sure, that's what I want. Us getting back together is the only thing that's worth a shit in my life. Kid, there's gonna be changes aplenty when Triboro takes over. Huge goddamn changes. And they may not bode well for the likes of me."

"What do you mean?" Robert asked, feeling guilty that Mary-Anne had already provided him with the news. If the Dealmaker could see it as well then, without doubt, trouble lay ahead.

"Those Manhattan fucks don't want me. You? You're aces. But me? Not so much. And that goes for Dixie as well."

Robert went to share his news about the future of TeleShop from Mary-Anne, but a sudden, echoing announcement from the house PA stopped him in his tracks.

"Dealmaker, where are you?" said the voice. It was John. The band had remounted the stage and were searching for the Dealmaker. "Somebody find the Dealmaker and get him up here!"

The Dealmaker was never a hard man to find —at least when he wanted to be. Within seconds people pointed him out and motioned he should get to the stage. With the flick of a switch, last moment's pained look disappeared. The Dealmaker turned on his "party" mode and lit up. He ran to the stage and mounted it.

"What's going on Johnny-man?" asked the Dealmaker, taking immediate charge of the mic. The crowd followed him with cheers. He walked across the stage with his arms raised, beckoning applause.

Christ, can't they see it? He looks like fucking shit. The man's sick. This isn't funny.

Sára Mender stood next to John, holding a magnum of champagne.

"Dealmaker," John announced, taking the mic, "the band wanted to tell you how much we appreciate all you've done for us. You've supported our gigs, mentioned us on-air and even worn our T-shirts. It's meant something to us all. Before the show, we bought you a gift from George Powless Spirits. They've assured us this bottle of 1975 Dom Perignon Champagne Brut is a classic. It's for you, Dealmaker. Thanks for everything."

Sára handed the champagne to the Dealmaker and raised the microphone to her lips. "Three cheers for the Dealmaker! Hip hip, hooray! Hip hip, hooray! Hip hip, hooray!"

The crowd thundered in response. The Dealmaker's already red face turned an even darker shade of scarlet. Instead of his typical, boisterous reply, he affected a smile of true sweetness. The Dealmaker bowed his head and raised the bottle to the audience. Slowly, he walked off stage as if the very act drained the energy from his soul.

The Nomadic Cowboys went on to perform a scorching final show. Robert lost the Dealmaker after he left the stage. As the clock passed midnight, the audience frenzy hit its peak. The Lucky Charm Saloon closed the buffet. True to their word, they'd provided a fabulous spread.

Robert spent the last hours speaking with his fellow show hosts. He had his first long conversation with the very pretty Cyd Steinberg. She had a husband, but they had chemistry regardless.

Stale Chili wandered about looking like Stale Chili. Kirk Glazer engaged in conspiracies with Joe Giannini. The lovely Alexandra McMurdo elected to go home at midnight. She was by far the sanest of the lot.

A sudden and urgent voice intruded. "Robert, we need your help." It was Sára, hustling over to him, wearing a concerned expression. "The Dealmaker's passed out. He's muttering and going on about the Dragon

Lady. We need to get him home."

Following Sára, he walked backstage. The Dealmaker leaned against a battered sofa, his magnum of Dom Perignon cradled in his arm.

"Kid, ah gotta ga homa … " This was as drunk as Robert had ever seen him. He didn't know the Dragon Lady's address, but had to get the Dealmaker there in a hurry.

"John, let's get him to a taxi. Grab an arm."

In a repeat of his first time at Lucky Charm Saloon, Robert pulled the Dealmaker to his feet. John grabbed his other shoulder and the pair humped the drunken show host out the bar's front door.

It wasn't a pretty sight. Some drool trickled from his mouth. A small amount of dried blood had caked on his face and collar. Robert raised his arm for one of the taxis.

"Help me get him in the back," he said to John. "I'll get him home."

"Big Mack, I love this guy. He's been great to our band. But this fucked up shit can't continue. The Dealmaker has got to clean up. He's looking worse every day."

Robert acknowledged the obvious. He slid the Dealmaker into the back seat behind the driver. "Thanks, John. I'll get him home. Thank Sára as well."

John said he would and shut the rear passenger door, heading back to the bar.

"Where to buddy?" asked the driver. "Give me a sec," he replied. "Feel free to turn on the meter." The driver pushed the engaged button.

"Dealmaker, where does Dixie live?"

"I love that woma … " The Dealmaker fell asleep against the rear, driver's side door. He started to snore.

Frustrated, Robert looked to the driver who met his gaze in the rear-view mirror. "Best Value Inn. It's on … "

"I know where it is," said the driver, who pulled out of the parking lot toward the highway.

Heading down the bleak road, the intermittent traffic pulsed against the masted lights. Robert felt an acute sense of déjà vu. He didn't have the Dealmaker's keys. Besides, he couldn't dump the man alone in his room in his current condition.

Tonight and tonight only, he'd have a new roommate.

§

Robert MacKenzie

Robert woke up late on Sunday morning. The clock read 10:47 a.m. He didn't feel that bad, just the usual ashtray mouth and dehydration. His head thumped, but it was bearable. Next to him lay the Dealmaker, still dressed as he'd been at the club.

The pair had exited the taxi as Robert schlepped the Dealmaker to his room. His friend did not cooperate. It was like carrying a gigantic bag of vodka Jell-O.

There was only a single, queen-sized bed in the room. The Dealmaker crashed to the mattress, face down. Robert thought he might have had to spin his friend around if he lay on his back. He didn't need a Jimi Hendrix moment. But seconds after landing, the Dealmaker began snoring.

Robert emptied his bladder and stripped down to his underwear. Sleep came for him without effort. In the middle of the night, Robert awakened to take another piss. He checked on the Dealmaker who still lay face down, snoring away.

Jesus, this has to stop. Drinking is one thing. Drinking all the time combined with constant smoking and snorting coke is another. He'll kill himself at this rate.

As the realization dawned he was in love with Yasmine, so it came that he loved the Dealmaker. He may have been a very flawed man, but he had a good heart. And he'd been more than good to Robert. He had a difficult relationship with his own dad, a smart man with unachieved dreams. It was only years later Robert understood how hard his father's death had hit him.

When he wakes up, I need to speak to him about what Mary-Anne said and tell him about my own plans. He's already on shaky ground. Losing his job will kill him.

Feeling grimy, Robert got up to grab some aspirin. From outside came a muffled voice and banging. It was an upset woman, but he couldn't make out what she said. As he walked to the draped window to take a look, there was a loud bang on his own door.

"Robert, open the door. Open the goddamn door!"

He recognized the voice in an instant and reached for the knob. Robert opened the door wearing only his underwear. Standing outside in a panic was the Dragon Lady. They stared at each other for a second.

"Where's Dave?" she said in a clear but strained voice. "He didn't come home last night and I'm worried." The Dragon Lady couldn't see the Dealmaker's inert form on the mattress.

Robert pulled back, turned and gestured to the bed. The Dragon Lady saw the Dealmaker and without asking barged into the room. She got down on her knees and embraced his sleeping form.

"Baby, are you okay? Mami, it's me. Wake up. You had me so worried." The Dragon Lady hugged the Dealmaker and rocked him until he awakened.

"Babe, what are you doing here?" he asked groggily, opening his eyes and glancing about. "Wait a minute, where the hell am I?"

"You're in my room, Dealmaker. You got really drunk last night and I had to get you home. You were too blasted to give me Dixie's address so I brought you to the motel. You were also too drunk to leave on your own so that's why you're with me."

The Dealmaker shook his head and moved to get up. He swung his legs over the edge of the bed. "Dixie, I need to take a shower."

"It's okay, hon. I've got the Caddy here. It's right outside. Take the keys and meet me there. We'll grab a shower at my place."

"You dirty fox," the Dealmaker replied. "I love you, babe."

"I love you too," whispered the Dragon Lady in return. "Get out of here. I'll see you in a minute."

"Kid, ya got any aspirin? And by aspirin I mean Percodan. Or codeine. Or a handgun. Jesus, is my head sore!"

"Sorry, Dealmaker. I only have aspirin."

"Yeah, so I figured. I got some pills in my room. Dixie, I'm going to get some painkillers, then I'll see you in the car."

"Okay, hon. I'll be with you in a sec."

The Dealmaker walked out of the room and shut the door behind him. Robert stood in front of the Dragon Lady, still wearing only his underwear. It was less awkward than expected.

"Thank you for getting him home, Robert. And thank you for letting him sleep in your room."

"You're welcome, Dixie. I love him too."

"It's that obvious?"

"Yes."

The Dragon Lady made a brief smile and walked toward the door. "I'm sorry for the way I've treated you, Robert. I don't have an excuse. I'm not that nice at my best, but I've been way over the top for a long time now."

"Thank you, Dixie. I appreciate the apology."

She walked outside after shutting the door. Robert stood in his underwear in the mute room. He would have gone to see Honest Phil, but state law closed car dealerships on Sunday. Instead, he took off his underwear, tossed it on the bed and headed to the shower.

Sitting on top of the dresser, a lonely bottle of Dom Perignon watched the entire affair. It had a massive tear in the foil around the cap. Twelve years it sat undisturbed and pure. One night with the Dealmaker and it was already despoiled. That was par for the course.

§

Robert MacKenzie

There was no particular reason Robert didn't visit Honest Phil on Monday. Or Tuesday, for that matter. Now that he was back on Show #8 he had his mornings and afternoons free. He called on Wednesday and showed up on Thursday before noon.

Honest Phil greeted him as Diana ushered him into his office. His assistant gave Robert a bright smile.

"Robert, y'all are lookin' fine. How's that Alfa Romeo doin' for ya?" Honest Phil wore the same attire as he had during their last visit. He was a man who knew his image and his customer.

"It's great, thank you. I appreciate your help."

"I told you, any friend of Billy-Ray is a friend of mine. Now I know why you're here. How much more help do you need?"

Robert pulled out the attaché case and handed it over. It contained the original fifty plus the extra ten thousand dollars. "Sixty grand."

"Okay, it's time for Honest Phil to make it right. Diana told me you gave her the bank information. To remind you, I'm taking six grand for myself."

"Noted."

"Good. Today's Thursday. It's probably too late to get it to you by this week. Possible, but not likely. But Monday afternoon should be a lock. Is that alright?"

"That would be fine. Something tells me I'm not getting a receipt."

Honest Phil stared in confusion for a moment until Robert broke out in a smile.

"Y'all have a sense of humor. You sure do. How 'bout I give you one more deal? Another special buy for a friend of Billy-Ray."

Robert raised his eyebrow.

"Do ya know the one thing your magnificent Alfa Romeo needs to make it perfect?" asked Honest Phil.

"Go ahead."

"A car phone. I happen to have the latest Motorola unit in stock. Usually, it runs sixteen hundred dollars plus taxes and installation. You want one, I'll give it to you installed for thirteen hundred dollars all in. Leave the car here. I'll have one of my staff drive you over to TeleShop. Then I'll have your car dropped off in the parking lot by 6:00 p.m. I'll leave the keys with Hank. What'd ya say?"

It should not have surprised Robert that Honest Phil knew Hank's name, but he was nonetheless. Since becoming flush, he always walked around with a lot of cash. It was either carry it or stash it.

A car phone. Now that's something I want but never thought I could afford. Yes, that would make life easier. Especially if I have to make changes.

"Done." Robert reached into his pocket and started pulling hundreds off a roll. When he counted out thirteen, he handed them to Phil.

"Great. Let me have Diana take your keys and write up your phone company application. Then she can give you a drive to your office. Always a pleasure doin' business with a friend of Billy-Ray. Say hi when you see him. Billy-Ray knows I always make it right."

Robert shook Honest Phil's hand and left the office. Without any notice, Diana waited for him. She smiled the entire time as he completed the application. At the end, she gave him his new telephone number and added her own in case he needed help.

Phoenix now felt like a whole different life.

§

Robert MacKenzie

With the switch back to regular, three hour shows and his returning to Show #8, Robert didn't see the Dealmaker. He would walk past the Dragon Lady a great deal. While she no longer scowled when they met, she didn't strike up conversation either. It was more a mutual nodding of recognition. He'd asked about the Dealmaker on one occasion. The Dragon Lady replied he was fine and said nothing else. Robert chose not to push the issue. The peace between them was far preferable to the constant animosity.

Mary-Anne had decreased her presence since the party—a bash still talked about by staff. Two weeks afterward, she now made irregular appearances.

Mary-Anne starts her new job on the first of September. She's going to disappear forever by next week. Plus, I have to take care of things—and soon. TeleShop doesn't feel right. It hasn't since the beginning of August.

Of all people, Cyd Steinberg became Yasmine's temporary replacement. She did a good job of juggling the position's various hats. No host had ever transitioned into a managerial role. Cyd wanted to be the first. But with Triboro bringing in their own team in a month, there was no guarantee. Robert hoped Cyd pulled it off.

The week passed by. That was the best way of describing it. The desperation of July was *Top 40 Radio*. August was more *EZ Listening*. Robert finished a successful but uneventful show on the fourteenth. He said goodnight to the crew and jumped in his Alfa Romeo. On occasion, Benjamin Braddock still hung around, looking at Robert and smiling.

Honest Phil had transferred the money as promised on Monday afternoon. He had fifty-four thousand dollars in his account with thousands more in cash. When he got the car phone, Robert's first call was to Yasmine. It was also their last.

"Yasmine, what's up? Aren't you happy for me?" Frustration filled both his thoughts and words.

"Robert, I'm happy for you. I am. What's happening is what I knew would happen. You're going to be great. That's why I can't do this anymore. I told you, if you were like my prior boyfriends, I could deal with it. But you're not like them at all. Not seeing you combined with these phone calls tears me apart."

"Yasmine ... "

"Robert, I got the job. The bank is going to file for a visa change after I start work. In the interim, they want me to report next week. They're paying for my relocation. And they'll put me up in a hotel while I find an apartment. No matter what, I'll be in Manhattan and you'll be in Oklahoma City. Please let it go. Please." The emotion in her voice matched his own as she said goodbye and hung up.

That call was over a week ago. Now, driving back to the motel, his victories — the cash, the sales, the car — rang hollow. He couldn't even vent with the Dealmaker. He'd as good as disappeared into the lair of the Dragon Lady.

His car pulled into the motel's parking lot, always quiet this time of night. Robert turned it off and sat for a moment before heading into his room. It had been a very long time since he'd felt this alone.

§

Robert MacKenzie

Robert's motel phone rang on Saturday morning. He wasn't one to receive a lot of calls. With his new car phone installed, he didn't use his room's phone much at all.

"Yeah?" Robert announced, groggy and tired. He went to sleep past 3:00 a.m. and wasn't in a cheerful mood anyway. "What'd ya need?"

"Big Mack, it's John. The Dealmaker hasn't shown up and we can't get a hold of him. His show goes live in a bit over an hour."

"So, who's going on afterward?"

"Alexandra and she's not here either. And before you ask, Stale Chili is on now."

"So tell him to run long."

"He won't do it. Says he has some personal matters to attend."

"Asshole! Did you call Mary-Anne?" Robert was about to add "or Yasmine," but checked himself in time. "What about Cyd or the Dragon Lady?"

"No answer, no answer, and no answer."

"So what do you want?"

"You know the drill. Get your ass here in a hurry and take over his show." John said the words as if they were obvious—which they were. Not pleasant, but obvious.

Robert did *not* feel up to going in but knew he had no choice. The Dealmaker had been late for the odd weekly show and missed an entire one three months back. But he never missed a weekend show. They were too important. Robert prayed he was sick with the flu and not with a bender.

"Okay. I need a shower. I'll be there in forty minutes; have everything ready."

"Thanks, Big Mack."

Robert hung up and headed for the bathroom. Twenty minutes later, after a quick shave and shower, he was on the highway. His Alfa Romeo was so much nicer than his old Civic that there was no comparison. It rode quieter. It rode smoother. It rode easier. And it had air conditioning. No comparison at all.

He hustled through the employee entrance and headed to production. Susie saw him and came running with a show printout and a headset.

Does she know I saw her with Frank at Lucky Charm Saloon?

"Hi, Robert. Here's the show. Did you bring your headset? I have a backup."

"I'm good, Susie. I have my own headset. How's the show?"

"Nothing special. John wants to have your production meeting right away."

"Okay. Ask him to meet in the prep room and we'll go over the show."

"No problem." Susie flew back to the set. For such a tiny woman, she knew how to run.

Robert looped his headset around his ear as he walked to the prep room. A minute later, John walked in.

"Hey, Big Mack," he said, pulling up a chair and sitting down.

"Hey, John. How's it going?"

"Not great. You haven't seen the Dealmaker much of late, have you?"

"No, he's found new digs."

"With the Dragon Lady?"

Robert wondered how he could have figured it out. But the crew heard and saw all. If you wanted gossip about a host, ask the crew.

"Yeah. How did you know? Is it obvious?"

"Oh, yeah. They try to hide it, but a blind man could see the truth."

"A blind man?"

"A blind man with special needs!"

The pair laughed and went over the show. It was basic at best. Since the end of July, passion had gotten up and left the building. Sales reflected the lackluster environment, but nobody much cared about that either. At least on the surface.

During the second break, he saw and waved to Alexandra. She'd arrived a bit late and now hustled between Scheduling and the prep room. Stale Chili had left TeleShop with his usual "What, me worry?" look to deal with his "personal matters."

Robert managed to hit target. He sold a couple of rings, the "Crystal of the Month" and the new Vicki Lester signature doll. Wishing Alexandra luck, he walked away from the set, thanking everyone for their effort.

When he entered the prep room, it was empty. The Dragon Lady should have been either there or in Scheduling. He headed down the hall to check.

"Linda, have you seen the Dragon Lady?" he asked the Scheduling office's sole occupant.

"No, I'm sorry. We don't know where she is. She's not answering her phone. If we don't hear, Alexandra will have to run long. We got a hold of Cyd; she'll be here at any moment."

"Okay, thanks," Robert replied with caution. This was unusual. Say what you would about the Dragon Lady, she was *never* late. He left Scheduling and headed back to the prep room. He'd check there and the cafeteria before he left.

But, the prep room was also empty when he arrived. Something felt wrong. While the Dealmaker was a hellion, the Dragon Lady was almost a teetotaler. He was about to turn and leave when the phone rang.

"Hello," he said.

"Robert, it's Dixie. Dave is dead."

§

Robert MacKenzie

Robert wanted to believe the Dealmaker went out with style. Some insane act of partying. An orgy of gluttony spread over days. Finding a hook for an obscure product and running with it toward oblivion. Instead, he simply didn't wake up.

He'd been with the Dragon Lady. The couple watched television after she completed her Friday show. They went to bed around midnight. She got up about 8:00 a.m. He never did.

When the Dragon Lady told Robert that Saturday of the Dealmaker's passing, he couldn't move. Like the cliché, color drained from his face. Cyd Steinberg walked into the prep room and started to say hello. But, from Robert's frozen expression, it was clear something was very wrong.

"You okay?" she asked, knowing he wasn't.

The Dragon Lady spoke in the background with scant details and a flat affect. Robert looked to Cyd and shook his head with minimal expression.

The rest of Saturday passed in a haze. A cliché again, but true. The Dragon Lady spoke to Cyd, explaining she wasn't coming in for the next few days. Robert said he'd work the Dealmaker's shift on Sunday and any extra shifts needed to fill his absence.

The news of the Dealmaker's death spread throughout the building. The crew got the word first, and they passed it to the operators. Cyd phoned the hosts, looking to fill two slots. In turn, the hosts phoned each other. He had no idea who contacted the Dealmaker's family. The police? The coroner?

The Dealmaker's obituary appeared in *The Oklahoman* on Sunday.

David Nathan Lieber

Known to all as "Dealmaker Dave Leonard," David passed without warning on Saturday. Born in Tacoma, Washington, David worked in sales across the United States. Since 1982, he was a show host at TeleShop USA. Survived by his wife of twenty-two years, Eve (Goldberg) and his daughters, Shoshana and Esther. Private service at Hahn-Cook/Street & Draper Funeral Directors on Monday. To honor David, please consider a donation to the United Jewish Appeal.

Robert knew his friend was Jewish. And the Dealmaker told him he was born at Fort Lewis, Washington during the war. But Robert couldn't believe he didn't know the Dealmaker's real name. That should have bothered him, but it didn't. The mystery only added to the Dealmaker's appeal.

David Lieber? For Christ's sake, Dealmaker, even in death you get the last laugh!

Billy-Ray took the news hard. He came into the studio on Sunday to shoot a special promo.

"Friends, I had the honor of knowing Dave for the last five years. He had a huge heart and I never met a single soul at TeleShop who didn't think the world of him. His absence leaves a giant hole in all of us."

Billy-Ray looked into the camera against a plain set. Maria Tissot ran graphics. In the upper right-hand corner, she inserted the Dealmaker's picture. It was his official company portrait.

"A spirit that big deserves a big sendoff. But, how? If you knew the Dealmaker, you knew how often he was in my office fighting for bargains." While Billy-Ray spoke in eulogy, he couldn't help but run with the accepted narrative. This was not the time to correct the historical record. "We're going to have a sale. That's right, a sale. In the Dealmaker's honor. Before you say this is crass, let me tell you something. TeleShop USA will donate all profits that day to charity. Every dime. Stay tuned. Saturday, August 22nd will be Dealmaker Dave Leonard Day. Our biggest sale ever!"

If there was a heaven and the Dealmaker was there, he would be laughing like a hyena. "Profits" was a relative term. By the time you added in the cost of goods, you never knew where their profit may lead.

Billy-Ray finished shooting the promo and left the production area. He saw

Robert and motioned for him to come over.

"How y'all doin' son? I know you and the Dealmaker were close."

"I'm okay, sir. It's a bitter pill to swallow. I wish there was something I could have done that would have helped him."

Billy-Ray was alone in the studio. Other than the party, Robert had never seen Billy-Ray without his secretary in tow. The president put his hand on Robert's shoulder.

"Son, there ain't nothin' nobody could've done. Nothin' at all. I had only praise for the Dealmaker. But he was a lost soul who rushed to his destiny a long time ago."

Robert shook his head. The Dealmaker was his own worst enemy. While that may have been the truth, regardless his absence still hurt.

"I know you're leaving us at the end of the month," Billy-Ray said.

"Yes, sir. I'm sorry. I've received an offer I can't decline."

"Don't be sorry. We wouldn't have made target without you. Hell, I owe you. Don't worry about TeleShop. Take Mary-Anne's offer and go with my blessing."

"You know?" Robert asked, making himself look naïve.

Billy-Ray smiled. "Son, there ain't nothin' I don't know when it comes to my on-air people. Let me make you a deal."

"Okay."

"Your last day is August 31st. Stay and host all day for the Dealmaker's sale this Saturday. If you do, you can leave on Sunday with your full pay and a hearty recommendation. What'd ya say?"

"I say yes, Billy-Ray. Yes and thank you."

"Good. I'm off. Be sure you give me a performance and a half on Saturday. I want the Dealmaker lookin' down on us and laughing."

"Yes, sir. I'll do my best."

"I know you will, son. Anyway, I got a late lunch with my wife's women's club at the Skirvin. God I hate those affairs. But what's a man to do?"

Billy-Ray walked toward the exit. Robert watched him go and headed back to the prep room. He had to work all day to fill in the absences caused by the Dealmaker and the Dragon Lady.

One more week. And one more big sale …

Dealmaker Dave Leonard Day? Christ, the Dealmaker would shit himself!

EPILOGUE

Robert MacKenzie

The temperature was in the low seventies and the skies were clear, without a hint of rain. It was Tuesday, September 1st at 12:03 p.m. and Robert walked along Liberty Street in Manhattan's Financial District.

"Dealmaker Dave Leonard Day" had gone better than expected. In truth, much better than expected. Cyd ran strategy and did a hell of a job. She gathered every piece of low quantity jewelry and bundled them together. Then she cut their price.

There was the Dealmaker Celebration Ring Special. The classic ring matched with a gold chain. Or a silver chain. Or two chains. Or an extra ring. Or whatever. The tiny quantities of each guaranteed sellouts. And the sellouts created more sellouts.

Every host and select members of the crew had prerecorded a "Dealmaker memory" segment. They'd tell humorous and often true anecdotes.

TeleShop established a special line for shoppers to call in to record stories of their own. Most were boring. Some were salacious. A few disjointed. But many were quite touching. TeleShop ran them in every show and they also helped sales.

The Dragon Lady finished off the day with her show from 9:00 p.m. to midnight, Eastern Time. Now that he was in Manhattan, he was in Eastern Time and didn't miss having to add the constant reminder.

As the clock approached 11:00 p.m., the Dragon Lady repeated the Bismarck Satin wedding bracelet. By special authorization of Billy-Ray and in honor of the Dealmaker, enchantment returned …

Bismarck Satin Platinum Wedding Bracelet
Seven Inches, Lobster Clasp
Sale Ends at Midnight!
Regular Price: $1,819.99
For the Dealmaker: $899.99!!!
Tonight only in honor of our late friend, Dealmaker Dave Leonard
The last ever Dealmaker Select Buy

TeleShop brought in one hundred fifty chains. TeleShop sold one hundred fifty chains. With the Dragon Lady on a roll, he didn't know if her tears on-air were real or shtick. And in the end, did it matter?

Robert entered the atrium of Chase's headquarters. Scores of people walked past and in a hurry, speaking with thick New York accents. The difference between Lower Manhattan and Oklahoma City was never more evident than the way people moved. The time was almost 1:00 p.m. and he was still at a loss how to proceed.

Calling up to the office and asking for Yasmine sounded desperate. But bumping into her by "accident" in the lobby looked even worse. He paced about for forty minutes, wondering what to do. As it turned out, fate intervened.

"Robert?" came a voice from behind. "What are you doing here?" It was Yasmine.

He'd forgotten how beautiful she was. Tall with piercing eyes and confidence to spare. Yet, if you looked close enough, fragility at the same time.

"I was in the neighborhood," Robert replied, hoping she'd melt when she saw him. She didn't, instead expressing a look of worry and concern. Yasmine wore a light blue linen suit with a matching linen skirt and low-rise heels. On her right wrist lay a Hublot watch. "Is that a new watch?"

"Yes, Mom gave it to me as a present for getting this job."

"It's beautiful, your mother has—"

"Robert, why are you here?"

"I left TeleShop."

"Left? Why?"

"I have a new job," he said. It was time to throw down and cut the timid bullshit. "I'm working for Mary-Anne."

"Mary-Anne?"

"Yes, Mary-Anne Warner, late of Welch, West Virginia and Oklahoma City, Oklahoma. Now of Greenwich, Connecticut.

Yasmine's eyes squinted in confusion. This would be temporary. She'd figure it out in a minute.

"Do the math, beautiful Yasmine. You were right. I'm a unicorn. I have a talent for one thing and one thing only. But that thing pays very well. In this case, one hundred grand per year. Plus a twenty-five grand signing bonus. Today is my first day. My new company thinks I'm looking at apartments—which I am, if not this exact moment."

The noise of the crowded lobby disappeared. Yasmine focused on Robert as he focused on her. The space between them narrowed. He reached out and took her left hand with his right. As they got closer, he inhaled her scent. It had been a long time.

"AVN?" she asked with a whisper.

"AVN," Robert replied with a smile.

Yasmine reached and pulled against him. Robert responded and allowed her yielding form to mold itself around his body. They had so isolated themselves from the crowd they didn't notice the stares.

"I love you, Yasmine. I liked the job in Oklahoma. I liked my coworkers. Unlike you, I liked the city. And I was making great money. But when you left it was torture. You were on my mind at all times. When I made that first call from my car and you said we couldn't continue, it crushed me."

"I'm sorry, Robert. I am so sorry. I love you. I do. So much! I cried when I asked you to stop calling. My mother heard me, but pretended not to. She's too proud to let me even think about failure. My sister couldn't pretend. She came into my room and held me while I wept. It was awful. I almost called you many times, but it couldn't have worked out if you had stayed in Oklahoma."

"Yasmine, I know. You were being realistic. I knew that and it made me even crazier. I was the one who dropped out of high school. But I was the one who flitted about the country for almost a decade. It ate away at me. Once I tasted the freedom having money gives, I couldn't go back."

Oblivious to the crowd, Robert embraced Yasmine and the pair hugged. He didn't know what he would have done if Yasmine rejected him. While women now looked him over with regularity, Yasmine was the only one he cared about.

"I heard about the Dealmaker," Yasmine said as they relaxed for a moment. "I'm sorry, Robert. I know how much you liked him."

"Thank you. I miss him. He helped me with everything. Including you. He liked you, you know. Said if you didn't learn to relax more you'd combust."

Yasmine laughed. It was so good to hear her laugh. He felt free for the first time in forever.

"What are your plans today?" she asked.

"I told you. AVN thinks I'm looking for an apartment. Either here in the city or in Greenwich. It's only a forty-five-minute drive or an hour on the commuter train. I checked into a hotel not far from here last night. I've started work but there isn't much to do this week."

"Technically, this is my first day of work too," said Yasmine. "I've been here since last week. I need to find an apartment as well. My hotel is about five minutes away on Washington Street."

"Is it nice?" Robert asked with raised eyebrows and much innuendo.

"It's okay," she replied. "Why would you like to see it?"

"If it's not too much trouble."

"Oh, no trouble. Give me a minute." Yasmine reached into her right jacket pocket and pulled out a brick-like telephone. It was a Nokia cell phone. She punched in some numbers and made a call.

Robert noticed that people had paid more than a little bit of attention to the couple. Yasmine said something to what sounded like a secretary before hanging up.

"I spoke to my boss's assistant. I told her I had found a potential apartment and needed to go see it."

"So ... "

"So, Robert, let's go check out my hotel."

"That sounds great. If I recall, the last time we were out, I stopped myself before I even started. Today, I'd rather keep going."

"Yes, that sounds nice. Please feel free to continue. And continue. And continue."

Holding hands, the couple exited the bank's lobby and headed to the future.

Toronto
September 1994 to March 1995
Tokyo
July 2022 to May 2023

www.ingramcontent.com/pod-product-compliance
Lightning Source LLC
Chambersburg PA
CBHW031428240626
47154CB00001B/248